T0268294

Praise for
Straw Dogs of the Universe

"Hauntingly beautiful and exquisitely written, *Straw Dogs of the Universe* shines much-needed light on a historical period that we must not forget if we want to do better as a human race. This book is a treasure, to be read and reread, as the best poems should be."

—Nguyễn Phan Quế Mai, internationally bestselling author of
The Mountains Sing and *Dust Child*

"A visceral and poetic work of art—Ye Chun's grasp of our shared history, of her unforgettable characters, and of the vast sweep of this narrative can only be marveled at: Who else could tell us the story of Chinese settlement in California as if it were an adventure tale filtered through the lens of Thomas Hardy? That the writing here is so insightful, so clear and vibrant and heartbreaking, is a testament to the overwhelming talent of one of our finest authors."

—Brian Castleberry, author of *Nine Shiny Objects*

"Ye Chun writes with depth and precision about the power of the human spirit—its resilience, tenderness, darkness, and yearning—even under the harshest of circumstances. *Straw Dogs of the Universe* is a luminous, unforgettable story about the terror and beauty of life for Chinese immigrants in the early American West. It will leave you aching by its end." —Alexandra Chang, author of *Days of Distraction* and *Tomb Sweeping*

"Impressive in scope, with unflinching historical detail and effortless storytelling, Ye Chun's *Straw Dogs of the Universe* is a magnificent addition to the growing tradition of historical fiction that rectifies the gaps and silences around the contributions of the Chinese workforce to the nineteenth-century American West. An unforgettable story of people who, despite horrific violence, betrayal, and loss, grow into the truest and strongest versions of themselves."

—Melissa Fu, author of *Peach Blossom Spring*

"Ye Chun's riveting debut novel, *Straw Dogs of the Universe*, moves seamlessly through several decades in the late nineteenth century, following four Chinese immigrants as they attempt to start anew in Gold Mountain. The constant search for home and for family underlies it all, and Ye Chun's mesmerizing prose brings their stories—of hope and hardship and love—to unforgettable life."

—Laura Spence-Ash, author of *Beyond That, the Sea*

Praise for
Hao

Long-Listed for the 2022 Andrew Carnegie Medal for
Excellence in Fiction
A *Literary Hub* Best Book of the Year
An *Electric Literature* Best Book of the Year

"Ye's writing thrives when dissecting the contradictions in life and in language." —Javier C. Hernández, *The New York Times*

"Gentle . . . Slow, somber and often elegant, *Hao* thematically foregrounds language . . . Ye shows how words operate as weapons, comforts, memories and insufficient—if sometimes beautiful—representations of intent."

—Tracy O'Neill, *The New York Times Book Review*

"Stunning . . . A powerful collection that explores what happens when lives break down, when it becomes hard to find a word—any word—to express profound loss and anguish . . . There's not a story in *Hao* that's anything less than gorgeous."   —Michael Schaub, NPR

"Words are Ye Chun's superpower. A translator and poet, she uses them sparsely, delicately, aware that each one carries unseen weight . . . These stories are immaculate, beautiful, tattered—like their characters."
                                        —Hillary Kelly, *Vulture*

"Ye powerfully renders the displacement felt by recent immigrants fitfully learning the language, to further highlight the cultural divide they face, and to demonstrate that they seem to have no way but forward . . . Universal and poignant."
                            —Kristen Yee, *Asian Review of Books*

"Lapidary, understated, unflinching and intimate . . . Haunted and haunting . . . Ye's sentences are both lyrical and muscular: spare and acutely alive."   —Lisa Russ Spaar, *On the Seawall*

STRAW
DOGS
OF THE
UNIVERSE

ALSO BY YE CHUN

Hao

STRAW
DOGS

OF THE

UNIVERSE

A Novel

YE CHUN

Catapult
New York

STRAW DOGS OF THE UNIVERSE

This is a work of fiction. All of the characters, organizations, and
events portrayed in this novel are either products of the author's imagination
or are used fictitiously.

Copyright © 2023 by Ye Chun

First Catapult edition: 2023

ISBN: 978-1- 64622-062-5

Library of Congress Control Number: 2023936798

Jacket design by Robin Bilardello
Jacket images: watercolor landscape © Asya_mix / iStock;
mountains © keiko takamatsu / iStock
Book design by Wah-Ming Chang

Catapult
New York, NY
books.catapult.co

Printed in the United States of America

1 3 5 7 9 10 8 6 4 2

For those who came before me

Contents

STRAW
DOGS
OF THE
UNIVERSE

1

To the Land of the Lost

*

1876

THE CHILD STOOD BY THE SHIP RAILING, WIND AND SALT ON HER
face. There was nothing but sky and sea at this moment, not even a gull
or a flash of fish: the sky spread blue and luminous; the sea glimmered
but did not conceal its cold carelessness. The night before, a storm had
thrown her and the other passengers in the hold off their berths and rolled
them back and forth across the dank floor. Through the porthole, she had
seen a slice of sky, lightning-lit and starless. Foamy water poured down
the hatchway: drops splashed into her mouth with the taste of bile.

Although this was her first time on the sea, ten-year-old Sixiang
was no stranger to fickle waters. The past summer, a typhoon had hit
her village, Yunteng, where the river jumped the bank and kept surg-
ing. Her grandmother teetered in indecision about what to save in her
tub: the ancestral tablets, the Guanyin statuette, or the antique bowls
and cups reserved for the deceased, which were also the household's
last valuables not yet traded for food. It was Sixiang's mother who
grabbed the jar of rice, the five sweet potatoes, and two salted fish; who
picked up the sheets of oilcloth for covers and the shoulder poles for
oars; and who asked her grandmother to leave the other things where
they were: "We can't eat those when we are starving."

Sixiang and her mother huddled in one tub, her grandmother in

another. They swirled in the currents of muddy water with other villagers and livestock animals, dodging branches, debris, and courtyard
furniture. Before nightfall, the flood had dwarfed tall palm trees and
erased houses, leaving only their tiled rooftops no bigger than grave
vaults. Under the oilcloth, Sixiang pressed against her mother's thumping chest. The water lapped and licked, rumbled and hissed. Darkness
wrapped them like fur.

After the third night, Sixiang awoke to a cool morning of light
rain. Her mother was pushing something away from the tub with the
pole. A body, face down, floated in the water, long loosened hair spread
like spent wings. The current lifted the drowned woman's dark blouse
and bared her lower back, pale as the weak sun. Jaw clenched, Sixiang's
mother was trying to push their tub away from the body, but it followed, head knocking, hair netting their tub. After a while of such futile maneuvering, her mother put down the pole, hugged her knees,
buried her face to her chest, and sobbed. Sixiang's grandmother was
floating in her own tub a little way ahead of them, in the direction of
their roof that now resembled an old buffalo's scrawny back. She was
chanting *Amituofo*, lips shuddering.

Sixiang had heard stories of water ghosts, how they crept into the
living and took hold. She picked up the shoulder pole, dipping it back
into the water. "I'm pushing it away, Mama," she said. "Look, it's away."

Her mother looked up, nodded at her, and took over the pole again.

NOW NO MOTHER was with Sixiang, nor anyone she could call kin.
Madam asked her and the four other girls in the group to call her *Loumou*, because, she said, she would be taking care of them like their own
mothers until they arrived in Gold Mountain and moved in with their
new families. Madam had changed from her silk blouse into a coarse
cotton top before they boarded the ship. She no longer wore powder
and rouge either: just a plain, bare face. "When the ship arrives, there
will be white men asking who you are," she said, moving her eyes

down the row of girls one by one. "If you don't say you're my daughter, they'll lock you up in a dark room filthier than this hold."

The hold held hundreds of Chinese men and thirty or so women and girls who were squeezed in its dimmer and fouler end, away from the porthole where the only fresh air was let in. The girls were divided into several groups, each led by a madam. Sixiang's group consisted of little Ah Fang, a year and half younger than Sixiang; two teenagers who had soon become inseparable and whispered everything in each other's ears; and Ah Hong, the oldest among them, who had not stopped crying since Sixiang first saw her several days earlier in the boat cabin, before they were brought to Hong Kong to board the steamship. Hands and feet tied then, Ah Hong had to raise both her arms to wipe away tears from her face. The sight of her had momentarily shocked Sixiang out of her own sobbing, sobering her as she was led into the cabin, which she had originally thought would only hold buckets of fragrant rice.

The group occupied two narrow berths in the hold: Madam, Sixiang, and little Ah Fang on the lower bunk; the older girls on the upper. All of them save Madam were struck by seasickness, and for the first three days of the voyage, Sixiang had curled into a ball on her bedroll, enduring the churning in her stomach. She got up only briefly to vomit in the waste bucket that kept refilling to its rim.

She also got up for the meals, yearningly. Even with nausea, her hunger would resurge. Two meals were served a day: morning, rice porridge; night, steamed rice—each topped with a few slivers of salted fish and a few pieces of sautéed cabbage. Sixiang chewed carefully, not taking a single bite for granted. The crying girl Ah Hong, however, would only eat a little, the rest of her food soon divided up by the two other teens. "You all are lucky," Madam said, glancing at Ah Hong. "Just a few years ago, folks had to bring their own food onboard. And they'd starve if they didn't bring enough."

Sixiang and little Ah Fang lay face to face on their bunk, and when less sick, they would talk about life before the flood. Their favorite dish: roasted duck for Sixiang; barbecued pork for Ah Fang, though it had been years since they last tasted them. Ah Fang had been bought by Madam on the same day as Sixiang, from a neighboring village down south, and had the look of a startled hare when she was dragged into the cabin. But at night, each time Sixiang reached for her mother in her sleep and felt Ah Fang's sharp little shoulder instead, she would find Ah Fang sound asleep as if without a care.

With caution, Sixiang approached the topic of ending up here. "What about your mama?" she asked Ah Fang in a casual voice, like it was an everyday question.

"What about her?"

"Why did she sell you?"

"She's dead."

"Your baba?"

"Dead too. Yours?"

"My mama is not dead," Sixiang said. "My baba, I don't know . . . He shouldn't be dead either." Sixiang decided not to pursue the subject any further, as she was clearly the luckier one between the two of them.

That night, when the storm hit, Sixiang and Ah Fang held hands while being tossed about on the soggy floor. Later, after they climbed back onto their berth, Sixiang started to hum a tune her mother used to sing to her at night. Ah Fang asked her to hum louder so that she could hear too. Sixiang did so and patted Ah Fang on the back as well, the way her mother had done. They fell back asleep that way.

In the morning, waking up to the hold's rustle and a quiet blue trickling down the hatchway, they both felt better in the stomach. After breakfast, they followed Madam past the men's bunks and up the slimy ladder to the steerage deck. It was smaller and more packed than the main deck above, which was off-limits to them, reserved only for first- and second-class passengers. Sixiang stood stunned by the sun for a moment. Then, one hand held in Madam's and the other holding Ah Fang's, she needled through the crowd to an opening by the railing.

She let go of both hands and grabbed the cool metal bar and, tilting her face to the wind, breathed.

In all directions within her vision, only sky and sea, and in all directions, a thin line between the two sheets of blue. Far, unceasing, a hollow medium, a phantom shore, where lands vanished, villages disappeared.

When Yunteng Village finally emerged from water, their house was reduced to a dripping cave with a dead fish on the floor. Each remaining grain of rice they'd saved in the tub was now countable. They divided a sweet potato three ways for three meals, cooking each with a spoonful of rice in a potful of water so the quantity appeared to expand tenfold. But their stomachs wouldn't be fooled.

They had a fan palm in the yard that the family had planted when Sixiang was little. They picked its seeds and cooked them like rice. They were saving the palm's heart for last to delay the killing of the tree, but one morning when they stepped out of the house, only the stump was left.

Sixiang dreamed of bowls of rice turning into pebbles and roasted duck bursting into fire the moment she reached them, as if she were a hungry ghost in the underworld, condemned to eternal starvation. When she woke in the middle of the night aching with hunger, she would sometimes see her mother staring blank-eyed at the ceiling, with the look of the dead fish stranded on their floor, as if the soul of the drowned woman clinging to their tub had indeed crept its way into her.

Sixiang's grandmother asked Sixiang and her mother to kneel with her in front of the altar, its wooden shelves now warped after days of soaking. The wooden tablets with their ancestors' names carved on them were cracking and peeling, standing limp on the uneven top like a small, ruinous graveyard. Sixiang's grandmother handed three sticks of lit incense each to Sixiang and her mother. They bowed and prayed. The bronze Guanyin statuette cast her all-knowing eyes upon them.

Villagers were leaving. Some carried their valuables on shoulder poles or pushed their old and young on wheelbarrows out of the dragon gate. Some left with nothing, having eaten their last edibles and spent their last pennies burying their dead. Some left their dead covered with grass mats, too weak to dig graves. They were heading north to the mountainous areas to beg. Sixiang went to the now-tamed river, hoping to catch a fish with an earthworm, but the water stank of death and rot. The earthworm wriggled in her palm. She tore a bit off its tail end and put it in her mouth. It tasted like mud, but that did not stop her from eating the rest. She went home, dug up more worms in the yard, and brought them to the kitchen where her mother and grandmother were boiling weeds into a green gruel. She asked them to try.

"We can't eat that," her grandmother said. "We're not savages."

Her mother looked away, as if even saying *no* took too much effort.

They couldn't leave. Both Sixiang's mother and grandmother had gotten their feet bound when they were six and were unable to travel far. They'd tried to bind Sixiang's when she turned six too, folding her toes beneath her soles despite her screaming. But each night, Sixiang would wake up in the middle of sleep and unwind the strangling bandages. After a while, her mother gave up trying to stop her, and eventually her grandmother did too, although she continued to bemoan the future of a low farmhand's wife destined for Sixiang with her fast-growing feet. Now, it occurred to Sixiang that she was the only one in the family who could walk long distances. And who would eat earthworms if she had to.

As the village emptied out, a man in a fisherman's bamboo hat rowed a boat down the river to their shore. A woman in an embroidered silk blouse emerged from the cabin, her face powdered, her forehead shaved high. Sixiang had been trying to catch a frog or crab by the shore. The woman eyed her before disappearing into the cabin again. She reemerged with a steaming bowl of rice and waved Sixiang over. "Here, little one, eat this." She handed her the bowl and a pair of chopsticks.

Sixiang had not touched a grain of rice for three months now. She took the bowl with shaky hands and stuffed a chunk of rice into her mouth. She did not stop until she had her third mouthful. Then she looked up at the woman: "My mama and grandma?"

"Don't worry." The woman smiled. "Eat it up. There's more."

The woman went back to the cabin and came out with a larger bowl of steamed rice. "Take me to your family," she said. Her other hand clutched a small gunny sack. Judging by its shape and the lovely *shasha* sound it made, Sixiang could tell it was a bag of rice, enough for them to live on for a month if they were careful to make it last.

Sixiang thought maybe the woman was Guanyin Goddess disguised in flesh, descending to answer their prayers.

UNLIKE SIXIANG, HER mother seemed to know right away that the woman wasn't Guanyin in any manner. Even while Sixiang jumped and hollered at their doorway, saying, "Rice, this kind lady has brought us rice," her mother's eyes were turning mournful. When her mother and grandmother finally sat down to eat the rice, trying not to gobble too greedily in front of the stranger, her mother's face was straining hard to hold back tears.

The woman sat across the table from them, sipping the water Sixiang's grandmother had poured from their kettle—they'd run out of tea, her grandmother had apologized. The woman sighed. "Life is too hard here," she said. "I've seen so many deaths along the river, people of all ages, not just the old but those in their prime. But the hardest to see were the little kids." She sighed again. "We all want our kids to live, don't we? We want them to live a better life than us. I know you all do. You love your child, I have no doubt." She looked at Sixiang. "What a sweet girl! When I gave her a bowl of rice at the river, the first thing on her mind was her mama and grandma." She took Sixiang's hand, stroking it. "She deserves to live better. You all must know Gold Mountain, the land of fortunes and riches. I live there most of the time, and I tell you, no one ever starves there. I give you my word: I'll find her a good family who will treat her like their own."

Sixiang's heart tightened as the woman's hands fastened around hers. Ever since she was little, her grandmother had called her *peibenhuo* when she was mad at her for one reason or another, like the time Sixiang dropped a hot teapot on the floor. *You peibenhuo!* Something to be sold for less than its cost, something that, instead of profiting the family, would bring a loss. Over the years, Sixiang had asked her mother many times if her grandmother would indeed sell her one day. And her mother's answer would vary, seemingly depending on her mood. Often, she would say it was just an expression for girls, all girls: "Don't mind your grandma. She's bitter. What good words could come out of a bitter woman's mouth?" But sometimes her mother's words seemed to be steeped in the same anger that lived in her grandmother: "Yes, if you don't behave, you'll be sold to a mother-in-law just like your grandma and to a husband just like your father who will leave you and never come back." In moments like this, Sixiang would almost blame herself for not knowing when to ask, as if her future depended on her mastery of timing.

But there was no question of timing now. This well-dressed, well-fed woman who had come out of nowhere was offering to give them the bag of rice she'd put on the table, plus six silver coins to weather the famine, and a good life for Sixiang beyond the corpse-strewn village. They would sail away to Hong Kong, where they were to board a steamship to Gold Mountain. Sixiang's grandmother watched Sixiang across the table, as if to appraise her value, a shimmer in her eyes that could have been greed, or hope, or a flash of fear. Sixiang pulled her hand out of the woman's grip and came to bury her face in the curve of her mother's neck. "Don't sell me," she whispered.

But her mother said nothing. She eased Sixiang into her arms, held her and patted her on the back as if she were a baby.

The woman asked them to prepare a bedroll and some clothes for

Sixiang. "I know this is hard, but it's better for everyone." Seeing no one move, she pressed on, "The boat is waiting. The ship is leaving the day after tomorrow. It's difficult, I know, but trust me, I'll take care of her and make sure she ends up with a good family."

Sixiang's mother gave her a little shove. "Come with me," she said, rising. She led Sixiang to their room and opened the wooden trunk at the end of the bed that they'd shared since Sixiang was born. Inside the trunk were their clothes and linens, most old and worn, the better ones long traded for food. Her mother lifted a corner of the linens, reached a hand to the bottom, and retrieved a flat, palm-sized thing wrapped in a silk kerchief. She unfolded the silk to reveal a photo: the portrait of Sixiang's father. At one time, for as long as Sixiang could remember, it had sat in a frame on their bedside table, but a couple of years before, it had mysteriously disappeared. When she asked where it had gone, her mother simply said, "Lost." Her father had mailed the photo home along with one of his first letters, and it had arrived on the exact day Sixiang was born. "Because your father wanted to be here for your birth," her grandmother had told her. She'd also told her that in the same letter her father had chosen a name for her—Sixiang, meaning "remember home," so that she would never forget where she came from. On every holiday before the famine, her grandmother would place an extra chair by the dinner table, along with an extra bowl of rice, topped with a portion from each plate, for the father who had given Sixiang her name and whom she had never seen except in the photo.

Now her mother held Sixiang's hand open and placed the photo on her palm. Her father's face looked young, even boyish, much younger than her mother now—maybe not that much older than Sixiang herself.

"Sixiang, go to Gold Mountain with the woman. You will find your father there, and he'll take care of you."

Sixiang tried to give the photo back. "Don't make me go. I want to stay here at home."

But her mother folded Sixiang's fingers over the photo. "Listen to me. We won't be able to do this for long, you know that. Now, you go to Gold Mountain and find your father. You bring him home with you. I will be here waiting. Your grandma will be waiting too."

"But how? How can I find him?"

"You will find a way. You are growing up fast. You are strong, stronger than me." Her mother held Sixiang's face in her palms, looking into her eyes as if to plant the belief in her.

Up close, Sixiang saw something she had avoided seeing before—her mother's sunken cheeks, her wan lips; her eyes, though held steady to hers, were dim and gray. Her mother would need that bag of rice.

Sixiang knew that Gold Mountain was not all gold or all mountain. It was where people disappeared, where both her grandfather and father had gone and never come back. She imagined dark holes in mountainsides camouflaged with mats of grass or a thin layer of rocks. People stumbled in, never to climb out again.

But she also knew there were laundries where men like her grandfather bent over, the way women did here, and rubbed and scrubbed. And iron roads built by men like her father where fire-spitting wagons glided along. She knew there were people of all kinds, their skin ranging from bone white to coal black, some eating raw beef, some speaking languages that sounded like bird calls.

It was also perhaps a place where Chinese men were chased like rabbits by *gweilo*, the white men, where they got their braids cut off and wrapped around their necks as nooses. Granduncle Di told these tales after the bandits attacked their village last year, targeting the households with Gold Mountain connections. During that ransacking, Granduncle Di's gold tooth was twisted out of his gums and his wife's finger was chopped off for the gold ring she couldn't slide off. Afterward, Granduncle Di would sit below the centuries-old banyan with its aerial roots hanging like wild hair and talk, as men and children gathered around him to imagine the world across the waters.

Granduncle Di was the only one among his group of six to have survived a raid by gweilo and to secure his gold and return home with it. The others were either shot or robbed or hanged. "To survive," he said, "you have to hold your fate in your own hands. Even when odds are against you, you can turn the signpost of your fate to a different angle and mislead Yanluo Wang so he'll chase another in your place."

But then, maybe remembering the bandit attack and the eventual loss of his gold here, he would lower his head and sob till his stiff-faced wife came to lead him home.

Sixiang didn't know how to make sense of these tales of horror alongside Granduncle Di's earlier stories of fabled sights, or the bits and pieces her grandmother and mother had gathered from letters sent to the village from so many long-departed husbands. But in Sixiang's imagination, dark holes in that faraway land persisted. She couldn't know if her grandfather and father had stumbled into the same hole and finally met each other, or if their holes were separate and they had remained strangers.

Like Sixiang, her father had been born after his own father had departed. In his father's last letter, sixteen years after he'd left, he'd asked Sixiang's grandmother to arrange a marriage for their son, and, once wedded, send him to San Francisco to help with his father's laundry business. Sixiang's grandfather had sent money for the wedding and promised to send more for the passage with the next letter, but neither that letter nor the money ever arrived.

Sixiang's grandmother consulted the *shenpo* in a village to their east, a known spirit medium in this part of Xinhui. She told Sixiang how the shenpo threw the rice she had brought with her into the air, while chanting verses and rolling her eyes back in their sockets. Sixiang's grandmother had hoped that the shenpo wouldn't be able to find her husband's spirit in the underworld because he hadn't passed yet, but the shenpo's body shook and burst forth with a man's voice. It was Sixiang's grandfather's voice, aged and forlorn. Chills shot up

Sixiang's grandmother's back, as if her now-deceased husband had touched her with his cold fingers. He beseeched her to set up a tablet for him on their family altar and burn incense twice a day so that his soul could cross the ocean and reside in peace with the other ancestors.

"What happened to you? How did you die?" Sixiang's grandmother asked her husband in the shenpo's body. She had spent only six months with him before his departure and had waited for his return for the last sixteen years.

"It doesn't matter now. It's over. I'm ready to come home," the voice said.

Sixiang's grandmother felt more at ease after she set up his tablet by his ancestors' at the altar. She made a routine of burning incense for him and serving him a cup of tea in the morning, a cup of wine at night, and a bowl of rice at each meal. But the chill, she told Sixiang, had stayed with her for a long time.

She hadn't wanted her son, Sixiang's father, to go to Gold Mountain in the first place, but the idea of going was already rooted in him. Without asking her, he signed a contract with a Gold Mountain railroad company—the contractor had been traveling village to village, peddling fabulous dreams to young men and handing out ready loans for their passage. Sixiang's father-to-be came home one day and kowtowed to her grandmother three times on the brick floor, saying he was an unfilial son who disobeyed her will, but he would make up for it. He would mail money home so the family could live a good life again.

Sixiang's grandmother told him it wasn't money she wanted, but for him to stay home with her. But there was already no turning back.

With the money Sixiang's father sent home, the family was able to buy back a few *mu* of fields—the price of land ever hiking—and hire back a couple of farmhands. But what Sixiang's grandmother feared most came true: her son vanished in the same manner as her husband, and this time after only seven years. No more letters or money, just a man swallowed by a land beyond her reach or imagination.

When the flow of money ceased, they fell back on selling their fields one mu after another and letting go their hired hands till only one remained. The family of three then survived a year of drought by selling everything they could. They survived the bandits who'd robbed all the gold from Granduncle Di and found neither caches of treasure in Sixiang's house nor jewelry on the women. The outlaws even searched their pigsty, which had been empty since their last pig was slaughtered for food. They swung back into the house and quickly eyed Sixiang, whom her mother clutched in her arms, but decided it wasn't worth the trouble to kidnap a skinny little girl who would bring no ransom.

Since her father's disappearance, Sixiang's mother and grandmother had taken to making fans and baskets with leaves from their palm tree. They also sewed shoes and embroidered pillowcases and kerchiefs, which their hired hand sold for them in the marketplace. For the first two years, they continued to wait by the river for the letterman to arrive on his monthly boat delivery. Then, only Sixiang's grandmother would go, taking Sixiang with her, and month after month they would stand, in vain, in the outer circle of the hopeful wives and mothers.

When Sixiang asked her grandmother why she hadn't consulted the shenpo about her father too, her grandmother slapped her and spat on the ground: "Don't you ever say that again, or ever think your father is dead, because he is not!"

Afterward, whenever Sixiang thought of the dark holes in the mountainsides across the ocean where her father might have fallen, she would remember her grandmother's words—and the burn from her grandmother's enraged fingers on her face.

SIXIANG'S MOTHER SELDOM talked about her father. One year, when it rained after the Qixi Festival, she said the rain was the weaver girl's tears. "Because her husband, the cowherd, didn't show up to meet her over the Magpie Bridge again."

"Why didn't he show up?" Sixiang asked.

"Because he is just like your father," her mother said lazily and dropped the subject there.

Now, though, Sixiang thought her mother must still care about her father. Otherwise, she wouldn't have kept his photo, or asked her to find him in Gold Mountain and bring him home. But how on earth could Sixiang do that?

The night after the easing of her seasickness, Sixiang took out her father's photo from the inside pocket of her blouse that her mother had hurriedly sewn before the parting. She unfolded the silk kerchief, and by the dim light of the oil lamp hung from the hold's ceiling, she squinted to study the photo. Her father's face looked even, his eyes and mouth forming two horizontal lines, showing no hint of a smile nor fear or nervousness. Seated on a carved high-back chair, his elbow resting on a small side-table beside a pot of white narcissus, he wore a Chinese cotton jacket, a Western hat with a round crown and brim, and a pair of calf-length leather boots that looked worn but sturdy. His feet were flat on the ground, spread evenly at shoulders' width.

He looked very alive. Maybe he hadn't fallen into a dark hole after all. Maybe something had happened that prevented him from writing more letters or sending more money home. Maybe if Sixiang looked at this photo every day and prayed, he would appear on the shore of Gold Mountain when the ship arrived, standing with his big, solid feet, waving. She would ask him to come home with her. Would tell him that her mother and grandmother were waiting for them to return. Then she would not mind spending another month on the ocean, as long as they were heading home.

ON THE FIFTH day at sea, when the whole group was on deck—the three other girls now also feeling well enough to leave their berths—several dark blue masses broke through the water. One jumped into the air, spinning its flippers and giant body. One clapped its wing-tail on the water, making sparkling splashes.

"They are whales," said Madam, "the largest fish in the world."

"Do they eat people?" little Ah Fang asked.

"Of course," Madam said, "they eat everything."

"You don't want to fall off the ship, then," one of the teens said. Her friend giggled and whispered something in her ear.

When they returned to their berth, Sixiang and Ah Fang couldn't help but speculate on the whales' feeding habits. The sharpness of their teeth, the strength of their bowels. Could they swallow a whole pig, an entire cow? Sixiang had first thought they were happy, harmless creatures because they looked that way to her, but she had learned that first impressions were not to be trusted—as was the case with Madam, who had first appeared nothing but benevolent. Now Sixiang tried not to shiver at the thought of the deceiving animals hunting out there, separated from them by only a thin hull.

On the sixth day of their voyage, after Sixiang's group climbed onto the deck from the airless hold, the crying girl Ah Hong pushed through the crowd to the railing. The next moment, she rose up and swung a leg across the metal bar, casting a dark, startling silhouette against the pale sky. But Madam seized her arm just in time and yanked her back down. She clutched Ah Hong's shoulders, staring into her face for a long moment, and then pulled her into her arms, saying, "I know, I know how you feel."

When Ah Hong started to cry again, the rest of the girls cried too. Sixiang tried to hold back her tears for a few seconds before surrendering also to the lure of sorrow. That night, before she drifted into her first sound sleep since boarding the ship, she vaguely felt there was almost nothing that could not be withstood, and if it did become too much to bear, there was always the bottomless ocean.

HER MOTHER HAD walked with her to the boat that afternoon. Her steps faltered on her small feet, as if her remaining energy was spilling out of her with each footfall, leaving her even emptier than before. As Sixiang continued to cry, she also held her mother's arm to steady her. The woman whom Sixiang would soon call Madam carried Sixiang's bedroll for her. The man who had rowed the boat to their shore was sitting on the bow smoking a pipe. He got up to take over the bedroll and put it on the bench behind him. The woman untied a small pouch from her string belt, picked six silver coins from it, and placed them in Sixiang's hand: "Give them to your mama. She loves you and only wants the best for you."

But instead of taking them, her mother closed Sixiang's fingers around the coins, the way she had done with the photo. "You keep them with you," she said. Then, turning to the woman and looking her in the eyes, she said, "Let her keep them." She didn't look away until the woman nodded.

It took both the woman and man to pull Sixiang onto the boat. Her mother stood on the riverbank, not helping her, just saying, "Remember what I said. Remember you are strong."

As the boat rowed away from their shore, widening the braided water between them, her mother raised an arm and waved. Above her, the white clouds were slowly disintegrating; behind her, the dirt path, baked hard by the September sun, led to the house where Sixiang had lived all her life. Her mother continued to stand there on the shore, waving, balancing on her frail legs and crippled feet, until the boat turned the bend. Then, her mother was gone. So were Sixiang's house and her village Yunteng.

WHEN SIXIANG HAD lost count of the days at sea, little Ah Fang fell ill. She vomited all over her bedroll and Sixiang's too. Her face burned, her lips chalky, her breath heavy as if she were pulling a plow. One night, Sixiang woke up from a fitful sleep to see Ah Fang with her eyes and mouth still and open, no longer making a sound.

Under the oil lamp, Madam wiped Ah Fang's face and hair with a wet towel—and Ah Fang looked almost once again like the orphan-child who had slept soundly, not reaching for anyone in the middle of the night. Madam wrapped Ah Fang in her vomit-stained bedroll and by the first light of dawn, with the help of a male passenger, carried her up the ladder to the deck. There, after tying a link of old chain around Ah Fang's feet to make her sink, they lowered her to the water.

Soon, Ah Fang would end up in a whale's belly, its bowels closing around her till her bones cracked. But what if a whale was more like an ocean carriage? Maybe it would ferry Ah Fang back to China, where she would meet a good family who would treat her like their own. Or maybe Ah Fang would be reborn as a child with a mother and a father who wouldn't die on her again. But Sixiang didn't believe the whales would do any of that. She thought it would be good enough if they just left Ah Fang's body alone.

The ship kept going, day and night, sunup and sundown. Sixiang's bedroll was stained with Ah Fang's vomit, and whiffs of it would enter her nose as the ship tossed and heaved. The two older girls kept their distance, watching her as if she would soon catch what had killed Ah Fang and end up in the bottomless sea as well.

In her half sleep, Sixiang turned to Madam, who had let her keep the six silver coins and had patted her shoulder after Ah Fang's death with what seemed like tenderness. Sixiang put a hand on Madam's arm, tentatively, but the woman pushed her away, even in sleep.

It was Ah Hong who climbed down from her top bunk to lie beside Sixiang. She let Sixiang bury her face in her arms and held her gently. Maybe Ah Hong thought she was holding death: maybe after her failed attempt to jump into the ocean, she thought it would be more convenient to die of Ah Fang's sickness. But Ah Hong had been eating up her share of food, even complaining like the two other teenagers that the break-fast congee was no thicker than rice-washing water and the dinner was blander than pig feed. Maybe death, after she'd been denied it, had lost its terror and allure, and she was able to live braver, kinder, than others.

"Where do you think Ah Fang is now?" Sixiang asked Ah Hong. "So far away from everything, how will she be reborn?"

Ah Hong thought about it for a moment and then, with a tinge of laughter in her voice, said, "Maybe she'll be reborn as a whale. They look happy, don't they?"

In her head, Sixiang saw the dark blue arches again, the family of whales frolicking like they hadn't a care in the world. Sixiang wasn't wrong, then, to think they were happy.

THE NEXT TIME Sixiang thought she'd spotted a whale, a couple weeks later, Madam told her she was looking at Gold Mountain. Sixiang stared at the dark shape till it filled in with hills and trees. Then, entering a gateway between two sheer cliffs, she saw little houses, little people and horses. She touched her inside pocket to make sure her father's photo was still there, along with the six silver coins that clinked like far-off bells when she moved a certain way. She had been looking at the photo every day when no one was watching. Perhaps her father would be there among the men on the wharf that was quickly enlarging. But Sixiang knew that nothing had been easy before, and nothing would be easy now. She knew that white men would soon be questioning her, forcing her to lie about who she was, and that the family buying her could be cruel. There would be grass and dirt under her feet, but also dark holes she could stumble into.

A flock of seagulls swarmed over from the shore, countless of them. They hovered above the ship and cried like orphans, like nothing could console them.

2

On the Sierra

✳

1867

THIS FALL WAS PERHAPS THE LONGEST MOMENT OF HIS LIFE. AS HE tumbled down the mountainside, bouncing, somersaulting in the whipping snow, Guifeng thought of his village Yunteng, and the girl known as Feiyan running fast on the riverbank. She had outrun every child in the village, and he, a year younger and half a head shorter than her, imagined that one day he would grow tall and outrun her. He would reach that *yulan* tree first, only to turn his head and watch her run as if the wind were carrying her, her body condensed into a simple, single-minded, swift dance. Now, as the snow carried him, the wind blowing and whistling around his body, he learned speed, the breathless speed he'd yearned for in his childhood.

He had lived eighteen years on the earth and had loved Feiyan since he was twelve—the girl known first for her fast legs, and then for her misfortune and disappearance. The old man she was wedded to was found dead in their shack and she was nowhere to be found. Rumor had it that she'd either been kidnapped by the bandits or sold by the flesh traders—for what else could have happened to a young, pretty girl like her? Guifeng expected never to see her again, until he did, on his first day in Gold Mountain.

Fated it felt to see her on that exact day—after he and other newcomers had been picked up on the wharf and led in a single file to Chinatown, carrying their possessions on shoulder poles, feet not yet accustomed to solid ground after two months' sea tossing. Much like the hold of the sailing ship, Chinatown seemed to be only occupied by Chinese men—until they arrived at an alley where several Chinese women stood conspicuously by doors left ajar, under red lanterns that looked lusterless in the afternoon sun. One of these women was Feiyan.

Without the slightest smile, she moved her eyes down the men as if inspecting a disorderly army, her stern eyes pausing on Guifeng for only a second, and if she recognized him, she showed no sign. But when Guifeng turned his head to look back at her, to make sure she was indeed whom he thought her to be, she was gazing at him. Her eyes seemed to be losing their hard edges, her face softening.

That was two years ago. Guifeng had not yet found the courage to go back to that alley and look for her. But now, falling with white burning speed through wind, air, and snow, he thought of her back in their village. There was no sorrow: she was just running.

He thought it must have been the *wuwei* that Daoshi had been talking about, which did not mean no action, as Daoshi told him, but rather, action done according to Dao, so that it felt easeful, unburdened by contriving or striving. That was how Feiyan had run, all ease and joy, which filled the twelve-year-old Guifeng with a longing that he had known was more than childish want. It felt wholesome, like an opening, like his heart was breaking into blossoms.

When two years later she was married off to that old man across the mountain, Yunteng became static without her motion. The village felt like a tomb with its dullness, its same sky, same fields, same dirt and dirt houses and days. Guifeng imagined what the old man would do to her. He observed old men in his village with a bad taste in his mouth: What did a toothless, hairless man have to do with a young girl who could easily outrun him, who was all rhythm and grace?

Guifeng's lovesickness did not cure itself with time, but instead branched into a more manageable longing for the larger world that stretched far beyond his village. At fourteen, several months after Feiyan was married off, he wrote a letter to his father expressing his wish to join him in Gold Mountain. "Not until you turn sixteen," his father wrote back. "It's a hard life here, but you can help me with the laundry business when you're older." The laundry business, in Guifeng's imagination, would be nothing like the kind of mundane, undignified clothes-washing done here by women on the riverbanks. American laundry had to be a more manly, industrial endeavor; otherwise, it wouldn't be something his father had pursued or which made enough money to provide for the whole family year after year.

At sixteen, Guifeng got married according to his father's will, to someone his mother had chosen for him—a small-footed, big-hipped girl who could hardly walk, much less run. His father's next letter was long overdue, but Guifeng had dreamt for too long of leaving to be dissuaded by his mother now. After two months' rocking in a sailing boat that had felt like a prolonged, restless sleep, he arrived in San Francisco, or Big City, as everyone called it. He only got to spend a couple of hours there—first at the Tin How Temple to give thanks for a safe voyage, and then at his clan association, Kong Chow, to register. Next, he was brought on a boat to Sacramento, Second City, and from there in a boxcar to the Sierra. Which was not gold but silver, a snow-capped mountain range that made him shiver with its sheer height and whiteness. The railroad he was contracted to build would go up and around and through it.

GUIFENG WAS AFRAID of heights, even though he was named after the mountain back home, Guifeng Mountain, which was the tallest in Xinhui but, compared to the Sierra, seemed more like a hill now. When he was little, his grandfather had taken him up the mountain for a Chongyang Festival. Tripping on a step, he almost rolled down a steep slope and had since dreamed of falling, his nightmares replete with stone steps turning into a cliff or solid ground caving into a bottomless pit. Now the Sierra, with its snowcaps wreathed in clouds, spread miles in front of him. The scale of things had changed. He was now one of the thousands of Chinese men brought here to nibble through the hard granite, an ant, no bigger than the numerous pinpoint stars below which they pitched their canvas tents.

He joined a gang of thirty, all of them from the Siyi area, all speaking similar dialects. A headman, whom people called Chang'er due to his long earlobes, translated orders from the white foreman who rode on his horse and called everyone John. A cook, Li Shu, made their hometown food on the open firepit, serving fish and poultry shipped in boxcars from Sacramento. Guifeng could now eat more meat in a day than what had lasted an entire week back home, but he paid for his food out of his own wage, which was thirty dollars a month if he worked from sunrise to sundown, every day except Sundays. Another portion of his wage would be going to the company for the next seven months, to pay off his debt of seventy-five dollars for his passage plus interest. Until the debt was clear, he wouldn't be able to save or send money home. He also had to buy a pair of leather boots on credit, as his fellow workers had warned him that the cotton slip-ons hand-made by his wife wouldn't last a week for this kind of work.

Guifeng shared a company-issued tent with Headman Chang'er, Chang'er's son Ah Fook, and Daoshi, who was in his late twenties and, like Chang'er, had been in Gold Mountain for over a decade. People called him Daoshi because he had tended the altars at the temple in Big City before joining the crew. Guifeng didn't know if he was a real Daoist priest or not, but he did like to quote from *Laozi* and *Zhuangzi*. Only Guifeng, Ah Fook, and a few others who had arrived on the same ship were new to the Sierra. The rest of the gang had been building the iron road since the previous year, when Chinese workers had only been hired on a trial basis. Now, ninety percent of the Central Pacific workforce were Chinese.

Their current job was to hew out a ledge for a roadbed along the cliff of Cape Horn, which dropped twelve hundred feet into a torrent of water below. With a rope tied around his waist, Guifeng was lowered over the cliff edge down the slope that was almost vertical. He tried to focus his eyes on the rockface in front of him, its creases and veins magnifying as his hands and feet groped for a firmer hold. He imagined himself as a small tree taking root in the rock but was certain a breeze could blow him away should the rope break for one reason or another.

Daoshi was lowered beside him. Together they were to drill holes into the rockface, insert black powder into the holes, and light the fuse before being hauled back up. Guifeng volunteered to do the hammering first to take his mind off the height, but his first strikes were soft and crooked. Daoshi, however, didn't comment. He said something else instead, a quote from *Laozi*: "天地不仁，以万物为刍狗。"

Guifeng asked him what it meant.

"It means heaven and earth do not pick and choose. They see everything as straw dogs."

"Straw dogs?"

"They're dogs made of straw our ancients used for sacrifices. Real dogs were too expensive, so they made straw ones to serve the purpose. A straw dog was prized as a sacrifice, and then burned or tossed away afterward. Prime or decline, heaven and earth do not favor or disfavor. In their eyes, all are the same. We are all straw dogs. Which makes me wonder what heaven and earth think of us now? Is what we're doing to the mountain no different from flicking off specks of dust? Do they neither approve nor disapprove?"

Guifeng let down another strike, steadier now, but the spike went in less than an inch. "This doesn't feel like dust to me," he said.

"And our bodies don't feel like straw," Daoshi said.

When they changed position, Guifeng's legs shook again, separated from the void by only a jutting sheet of rock. Soon he also became aware of a pain in his hands clutching the spike, which were cracking under the force of Daoshi's hammer strikes.

"You need gloves," Daoshi said. "It would be nice if our bodies did not feel pain, like straw."

By the time they were hauled up, Guifeng's palms were bleeding. A hawk soared past him, heedless of gravity, up and up into the sunlit blue that was cold and brilliant, welcoming nothing and everything. Guifeng threw himself on the ground the moment he reached it, as explosions boomed below him, shaking his body as if it were hollow as straw.

A DEATH OCCURRED a week later. A pulley got stuck, and a man surged into the billow of dark smoke before plunging with the blasted rocks into the torrent below. No one wanted to go down the cliff again, but the foreman yelled out threats to withhold pay for the day. Headman Chang'er spat and cursed and let himself be lowered down. One by one they resumed work. When Guifeng was lowered again too, he put his forehead to the flat rockface that trapped millennia of sun-heat and ice-chill. He'd seen a fern fossil imprinted in a rock that he'd drilled into and blasted away. It could be him next, blown asunder, with pieces of him revealed as fossils to a future eon.

At night, they sat around the campfire talking quietly about the man's death. They'd buried him at sunset. Several of his friends and tentmates had climbed down the cliff, wrapped his remains in his bed-roll, and carried him up to a burial ground. As they built the railroad, they were also building graveyards alongside it, marking each grave with name and dates carved on a stone for the clan associations who would eventually come collect the bones and ship them back home. Daoshi had burned incense and chanted incantations for a smooth passing of the deceased soul, although they all knew that those who died a violent death could not be easily appeased.

Chang'er pulled on his pipe before starting a story. He spoke of a time from his mining days. A tentmate of his went out to pee and saw a man stoking the dying fire—"a man, mind you, with nothing left for his face but a bloody pulp. But my buddy, Ah Xing, still recognized him to be Ah Deng, who had departed a few days before with his share of gold—not a huge fortune but enough to build a two-story house back home and buy a few mu of land. Ah Xing came running into the tent, screaming that he'd seen Ah Deng's ghost, and said the ghost had told him he'd been shot and robbed by a gang of gweilo down the stream.

"We went out to look but saw nothing save the dark night. When we came back in, Ah Xing was grinding his butcher knife. 'What are you doing?' we asked him. 'Revenge,' he said. 'You all should come with me.' 'How?' we asked him, shaking our heads, 'How can knives fight guns?' Ah Xing spat and called us a bunch of cowards. We didn't respond because we had the feeling that it wasn't Ah Xing talking anymore; he hadn't ever talked in that throaty way, like he'd smoked a pipe every single day of his life, the way Ah Deng did. Ah Xing was not a smoker. We saw his body the next morning, dead, dumped by the stream where we'd been panning."

Chang'er paused to rekindle his pipe in the fire. The pause was long. "You'll never want to see what we saw," he said at last, "but I'll tell you what the gweilo had done to him, so you know what they're capable of." Chang'er looked at them one by one around the fire, from Daoshi who sat cross-legged and straight-backed as usual, to Li Shu whose hand hovered above a sizzling teapot, all the way to Chang'er's son, Ah Fook, who wore a pained look on his face as if he were already suffering what Ah Xing had suffered.

"They'd beaten him to a pulp, and they'd cut off his, his—" he paused to point at his crotch, "and stuffed it in his mouth." Chang'er shook his head hard before clearing his throat to continue, "I'll tell you this: Ah Xing's ghost is still haunting. Both Ah Xing's and Ah Deng's. They're still looking for someone to avenge them."

He spat into the fire, which hissed and leapt.

When only Daoshi and Guifeng were left by the fire, Daoshi took out a book from under his jacket, opened it to a seemingly random page, and read a quote out loud: "为者败之，执者失之，是以圣人无为故无败，无执故无失。"

Guifeng waited for Daoshi to explain, but he did not, only looking into the fire, so Guifeng asked him to translate the quote into plain words.

"This is the literal translation: Those who act fail, those who grasp lose, so the sage does not act and does not fail, does not grasp and does not lose. But the tricky thing here is wuwei. If it means not acting at all, then a sage is no different than a rock." He picked up a palm-sized rock by his feet and looked at it. "This doesn't look like a sage, does it? For that reason, wuwei cannot mean not to act, but to not act against Dao. It is acting according to Dao, and Dao acts as if it doesn't act, while all is being acted upon."

Guifeng thought about this. "I'm not sure these words are plain enough for me, but tell me, Daoshi, what is the act according to Dao in Chang'er's story?"

"If I knew, I'd be a sage," Daoshi said. "But I do know it's not what his possessed friend did—going for his own death with a butcher knife is surely not Dao." He rose to his feet and tossed the rock toward the valley. The firelight caught a glimpse of its arc before the rock vanished into the darkness. Guifeng listened for it to hit, but the sound never came, as if the night had swallowed it whole.

SNOW FELL A few weeks later. Flakes poured down, soft at first, then ruinous. Within hours, the snow had covered pines, rocks, roadbeds, and tents that creaked under its weight and collapsed. At a nearby worksite, a locomotive-driven snowplow triggered a snowslide that tossed a man into the ravine below. Guifeng's gang were ordered to clear the tracks and roadbeds by hand, but the snow came down faster than their arms, piling higher than their shovels' reach.

They were then ordered to move to the east of the mountaintop, on foot or sled, to Truckee Canyon, to fell forests that were blocking the railroad route. They cut down pines thicker than a dozen men combined and blasted out stumps from the frozen ground. Each treefall was a small earthquake, each blast a battlefield. But without the proximity of precipices and immediate threat of falling, this felt like an improvement to Guifeng.

At camp, the men drank, gambled, and told tall tales. They made those who were married talk about their wedding night. Those who didn't have sons or nephews with them talked about girls they'd visited in San Francisco, Sacramento, Auburn, Green Valley, Cisco, and the girls they were about to visit in Truckee. They seemed to know all about the girls.

Guifeng had never learned her real name. He'd only heard her go by Feiyan, a nickname used by her parents too—maybe because she was fast like a flying swallow even as a baby? Guifeng was certain that she went by a different name now, likely one of those floral names befitting her trade. He had once imagined that even if she'd been kidnapped or sold into a brothel, she would have somehow managed to run away, given her talent for running. It had never occurred to him that she'd end up all the way here in Gold Mountain, and that he would see her on the day of his arrival. As if without knowing it, he had come here, so willfully against his mother's will, to meet his destiny.

But wasn't his destiny already decided for him? To be a dutiful provider for his family who depended on him and waited for his return. He should think of his wife instead, who was his and his alone, a good-looking girl always warm in bed: holding her in the winter was like holding a stove. She was six months pregnant when he left, her belly a glowing dome where he'd put his ear and heard soft wing-like rustlings. He'd felt awed by the sheer fact that he could father a child—most men could, no doubt, but it was still marvelous to know that a life descending from him was growing inside his woman. And for that reason, he could no longer think of her as just any girl his mother had happened to choose for him. At his departure, his wife had taken his face in her hands and looked into his eyes until he promised to come back to her. "Yes," he had promised.

But as he lay on his bedroll, feeling finally closer to the ground, even though they were still thousands of feet above sea level, he couldn't help but see Feiyan trapped behind the narrow door she'd stood by that day, pressed down by man after man. Had she not tried to escape? Could she not? Or perhaps the real question was: Even if she'd tried, where, in this strange land, would she have escaped to?

Had he not seen her that day—had it happened that she was behind the door, or that he and the other newcomers were led down a different alley—he would probably not be thinking of her right now. He would have thought of her less and less, as during the months when he was with his wife, until eventually Feiyan would have just faded away. Like his own childhood self, a shed skin dissolving into the air. But would that have been better? He wondered. Would he still be yearning for something, only without knowing what it was?

ON SUNDAY, HE walked with Daoshi a couple of miles east to Truckee, a logging town where Chinese miners had been holing up in the winters since the previous decade. Its Chinatown was a triangular area adorned with red lanterns and yellow flags and Chinese signs that warmed his heart to see. They came to a bathhouse where hot steam rose above its shingled roof. The tubs had a jovial atmosphere, where men, mostly loggers and railroad workers like themselves, chatted and laughed and exchanged news as they soaked their aching muscles and rubbed away their weeklong dirt. After the bath, Guifeng and Daoshi put on the clean clothes they'd brought with them and sat in front of the barber's next door to have their faces and foreheads shaved, their queues rebraided.

Then Daoshi headed to the brothel, where two girls in thin pastel blouses stood on the lantern-strung porch, like early harbingers of spring. With his upright posture, Daoshi went to the girl in peach. The girl in mint, tall and slim like Feiyan, beamed a smile at Guifeng. But he turned his eyes away and kept walking down the part-plank, part-dirt street under the post-noon sun, which was almost warm on his cleansed skin.

A man standing by a doorframe painted bright gold and violet nodded at him. "Young man," he said, "you look nice and clean, just right for a photo portrait."

Guifeng paid the man thirty cents and sat down on a carved high-back chair, against a light blue cloth hanging down the wall. On his right was a small side table with a porcelain pot of blooming narcissus, its fragrance reminiscent of women's powdered flesh, of his wife on their wedding night, and the girl smiling at him just a moment ago, whom he could have held in his arms by now had he chosen to. The photographer asked him to rest an elbow by the flower, look at the glass lens in the middle of the black barrel, and hold.

Fifteen minutes later, the photographer emerged from the corner of the room that was enclosed with a dark curtain draping from ceiling to floor. "Now your youth is forever captured," he said, handing Guifeng the photo. "You got a wife back home?"

"Yes," Guifeng said.

"Send it to her, so she won't be too lonely." The photographer winked.

Guifeng looked at the small black-and-white face in the photo. It looked plain, with nothing striking about it, nothing that suggested an appetite for the extraordinary or any deviation from an ordinary Chinese man's ordinary destiny. Except perhaps the glimmer in his eyes that seemed to be seeping through the face's dull regularity, a glimmer that made him think of Feiyan's gaze that day.

Following the photographer's direction, Guifeng came to the grocery store across the street, which also provided postal services. He bought an envelope and a piece of ruled rice paper, borrowed an ink well and a thin-tipped brush from the shopkeeper, and began to write:

> *Respectful mother and wife:*
>
> *Hope you are both safe and well. Since my last letter relating my safe arrival in Gold Mountain, I have been building the railroad in the Sierra Mountains. Food is good and plenty, and my co-workers are all from our Siyi area. I will be paying off my debt in spring and begin mailing money home monthly.*
>
> *I am counting the days until the baby's birth. I have thought more about names. If it is a boy, call him Siqiang, so he will grow up strong. If it is a girl, call her Sixiang, so she will always remember her home. This enclosed photo represents my wish to be there with you all.*
>
> *Guifeng*

IN SPRING, THE men moved back up the mountains, this time all the way to the summit, to be part of the army that was clawing out tunnels in the granite. Now the ground was seven thousand feet above sea level. There were no trees at this height, only snow and ice-draped rocks. Guifeng's gang was stationed at the west portal of Tunnel No. 6, over fifteen hundred feet away from its east portal, or half the length from the shaft at the midpoint where workers attacked the rocks on both fronts. The superintendent, James Strobridge, wore a black patch over his right eye, allegedly lost in a black powder explosion.

The rock up this high was solid granite, even harder than that of Cape Horn. A team now consisted of three men: Daoshi would find a seam or crack to position a three-foot-long flat-tipped pole drill in; Guifeng and Ah Fook would take turns wielding their sledgehammers and pounding the top of the drill. After every two bangs, Daoshi would rotate the bit a quarter turn to lodge deeper into the rock. It took a team two to three hours to drill a hole a palm wide and an arm deep. Then they filled the holes with black powder and a fuse and packed the opening with wet sand. Then they lit the fuse and fled.

Guifeng thought of a story Daoshi had told them one Sunday, when they were still in the canyon, as they sat around Li Shu watching him chop a roasted duck on his makeshift counter. A story by Zhuangzi about a cook who mastered the art of cutting up oxen. Impressed by his skill, the king asked how he did it. The cook, named Ding, said, "When I first started this line of work, I saw a whole ox. After three years, I saw chunks of an ox. Now, I see not with my eyes but with my mind. I see crevices between an ox's bones and joints, and the blade of my cleaver finds those crevices with ease. Other cooks replace their cleaver every month, while I've been using mine for nineteen years. When I come across a tough joint, I slow down. I keep my eyes focused, my hand steady. I insert the blade lightly, and *hu-la*, the meat falls apart like a lump of earth. I stand up and let joy fill me. I clean my cleaver and put it away. What I follow is nothing but Dao."

Li Shu waited for Daoshi to finish the story and handed him his cleaver: "Okay, I'm not Dao enough for you. Why don't you chop for us? Let's see how you make it all breezy and joyous." And Daoshi just laughed.

Now hammering away on the unyielding rock, Guifeng wondered if it was ever possible to make this back-breaking swinging, this slow holing, this tamping and fusing, an art, or an action aligned with Dao. The Way, the ultimate principle of the universe, which, according to Daoshi, or Laozi, was beyond naming or defining. As Guifeng scampered toward sunlight praying nothing would go wrong, all he could feel was the tight rattle of fear in his small thumping heart.

IN SEPTEMBER, THE night of the Mid-Autumn Festival, each of them got a mooncake special-ordered from San Francisco Chinatown. They savored it with rice wine by the campfire. The same filling of lotus seed paste and salted duck egg yolk, the same full moon their families back home must have seen twelve hours ago. But this moon rising above the ragged mountain peaks looked cooler, paler than the ones Guifeng remembered from the past on this particular night. It looked as if it couldn't care less about what those watching and admiring it were thinking.

The men by the campfire talked about the mooncakes: the best they'd had, the varieties of fillings, and how the cakes had come about. Ah Fook said they were made to look like the full moon, of course. Li Shu said that was what children were told: they were made to look like women's breasts, or if not that, their bellies when they were with child.

Chang'er dismissed them both. "I'll tell you the true origin of mooncakes," he said before gulping down his cup of wine. "It was at the end of the Yuan Dynasty. Zhu Yuanzhang got this brilliant idea. He had his soldiers put paper slips in small cakes and distribute them to all his followers. What was on the slips? A message: *On the fifteenth night of the eighth moon, we kill the barbarians.* That was how we Han people drove out the Mongols and took back our country."

"Not forever," Daoshi said.

Chang'er looked at him. "For almost three hundred years."

"Then the Manchus took over," Daoshi said.

They all went quiet. Guifeng suspected they might be thinking the same thing: the decade-long Taiping Rebellion that had recently failed. When he was a child, he'd seen soldiers razing his village, beheading a dozen villagers thought to be rebel supporters. For months afterward, he'd had nightmares about bouncing and rolling heads. Anti-Qing conversation was not safe to have, not even up here in the Sierra, half an earth away from Middle Kingdom.

"Then what are you saying?" Chang'er said. "Wuwei? Do nothing? Let the barbarians treat us like rats?"

"I never said wuwei was doing nothing."

"What is it, then?"

"It is—" Daoshi paused, as if he had second thoughts about what he was going to say.

Chang'er was going to say more before Li Shu stopped him. "Hold on. You two save your spit. I have a story, which I guarantee will bring a laugh. I have a buddy who is also a cook—not your enlightened Cook Ding, just so you know." He gave Daoshi a teasing look. "My buddy, unluckily, cooks for the white gang building those snowsheds." He jutted his chin to the west where sheds were being built to cover the track before the new season of snows pressed in. "These gweilo are a mean bunch, as you may have guessed. They made it a sport to torment my friend: they called him names, pushed him around. Once they snuck into his tent and tied his braid to one of the sticks he pitched his tent with. When they didn't like the food he made, they poured it on his face. One day, my buddy finally had it. Guess what he did?" Li Shu started laughing, and in between his laughs, he said chokingly, "He peed into a pot of beef stew before serving it to them! And guess what they said? They said the stew was the best my buddy had ever made!"

Chang'er slapped his knee. "Ask your buddy to shit in the stew next time. They'll like it even more."

All laughed except for Daoshi, who said quietly after the laughter died down, "I'll tell you what wuwei is for us. It's that we sit here and not go back to work, until they pay us the same as the whites, and treat us like men, not rats. We will be at once doing nothing and doing something that should be done. That's wuwei."

They all went quiet again. Guifeng had heard that white men would go on strike demanding higher wages than they'd already got, and their bosses would bring in Chinese men to break their strikes. As a result, the Chinese had been known as strike-breakers, the very opposite of strikers. It was a novel idea to think they could go on strike too—especially when they were supposed to feel grateful for having a job at all, and for making several times more than they would have made in China. But on the other hand, being a farmer in China didn't involve flirting with death moment by moment.

"Why do you think they won't just fire us?" Chang'er said.

"They'll get hundreds more to replace us. China is poor in everything but its number of people."

"If all the thousands of us stop working together, they can't find so many replacements, not for a while."

"How can we get the thousands of us to all stop working?"

"By organizing."

"How? Putting paper slips in mooncakes?" Chang'er raised the last bit of his cake and looked at it: no slip, no message.

Everyone turned their eyes back to Daoshi, who sipped his wine and shrugged. "Why not?"

But that was barely reassuring. As far as they knew, Daoshi had never mentioned his family back home, nor had he sent anything when the delivery man came to collect their letters and money bound for China. He drank and frequented brothels despite his scholarly habit of quoting inscrutable texts. It probably wouldn't matter much to him if he lost this job, unlike the rest of them, each with multiple mouths to feed.

"Well, it'll be another year before we have mooncakes again," Chang'er finally said, lifting his face to look at the moon, which had risen about mid-sky but appeared neither brighter nor warmer. Instead, it looked almost ghostly, like an undernourished, cheerless version of itself. "Let's get some sleep before another shit day in that asshole." He looked at the tunnel behind them, its portal half lit by an oil lamp. The night shift's hammering had not stopped clanging out.

Under the pallid moon, the tunnel crouched like a primeval beast, all mouth and pain and loveless hunger.

THE WINTER TURNED out to be even colder and snowier than the last. They dug out a maze under the snow to connect the tunnel entrances, the dumping and storage areas, and the wooden shacks where they now slept. They no longer knew the difference between day and night, sun and moon. Height also became irrelevant, as Guifeng felt as if he was deep inside the earth's bowels. The tunnel's entombed smell oozed out of the dark, damp rock, which was compounded by the static profusion of explosion fumes and granite dust that burned their lungs. Icicles hung on rock, dropping frigid water—the piss, they called it— which, mixed with the frosty water pulsing out of the rock below, covered the ground with sheets of ice on which they tried not to slip as they hammered and drilled, while the frozen rock bounced their exertion back.

In between shifts, they squeezed into the small wooden shacks shipped in whole from Sacramento, in which bunks were piled three tiers high. Despite the small stove in the middle of the shack and the crumbled newspaper Guifeng stuffed inside his cotton-padded jacket, the cold followed him to his top bunk. He longed to sleep on his own bed in his village that seemed to exist only on a cloud now, a warm, green, moist bubble where three women were waiting for him—his wife whose body heat he keenly missed; his daughter who had just taken her first steps as related in their last letter; and his poor mother who had to make a living out of waiting. Would his own fragility infect them? If he was to blow up in an explosion, or if his blood froze in an avalanche, would their green bubble burst, too?

He had inquired about his father during his registration with Kong Chow Clan Association on his day of arrival. They'd found his name in their records: "Missing, likely dead" was what had been written down. According to their notes, Guifeng's father disappeared one November day in 1864 during his laundry delivery, and his laundry business, which was located outside of Chinatown in a white neighborhood, as many of them were, got ransacked and burned. Guifeng did not want to imagine how his father died. It could be any of the myriad ways a Chinese man in Gold Mountain met his demise, which ran a long list in the Chinese-English phrase booklet from which Ah Fook was learning English:

He came to his death by homicide.
He was murdered by a thief.

He was choked to death with a lasso, by a robber.
He was strangled to death by a man.
He was starved to death in prison.
He was frozen to death in the snow.
He was killed by an assassin.
He was shot dead by his enemy.
He was poisoned to death by his friend.

. . .

Guifeng and Ah Fook had marveled at the list, which filled an entire page of the fifteen-page booklet, placed side by side with the more
typical entries on self-introduction, business transactions, and police
and court dealings. Was it out of perversion or admonition to include
something so morbid? They talked about it and decided it was probably neither. It was more likely matter of fact. Because, as they were
learning quickly, death for the Chinese in Gold Mountain was always
looming and frequently gruesome. They couldn't help but predict that
the list would continue to grow in future editions of the phrasebook,
to include the new ways of death that the railroad had been inventing
for them.

IN SPRING, THEY stumbled out of the tunnels into the glinting sun:
the air was cuttingly fresh, the pines still jostling to point their fingers
at the sky. They tallied calamities and losses: a camp nearby had been
swept away by an avalanche; one down west had been wiped out by
smallpox; another had lost half of their men to a tunnel cave-in; another
lost a quarter to a dynamite misfire.

Daoshi no longer stayed with the gang. He'd been traveling up and
down the thirty miles of the line from Cicero to Truckee to preside over
funerals. He'd become known as the person to ask. If in the past, he had
not been a real Daoist priest, he'd become one here on the Sierra. He
now wore his hair up in a topknot as a real daoshi did and wore a black

robe and cap for ceremonies. He even set up altars when death claimed many at once. Chang'er no longer handled his pay. Their foreman had simply deducted one man's wage when he gave Chang'er the gang's total to allocate.

From time to time, Daoshi would pass through, bearing news. He told them that white workers from the Union Pacific Railroad, those laying tracks from east to west in the opposite direction, had kidnapped their boss for delaying their wages. The news made the gang sigh and shake their heads, as they remembered bitterly that they'd once been delayed wages for two months in a row and had done nothing more than curse and swear among themselves. Daoshi also told them that their boss, Charles Crocker, had commissioned a contractor to design a poster for more recruitment from China: they needed five thousand more workers to win the race against the Union Pacific, but Chinese workers were leaving.

"There are other jobs for us now, better paid and less treacherous," Daoshi said. "Three hundred workers near Cisco have just decamped for a quartz mine up north. A foreman tried to whip a gang into staying, and it turned into a fight. The bosses are learning that we're not so docile after all."

Because of the news Daoshi had brought with him, when Crocker raised their wages in mid-May from thirty to thirty-five dollars a month, they were not surprised. Nor were they grateful. The raise was long overdue and not enough. The white workers had been paid forty dollars a month, provided free food, and slated fewer hours, and they had outright refused to do the tunnel work: "That kind of work is for Chinamen," they said, "not us."

Meanwhile, Strobridge continued to yell at them, "Too slow, you rat-eating, pig-tailed chinks! Are you all slow like your small-footed women?"

It didn't surprise them either when the company started to use nitroglycerin, the newly invented dynamite far more powerful than black powder—even though five Chinese men and one white man had died in a misfire the previous spring when the company first experimented with the chemical. Now, Strobridge and the foreman stood outside the tunnel as they watched Chang'er carry the cart of vials in, Strobridge's black eyepatch ominous.

Guifeng was still teamed up with Ah Fook. Since nitro required smaller drill holes than black powder, teams had shrunk back to two workers each. It was the gang's second time using the new explosive. The first blasts had made such gigantic bites into the rock that Guifeng had almost felt cheerful—because of both the fact that he'd survived them unscathed and the prospect of being released much sooner from the tunnel's hellhole at this escalated speed.

After his training with Strobridge, Chang'er, being the headman, was handling the explosive exclusively, since no one else in the gang wanted to touch the deadly vials. Hands trembling visibly in the lamp light, he slid a canister into a drill hole, lowered the blasting cap into the nitro, filled the hole with wet sand, and attached the fuse. Guifeng, Ah Fook and a couple of other workers staying in the tunnel to assist him watched with their breath held as Chang'er repeated the same motions with the rest of the canisters. Then, before Chang'er lit the fuse, everyone fled the tunnel. Chang'er ran out after them. They crouched behind the boulders and listened to one another's shaky heartbeats. Then the mountains shook and their bodies sprang up, their hearts somersaulting.

"Now get in and clear the rock," Strobridge shouted as they were still patting dust off their heads.

Guifeng went in with Ah Fook, one pushing a wheelbarrow, the other holding a lamp and a shovel. Guifeng would soon be asking himself again and again why the two of them were the first to step back into the accursed tunnel. Was it possibly because he had said to Ah Fook, "Let's go"—in English, as if to impress Strobridge standing by?

Guifeng had expected an easier cleaning job, since the chunks left by nitro blasts were larger than those left by black powder, meaning fewer stoops to fill a barrow. For once, he was not on his guard. Instead of fearing imminent death as he should, he was thinking ahead to someday when he would be recounting all this to someone—maybe Feiyan—leisurely, away from any form of danger, describing these outlandish experiences that could be remembered as adventurous, even heroic.

He had not sensed it coming when it came, and it came all at once—the flash of light, the torrent of heat, the gush of dust and rocks and chips that together hurled him into the air, with such a force he felt propelled out of his body, which hit the rock ceiling and then hovered in midair for a moment before dropping—toward another body twisted on the rock below. Bones hitting bones, cushioned only by hardened muscles. It was Ah Fook below him, his eyes open, one of his arms bent in an odd angle, next to the lantern, where oil pooled out of the shattered glass, spitting little fires along its way. Blood from under Ah Fook's head was coursing toward the little flames, extinguishing them as it advanced, dark and unrelenting. Without thinking, Guifeng brushed his palm over Ah Fook's eyes to close them. Ah Fook, who had worn other people's pain as if it were his own, who had taught Guifeng English with the booklet that listed dozens of ways to die but not yet his, had saved Guifeng's life with his death.

Strobridge took off his hat when Chang'er carried his son out of the tunnel. "I'm sorry," he said. "Sometimes air bubbles in the cartridge can delay the charge."

THERE WERE NO coffins left at the summit camps. The next shipment of supplies was not due to arrive for another week. Chang'er asked to be left alone with Ah Fook inside the tent. Guifeng waited outside. Besides a sprained ankle and some cuts and bruises, Guifeng appeared intact. But his ears rang with a constant buzz. His head ached as if it were held on the tip of a spear. When Chang'er finally stepped out of the tent, he walked away without looking at Guifeng. Ah Fook's body was lying on his cot, covered by his bedsheet from head to toe. Since they'd moved out of the crammed shack into their old tent at the end of the winter, Guifeng's cot was once again next to Ah Fook's. Guifeng sat down on his cot and looked at the motionless Ah Fook. Then, wiping his eyes with his sleeve, he kneeled down beside Ah Fook's cot.

Chang'er came back hauling on his shoulders two long wooden boards, which looked like leftovers from last winter's lumber for the snowshed. He set them down on a bench outside the tent and started to saw and hammer. When Guifeng offered to help, Chang'er waved him away. He had still not said a word to Guifeng, nor looked in his direction. Explosions continued to erupt across the mountains.

Daoshi came before sunset. Clothed in his ceremonial robe and cap, he talked with Chang'er in a low voice by the coffin. When the rest of the gang returned from the shift, a few helped Chang'er carry the coffin down the western slope. Facing west was not usually good *fengshui*, Daoshi explained, but in their case, it was the direction of the ocean and China. They came to a clearing where mounds of newish dirt were lined up in rows, each marked by a rectangular stone with name, dates, and home village carved into it. Though no ocean could be seen from here, an alpine lake lay in a pine-encircled valley, its rippling water reflecting the golden sunset. If not for the blasts that hadn't stopped shaking the mountains, Guifeng could almost imagine a heavenly abode for the spirits of Ah Fook and all those buried here, lying so close to the vast sky and the clear mirroring water.

On their way back to the camp, Daoshi lingered behind with Guifeng, who hobbled on a stick. "How are you?" Daoshi asked.

"I'm fine." Guifeng fought back a new surge of tears.

They walked quietly. Daoshi kept a slow pace with him. After a while, Guifeng asked, "Is heaven punishing us for what we're doing to the mountains?"

"Maybe, maybe not." Daoshi looked at him. "Just know that it wasn't your fault. It was none of our faults."

"We're all straw dogs."

"It does feel that way sometimes. But you're not straw, nor dog, nor made for the purpose of sacrifice. Don't be too hard on yourself."

Guifeng looked away from Daoshi's gaze. Behind them, the sky was aflame with wild streaks of sunset clouds—red, purple, black, gold, like it was a giant altar, waiting for its sacrifice.

THE NEXT MORNING, when Guifeng opened his eyes to the first light of dawn, he didn't hear the routine clatter of Li Shu's kettles and pots, or the usual rustle and chatter of early risers. Daoshi was sleeping on his old cot, which they'd kept for him although his visits hadn't been as frequent as Guifeng had hoped. Chang'er lay still on his, facing the tent's canvas wall. He'd turned in late last night, and then for hours sniffled and tossed.

Last night at dinner by the campfire, Chang'er had said only one thing: "I'm not going back to work. You all do what's best for you."

Daoshi was by the fire with them, sitting upright, the way he'd been in the fall, under the pale full moon, when he'd introduced the notion of a strike to them. They must all still remember what he'd said about wuwei then—the action of nonaction, the doing of not doing what one shouldn't do.

Now lying in the tent, Guifeng was certain that everyone was awake by this hour, was listening and waiting like himself. When the sun shot straight through the tent from the east, the time they normally headed to the tunnel, Guifeng finally heard Li Shu walking to the stone hearth to rekindle the fire, and someone step out of the tent next door, saying, "Morning," all in a quiet, probing manner. Then, a few minutes later, came the expected clomping of boots and spew of curses: Strobridge and the foreman were outside their tent.

Chang'er took his time to get up, his shoulders stooped, eyes bloodshot, but before he stepped out of the tent, he took a breath and lifted his chest. Daoshi followed him out. So did Guifeng. Strobridge measured Chang'er with his good eye. "I'm very sorry for your loss, John," he said. "But this work cannot be delayed. You've got to understand: this railroad is bigger than you and me. No death will ever stop it from being built."

In the afternoon, the foreman came alone. "I'll tell you what," he said to Chang'er, "ask your gang to go back to work and we'll still give everybody a half day's pay. You all just need to do the drilling and cleaning. We've got someone to handle the nitro and check for misfires, someone we pay extra."

Chang'er translated the foreman's words to the other workers before stepping back into the tent. Guifeng followed him in. He listened to the sounds outside: the querulous mumbles among the rest of the gang, feet shuffling, tools clinking.

"They need the pay," he said to Chang'er, somehow feeling responsible to explain for them.

"No." Chang'er lay on his cot, staring at the seam of the tent where they'd added several new patches since the spring. "They are just cowards, and you should go join them."

DAOSHI HAD LEFT in the morning to preside over a mass funeral near Cisco to the west of the summit, where an explosion had just taken five more lives. When he returned a week later, he brought a stack of flyers. On each of them, the note: *Monday, third day after Summer Solstice, we go on strike.* As he traveled up and down the thirty miles of summit area, Daoshi had been organizing with other gang leaders for a collective strike. An agreement had been reached, Daoshi told them, and over three thousand workers in a hundred or so gangs would go on strike at the same time. "The flyer is to let everyone know the date, like what Zhu Yuanzhang did with the mooncake slips," he said, nodding at Chang'er, "but there's no need to hide them—even if we held this right in front of Strobridge's good eye, he wouldn't know what it says."

Chang'er nodded back without saying anything.

STRAW DOGS OF THE UNIVERSE 45

"Summer Solstice," Li Shu said, filling Daoshi's teacup, "an auspicious date—peak time for yang energy."

After dinner, Daoshi continued east to bring the remaining flyers to the rest of the summit camps. Chang'er left with him. Guifeng had wished to join them but did not ask. He knew that Chang'er, who had refused to look at him at all, wouldn't want him along. Guifeng went back to work the next day with the rest of the gang. He loaded and carted rocks mostly, as he couldn't stand still on his twisted ankle for the drilling work—although the pain was a welcome distraction when thoughts of Ah Fook took hold.

All through Friday and Saturday, hammering and blasting rumbled on across the Sierra, but there seemed to be solidarity in the sounds. Soon, all three thousand Chinese workers would refuse to raise their hammers or hold their drills, to insert nitro or black powder into the holes. They would neither run nor scamper. They would just sit and breathe. If only this had happened when Ah Fook was still alive.

MONDAY'S SUN SHONE splendidly upon the mountaintop. It had been almost two years since Guifeng arrived on the Sierra, but this was perhaps the first time he was glad to be here. As he sat with his countrymen in front of their tents, the crisp morning light all around them, he felt as if a piece of sky were slipping inside his chest as he breathed. He could not imagine the air ever clearer than this, and without the blasts he could hear the breezes brushing across the bare rocks and through the dense pines and spruces along the slopes. He didn't even mind the height, as there was no danger of falling, not on this day.

But in the late afternoon, the clouds darkened and hung in the sky like the tattered laundry flapping on the ropes strung between their tents. By the time Daoshi, Chang'er, and the other representatives returned from their negotiation with Charles Crocker, in front of his lavishly outfitted railcar parked by the newest laid track, a gray flurry had begun to fall. They'd brought two demands to the meeting: an increase in wages to forty dollars per month, the same rate as the white workers, and reduced workdays from eleven to eight hours, also like the white workers. They came back with Crocker's answer: "John Chinaman no make laws for me; I make laws for Chinaman. You sell for thirty-five a month, me buy, you sell for forty and eight hours a day, me no buy." One headman imitated his voice, although they recognized that Crocker had imitated their English in the first place. To humor or humiliate them further?

"They call us Crocker's pets. Don't forget that," Chang'er said.

The next day, Strobridge and the foreman rode up on their horses and informed them that their food supplies had been cut off. "Let me make this clear," the foreman said, as Strobridge's good eye glared across them like a search light, "if you don't go back to work, you get no food and no pay for the month of June. If you go back now, we won't dock your wages."

On the fourth day of the strike, the camp's remaining provisions had trickled down to watery congee for each meal. Li Shu had tried to be resourceful by bringing some men to fish with him at the alpine lake overlooked by their graveyard. But when they arrived one day, several foremen were drinking and playing cards on the bank. They reached for their rifles. "Get lost," they said. "This here is company property."

On the fifth day, Guifeng felt faint. He had never saved food, nor had he had any extra to save. He had, in fact, always felt hungry and would devour every meal as if it were his last. A hearty meal at the end of hours' toil had been, in a way, what he'd lived for. Now his body wanted to go back to that old basic rhythm: work, eat, work, eat— which was easier to sustain than this doing nothing, this suspension and nonaction. Work, after all, was what his body was used to. It was his duty and destiny: he had learned to endure the drudgery and grind, and then he tried to master it like Cook Ding cutting an ox in the *Zhuangzi* story. But Guifeng also understood that the kind of work he'd been doing would likely never bring mastery or joy, and part of him never wanted to step back into that dark, cold, blood-sucking tunnel again. As his body longed for action, it also longed not to suffer its impact and the constant threat of breaking.

"What do you say, Daoshi?" Li Shu sprinkled his last handful of rice into the pot of water. "What's wuwei now?"

Daoshi shook his head. "It's not sit here and starve, I know that."

"If we go back to work," Chang'er said without looking at Daoshi, or anyone in particular, although the heat in his eyes could be felt by all who heard him, "my son and all the other sons and fathers will have died in vain."

"We have fought," Daoshi waited for a while before saying. "We did what we could do, but let's not go against nature now. That would be the opposite of wuwei."

"Oh, cut your wuwei bullshit," Chang'er said. "This has nothing to do with that. This is about our face, our dignity. We can't show them we are what they think we are, a bunch of cowards and coolies. We must die fighting."

Daoshi shook his head again. "That's headstrong striving. We don't want to go against the natural course of things."

What was the natural course of things? Guifeng asked himself. To do what he needed to do to eat, because the body was naturally hungry and needed nourishment. And the natural course after that was to find the girl whom he had loved since he was a child and be with her. He had told himself every time death loomed large that he would go find her if he lived through this. He would save a Sunday and take the train down the tracks he and his countrymen had laid to Sacramento, Second City, and then a boat to Big City. He would find the alley he had marched down on the day of his arrival and the door by which she had stood and met his eyes. Would she still be there? Would she be gone? Either way, he would have to go find out and see if there might be a way for them to be together. There should always be a way that was Dao's way, shouldn't there?

The next day, when Guifeng and the rest of the gang came back from their shift in the tunnel, Chang'er was gone. They'd had an early lunch of freshly cooked rice, roasted pork, and sautéed cabbage carted to the worksite by Li Shu, and Guifeng had gorged himself without savoring the bites. He had tried not to dwell on how Chang'er was still suffering from the hunger that he himself had known so well just a moment before. Each time Chang'er's face surfaced, so did Ah Fook's wide eyes.

THEN THE SEASON circled back to the relentless snows. Guifeng once again found himself cutting out caverns through the snowdrifts with his fellow workers. He felt as if his blood had frozen over along with his thoughts. A numbness trailed its ice through his body even as it eased the ache and itch of the frostbite in his fingers and toes. He was too numb to move when he saw it coming: the snow overhang on the cliff, looming sheerer above them with each passing hour, had suddenly let loose. Phantom horses of snow galloped toward them, and in less than a second, he was carried off his feet, carried down the slope that he had, in his nightmares, dreamed of falling down and down without hitting bottom, where only Ah Fook's eyes would eventually meet him.

But when he understood that he was indeed falling, tumbling at a speed he'd never known before, it was not Ah Fook who appeared in his mind, but Feiyan. She was running fast in their warm green village toward the blooming yulan, its sweet fragrance enchanting the air. As the wind howled and the snow and ice clashed, Guifeng felt a strange ease. He felt unhindered, as if an energy had taken over him and he was simply moving with it, without resistance or fear. Falling was a stillness, a wuwei. That was something he hadn't imagined before.

3

Fortune

*

1877

Daoshi

HE HAD SEEN THE LITTLE GIRL WATCHING HIM FROM ACROSS THE street. Either with a younger child not much smaller than her strapped to her back, or with a hunch as if the child's weight were still on her even though the child temporarily wasn't. A *mui tsai* with a perpetual hunch. What would happen to her? Could he tell her fortune? In three or four years, she would be sold to a brothel at five times the price she'd been purchased for, or to a laborer who had finally saved enough for a wife or concubine. If she became a prostitute, she would live perhaps to her twenties before coming down with an incurable disease. If she became a wife or concubine, she would work and bear children. Either way, she would continue to be burdened, beaten down.

It surprised him one day when the girl took the fifty steps across the street, extended her palm, and bared a photo to him: "Can you tell this person's fortune?"

Daoshi looked at the photo and, for a second, thought he was looking at a younger version of himself. He'd had a similar photo taken during his mining days, sitting on a similar high-back chair by a small

table with a pot of fragrant narcissus. He could still remember the
flowers' delicate petals and the nostalgia they'd brought him—of days
in his childhood, Spring Festivals, firecrackers and feasts, days spent
with his family that were long gone. It was his first and only photo,
which he'd misplaced years ago. Even in the next moment when he
recognized the face to be someone else's, someone he'd once known,
the echo of himself was still there, cast back from times past. "Who is
this person to you?" he asked.

"My father," the girl said.

LONG BEFORE HE was called Daoshi, he was Fuyao, born to a family with five-generation Daoist priests. Fuyao had watched his father
perform rituals since he was little. His job was to beat a wooden fish
in a slow steady rhythm as his father and uncle, later joined by his
older brother, chanted incantations. When he turned twelve, he began to assist them in the hell-breaking ritual, a funeral necessity unless a family was too poor to afford it. They set fire to joss paper and
a plaque with the name of the deceased written on it, which were
encircled by nine tiles facing the nine directions, signifying the nine
hells underground. Fuyao's father led the dance around the fire, with
interlacing steps as if to evade the hell flames from down below. His
uncle struck a handheld gong; his brother beat a waist drum; they followed his father's steps around the fire, while his father strung more
pieces of paper onto his bronze rod and dipped them into the flames
to keep the hell fire strong. Then he jumped across the fire and, with
the rod, broke the tiles one by one. He had gone down into the hells
to guide the spirit of the dead on a smooth, speedy passage, each step
a step through the punishing flame, each tile-breaking a breaking of
a stubborn attachment in the dead man's life. Then his father shifted
into suturing steps to walk the *bagua* trigrams, the steps up toward
the heavenly realm.

The fire dance, the loud crude instruments that were not music to the ears but a soundscape for the enacted hell journey, had kept Fuyao spellbound. He watched with fear that his father's robe would catch fire as he jumped across the burning pit, sweat beading on his forehead, the white tiles staring up at him, his eyes cast low as if a misstep would leave him entrapped down below.

In other ceremonies, Fuyao watched his father exorcise evil spirits from folks who were sick, possessed by hungry ghosts who couldn't rise to the sky realm but lingered behind for their unfinished business. Just as he had never seen the real torturing hells construed with paper, tiles, and flames, Fuyao wasn't able to see the evil spirits that his father shifted his bronze mirror to capture and waved his peach-wood bludgeon to expel. "What do they look like?" he asked his father.

His father shook his head: "It's not important what they look like; it's important that you learn what you're supposed to do." Which meant memorizing the verses and incantations and practicing the steps and dances to lead the dead where the living wanted to see them go—the clear space where they would rest and hold no more grudges against the living.

The first book his father asked him to recite was Laozi's *Dao De Jing*. "道可道，非常道；名可名，非常名。" Fuyao read the entire book but could not find a single word about hells or hell-breaking or evil spirits or exorcism. What had this book about Dao and wuwei to do with all the rituals he was supposed to learn and perform—the family business that depended on others' belief in the hells and wishes to escape them? The founding text of their religion seemed to have nothing to do with any of that.

"Enacting Dao needs concrete forms," his father said. "Joss paper is made of wood and water; the golden threads on it are metal. When you burn it, it turns to ashes, and ashes' eventual form is dirt. All five elements of the universe reconfigure as they change from presence to absence, traveling from the yang world to the yin world, and then back to presence again. This realm-crossing through the transformation of the five elements is how we communicate with the dead. We Daoists believe in change, in the diverging and converging of the opposites. All are changing but never lost."

Fuyao listened to his father but remained skeptical. When he became a teenage apprentice at thirteen, his mother fell ill with a lung disease that no exorcism could cure. After she passed away, his father embraced opium. Once, his unsteady steps indeed got his robe caught on fire. Though he didn't get stuck in the hells as the younger Fuyao had feared, his father, more and more, became either too high or too low to get out of bed. Maybe he was experiencing the presence of Dao, the ultimate harmony and way of the universe, in his opium stupor. But if that was wuwei, Fuyao thought, it would be nonaction in a most superfluous and squandering way—doing nothing but smoking the family's wealth away. Luckily, Fuyao was not the firstborn son. He left his older brother to tend to the mess at home and ran away.

He wanted to find his own truth—in an unlikely place, Gold Mountain. Gold could be it, real, glittering, undeniable: a truth he could hold in his hands. But first, he needed to learn that he was nobody: he was no longer somebody's son or brother, or somebody with a family trade to inherit and rely on, or somebody with a name and facial features to be distinguished from another. He lost all that in Gold Mountain as he became a nameless prospector, a Chinaman who sifted through the leftovers of white men's mines, hoping to feast on their food scraps.

Besides being nobody, he had no luck. Months of toil in placer mines yielded no more than a bagful of gold dust to pay off his debts for the crossing. And then months more went to the barter for the comfort of women. One girl, Ah Ju, to whom he would return again and again, had a curious composure he couldn't quite put his finger on. Even more of a nobody than himself, she nevertheless seemed at ease that way. She maintained a nondifferential friendliness with every man, which seemed to be out of neither compassion nor calculation. Her eyes looked neither dull nor passionate, driven by neither poverty nor need. They were profoundly unagitated. And during lovemaking, she was neither detached nor given to displays of fake or genuine pleasure. She was just there, with a neutral face that suggested no rejection or desire, her sparse yet melodious body movement an effortless flow. Daoshi thought of Dao, of wuwei. In all places, of all people, he had finally seen it in this lowly girl.

To say that he fell in love with her wouldn't be as true as saying that he fell in love with what he thought she possessed. A natural profundity she might not even have known she had, but which Fuyao knew for sure that he did not, nor did his father or uncle or older brother who must still be performing their rituals for the living and dead, entitled as the practitioners of Dao. While this girl, who had no freedom nor future, knew neither verses nor incantations, simply had it in her, without having to strive or perform.

He resolved to buy Ah Ju out of her servitude, not only to make her his, but to spare her life. She would otherwise die young where she was, along with her rare essence, for which he needed to procure solid gold to barter, not leftover dust or specks. He needed the real thing to preserve what this girl had. He needed to take risks, to trust luck was there for him if he believed he was lucky. He left the placer mine with two other men. They decided to venture deep into the mountains, to riverbanks not yet mined, which white prospectors had claimed as their birthright. Why? Fuyao and his companions asked. Wasn't this a free country where everyone had equal rights? Wasn't that written in the constitution? Blinded by an extravagant faith in luck and a misguided notion of freedom and equality, they camped at an upstream riverbank, sifting pristine water, until they were ambushed by a white gang who wielded revolvers and played their favorite game of tying the queues of Chinamen together so they were grasshoppers on the same string, roasted ducks on the same hook.

When Fuyao came back to Chinatown with nothing but a borrowed dollar to spend half an hour with Ah Ju, because more than ever, he needed her calm to heal him, she was gone. "Gone where?"

"Where do you think?"

"But just a month ago . . ." He could see her lying on the pink satin sheet rubbed threadbare by nobody-men like himself, in the cramped room she'd managed to keep clean, with a lemon scent she'd spray after each customer, a thin, beguiling layer of sun and summer light. Her unfeeling body lay by itself, encircling its own void, which was now nothing more.

Fuyao was struck by a longing for the consoling dance his family had performed for the dead. At night, he found Ah Ju's mound in a corner of the graveyard. He made a small twig fire and burned joss paper in it. Then, standing up, he began to dance around the fire in the hell-breaking steps he recalled from memory. He imagined holding Ah Ju's hand, leading her down the ether through the bewildering flames, and then up to the clear sky, where her essence would find its true home.

He stayed in Big City and got a job tending altars at the Tin How Temple, in exchange for a small wage and a mat on the floor. He had free food too, sourced from people's offerings to the gods and goddesses. He continued to visit brothels for the skin-to-skin contact and was sometimes saddened to see another girl fall ill and be disposed of. Sometimes he wondered if Ah Ju was someone he'd conjured up, her perceived wuwei nothing but a willful acceptance of defeat. Not unlike himself, as he drifted from sunup to sundown, and as folks began to call him Daoshi, in a kind of good-humored mockery, because he was merely a humble attendant. He refrained from letting them know the true irony of the nickname.

THEN CAME THE Chinese exodus to the Sierra. The railroad building, muscle work, good pay, and Fuyao, now half jokingly called Daoshi by many, was grateful for the change. It might have been a Daoist's dream to be up there in the high mountains, close to the sky. The Sierra's trees, rocks, fossils, rivers, lakes, its grasses and vines, clouds and stars, mosquitos and thunderstorms, ticks and blizzards—its entire ecology might instill in him divine knowledge. Up there on the peak, he sometimes felt he could see the circling movement of Dao as manifested in the sun and moon's unfailing orbits, the stars' perpetual glistening, and the indiscriminating cruelty and bounty of the universe.

But the work they were doing—changing the rock, rather than utilizing what was already there—felt like blasphemy. And men dying no less gruesomely than at the gold mines, in much larger numbers, felt like a punishment. The rock that took millions of years to form, to compress into a solid, indestructible mass, could be destroyed along with a man you'd just had tea with, a man who had just told you a joke or laughed at one you'd told. And that laughter would echo in your ears as you pieced together his body parts and buried them in a rush by the rail track.

Daoshi's nickname soon became a real title, as people from camp to camp began to ask him to preside over funerals—quick, pared-down ceremonies, with no reenactment of the nine hells or interlacing steps through them. Nevertheless, he burned joss paper he'd ordered from Big City and uttered with sincerity the half remembered, half improvised incantations to soothe the dead, to help them navigate the treacherous maze of hells made real by the railroad. If life had been unendurable, the afterlife demanded some solace.

He traveled from camp to camp to do what he had run away from doing in Middle Kingdom. He kept his forehead unshaved, unbraided his queue, and tied his hair up in a topknot, the way his father and grandfather and all daoshi had done for two thousand years. He debated with himself whether it was the right thing to do. When the Manchus conquered China two hundred years ago, they'd forced Han men into allegiance by ordering them to wear their hair in the Manchurian style. Those who refused to shave their foreheads and braid their hair lost their heads instead. But here in Gold Mountain, the queue had developed entirely different meanings. It was an object of ridicule to the whites who cut and collected them as souvenirs, the way they did with the Indians' scalps. To wear a queue here meant you were Chinese, and to keep wearing it meant you were not afraid of being a Chinese man in the white men's world. From a sign of submission, it had somehow changed into one of resolve and resistance. And for those who were planning to return to China, it was also a necessity to preserve, as they could still get beheaded if they went back without one. Only Buddhist monks and Daoist priests had been exempted from the Queue Order, a privilege Daoshi's family had not hesitated to exercise. Daoshi was now aligning with his family by returning to that hairstyle he'd worn as a child. Not out of fear or shame, he decided, but because here in the mountains where his service was keenly needed, he had, unwittingly, become a real daoshi.

When he helped organize the strike, bringing news with him as he traveled from camp to camp and working out details such as devising the flyer borrowed from Chang'er's story, he secretly wished that the whole wrongful endeavor would be annulled, this violation of the mountains, the bones of the earth. Sitting by a campfire talking to a new group of men he might soon need to help navigate to the underworld, Daoshi wished for a permanent strike, a lasting wuwei, even if it cost three thousand Chinese their jobs and livelihood. How would he know what was right or what was wrong? What was flowing with Dao or striving against it? What did he know, after all? He knew change was constant. The strike, not going to work, was a kind of wuwei. And the end of strike, not continuing to fight hunger, was also a kind of wuwei. He knew very little beyond that.

THEY LEFT THE Utah desert after the final spike had been hammered in—the real spike, not the gold one Leland Stanford had pounded in for the camera. The ghosts of the dead were left roaming in the deserted campsites, the tunnels, the snow caves, the rockfaces. Daoshi couldn't guarantee the rituals he'd performed would ferry their souls across the nine hells and eventually, when their bones were collected and sent home, guide them across the monthlong ocean back to their villages' burial grounds and their family altars, where their women and children would burn incense and offer spicy wine and sweet meats so that their souls would finally rest in comfort. Daoshi could guarantee nothing except the sincerity of his wish.

He, Guifeng, and many other railroad men carried their bedrolls and boarded the westbound train. They'd find another line of work, they said, something less prone to maim or kill them. Perhaps they would be more respected, or at least tolerated, now that they'd built the railway across the insurmountable Sierra. Although they had not been invited to the photo-taking at the Promontory Summit, they were praised in the papers as the ones who had "achieved the impossible," "the greatest feat in the American history." They had done something and proven they were not to be taken for granted.

But what followed in California was a labor movement that excluded Chinese laborers. Daoshi and the others watched as white folks poured into the West Coast from the rest of the country and from all over Europe, many as poor as, yet united in their hostility toward, the Chinese. And the politicians would soon seize upon this hostility to reap their own profits. But that didn't concern Guifeng yet. He had fallen head over heels for a girl who worked in a brothel, famed for her many runaway attempts. They were headed back west to Truckee, across the mountains again, Guifeng told him before their departure. Maybe the *tong* soldiers wouldn't find them there, and they could start a new life: he would get himself hired back by the company, cutting wood this time, the green gold.

Soon a bounty appeared on the Chinatown billboard, and then a couple weeks later a notice pronouncing both the kidnapper and the girl, property of the brothel, dead, shot by a tong soldier.

That was eight years ago. Daoshi had since concocted a new way to make a living: fortune-telling. He bought a desk and chair from a pawnshop and asked the owner to let him set up his station by the door. At night, he tended the shop in exchange for board in a small backroom converted from storage. He read his customers' palms, checked their *bazi*, and deciphered the words inscribed on the sticks they shook out of the bamboo cylinder. He foretold likely predicaments and recommended tenable remedies: avoid watery areas for the coming week; be wary of possible food poisoning; do not quarrel to calm your liver fire; eat only warm food and drink hot tea to keep stomach illness at bay; start something new, as there is no calamity in the foreseeable future. Things that his often-unlucky countrymen could bear to hear.

He realized that he hadn't thought of Guifeng for a while, not until his daughter appeared with his photo on her little palm. Her small back hunched, forearms bruised, the child answered his questions one by one: "What's your name?" "How did you end up in Gold Mountain?" "Why were you sold?" "When was the last time your family heard from your father?"

"When I was seven," she said to the last question, counting on her fingers. "Four years ago."

That must mean that Guifeng had not been killed by the tong in 1869, as the bulletin had claimed, and it also meant he was alive at least till 1873. Perhaps Daoshi shouldn't be surprised, because just last fall, as he'd followed the news about the Trout Creek shooting near Truckee and the subsequent trial, Guifeng's face had surfaced in his mind, as if he was not only alive but also somehow involved in the whole awful deal. But Daoshi had not looked into it further. Had he not cared? Or had he come to accept that whether or not Guifeng was still alive, ultimately the young man's fate wouldn't be unlike the rest of theirs? Bypassing one death would only bring you face to face with another.

But clearly, the child believed that her father was still alive. Why else would she ask Daoshi to read his fortune?

"I know your father. We built the railroad together," Daoshi said, looking at her, "and he's doing fine." He wanted to believe it too.

Sixiang

"WHERE IS HE?" SHE ASKED THE FORTUNE-TELLER. ONLY RE-cently had the Chens started allowing Sixiang to run errands outside of their supervision—be it buying herbs from the drugstore or groceries around the corner, and when she had much to carry, they would let her go without the burden of their child. During these trips, Sixiang would see a man sitting at a desk in front of the pawnshop. Sometimes, a few men would hover over him; sometimes, when nobody was there, he would read a book or rest his head on a hand and doze off. Everything about him looked neat. Even when he was dozing, he looked nice and tidy. She heard people call him "Daoshi."

Daoshi took another look at her father's photo. "Across the moun-tains, I think."

Sixiang looked around her but only saw the hilly streets tilting up and down. "Where are the mountains?"

"To the west of here. You will need to take a ferry and then a train."

"I have six silver dollars." Sixiang touched her blouse where the inside pocket held the coins. She hadn't told anyone else about them before now. "Will you take me to see my father if I pay you six silver dollars?"

Daoshi did not answer right away. He put her father's photo back in her palm, and glancing at the new bruise on her forearm, which she'd gotten yesterday from Mrs. Chen's pinching, said, "Let me think about it."

SEVEN MONTHS EARLIER, after the ship had finally anchored, a black-suited, mustached white man took a stack of papers from Madam, shook his head, and snickered. He said something in English to the Chinese man who'd followed him onto the deck. In a Western suit and without a queue, the Chinese man said to Madam in Cantonese, with a straight face, "The officer asked how many daughters a Chinese woman can bear."

"I don't know about other women," said Madam, who had changed back to her silk dress, "but all four are mine."

The translator relayed this to the white officer, who called out the names on the paper one by one, his pronunciations so off the girls hesitated before answering, although they had been quizzed numerous times by Madam during the voyage. The officer shook his head again and then surprised them all by saying in Cantonese, accented but not incorrect, "Is she your mother?"

To which all the girls uttered yes.

They were then led onto a horse-drawn wagon, which made its way over a cobblestoned road, turned a corner, mounted several slopes, and then stopped at a doorway with peeling red *duilian* glued on the wooden frames. They were led down a flight of dim stairs to a basement, which was low-ceilinged and windowless like the ship's hold. Also like the hold, it was packed with men, cluttered around a crate upon which stood a girl who Sixiang recognized as coming from the same ship as her, though from a different group. The men were chatting and joking loudly, chewing salted peanuts sold in paper cones and shouting out numbers.

Madam ushered the four girls behind a screen and patted a thick layer of white powder over their faces and necks and two round rouge patches on each of their cheeks. "Try to look your best," she said. "This is your one chance to score a good master."

When it was Sixiang's turn to step onto the crate, she had to balance herself so as not to trip, her body still enthralled in the tumbling motion of the monthlong voyage.

"What's the use of a little one like this?" someone said. "She needs a loumou."

"Wait for a couple of years, then she'll be useful."

Numbers were shouted out three different times, until there was silence after two hundred and fifty. Sixiang peered up at the man who had called out the number. He was clearly not her father—too old, too many droopy corners in the face, without a trace of her father's even features from the photo. Madam helped Sixiang down off the crate and counted the money Mr. Chen handed over. He didn't look cruel. He looked like Sixiang's next-door neighbor back in her village, who yelled at his wife and children from time to time but was amiable to others in general.

"This man will be your master from now on." Madam put a hand on Sixiang's shoulder. "You'll go serve him and his lady. Be respectful, and they'll treat you well." Her voice was soft like that time by the river, but when the next moment she took Sixiang in her arms, Sixiang stiffened. Madam looked into her eyes with something like hurt before letting her go.

Mr. Chen carried Sixiang's bedroll and took her out of the basement into the sun. Then, after rounding a corner, hiking up a steep street, and turning once more onto a flatter and busier street, they were in front of a store, where baskets of salted fish, dried oyster, and shriveled mushrooms were on display at the door. They walked past shelves of preserved fruits and pickles and peeled shrimp and up a flight of creaky stairs to a closed door. On the door hung an upside-down 福 character, but the red of the paper and the gold of the word were both fading, as if whatever fortunes or blessings imparted on the household were running out. Mr. Chen opened the door to a room of mismatched furniture, where a round lady sat in a rocking chair, holding a fat baby in her arms. A toddler, also chubby, leaned against her knees.

Sixiang had never seen an adult so plump or babies so fat. Back in her village, hunger had ground the flesh off people's bones, chipping them down to almost nothing. While here, inside this door, there must indeed be plenty to eat, as Madam had promised. As Mr. Chen led

Sixiang in, the woman stood up for just a second before sinking back down in the chair, which whined beneath her.

"You've been asking for a mui tsai," Mr. Chen said charitably. "Now I bought you one."

AS IT TURNED out, Mr. Chen would indeed yell at Mrs. Chen and Meimei, their toddler daughter, but not directly at Sixiang—maybe because he saw it only fit for his wife to punish a mui tsai. It didn't take long for Mrs. Chen to do so. About two weeks in, Sixiang was washing dishes in the kitchen when Meimei tugged at her arm, causing a bowl to slide out of Sixiang's hand. Mrs. Chen, who was nursing her baby son in the rocking chair, darted over with surprising speed given her small feet, and slapped Sixiang in the face. "I've treated you well, right? Giving you food to eat, clothes to wear. What do you do in return? Break bowls and destroy my things?"

Sixiang was almost not surprised. She had not trusted Mrs. Chen from the beginning. There was something odd about her, as if the abundance didn't quite belong to her but instead held her down. She spent all day long in her whining chair, listlessly giving out orders, or absently watching Sixiang while nursing her son. Even her scolding sounded sluggish: "That scrubbing is giving me a headache. Can't you just get it done with?" Sixiang had not trusted her languid ways.

The two children were bullies too. Meimei, already fourteen months, always wanted to climb onto Sixiang to be carried like her infant brother, whom Mrs. Chen would dump onto Sixiang after nursing. Even as she cleaned, cooked, washed, and peeled bags of shrimp and rolled cigar parts that Mr. Chen brought up daily from his dry-goods store downstairs, Sixiang had to carry the fat baby on her back.

There were only two rooms in the apartment. A corner was partitioned off from the outer room with a screen, enclosing a low bed patched together with wooden boards, where Sixiang and Meimei slept. The toddler liked to toss around in her sleep. One night, when she landed a foot on Sixiang's belly, Sixiang, without thinking, slapped her pudgy leg away and then gave her chubby flesh a hard pinch. Meimei woke up, looking at Sixiang in the dark, too startled or hurt to cry, while something like betrayal spread across her little face. Sixiang stopped pinching and took Meimei in her arms.

IN THE AFTERNOONS, they let Sixiang take the children out for an hour to get some sun. With the baby strapped on her back and the toddler's hand in hers, she would pace the children up and down the street by the storefront, within sight of Mr. Chen attending the store and Mrs. Chen sitting by the upstairs window. When he was not busy, Mr. Chen would take the baby and let Sixiang jog along the street with the toddler. Meimei liked to point at things, asking what they were. "That is a carriage drawn by horses," Sixiang would say, "and that is a gweilo driving the carriage," and lowering her voice, "Don't point your finger at him, or he'll get mad and beat us." Most of the gweilo on the street were younger men loitering in front of stores, shouting out things and laughing among themselves. They wore unwashed clothes, their hair oily, their faces sporting various cuts and scars. Whenever they came around, Mr. Chen would rush Sixiang and Meimei inside the store and spit on the ground with venom.

Sixiang looked forward to this hour of open air. She hoped to see her father, a man whose face would appear as an older version of the one in the photo, which she still looked at every night before sleep. Now she prayed that her father would pass this street called Tang People Street one afternoon when she was out with the children. He would pause in his walk and recognize her, or in any case, he would think to himself that this girl looked like his daughter. Even though he had never seen a photo of her, as no such photo had ever been taken, he would maybe think that the girl looked about the same age as his daughter and stop to talk to her, while pretending to look at Mr. Chen's store. He would ask what her name was, and she would tell him

"Sixiang," the name he had given her in the hope that she would never forget her home.

But had he forgotten? Sixiang couldn't help but wonder. If her father had wanted to keep in touch with them, all he needed to do was send a letter. Why did her mother think he was still alive and that Sixiang could find him and bring him home? Perhaps her mother knew something that Sixiang did not, and Sixiang would have to trust her.

SHE WAS INDEED given plenty to eat. Sometimes after feeding Meimei, Sixiang got to eat alone in the kitchen. Sitting on a stool and holding a bowl of rice topped by pieces of vegetables and meats, Sixiang imagined dividing her food into three portions and offering her mother and grandmother each a share. On the ship where the meals were meager, Sixiang had not thought of such a ritual. Now she would eat her portion, imagine her mother and grandmother eating theirs, and then she would eat theirs as well. It was just like what people do with the food offered to their ancestors: they wait till their ancestors ingest the flavor out of the food, and then eat the food so as not to waste it.

It was not until late spring of the following year that the Chens allowed Sixiang to run errands out of their sight. One day, on her way to the grocery store on Stockton Street, she took out her father's photo from her inside pocket and crossed the street to where Daoshi was sitting.

Since then, all through the last weeks of spring and first weeks of summer, whenever she got a chance, she would cross the street again and asked Daoshi the same question: "Will you take me to see my father?"

But he wouldn't give her an answer.

MRS. CHEN KEPT her fingernails long, pinching not only Sixiang's arms but her face too.

"Are you stupid or what?" Mr. Chen shouted. "Do you want to

show everyone how badly you treat our mui tsai? People talk, and those white women are looking for reasons to take girls away."

Sixiang had once seen a white lady shopping at Mr. Chen's store, who looked at Sixiang in a way that made her feel timid and small, as if she were no bigger or stronger than the children in her charge. Another time, Sixiang saw the white lady and a Chinese teenage girl, one in front, the other at the back, leading a group of younger Chinese girls down the street. Some of the girls were around Sixiang's age, some smaller. Mrs. Chen told Sixiang that white women would fatten up the poor Chinese girls before barbecuing and eating them. As they walked hand in hand in a chain that made some of them stagger, the girls didn't look happy or unhappy, nor did they look scared. They mostly looked clueless. Did they not notice as each of them went missing, one by one, like pigs taken off to slaughter? Mrs. Chen said they were put under a spell by the white women, who forced them to recite verses about their god.

"Their god is angry," Mrs. Chen said. "He threatened to destroy the world with flood and fire and send those who didn't believe in him to hell. Our Guanyin Goddess would never do that to people." Sometimes, after Mrs. Chen muttered prayers and burned incense at the Guanyin altar in the outer room, she would give Sixiang a piece of mung bean pastry or a handful of raisins as a treat. Occasionally, she would even ask Sixiang to take a break or ask Meimei to stop nagging her. But just as Meimei would go on nagging, Mrs. Chen's anger would always return. There was always something not right. The food Sixiang cooked was either too salty or too bland. The laundry was not clean enough. The children were crying too much. The floor had sticky spots. The cigars were not rolled fast enough. The raw shrimp was making Mrs. Chen, who was expecting again, nauseous.

"Are you doing this on purpose? Just to make my life miserable and force me to punish you and act like a bad mistress? You know what's going to happen to you if you stay bad? We'll sell you to a brothel! That's where you'll end up," she said between her teeth.

A brothel must be where Ah Hong had been sold to. At the basement auction, Ah Hong was the first to step onto the crate, her face powdered so thick, her head bent so low it looked severed from her neck. When she was taken away by a woman dressed in a silk blouse like Madam, Ah Hong didn't look back at Sixiang. Not a nod or a smile for goodbye.

Once, stepping out of a grocery store, Sixiang saw Ah Hong strolling with two other girls on the street. They were all dressed in light-colored blouses. Men whistled at them, and they responded with a wave of a kerchief and a teasing grin. Ah Hong did the same, awkwardly, not so much doing it as copying it. A man in a brimmed hat and a black jacket strolled behind them, looking around as if people might jump out and spirit them away. Sixiang followed them down the long route despite the heavy basket she was carrying. But when the man turned to look at her, moving his narrowing eyes over her body, she quit following.

ON A LATE July day, before dusk, Sixiang was sent to pick up a few turnips from the grocery store. Across the street from the store, several men stood in front of Daoshi's desk, blocking his face. At the entrance of the pawnshop, the old shopkeeper in gold glasses was greeting a customer. When they turned their backs from the door, Sixiang ran across the street into the shop.

The shop was cluttered with pieces of furniture piled on top of each other, shelves of bowls and pots, walls covered by clothes and utensils. Against the inner wall, next to a mound of wooden trunks and below a display of swords and knives, stood a large silk screen. Sixiang slipped behind it. Its four panels featured the Four Great Beauties of the ancient time. Right in front of Sixiang was the painted face of Zhaojun, the musician beauty, holding a pipa. Sixiang's mother had told her the story: how Zhaojun was sent away by the emperor to marry a barbaric king in a foreign land and ended up dying of homesickness. "It's all the same for women," her mother had said. "Whether sold to a king or a peasant, she will find herself far from home." Sixiang had been sent away to the farthest place, and she was only a child. But her mother had not sold her, Sixiang must remember. Her mother had insisted that Sixiang keep the six silver coins, her sale money. And she was awaiting her return. *You are strong*, her mother had told her.

From behind the screen, Sixiang saw a door at the back of the shop. She had asked Daoshi where he lived—"Right there," and he'd pointed at the shop. She had devised a plan as soon as Mrs. Chen talked about selling her to a brothel. Sixiang would run away at the next opportunity, bringing nothing with her except her father's photo and the six silver dollars, which she always carried with her. When the old man in glasses turned to send off the customer, Sixiang snuck to the door and tried the knob. It opened to a small room that she knew right way was Daoshi's: a black robe hung from a nail on the wall, a few books lay on a wooden trunk next to a smoothly made single bed, all spare and tidy, like Daoshi himself.

Sixiang closed the door behind her and sat down tentatively on the edge of the bed. After a while, she heard words exchanged between the shopkeeper and Daoshi, and then the sound of footsteps and furniture moving. Daoshi must be bringing in his desk and chair for the evening.

She was looking at one of his books on the wooden trunk when Daoshi opened the door. In his hand were two steam buns wrapped in a piece of paper. He didn't appear surprised to see her. Although why would he be? Being a fortune-teller, Sixiang thought, he must have already known.

"Eat these, and then go back to your owners."

"I can't. They'll sell me to a brothel."

Daoshi looked at her and for a moment seemed to be assessing the accuracy of her statement against his own foretelling. He handed her the buns. "Still, eat these. We'll talk later."

He went back to the shop. Sixiang ate the barbecued pork buns.

But before she could finish, she heard noises from the street. People were running and shouting. Were they hunting her down? Did the Chens summon a mob to catch her? She considered hiding under the bed but instead opened the door a crack and peered out. Daoshi was standing by the shop entrance, looking down the street where people were scuttling past, yelling, "Gweilo are coming, hundreds of them!"

Daoshi closed the double-framed door, barring it from the inside with a chain lock. Then he looked around and pushed a table against it. Looking around again, he directed his eyes at the swords and knives hanging on the wall. He took a sword down, and clutching it in his hand, he blew out all the oil lamps in the store. He came to where Sixiang was peeking out. "You'll stay here for now."

"What do the gweilo want?"

"They want to feel better about themselves. It makes them feel less weak to tear us down."

Soon they heard banging and kicking on the store door. Sixiang remembered the bandit attack in her village—how her mother had held her in her arms when the men broke in and how, despite the horror, her mother had kept her safe. After Daoshi blew out the oil lamp in the room, he sat down on the bed with her. Sixiang leaned against him, and he put an arm around her. They sat in the dark, listening.

The shop door broke open and clamors poured in from the street. Daoshi picked up the sword by his feet. Sixiang buried her face in his chest, focusing on the pounding of his heart, which was no less forceful than her mother's when they had huddled in the corner of their room as the bandits ransacked their house. She could feel Daoshi's arm tightening around her, as if he was keeping the whirlwind at bay through his firm hold.

Hours passed and Sixiang must have fallen asleep this way. When she opened her eyes, morning had come in through the small, curtained window. She was lying in the bed covered with a blanket. Daoshi was no longer in the room. Sixiang got up, again opened the door a crack, and saw Daoshi standing alone in the middle of the shop. It was gutted, most of its contents gone, what little was left either broken or ruined. A pile of human feces gathered flies on a textile couch. The screen featuring the Four Great Beauties was punctured and slashed, a knife gash running through the face of Zhaojun, the girl sold by her emperor to the barbarians.

They could still hear sporadic shouts down the street. "Not much left for them to rob or destroy," Daoshi said, walking over to the small kitchen next to his room, where a pot of congee was simmering on the stove. He filled a bowl for Sixiang, one for himself. Then, they went back in his room again, closing the door.

"What does this book say?" Sixiang pointed at the book she'd picked up the previous night. On its cover was a drawing of an old man with long flowy beard, his hair tied into a topknot like Daoshi. Sixiang had seen portraits like this before and knew it was Taishang Laojun, the Daoist god. She'd been looking at the words in the book before the riot: some of them looked the same but were put in different places.

"What do you think it says?" Daoshi asked.

"I can't read."

"I know. But what do you think Laozi would say in his book?"

"He would give answers to questions."

"What kind of questions?"

"Any questions we ask."

"Such as?"

"Such as what's going to happen? Will the gweilo leave us alone now?"

"Let's see if there's an answer to that." Daoshi flipped through the pages before stopping at one. He examined the lines and read out loud: "飘风不终朝，骤雨不终日。孰为此者？天地。天地尚不能久，而况于人乎？"

"What does it mean?"

"It means no storms last forever. Even gweilo run out of steam."

"Then what happens to us? Will you take me to see my father?"

"I don't know that yet. One step at a time."

He put down the book and asked Sixiang to tell him about her life in China. So she told him about the flood, about the unburied bodies under the grass mats, about their fan palm tree, and her mother who had placed the photo in her hand and let her keep the six silver coins. Then, she told him about her monthlong voyage and what had happened to Ah Fang and Ah Hong.

"What was my father like?" she asked Daoshi.

"He was a fine young man," Daoshi said.

"Are there holes on the mountains?"

"Holes?"

"Holes that people stumble into."

"Well, there're ravines and gorges, and tunnels we dug out of the granite. Come to think of it, your father did fall off a slope once, but he was a lucky man. He came out unhurt."

"Why did he stop sending letters home?"

Daoshi thought for a moment. "There must be a reason," he said, looking away from Sixiang. "I'm sure there was a good reason for that."

SIXIANG DIDN'T LEAVE the pawnshop with Daoshi until the next morning. The aftermath was hard to look at, the street so strewn with wreckage they had to watch their steps to avoid glass shards, squashed melons, broken jars. No door was left unbroken, most windows shattered. Two adjacent houses down the street had been reduced to charred skeletons, where smoke wafted out and darkened the air. People were picking up what was still salvageable, swearing out loud or silent with slumped shoulders.

As they turned the corner, Sixiang saw a man hanging down the eaves of a three-story building, his legs and arms dangling, his black queue snaked around his neck. Several men stood below, debating how to get him down. Daoshi put an arm in front of Sixiang to block her view, but it was too late. All she could see were the man's gaping mouth and half-open eyes, until they reached Mr. Chen's dry goods store.

Mr. Chen was pushing up an overturned shelf from the floor, which was littered with broken bottles and jars and their spilled-out contents. He paused to look at Sixiang and Daoshi, his eyes bloodshot, anger set in his hard jaw.

Daoshi stepped over to lend him a hand. "Your mui tsai took shelter at the pawnshop these last two nights," he said.

Mr. Chen nodded gravely, then without a word signaled Sixiang to help with the mess.

"I know her father. I'll be back to check on her from time to time," Daoshi added.

He patted Sixiang on the shoulder before walking away. She watched him leave. He'd said he would think of a way to help her, but that until then she must wait and not try to run away again. He asked her to trust him.

Mrs. Chen stared at Sixiang from the top of the stairs, as if she didn't quite know who she was. "I thought you were killed by gweilo," she said.

But as she ranted about the looting, the loss, her rage found its way back to Sixiang. "Now you know you have no place to go, right? Now you know that gweilo are on the street, slaughtering men, raping women, robbing us of everything we had. I hope you've finally learned how good we've been to you!"

They no longer allowed Sixiang to go out. After the cleanup, Mr. Chen brought upstairs more cigars for her to roll and more shrimp to peel. Mrs. Chen watched her, looking for reasons to dole out punishment. Meimei continued to be clingy, nagging Sixiang to carry her all day long, as if she too had made up her mind to torment Sixiang as much as she could.

Lying in the partitioned corner, Sixiang imagined pinching Meimei's fat cheeks and doughy arms and legs the way Mrs. Chen did to her, pinching the child hard until her eyes melted into tears. She would not stop like last time. She would slap Meimei's face too, pretending it was Mrs. Chen's, slapping away both her puny helplessness and her mother's meanness.

But these thoughts scared Sixiang. She counted the days. In a dream, her father came to her rescue in the guise of Daoshi, and it somehow made sense even though Daoshi was about ten years older than her father. They would go back to China together. And her mother would recognize him in no time.

SEVEN DAYS LATER, rolling cigars with the baby strapped on her back, Sixiang heard noises outside the door: a cacophony of voices, both men's and women's, in English and Cantonese, followed by stomping steps up the stairs and loud knocks on the door. "What do you want?" Sixiang heard Mr. Chen say. "I told you we have no slave here."

But the knocks carried on.

"Don't open it," Mrs. Chen whispered to Sixiang. "They're gweilo. Go hide under the bed in the inner room."

But Sixiang heard her name called in Cantonese: "Sixiang, we're here to help you." A Chinese girl's voice. "Are you in there?"

Mrs. Chen stared at Sixiang and slid a finger across her own throat as if to indicate what would happen to her. The baby strapped on Sixiang's back began to bawl, while Meimei, scurrying toward the inner room, stumbled and fell. Mrs. Chen's hands were reaching in all directions.

Now the knocks turned into kicks. The next moment, the door was forced open, and a big white man holding a baton stomped in. Just a week ago, Sixiang had heard dozens of gweilo smashing and looting the pawnshop, heard hundreds of them stomping and shouting on the street. Sixiang ran toward the inner room, but the man grabbed her wrist.

"Don't take her," Mrs. Chen cried. "She is my daughter." For once, Mrs. Chen looked at Sixiang pleadingly, as if begging her to confirm, to call her *Loumou*, and stay. But the Chinese girl stepped forth and, tak-ing hold of Sixiang's other arm, pulled her sleeve up to bare her bruises. Sixiang was made to look at her own pain.

"She's not my mother," Sixiang said to the Chinese girl who still held her sleeve up for the tall white woman to see.

"Poor girl." The white woman put a hand on Sixiang's head.

Sixiang had seen them both before. They were the ones leading the group of Chinese girls down the street and, if Mrs. Chen was right, had been fattening and barbecuing the children one by one. Now, one wrist clutched by the white man, the other by the teenage girl, her head pressed under the white woman's palm, Sixiang froze. She willed the same strength of endurance as when Madam had gripped her arms while the boat was rowed away from her mother, who stood waving, balancing on her bound feet. Except that then, it was her real and only mother from whom she had been taken.

SIXIANG SAW DAOSHI as they led her away. He was reading a cus-tomer's palm in front of the pawn shop, where the broken door had been replaced by a new one. He looked up and nodded at her, knowingly. Had he foreseen this? Or was *this* his plan to save her? To have her slaughtered and eaten? But Sixiang had never completely believed Mrs. Chen's words. The way the white lady held her hand as she talked to the white man walking by her side was gentle, and Sixiang had discerned no ill will in her eyes. But when she looked at Sixiang, she seemed to be seeing her and something else at the same time—some projection she was mapping out in her mind yet unknown to Sixiang, some scheme not necessarily cruel, but not altogether benign either. It was different from the way Daoshi looked at her. He looked like he was planning things too, but in a way Sixiang felt she could trust. She looked back at him, trying to read his eyes. *What is your plan?*

"How did you find me?" Sixiang asked the Chinese girl when she turned her head back to the direction they were leading her.

"Someone informed us about you," the girl said.

"Are you going to eat me?"

The girl laughed. "That's the stupidest thing I've ever heard."

The white lady and the girl exchanged something in English and they both laughed, both looking at Sixiang in amusement. "You're safe with us," the girl then said, somewhat stiffly. "Miss Moore came to your rescue. You should thank her. She saved all of us. Say *'thank you.'* It means *do ze* in English."

Sixiang mimicked the sound of the words, the first English words she'd ever uttered. She felt alone walking between them, as they led her farther and farther away from Daoshi, his face completely blurred now when she looked back. The pawnshop entrance by his desk led to the small room where they'd sat together on the night of terror, and she had fallen asleep held in his arms, held for the first time since she had arrived in Gold Mountain. The two of them in the whirling mayhem, like she and her mother in the flood, and she had fallen asleep feeling cared for, with the almost prescient knowledge that things would be okay.

The white lady said something for the teenage girl to translate to Sixiang. "From now on," the girl said in Cantonese, "you will live with us, with God."

4

Run

1865–1869

Feiyan

SHE LOOKED AT THE SKY ABOVE CANTONESE ALLEY. THE CLOUDS thickened but the wind stayed dry. She looked back at the column of new arrivals marching closer, their shoulder poles pulled low by trunks and bedrolls, their steps half drunk from the sea voyage that had newly brought them here. They turned their faces sideways to gawk at each girl standing by each narrow door. Some of the men would be dreaming of her tonight, but none would enter her dreams. She would have liked to set out running, in the direction the men were heading, to run ahead of them and let them take a good look at her running away. But she stood still.

Then she saw him among them, his face unmistakably familiar, though it took her a moment to place it. In her village where the air would be warm and moist and swelling with flowers this time of year, the boy's eyes had once followed her as she raced the village kids, out-running them all.

That was before her first bleeding, before her marriage to the old man three villages down south, across the haunted mountain. A gambler whose mood swung with the hand he was dealt and whose own hands turned to fists on her body. How she'd kicked in her sleep then, like a kind of nocturnal run, a midnight escape.

One night after the old man wore out his empty fists, his luck-forsaken arms, Feiyan ran out of the shack and up north toward her village, which meant she had to cross the mountain where the she-ghost reigned at night. It was said that the woman had been snatched away by the bandits and torn open night after night until her body broke into rotten pieces. But she grew powerful after death. She conquered the mountain where the bandits camped, haunting each of them, sowing discord and coaxing them to kill one another off. Now she seized men and women alike, hating them all, because men had dirtied her and women had thought her dirty. She would grab hold of your hair and force you to turn and look at her.

The night was lit by nothing but a cleaved moon and insipid stars. As Feiyan ran up the mountain, she heard howling like red whips flogging the dark. She tripped over a rock and as she fell, her hair was yanked back while a voice blew into her ear: "Run, run. Let me see how far you can outrun your fate."

Feiyan ran out of the ghost's grip, ran down the thistle-grown mountain, and ran home. Her mother warmed up a bowl of leftover congee and tended her wounds, muttering the tired wisdom about this life, past life, next life, about small feet, big feet. She regretted not having Feiyan's feet bound to bargain for a better marriage, as if one could wrangle some control out of life by controlling the size of one's feet. Feiyan needed her feet. She needed to run. She had run away from the old man, from the ghost, but in the middle of the night, her father and brother tied her feet and hands, put her on top of their donkey, and sent her back: "We're not the dishonorable type. Marry a chicken, follow the chicken; marry a dog, follow the dog."

This time she had to plan. The man kept her tied to his bed except when he needed her to cook and wash. She had vast spans of time to stare at the mud ceiling and the muted light filtering in through the papered window. She had her anger too, like the mountain ghost's. She said to the man in the middle of a night, "I need to use the outhouse, unless you want me to shit here. Would you like that?"

The man was in a fine mood. He had won a hand and had just climbed off her. She kept hearing the voice: *Run, run. Let me see how far you can outrun your fate.* In her head she could see a harbor where water spread to the sky, and a docked ship as big as a village except without paddies or trees. She knew men departed on it for Gold Mountain. No one would know her there. There, her fate wouldn't find her.

The old man had fallen asleep when she came back from the outhouse. She looked down at him, snoring through his few jagged teeth that had just a moment earlier bitten into her lips. "Do it," a woman's voice rang in her ear. She startled, surprised that the voice didn't wake up the man. "Do it," and this time she recognized it to be the mountain ghost's voice. She lifted the bucket of cooking ash by the stove. She'd heard stories of newborn girls pressed face down into an ash bucket the moment they'd made their way out of their mothers' wombs. She'd heard "Why didn't we choke you in the ash?" from her own parents when they were mad at her. Tied to the bed, she had more than once stared at the bucket with its accumulated remains of days of cooking. It seemed to be waiting.

He opened his eyes: the dark wicks of his pupils jumped. He would kill her, turn her into a hollering ghost trapped in this half-sunken shed. She dumped the ash onto his face, threw the bucket over his head, and threw all her strength, her worth, on top of it, until his body stopped moving. She heard the ghost laughing. "You did it, girl. Now you're in real trouble."

Feiyan trembled as she packed a few belongings and the leftover baked potatoes in a cloth bundle. But when she tied the bundle around her shoulders and started to run, she was steady and still. Her legs fell into an assured rhythm to take her away from the dead man and his ghost, toward the northeast where the delta opened to the sea. She hid in pigsties like an urn of coins. She picked through garbage in back alleys and begged for food on noisy streets. After two days, she came to the harbor where a ship almost as big as she'd imagined was docked. Men were embarking with trunks and bedrolls swinging under shoulder poles. A madam waited with sniffling girls for their turn, her eyes shooting around as if someone might steal her cargo before she could pocket her profit on the other shore.

Feiyan limped toward her. "I'm selling myself," she said, catching her breath. "Get me on that ship."

The woman looked at her big, bare feet: Feiyan had lost her cotton-soled shoes when she ran away from a gang of ruffians; now her feet were covered with dirt and dried blood. The woman then looked at Feiyan's face, and Feiyan worried she might see it too—the dead man with ash in his mouth, nose, eyes, and ears. "There are indeed all kinds," the woman said, as if to herself.

"We were hit by famine," Feiyan said. "My whole family starved to death. I heard about the ship, about girls going to Gold Mountain. I'll go. I'll do whatever you want me to do."

The woman now looked at Feiyan's neck, hands, and arms, and again as if to herself: "These bruises and scars should be gone by the time we arrive. You'll look like new."

AFTER FIFTY DAYS on the ocean, fifty days of rocking, vomiting, and awakening with the old man's dead eyes on her, Feiyan was sold to Red Peony. She was given a pair of embroidered shoes that pinched her feet, and their narrow platform soles forced her to walk with shaky steps and swaying hips like a small-footed woman. "You need to look more womanly for this trade," Madam Qian, the brothel keeper, told her.

Feiyan was also given some clothes, including a pink silk blouse that carried whiffs of soap and perfume, whiffs of musk and decay, and a stain at the hem that looked like old blood. She was put in a small

room with a bed, a one-drawer table, two chairs, and a clothes hanger.
On the table were an incense burner, a teapot, and two cups. A mirror
hung on the wall for her to reapply powder and rouge. A water jar and
a basin hid underneath the bed for her to clean herself.

It wasn't long before she heard the voice. She was lying in bed with
her first customer, in awe of his lithe body and glowing youth. He'd
arrived newly bathed and shaved and dressed in a clean linen shirt.
He talked to her before touching her, in a dialect close to hers but far
enough that he couldn't have heard about what she'd done. What were
folks saying about her back home? It didn't matter now. She was Ah
Hua here, a prostitute. Better this than wife to that now dead man.

Wrapped in the young man's sinuous arms, Feiyan was just about
to loosen her tight shoulders when she heard the voice. It was right by
her ear on the bed with her and the young man. A weak, wispy voice,
nothing like the mountain ghost's sonorant one. "You think this is not
that bad, huh? You stupid girl."

It all went downhill from there. Customers would come with their
weeks-long filth, odor, and bad temper. They were not only Chinese,
but white, black, brown, and all kinds. They filled the tiny room with
opaque stench and angst. But occasionally, when there came a clean,
gentle one, just as Feiyan felt an ease begin to fall over her, she would
hear the voice again.

She had learned to anticipate its coming. She listened. She waited.
She pleaded that the ghost wouldn't vent her grievances on her, knowing that no matter how miserable a woman's life might be, she became
more powerful dead than alive. Feiyan had gotten away from the mountain ghost who'd dared her to kill and run. But now she was trapped in
this narrow chamber with this new ghost who could devise ways to toy
with her life, as ghosts tend to do.

"I'll always be haunting here, because they only ship men's bones
home, and besides, who will put my name on a plaque and burn incense
for me?" the ghost said.

"I'll burn incense for you if that will calm you down." There was an altar in the brothel's foyer. Feiyan could pray on behalf of the ghost to appease her.

"Will you? Okay, maybe you can also get me a daoshi to guide my soul through the hells and find a nice family for my rebirth?"

"Where can I find a daoshi? They don't even let me leave the brothel . . . But where do you want to be reborn? Gold Mountain? I doubt even a daoshi could guide you all the way back."

"I want to be reborn into a rich family. It doesn't matter where it is. If you're born rich, you have nothing to worry about."

"I'm not sure about that. Even a rich girl can get kidnapped or sold to a drunk husband."

One day, a customer slapped Feiyan in the face for talking out loud. The man told her he'd first thought she was talking to him, but he soon realized that she was either out of her mind or possessed. He'd been in this same room before, on this same bed, and had even seen this same pink blouse worn by its original owner. He knew how the girl had died. Ah Li, was that her name? She'd used her smile on every man and driven two of her lovers into a duel. The one who survived ended up stabbing her to death. On this very bed.

DURING DAYTIME HOURS when business was slow, Feiyan and the other seven girls at Red Peony were assigned piecework. As they sat together embroidering slippers, sewing buttonholes, or lacing up undergarments, they evaluated their customers: types that were harmless, types to watch out for, types to steal from, types to leave alone. They all had four-year contracts to fulfill and then what? Marry someone? What was the chance of that? The chamber ghost would laugh whenever Feiyan flirted with a man who could be a marriageable candidate. Just as she was conjuring up a coquettish smile, she would hear the ghost's snicker: "Dream on, you little slut."

What else, then? She could work in a shop and sew. She could be a servant. But white families didn't want Chinese women, the girls said. They'd rather hire Chinese men to do the women's work, so Chinese women were left with nothing.

One night, a white man sat his big ass on her chest and spat words at her, which she didn't understand but knew for sure to be the filthiest kind. He was a large man, twice the size of the dead man whom Feiyan had been measuring all other men by: meaner or nicer, more vile or less vicious, more viable for her to strike back or to endure. The man was choking her, his cock in her mouth, his hand grabbing her hair, and he had not stopped spitting those ugly words at her. Feiyan had to shut her eyes so as not to see the hate in his, but it was filling her up until it became her own. She bit down on the man, who screamed and slammed her head against the wall. He could have killed her had the brothel guard not rushed in with an ax and knocked him out.

Feiyan had since kept a knife under her pillow, which she'd stolen from a drunk customer. The chamber ghost was aghast when Feiyan unhooked it from the man's belt. They'd argued that night as customers climbed on and off her.

"It will only bring you harm," the ghost insisted. "A knife is not our weapon."

"What's our weapon, then? Had you had a knife, you could've stabbed your lover before he did it to you."

"That's nonsense. Do you really think my arm was stronger than his?" And the girl-ghost was sobbing again.

DEATH SOON VISITED the girls literally. The oldest among them, Ah Jiao, who was twenty-seven, swallowed opium early one morning. With her smooth brows and round jawline, Ah Jiao had appeared untroubled, and the girls liked to seek advice from her. No one had imagined she'd been saving opium for such a way out. Another girl, even newer than Feiyan, developed a terrible case of syphilis and vanished one night. Then two other girls ran away together, despite the warning that all runaways would end up either gutted by men or mountain lions or caught and dragged back with their contracts extended another four years. The latter befell them, along with a beating that did not quit until they passed out.

It took effort to stay alive. Feiyan asked her customers to return with fresh lemons, from which she squeezed juice into herself to kill sperm and germs. She tried to look forward to something, some vague future at the end of her contract. She kept a tally of her days on the squeaky bed where the sorry girl had been killed. So acquainted with the girl-ghost and the death all around her, Feiyan sometimes didn't know if she was still in the living world or had already stumbled into the ether.

When it was her turn to stand by the door to entice customers, she looked down the narrow alley and the blue that opened where the alley met the wider Jackson Street. She imagined running down the alley and then up the street, not stopping until she outran this new fate of hers.

ON A SPRING day at the beginning of her third year, Feiyan was allowed to leave the brothel for a haircut on Dupont Street. When she was done, she saw the brothel guard sent to watch her waiting outside the salon, his head bent over a game of Go. She told the hairdresser she needed to use the privy at the back of the shop. The moment she was alone, she cut off the soles of her shoes with the stolen knife she'd carried in her jacket pocket. Then she opened the shop's back door and started to run. She ran northwest, away from Chinatown. She'd heard from a regular of hers about a farming village called Cow Hollow a couple miles from here, where Chinese could lease land and build their own farms. She had nothing except her knife and a little pouch of tips she'd saved away. She'd received nothing for selling herself other than a debt for the passage and a contract that unfurled endlessly in front of her.

A woman out by herself was not a common sight, let alone a running Chinese woman. Men gawked at her, but she kept running down the streets that dipped and climbed. She'd once thought she would stay put for the duration of her four-year contract, but it would never have been only four years. Menstruation periods had to be made up. Sick days, too. Once she'd had a fever for ten days, and an entire month was appended to her contract. Truth was that few could outlive their contracts. And on top of all that, she wanted to run. She needed it. She had been dreaming of running, of using her legs. She had occasionally watched tall, muscular horses galloping down the alley, while men whipped or kicked them with their spiked boots. She had wanted to run with those horses with no men riding on them.

Now as her body fell into the light, undeniable rhythm that made her heart pump, she was almost laughing inside. She ran toward the northwest while the sun shone in and out of sight. She would run until there were no more buildings, only land with green fields and cows and farmhouses. She knew all about farming, having helped her family since she was able to walk. She missed the dirt under her feet, between her fingers.

The guard must have borrowed a horse from someone. It didn't take him long to ride next to her. She ran alongside the horse until the guard jumped off and knocked her down. "You're not slow for a girl," he said as he snatched her arm.

She was whipped by Madam Qian herself. Her heel-less shoes were burned in front of her on the stove, her knife and money taken. Her contract was lengthened four more years because of her "dishonest action against her owner." She was eighteen. Most girls at Red Peony did not live to twenty-five.

THE CHAMBER GHOST laughed at her: "What an escape! You thought just because you had a pair of ugly big feet, you could run away from here? Stupid girl."

Feiyan ignored her. She lay on her belly to avoid rubbing the lashes on her back and buttocks. It was worth it. She'd done something for herself. She would not end up trapped here like the ghost, forever having to watch men ride the next woman and the next. Feiyan had run for a full half an hour. And these mere thirty minutes of running had rubbed all the rust off her joints. It had been worth it. To feel the wind and air and see the clouds that followed her and the open horizon that pulled her toward it.

Madam Qian no longer allowed her to stand in front of the door for fear she'd run away again. She had whipped Feiyan methodically, making sure that she hurt but wouldn't end up bedbound and cause business to suffer. Madam Qian did all the punishments herself now, not trusting the guard who had beaten the two previous runaways half dead the moment she was not looking, which had cost her two weeks of earnings from each of the girls. "You can't trust men to do the beating of women," she'd said to Feiyan as she whipped her, as if saying so could exonerate her.

Feiyan asked to have her door-standing privilege back: "Do you want me to get no sun or fresh air and die? Why don't you just put me in a coffin, then? Either way, you'll lose six years of money I would be making for you."

"That may be just what I'll do," Madam Qian replied. But two weeks later, she let Feiyan stand by the door again, perhaps figuring that with her thick heels and no knife to cut them off, she couldn't run anyway. And that with all eyes watching her, she wouldn't dare.

But Feiyan did. She bent down and in a second knocked off the heels and set off running toward the end of the alley and up Jackson Street. She ran without planning it, following the instinct that moved her feet up and down in the rhythm that was only hers. The chamber ghost would laugh at her after another beating. But for now, the wind was blowing behind her and through her and carrying her forth to the opening sky.

The guard ran after her, with no time to secure a horse this time. "Catch her," he called out. "Catch that whore!" Men stopped and watched. Some looked familiar, grinning stupidly. She was knocked down sideways by a black-jacketed man, a soldier of Hip Yee Tong that owned Red Peony. She knew because he was a regular of hers, not a bad man, who'd brought fresh lemons to her from time to time. "No offense," he said, reaching down to grab her hand. "I had no choice."

This time, Madam Qian let the guard do the beating. Feiyan had felt thankful when he knocked out the white man with an ax that time, but she soon learned that he didn't do it for her. He did it because he liked it.

"I'm tired of this," Madam Qian said. "I tried to be kind to you. You wanted some sun, I let you get some sun, and this is what *I* get in return—more betrayal, more trouble. Now, so you know, your term has been extended another four years. You try it again, you'll be here till you die."

"Unless he kills me first," Feiyan said.

"That would be too easy for you. I'm watching."

The man chuckled as he roped the end of the whip around his hand.

FEIYAN HAD YET to see Cow Hollow. The regular who lived there would stop by Red Peony once a week after selling vegetables door to door in Chinatown. Feiyan had been pressing him to tell her more about the place. Exactly how far was it? How many streets did he have to travel? How many women lived there in the village? What did they do? This man had a wife and two children. Even if he'd been single, Feiyan wouldn't have asked him to help her escape, for he simply didn't strike her as the type who had the guts to mess with the tong.

His wagon, on the other hand, could be useful. Through her barred window, she could see it parked on the side of the alley. But how could she reach there from this crib, which opened only to the corridor that led to the foyer and the front door where the guard and Madam

Qian never took their eyes off those coming in and going out? How could she get herself from underneath this moaning man to his wagon drawn by a bay mare?

Could she knock him out, change into his clothes, and walk out disguised as him? His brimmed hat was an asset, as was his habit of coiling his queue inside his hat's crown. But knocking him out was neither nice nor easy to do, which was why she'd been of two minds on this for the last few weeks now. But was there another option? What if something happened to the man and he would never come back to the brothel again? She must seize her chance when she still had it. As he came and collapsed on top of her, she reached down to the edge of the bed, grabbed the porcelain water jar, and threw it against his head. His body jerked and then stopped moving. She pushed him off her, jumped out of the bed, and put on his clothes, which fit her just fine as they were about the same height. She put on his hat and tugged her hair inside its crown. Then, covering the man with the sheet, she opened the door. She must walk down the corridor and exit the front door right under the watchful eyes of the guard and Madam Qian, and then walk right to the wagon across the alley, as if she'd done it every week. She'd never driven a wagon before but had watched men do it. She had been paying attention to these kinds of things, knowing it might all come in handy someday.

"Come back again," Madam Qian said to Feiyan, who nodded and walked through the door.

The bay mare was nibbling on the sparse curbside grass. Feiyan came to her, and, touching her face, whispered, "Be good," into her ear. Then Feiyan took off the rope halter and mounted the seat. The guard was eyeing her. Madam Qian was taking money from the next customer, who would soon be greeted by a bitter surprise. Feiyan tipped her hat at the guard and clicked her tongue. Then she was away.

After driving out of Chinatown, she turned to an unlit side road, which led to a wider road equally dark. She headed west, toward which

YE CHUN

the thin moon was inching, but decided against going to the farming village for now, as they would likely be looking for her there. She kept driving until she came to a woodland with heavy, twisted branches. She unharnessed the mare, left the wagon beneath a sweep of thick boughs, and rode the horse into the woods.

The night woods smelled dense with wildness. She kept her eyes open and her ears alert for the shifting shapes and sourceless sounds. She had not seen the dead man's ghost, but his ash-covered face had visited her often at night, alive and furious. Sometimes she thought she saw him in the faces of the men straddling her, as if he'd possessed them, tormenting her through them with all his hate. Almost every week, she'd thought one of them would kill her. But they wouldn't, not out of mercy, but to keep her alive so that she would continue to suffer. If it was unjust of her to kill the old man for what he had done to her, she had paid for it. For four and a half years now, she had been paying for this debt. Enough was enough.

She thought of the man she'd knocked out at the brothel. If he ended up dead, she wouldn't be able to cross another ocean to escape the killing. By now, she'd learned that crossing an ocean would not necessarily set you free and could just as easily bring you to another locked room. So she had to keep running, to outrun her fate as the mountain ghost had dared her.

But here in the dark woods, she couldn't run. The live oaks' gnarled branches interlocked to block her way in all directions. Even the sky was broken into pieces by the canopy. In the cracks, the thin moon hung, cold and glinting like a scythe. The mare trotted slowly. Feiyan leaned over and pressed her body over the mare's back. She stayed that way, taking in the body heat of the mare, whose large muscles and undulating gait felt like the most reliable thing in the world.

Feiyan was caught early the next morning. She'd fallen asleep on the horse's back and was startled awake by the first light trickling through the branches, or perhaps by the sinking feeling about what was to come. One behind the other, the brothel guard and the man she'd knocked unconscious rode through the twisted oaks. The man looked fine, albeit livid. As the guard aimed his revolver at her, the man dragged her off the mare and kicked and cursed. Then, with more curses spewing from his mouth, he stripped her down to her undergarments. He grunted as he changed back into his own clothes and returned what he'd been wearing to the guard. Then the two men tied Feiyan's feet and hands the way her father and brother had done years ago and threw her onto the spare horse.

The man spat in her face before mounting his bay mare. Feiyan shut her eyes to keep the spit from running in. She heard the mare trot away.

At the brothel, as Madam Qian watched, the guard beat Feiyan until she couldn't feel a thing. She was given no food for three days and a warning that they would cut her ankle tendon if she dared to run away again. Her contract was extended to the rest of her life.

Then, several months later, the boy came. She had vaguely expected him to come after she'd seen him march down the alley with other newcomers. The way he'd looked at her had made her think of her childhood, those green, free days, and the warm village she could no longer return to. It had been years since then, and she'd almost forgotten him, cataloging him, too, as a thing of the past. But on a mild May evening, she turned her head and saw him standing in front of her, grown and beautiful.

Guifeng

1869

HE TOOK A TRAIN ALONG THE TRACKS THEY'D BUILT. THE WHOLE endeavor now spread out in front of him. Not just track by track, railbed by railbed, each hammer, each chisel, each explosion, and each cartload of rocks pushed away—the humiliating work that had taken almost every waking hour of the last four years of his life. Nor just snowstorms, fast funerals, makeshift graves—so many deaths without much of a ceremony to honor or sufficient grief to spare them. In hindsight, it had been perpetual exhaustion and chill, but looking ahead at the iron tracks that the wheels were rolling upon through and across the mountains, Guifeng couldn't help but feel proud of what he and his countrymen had done.

During the last days of laying the last tracks in the desert, a race was staged between the Chinese workers and the Irishmen from the other side. Daoshi called it a dog race: white men were the breeders, gamblers, winners, and losers, and they the Chinamen their racing dogs. Yet, be it straw dogs or racing dogs, they couldn't help but put all their worth in it, couldn't help but win. At night, lying under a skyful of stars, Guifeng could almost sense Ah Fook's airy presence in the sandy air: no longer with a shape or a voice or a heart to hammer down its doubts and demands. While Guifeng was still here, lying on the sinking sand, breathing one vanishing breath after another, as the stars punched glistening holes into the sky as if to show the universe's eternity beyond eternity.

Then it was over. Guifeng was jobless but carried a giddiness in his head for having survived it all. With thirty dollars in his pocket—what remained of his last month's pay, which he had kept instead of sending home to his family—he took the westward train for the first time, along the tracks he and his fellow Chinese railroad men had built, toward Big City.

He came to the part of Chinatown where he'd first seen her. Cantonese Alley, or Alley of Joy, as the men called it. Dusty and gray on that day four years ago, when he was a young newcomer without muscles or will. Now it was evening. Red lanterns and golden lamps floated in the May air, silhouettes of beckoning girls, giggles and banter, incense and perfume, lush, yet foreboding.

He walked up and down the alley, avoiding eye contact with girls who were not her. Which door was it? Should he wait around for her to appear, or should he come back another time? But he wanted this to happen right now, so that he wouldn't wake up the next morning sobered up from this giddy feeling, and then drift away just like any other Chinese man. Work whatever job was available, live with no other dreams besides sending money home or returning with enough to build a two-story house. But that was not what he wanted. He'd known it when he rolled down the mountainside in the avalanche, thinking of Feiyan's childhood running and feeling fearless in his free fall. He'd known then what he was here for.

"Are you looking for a specific girl?" asked a middle-aged woman sitting on a stool by a door.

"Yes, a tall girl from Xinhui, about twenty-one," he said, and was going to add, "a girl good at running," but knew how irrelevant that piece of information would be.

"Oh, that must be Ah Hua. She's busy right now but will be done in a moment." The madam pointed her chin to inside the door, where a corridor led to a series of smaller doors on either side. "You can pay me now and be the next."

"How much?"

"A dollar for a quarter hour. A dollar fifty for half an hour. Two dollars an hour. How did you know her?" The madam's eyes shone with nosiness.

"I'm not sure if I know her," Guifeng said, already disliking the woman. "I'll have to wait and see."

The door that the madam had pointed her chin at opened. The person stepping out was a white man with matted hair and in a soiled work shirt, who, judging by his look, must not have had a proper bath for months. Guifeng, by contrast, had taken the time to give himself a thorough scrub at the bathhouse, which he'd learned from his camp-mates to be the basic etiquette for visiting a girl. This man being white also bothered him. How could Guifeng walk in and see only her and not also the men she'd served, especially this white man who had just sullied her, whose filth and stink were still on and inside her?

"She'll clean up." The madam seemed to have read his thoughts. "Our girls are very clean, especially Ah Hua. You won't smell a whiff of that gweilo. She will soon be all yours. Why don't you buy her for the rest of the night? Only eight bucks."

Getting no response, she went on, "What's wrong? This isn't your first time, is it?" The woman stood up from the stool and yelled down the corridor, "Ah Hua, a new guest."

"Can't you give me a break?" Guifeng heard a faint voice shout back through the closed door, a voice as right as the dirt and air in his village Yunteng, which was so far away but seemed to be miraging in front of him, here in this rowdy, heartbreaking alley.

"Our guest can't wait." The woman laughed, seeing that he had decided to stay after all.

Guifeng paid the madam two dollars, walked down the corridor to the door, now open. She was bending over a bed, smoothing a plum-colored bedsheet with a small hand broom. She looked tidy, dressed in a thin pink blouse, her hair combed into a neat bun. The air smelled of lemon, which she must have sprayed a moment earlier. He wondered how long the scent would stay and cover the residues of her previous customers. He refrained from breathing in deeply.

She turned and looked at him. Her recognition was like a sunset, radiant but disappearing even as it pulled him in. "So, you're the one who can't wait."

He heard the teasing in her voice. Was it meant to cool down and reduce him to just another man? Another young customer who didn't know what he was doing, a green hand who could easily fall for her, while she knew all too well how it would end, how no magic could ever happen in this cramped room with its gaudy colors. But the way she said those words, with the exact pitch and tilt that he knew in his very blood, again brought their village in front of his eyes, where yulan trees were blooming fiercely in this season.

He had imagined this encounter many times. What would he say? How would he act? Would he make love to her? Or would he just sit and talk? What would make him not look like the same puppy-eyed twelve-year-old craving her attention?

"Do you still like to run?" That was the first thing he'd thought of saying, while knowing it was the most terrible thing to say. He regretted the words as soon as they slipped out of his mouth.

"Yes, I do," she said, looking at him, the heat flickering back in her eyes. "And I'll never stop."

She sat down on a chair by the small table and gestured him to do the same. He sat down. The lemon scent was already fading, his recollected yulan fragrance now ghosting the air. "You used to outrun everyone."

"That's true," she said with a chuckle.

"That boy called Mouse—though he looked more like a donkey—tried to race you. Remember that? He almost dropped dead."

They laughed. She struck a match, lit an incense stick on the lotus-shaped porcelain burner. A pale smoke tendril rose, sandalwood's bittersweet scent.

"So you survived that damn railroad." Her eyes fluttered a faint accusation. Had she been waiting for him to come?

"How did you know I went to build the railroad?"

"Nine out of ten Chinese men worked on the railroad. They came here on weekends. Some said they'd come back but never did. I figured they were dead."

"Many did die," Guifeng said.

Then he began to tell her about the things he'd wanted to tell her for the past four years. Things he'd repeated to himself, pretending it was her he was telling, things that would have been unremarkable without her ears to listen or her mind's eye to picture them. The life-and-death events that had taken too many lives, including perhaps those who had slept with her on this very bed with its flashy colors and stubborn creases, which now lay empty a few feet away from them, inviting and terrifying, as if foretelling a darker fate ahead.

Guifeng sat tight on the squeaky chair and told Feiyan about his fall down the mountainside in the avalanche. How he had feared height all his life, but that fall, somehow, had taken the fear out of him. He seemed to have been brought back to their village where kids were run-ning, Feiyan the fastest among them. As he tumbled down the snowy slope, his body hit a thick pine and the interruption must have woken him: he began to swim as if in water, breaststroking to keep his mouth and nose above the rushing snow, but it piled upon him, gush after gush. When he finally stopped falling, he found himself tucked inside a white pocket. He punched and punched until his fist was hugged by wind.

She told him her Gold Mountain story too. She had not been kid-napped, no, not like what the rumor had said. Instead, she had run away from the drunken old husband and sold herself to a trafficker for the passage here. She had tried to run away three times since, and during her most recent escape attempt, she'd ridden a horse. "Remember the rich farmer Lu Ah Bo's horse? He'd let us ride sometimes. I guess I learned how to ride a horse then."

She laughed and lit another incense stick, the dark aroma now dense like the deep earth.

•

THE IDEA CAME to him before he fell asleep in his boardinghouse bunk. He would take Feiyan away. They would ride the train back across the mountains, along the tracks he'd built, and go live in Truckee on the other side of the Sierra. The town had felt the closest thing to home during his past four years moving from camp to camp. At least one third of Truckee's population were Chinese, and he'd seen several couples in Chinatown, husbands and wives working side by side in a grocery store or a laundromat. No one seemed to bother those women and they had the look that they wouldn't stand any bothering. He could get a job at a lumber company. They'd been hiring even when he was still on the Sierra. Several of his campmates, including the cook Li Shu, had moved back into the woods near Truckee. Guifeng would work and provide, and when they saved enough, he and Feiyan could open a store. Or they could buy some land and farm. Back when he was in China, Guifeng had not been keen on farming, but now, after four years of handling rocks, he missed the commonplace and reliable work with dirt.

The question was how to get Feiyan out of the brothel, where the guard had the vicious look of a killer, and the madam was already suspicious of him. "If you want to buy her, I'll give you a good price," she'd said to Guifeng when he left the night before.

"Why would I buy her?" Guifeng was on guard. "She's covered with whip welts. You shouldn't have done that to her." He had not seen Feiyan's body nor the scars on her back, but he could imagine the beating and whipping after each of her three runaway attempts.

"Young man, you do your business, I do mine. You're in no position to tell me what to do to take care of my girls. You don't own her and don't look like you'll ever own a girl. But if you ever change your mind and want to buy her out of her lifetime service, I'll give you a good price: eight hundred. Think about it. It's a bargain for a girl like Ah Hua."

Guifeng had certainly thought about it, but unless he struck it rich at a gold mine, he had no chance to get hold of that much money. Even gold was no longer possible, since gold, as he'd heard, had been mined out in this place, which was nevertheless still called Gold Mountain.

At nightfall, he came again to Red Peony, and again paid two dollars for an hour with her. "Leave with me," he said without giving himself time to hesitate.

It turned out that he needn't have come up with a plan himself. She had thought it through, and all she needed was someone like him to help her carry it out. This was how: she would slip a potion into the brothel's breakfast congee, make everyone sleep like a rock, and then she would untie the keys from the madam's waist string and walk out in men's clothes.

Naoyanghua. That was the name of the potion. They'd given it to a girl whose baby's head was too big for her fourteen-year-old hips. The midwife knocked her out with the drug before cutting her belly open. That was how Feiyan learned about it. Guifeng could get it in an herb store.

On the third night, Guifeng brought the vial of potion he'd bought from an herbalist, who had stared at him from behind his cracked glasses.

"For my wife, who is having trouble sleeping," Guifeng had said what Feiyan had instructed him to say.

He also brought Feiyan a set of his spare clothes, a pair of newly purchased flat-soled cotton shoes, and a brimmed hat like his own.

He bought the rest of the night with her. They needed all the time they had to plan out the details. They sat across the small table, within touching distance, but did not touch. He kept his hands on his knees or by the teacup. He glanced at the bed but left it alone. It would ruin what they had between them if he got on the bed and pressed her down like any other man.

He had to leave before the night was over to give her time to sneak into the kitchen and dump the contents of the vial into the pot of congee.

"Remember my offer. You don't have to pay to see her every night," said the madam, as Guifeng stepped out of the brothel into the thinning night.

Feiyan

HE HAD NOT TOUCHED HER. SHE COULD TELL THAT HE WANTED TO but had decided she was worth waiting for. But was she sure? Could she dare to believe she was wanted that way?

In this room, men's wants were as cheap as a dollar and as open and untethered as the odor that permeated the air, and that she had to fight with squeezes of precious lemon slices and incense. The battle of scents. She observed it as the next man freed his want on her. She couldn't care less about their crude ways. She was more interested in the quality of the air she was forced to breathe.

Lemon and sandalwood incense. Her nose desired them. Her nose also preferred those coming in with the smell of soap. Even before she saw him, she smelled his cleanness, and already it was a relief.

He sat down on the chair, talking about back home. The sandalwood smoke poured through the air, and Feiyan smelled her village, its dirt, river, burly palm trees, its morning dust stirred up by the chickens rushing to her feet, its pigsty sharp with new feces. She would feed the chicks and pigs first, and then head upstream to fill the two buckets with water that had run itself clean overnight. She would carry them home with a shoulder pole, a chore she'd done since she was nine, keeping her balance, challenging herself to not spill a drop. Then she would go out again for a run along the river.

She didn't touch him, just as he didn't touch her. She considered making the first move, as she'd done with young first-timers, guiding them to trust their bodies. She'd enjoyed those rare moments, rare because they wouldn't be the same the next time. They would pride themselves as the rein-takers and be crude and familiar and predictable like the rest. But she didn't reach out to touch him. The holding back was what held the moment, so it wouldn't grow old. She didn't touch his hands, which were calloused but tender-looking, the fingers long and sensitive without their knowing it. They were playing with the rim of his felt hat. In order to not touch his hands, she took his hat and put it on her head, as he talked about his railroad days.

"It looks good on you." He leaned toward her.

She took off the hat and hung it on the clothes hanger. "Keep going, I want to know more."

So they just talked across the small table as the incense sticks burned to stubs one by one. They rested their heads against the wall or shifted their bottoms on the chairs and left the bed empty. She had smoothed the bedsheet, but it still looked wrinkled, unclean.

He stayed seated on the chair until his time was up, and then the next night he came back and asked her to run away with him. She stayed calm, not wanting to reveal too much. Up till now she'd only been able to rely on herself, unless she counted the ghosts who were not always trustworthy, especially not the one in this chamber, watching them right now, full of envy, preparing her speech of mockery and admonition: "If you think he's really fallen for you and will do what he said he'd do, you're the stupidest girl alive. Get ready to never lay your eyes on him again. All that sweet smell and back-home talk does not mean a thing. Been there myself and look at what I am now."

But he came back the next night. They both looked calm, the kind of calm she recognized to be what one must muster even just for once in a lifetime. Again, they sat without bothering the bed, without touching, although their hands were so close she could feel the pull in the inch between their knuckles and skin. They didn't talk about what they would do after getting off the train at the town across the mountains. They didn't talk about it as if what they wished for would leak out through uttered words and vaporize like all the other wishes the idle mind could concoct.

They focused on the closer future and the night hours that were leaking away. As the morning approached with its quiet hunger, Feiyan felt as if their plan was already in motion, like back when she'd finally seen the harbor where the Pearl River flowed into the sea, and the ship with its dazzling system of masts. What she'd since learned was that being saved by no means meant staying saved, but still, as he talked about their escape, she felt it in her gut that this one would not fail. It had been promised to her, because he was with her, which would make all the difference.

The cooking woman, Ah Gu, was alone in the kitchen, bent over the steaming pot of congee she was stirring. Her face had been melted in a fire before Feiyan's time, an inferno that had burned down half of Chinatown. "Egg white, that was all I needed," Ah Gu had told her more than a few times. "Had I gotten hold of some egg white and spread it on my face, I would have been just fine. I'd seen it done back in my village. A girl was helping her mama cook, a pot of boiling water spilled on her face, and her grandma separated egg white from yolk and spread it on her burn. Her face was like new. Such a useful remedy, but we'd run out of eggs. No more eggs when you most needed them. That was my luck. Bad things must have happened in my past life, I'm paying for them now. That's how I see it."

"You will have a good life next time around," Feiyan had said. She'd tried to see Ah Gu's face beneath the mesh of scars—the old face that could have been saved if egg white had not been uselessly cooked and eaten; a face nobody could remember, least of all Ah Gu. Day after day, Feiyan never failed to be shocked by this faceless face in the pre-dawn hour when the last customers departed for their own precarious futures, and the last girls washed their overused bodies and paced into the kitchen one by one to get their bowl of congee, before returning to their overused bed for six hours of solitary sleep—shocked and re-minded once again that misfortune could strike anywhere, anytime.

"What's for breakfast?" She stepped to the pot, and as Ah Gu turned to remove bowls from the shelf, Feiyan dumped the contents of the vial into the soup and picked up the long-stemmed spoon to stir it.

"Same again?" she said when Ah Gu turned back to set the bowls on the table.

"What do you expect? Same day for same life, same breakfast for same day," Ah Gu said.

But it wouldn't be the same for Feiyan.

Guifeng

WHEN HE CAME BACK, THE ALLEY WAS WRAPPED IN A DAWN FOG. The lanterns, now off, hung anemic in the pale air. He sauntered up and down the alley so that he wouldn't appear to be loitering. It had passed the time they'd planned to meet. Pedestrians were appearing on the main street but the door to Red Peony stayed shut. Many things could have gone wrong and they had no contingency plan. "We won't need one," Feiyan had said, looking so sure, just as she looked when she ran. He was not like her but wanted to be. More sure, less doubtful. He could tell she'd begun to see him differently after he returned on the second night, asking her to leave with him. Now he just needed what he had proposed to happen in reality.

As the fog lifted partway and the sky began to clear, the door finally opened a crack. A men's hat poked out, and it took Guifeng a second to recognize her. She was wearing his clothes, plain but newish, which he'd bought months ago in Truckee, while most of his other clothing was brought from home, handsewn by either his wife or his mother and now spotted with various patches. The loose jacket and pants camouflaged her curves well. Her hat rim was pulled low, and beneath it, she must have rubbed something on her face to make it look darker, more weathered.

Quietly, she closed the door behind her and locked it with a key before slipping the key chain inside her jacket pocket. She walked toward him with a widening smile, and as they walked together out of the alley, she brushed her hand against his.

"Did everything go well?" he asked in a whisper.

"Yes, they're all sleeping like pigs, Madam Qian especially. She couldn't even make it to her bed, passed out right on the floor in her room." Feiyan laughed to herself under the hat brim. She was walking fast in the new cotton shoes, as if she could barely stop herself from breaking into a run.

DAOSHI WAS WAITING with Guifeng's luggage in front of the board-inghouse. Guifeng had told him about his plan, and Daoshi had not lectured him on folly, destiny, duty, or filial piety, as Guifeng had feared he would. Instead, he just listened, which must have had to do with his wuwei practice—not interfering with other people's actions, even if their actions might appear to be the opposite of wuwei. But how could wuwei be achieved here? Had Guifeng done nothing, Feiyan would be trapped in the brothel for the rest of her life. Wasn't he also following Dao and practicing wuwei? Doing what he was supposed to do and feeling as if the doing was non-doing? That was how it felt from the moment Feiyan turned her back on that brothel door and walked toward him, smiling from beneath her hat, his plain clothes almost elegant on her lean, straight body. It felt so right and effortless despite all their effort.

Daoshi's presence confirmed that feeling. He looked at them without judgment or question. He held his hands in front of his chest and bowed. "Take care," he said, and saw them go.

AFTER A RIDE in a ferry and then a stage wagon, they arrived at the Sacramento train station in the afternoon. Although he only had fifteen dollars left in his pocket, Guifeng decided to buy two second-class tickets for upholstered seats. The third-class passenger coaches, also known as the emigrant cars, which he'd ridden three days before, would be stuffed with benches and sweaty laborers. He wanted to give Feiyan a good experience for her first-ever train ride. She'd asked many questions about the train last night, including its speed: "How fast? Faster than a horse?"

"Yes, a lot faster. It's engine drawn," Guifeng had told her. "That's the whole point. One coal-burning engine draws the entire chain of carriages on steel wheels over wrought iron tracks." He'd felt proud.

They sat down across from a peasant-looking white woman and her two children, who seemed like safe passengers to ride with. Chinese men would start a chat, and Feiyan's silence would irritate them if they hadn't already seen through her guise. White men would provoke if not outright assault you. Black, brown, and native men were unpredictable and therefore better to keep at a distance as well. White women, on the other hand, would maybe throw disdainful looks at you but generally leave you alone, like this bonny-hatted, hard-faced woman busying herself with her children who wouldn't sit still. She furrowed her brows deeper when Feiyan and Guifeng sat down across from her but said nothing.

Feiyan turned her eyes to the views outside the window, where there were no buildings blocking the sky or breaking the sun into crawling patches on a wall, where hills of wild oat grass the color of harvest were giving way to blurring branches of pines and spruces. Guifeng could sense a lightness settling in her. He felt his heart strung to hers, tugged by every inflection of her moods. Such sharing was so astonishing it made him nervous. But he decided not to be. They were on a train, along the tracks he'd risked his life to build, and if he had ever doubted whether it was worth it, he did not now. This alone—fleeing with Feiyan on the world's fastest moving vehicle toward a future together—made the whole endeavor worthwhile.

There would be many unknowns at the end of the train ride, but they would make it somehow. They had both chosen to come to Gold Mountain and had made it this far. From this point on, they would not allow anyone to tell them what to do—to arrange love, direct passion, or list duties to fulfill. They would not obey the old schema of things anymore.

But even as he was thinking these audacious thoughts, an unease and a weariness were burrowing inside him. He saw the faces of his mother and wife when they sent him off, standing still on the riverbank till the boat turned the bend. This wasn't a good time to think of them, who must be worrying at this very moment about the overdue letter and money he had not sent. It wasn't a good time to think of his daughter either, whose face he had never seen, who should be three and a half years old now. Guifeng would rather not let guilt and sorrow run their course and rob him of his happiness, with Feiyan sitting next to him as the train took them farther and farther away from the old order of things. Had they been alone, he would have let his longing for her overcome all the other feelings, letting its rightness assert itself.

One of the white woman's children, the little one about the same age as Sixiang, was looking at Guifeng, intently, without a blink of her hazel eyes, as if questioning him, *Who are you? What are you doing?* Guifeng tried to smile at her, but even after looking away, the child seemed scornful.

Feiyan turned to him. Her eyes were not clouded like his. She was wide awake and looked determined not to miss a minute of her freshly obtained freedom. The light in her eyes troubled him a little. Under the renewed scrutiny of the child the same age as his daughter, who might be starving at this moment, he smiled at Feiyan with as much lightness as he could summon. He felt lopsided, as if he was in an inverted world, looking at Feiyan from a widening distance between them.

The train now carried them across the precipice at Cape Horn, where Guifeng had witnessed his first death in Gold Mountain. His fellow campmate whose name he hadn't yet learned had surged toward the brilliant sky before plummeting into the raging river. Guifeng looked out of the window and saw nothing but air. The mountain suspended them on its hip, like a giant mother who was going to drop them but changed her mind.

5

Clean Heart

1877–1878

Sixiang

THE GIRL ON THE NEXT COT REMINDED HER OF LITTLE AH FANG ON
the ship, who used to fall asleep as if without a care, but those sound
sleeps had also, all too quickly, led her to the final wakeless one. This
girl, Ah Jia, was small-boned like Ah Fang, although she was a few
months older than Sixiang. She'd asked Sixiang her age the first thing
after Miss Moore and Yizheng assigned her to be Sixiang's friend. Ah
Jia seemed pleased to learn that she was older. She said she'd come to
the Home a few months earlier than Sixiang too—she'd run away from
her owners by herself.

Ah Jia had a shiny scar the size of a medal on the inner side of her
forearm. Sixiang saw it when they washed together by the bathroom
sinks before bedtime. She tried not to stare.

There were twelve beds in the room, occupied by girls from age
five or six to late teens or earlier twenties. In the smaller adjacent room,
two older women in their mid- or late twenties slept with the four babies. Yizheng, the teenager who had accompanied Miss Moore to take
Sixiang here, was clearly the leader among them. Before bed, she'd

helped Miss Moore and the other white lady, Miss Webb, inspect every girl's face, teeth, and hands. The youngsters opened their mouths dutifully for the inspection, but some of the older girls muttered things under their breath the moment they turned away.

After the last oil lamp was blown out and the room snapped into darkness, Sixiang shut her eyes for a moment before opening them again—cautiously, as if the room might have turned into something frightening. She peered into the dark to make sure the shapes on the cots were still the same as before. Then she heard a whisper: "Are you afraid of hell?"

"What?" Sixiang started. Ah Jia's eyes from across the narrow space between their cots gleamed like a wild cat's.

"If we don't get our heads dipped in the water, they'll send us to hell. The older girls told me so. But Loumou said I wasn't ready to get my head dipped yet."

By *Loumou*, Ah Jia meant Miss Moore. Sixiang had heard several girls call the white lady that earlier today, which shocked Sixiang. Back on the ship, Madam had also asked the girls to call her *Loumou*, but no one wanted to do so. The girls here, however, seemed fine with it, especially the younger ones, who spoke to Miss Moore with sugary voices, like they really wanted her to be their mama. They must be real orphans, Sixiang thought. But she was not. She still had a real mother waiting for her to return.

"You try to lie quiet and go to sleep now," Ah Jia whispered again. "It's not too bad here—actually, it's not bad at all. You don't have to work as hard, and you don't get beaten up and burned. At most they'll scold you. And if you behave, they'll let you dip in the water."

Sixiang tried to stay still on her bed. Soon she heard Ah Jia's breathing even out, and the other girls' breathing, snores, and sleep mumbles rise and ebb. She felt as if she were back in the ship's dark hold again, except all the passengers here were girls.

"You're safe with us," Yizheng had translated Miss Moore's

words to her earlier today, after they'd turned the corner at Stockton and Washington Street and she could no longer see Daoshi when she looked back. It must be Daoshi who had informed the Mission Home to have her "rescued." He'd promised he would find a way to help her, but how could this be the way? How would this bring her closer to her father—and to home? She reached down into the basket under her cot for her blouse and groped for her father's photo in its inside pocket. She held the photo, its edges now furry after so many touches. She tried to picture her father's face in her head, but instead she saw Daoshi's face turning smaller and blurry as she was led away to this brick building. She thought of the face of God on the walls in every room she'd been led in so far—the elderly white man with deep-set eyes and willowy hair. Before bed, with Miss Webb playing the organ and Miss Moore leading the chorus, they'd sung English songs, facing the picture of God. The clear melody and soft singing had sent warm rivulets down Sixiang's spine.

Now, the hymns echoed back in her head, even though a vision of hell also lingered: images of faceless men shouting, stomping, smashing, scorching, killing, while she and Daoshi hid in the small, darkened room holding their breath. In the back-and-forth pulling between the soothing songs and searing riot, Sixiang fell asleep, without knowing what was lying in store for her.

The bell seemed to ring a moment later. She opened her eyes to find all the girls still on their cots, their faces seemingly soft and untroubled, smoothed by sleep. Even the scar on Ah Jia's arm stretched out from the covers looked less red and bulging.

Ah Jia showed Sixiang how to fold the corners of her sheet underneath the mattress, the Christian way of making the bed. "Only when everything is clean and tidy will God like us," Ah Jia told her.

Everyone had chores. Sixiang and Ah Jia were assigned to take care of the babies as the two women prepared the breakfast. One of the babies was Meimei's age and just as needy. When Sixiang held her on her lap, she wondered what was happening to Meimei—did she have to sleep alone on that partitioned-off bed, or did Mr. and Mrs. Chen allow her to sleep with them? Would Mrs. Chen start pinching her now that Sixiang was gone?

Breakfast was congee sprinkled with dices of pickled radish. The serving girl was exact with her scoops, measuring out the proper portion based on each girl's size. Sixiang saw that she would sometimes change her mind and scoop a little back from a girl's bowl. Sixiang was unimpressed by the food here. The night before, dinner had been rice with a small serving of bland, overcooked cabbage. At the Chens', she'd cooked three dishes and one soup for every dinner, and their breakfast congee was never without slices of lean pork or preserved eggs. "What's there to live for if not three flavorful meals a day?" Mr. Chen would say in his good moods. And despite Mrs. Chen's tormenting ways, she had never let Sixiang go hungry.

Sixiang saw some girls grumble under their breath about the food, but no one complained openly. Besides the two women eating and feeding the noisy babies in the kitchen, the rest of them all sat quietly around the long table in the dining room. Miss Moore and Miss Webb sat at each end. Yizheng sat right by Miss Moore. They all folded their hands and lowered their eyes as Miss Moore said prayers to God in English and Yizheng followed by translating them into Cantonese.

"There will be meat on Sunday," Ah Jia whispered to Sixiang. "Potatoes with beef. Each of us gets a piece of beef this size." She circled her thumb and forefinger to form a small round nothing. "You eat a tiny bite at a time to make it last."

"No talking while eating." Yizheng tossed a stare at Ah Jia down the table. Yizheng had been at the Mission Home for seven years now, the longest among them all, Sixiang had learned from Ah Jia. She accompanied Miss Moore not only to rescues but to court hearings, and on those occasions, she would put on a tight-chested Western dress and a lacy hat.

"Chew with your mouth closed," Yizheng said to another girl, "and do not smack your lips."

It seemed that Yizheng could read Miss Moore's face without Miss Moore saying anything. Miss Moore only needed to give someone a look and Yizheng would spell out the right reprimands, first in English and then Cantonese, so that they could both learn the foreign language and forego their old uncouth habits at the same time.

After breakfast, the girls formed double lines in the dining hall and marched out. As they passed the front door of the living quarters to the study room, each of them was again inspected by Miss Moore and Miss Webb, who scanned their faces, hands, and fingernails, tidied their hair with a comb, or flattened the collars at their necks. They were to study the Bible, God's teaching, Ah Jia whispered to Sixiang as they waited for their turn, so they must be very clean.

Two by two they sat down at a desk where a thick, leather-bound book was placed before each of them. The book had both English and Chinese words in it, neither of which Sixiang could read. In the Laozi book she had flipped open in Daoshi's room, the words were large and lined up from top to bottom. In this book, the words were small and numerous and lined up row by row. But whatever the words said, it was thrilling just to hold such a serious-looking book in her hands.

Miss Moore asked them to open the book to a certain page before reading a passage to them in English. Yizheng then read the Chinese passage underneath so that they knew what it was about. Then there was discussion of the passage, also both in English and Chinese. Then they all read the passage after Miss Moore and Yizheng until they could memorize it. At the end of the study, Miss Moore asked, which Yizheng translated, "What dirt will God clean from your heart today?"

One by one the girls took turns to say something. "Filth," said a girl who had earlier stalled the line of inspection because Miss Moore had held up her fingers and made her look at the dirt in her nails. Another girl said, "Laziness." Another said, "Heathen beliefs." Sixiang felt a pang of panic again, while the image of scalding and scraping a pig for butchering appeared in her mind. It was clear that everyone must say something bad about themselves. Some girls were able to say it in English. Some said it part in English, part in Chinese. Some depended on Yizheng to translate for them to Miss Moore. They all ended by saying, "I ask God to take the dirt from my heart. I pray to God and he can wash my heart clean." That was also what Ah Jia said, after confessing she was "disorderly" sometimes, as most of the girls did; it seemed to be the standard answer.

"Sixiang, what about you?" Miss Moore asked her. Her eyes were not unkind, but the projecting, scheming look was there again. Perhaps she wasn't all that different from Madam, who had come across as open and kind but had been, in reality, calculating Sixiang's price-tag. Was Miss Moore also planning to sell her? Ah Jia had told her that the girl who'd slept on Sixiang's cot before her was married off a month ago. Was she sold?

"Loumou is asking you," Yizheng said in Cantonese.

"I don't know what to say," Sixiang muttered.

"You must say something. Filth, disorder, arrogance, or heathen beliefs. I'm sure you have heathen beliefs. If you believe in Guanyin Goddess, you have heathen beliefs."

Sixiang thought of the hell Ah Jia had forewarned her of last night and nodded, mumbling, "Heathen beliefs," in Cantonese.

"You must try to learn to say things in English," Yizheng said, "so that Loumou can understand you."

Sixiang parroted Yizheng's words that were supposed to be her English answer to Miss Moore's question, and then she said what every other girl had said, repeating word by word after Yizheng, "I ask God to take the dirt from my heart. I pray to God and he can wash my heart clean."

Then something dawned on Sixiang. Maybe the reason that her wish hadn't come true was because she hadn't been praying to the right god. Maybe what governed in Middle Kingdom—Guanyin Goddess and Guanyu God—didn't govern here in Gold Mountain. The gods and goddesses back home might have lost their powers once you crossed the monthlong ocean. They might have lost some of their powers even at home, as Sixiang and her mother and grandmother had prayed every day, but what had been granted to them?

Sixiang closed her eyes to pray, trying to summon the image of the wavy-haired, deep-set-eyed God. But she saw Daoshi instead—his straight black hair tied up in a neat topknot, his black eyes steady and attentive in their listening way. She opened her eyes to get a better look at the portrait of the God on the wall, but after she closed her eyes, she continued to see Daoshi, who had held her in his arms on that whirlwind night—the way only her mother would do.

AFTER HOURS OF sewing in the late morning and most of the afternoon, which Sixiang learned was to help pay for their food and board as the donors' money wasn't enough, they got an hour's free time. They went to play in the fenced backyard, where a big oak tree leaned toward the three-story building. In between the branches lived a family of scuttling squirrels and two mourning doves whose coos Sixiang had heard in the early morning through the window. Sixiang asked Ah Jia if Miss Moore ever sold the girls—what had happened, for example, to the girl who used to sleep on her cot?

"I don't know if Loumou sold her or not, but she did have a wedding here under this tree. She was given a white dress instead of a red one. She made a big fuss about that, saying they were sending her away to die. But she calmed down when she saw her Christian groom. The man smiled at her like his mouth couldn't close." Ah Jia giggled. "Have you had wedding cake before?"

Sixiang shook her head.

"It's the sweetest thing in the world." Ah Jia licked her lips as if the cake's aftertaste was still there. "I hope we have more weddings."

Then, remembering something else, Ah Jia lowered her voice. "The girl used to squirm in bed at night and make gross sounds." She giggled again. "I'm glad you're here next to me now. You sleep quietly once you're done tossing and turning."

Ah Jia said the older girls here had been mean to her. Even her assigned "friend" was mean, although the girl had never admitted she had meanness in her heart when asked what she would pray for God to clean. She only said "disorder" again and again.

Shortly after Ah Jia escaped to the Mission Home, her "friend" asked her to steal apples for the older girls. The girl was only a few months older than Ah Jia but was a head taller and considered herself one of the older girls, claiming her role was to pass down instructions from the older girls to the younger ones. Their first task for Ah Jia was to steal apples that a donor had brought to the Home, not the whole dozen, just a couple so that Miss Moore and Miss Webb wouldn't notice. Ah Jia snuck into the kitchen when no one was watching and stuck two apples under her blouse. She was only given a thumb-sized cube when the two apples were divided among them. But the next day, at study, Miss Moore asked who had stolen the two apples. "I have never seen Loumou so angry. Her eyes were like a mad water buffalo's. She yelled something and Yizheng translated it to us: 'Honesty will be rewarded by God; dishonesty will bring you on the path to hell!' I didn't want to go to hell. I raised my hand and said, 'I did it,' and I said the only reason I did it was because my 'friend' asked me to, or I wouldn't have any friends here. After I said it, Loumou wasn't so angry anymore. She didn't punish me because I was honest," Ah Jia said with equal pride and trouble in her eyes.

She changed the subject back. "I don't think Loumou sells us. We are just being sent away by God when it's time. You get married, or you get sent to white families to learn about Christian ways of keeping house. Or you get sent back to China to spread the word of God. But wherever it is God wants to send you, you need to be a clean girl, not like the one up there in that room." Ah Jia pointed at one of the attic windows with a partially drawn curtain. "That girl," she said, lowering her voice to a whisper, "has been dirtied by hundreds of gweilo."

On the riot night, she told Sixiang, the mob had banged on the front door and thrown rocks at the windows, breaking three of them and cracking many more. The girls all went into hiding under their cots and ended up spending most of the night that way. In the early morning, they heard a different kind of banging on the door and a girl's crying and begging in Cantonese. They peeked out above the windowsills when Miss Moore and Miss Webb opened the door. "The girl crawled in without a shred of clothes," Ah Jia said with horror in her face, as if she was seeing everything right in front of her eyes again. "She was covered in blood and huge bruises, her face so swollen it looked like an eggplant."

"How old is she?" Sixiang asked.

"About Yizheng's age, but Yizheng wouldn't even touch her when Miss Moore asked her to help carry the girl to the sick room. Miss Webb wouldn't touch her either. She had to run back in and grab a blanket to cover her up first. Only the two women who used to be the same kind helped clean and feed her. But even they shake their heads when they talk about her."

"Can I take a look at her?"

"Why?" Ah Jia asked.

"I know an older girl who had been sold to a brothel."

"We're supposed to stay away from the sick room. Girls in it are contagious. Before this girl crawled in, another girl had died of consumption in that room. The girl taking care of that girl got it and died in there too. I don't want to get what this girl got. I don't want my face to look like an eggplant."

Sixiang nodded. She'd kept seeing Ah Hong in her head when Ah Jia described the girl, and she wanted to make sure it wasn't Ah Hong. But that night, she dreamt of Ah Hong, who was telling her that she wished she'd gotten what Ah Fang had on the ship and died then. She spoke with blood dripping out of the corner of her mouth, her face indeed purple and swollen like an eggplant. Sixiang awoke to a bottomless dark she seemed to be falling through, but when she adjusted her eyes and saw the sleeping girls taking shape on their cots, she tried to tell herself that even if it was indeed Ah Hong, she was safe now. If all the gweilo had done to this building was banging on the door and smashing a few windows, this was indeed a safer place than the rest of Chinatown. That must be why the girl, whether it was Ah Hong or not, had crawled her way here. It must also be why Daoshi—it could only be he—had arranged for them to rescue her.

THE NEXT DAY at the afternoon recess, Ah Jia asked Sixiang if she still wanted to go see the girl. Sixiang had kept peering up at the attic window.

"If I help you sneak up," Ah Jia said, "will you help me with something in return?"

"What do you want me to help with?"

"Can you sneak into the basement with me? Sometimes a carrot will slip through the crack of the kitchen floor. I went down there once with the older girls, but the moment they got their carrot, they said there were ghosts in the basement. They ran out and latched the door shut from outside to keep me there. Just to be bad and mean. I screamed for a long time before someone heard me."

"That was so mean of them," Sixiang said sympathetically. "Were they punished?"

"They didn't get to eat that night. But then they became meaner. They'll pinch me when Loumou and Miss Webb are not looking. They even said they would burn me with a candle like my old owner. Have you seen my scar yet?" Ah Jia pulled up her sleeve to bare the shiny medal on her arm.

"I saw it," Sixiang mumbled.

"Go on, you can touch it."

Sixiang touched it and felt a pang of pain, as she imagined Ah Jia's owner, who must have looked just like Mrs. Chen, clutching Ah Jia's skinny arm to the candle flame. Sixiang thought it was only right to show Ah Jia her own scars too, though none of them were as large or show-worthy.

She could tell the other girls were shunning them. They would pretend not to see them even when they were all seated at the same table sewing. When Ah Jia tried to join a conversation, they would simply not respond, or speak over her as if they couldn't hear. Even the older girls doling out meals seemed especially stingy with both their portions. For her proximity to Ah Jia, Sixiang was treated as an enemy as well.

"You don't want to be close to Ah Jia," a taller girl had leaned down to whisper in Sixiang's ear earlier today when Sixiang waited in line for the privy, "because she is a little liar."

But Sixiang had liked Ah Jia right away, as she'd liked Ah Fang on the ship. She even wondered if Ah Jia wasn't somehow Ah Fang's rebirth so that they could continue to be friends. Had Ah Fang been alive, she could certainly have been sold to an owner even crueler than Mrs. Chen and gotten a scar like Ah Jia's, and they could have both ended up here. Sixiang looked around the backyard: a group of younger girls were playing hand-clapping games, and beyond them, near the brick-walled fence topped with barbed wires, several older girls were chatting. One of them, the taller girl who had whispered her advice to Sixiang, was looking at her with a hand on her hip. Sixiang reached out and held Ah Jia's hand: "Okay, I'll go to the basement with you if you take me up there."

SHE EXPECTED TO see a dreadfully soiled and disfigured face as she climbed the stairs with Ah Jia, who led her up to the attic landing, pointing at the direction of the room, the last down the corridor lined with a few other doors. "Be quick. I'll watch for you," Ah Jia whispered.

When Sixiang opened the door a crack and peeked in, Ah Hong was staring straight at her. Her face was a little bruised and swollen, but nothing like an eggplant. There was nothing about her, leaning against a propped-up white pillow under a white sheet, to suggest dirtiness either. But she lay so still in the small, slant-ceilinged room and for a second, Sixiang thought she was not breathing.

"It's me," Sixiang whispered from the door, unsure if she should step any closer.

But Ah Hong continued to stare.

"It's me, Sixiang. Do you remember me?"

"Little Sixiang?" Ah Hong's face finally opened to a slight smile. She reached out a hand from under the white sheet, a pale wrist ringed with dark bruises. "You've grown so big."

"Are you feeling better? Can you still walk?" Sixiang asked, closing the door behind her as she stepped closer to touch Ah Hong's hand. She'd seen gutted shops, wrecked buildings, charred houses, and a hanged man noosed with his own queue. She still couldn't quite believe Ah Hong looked so clean.

"Why do you think I can't walk?"

"They said you had to . . ." Sixiang couldn't say the humiliating word *crawl*.

"Of course I can walk. I just don't want to get up. It's nice lying here like this."

"But you're all alone."

"I like it. I like to be left alone. But if you want, you can come visit me. I don't mind seeing you."

As Sixiang was going to say okay, the door flung open. Miss Moore and Yizheng stood in the doorway. Ah Jia was there too, her wrist clasped in Yizheng's hand. "Why are you in this room, Sixiang?" Miss

Moore and Yizheng were saying something together, one in English, one in Cantonese.

"I, I know her. She is my friend," Sixiang stammered.

"We have rules here we expect you to follow. Do you understand?" English and Cantonese.

"And you," they said, turning their eyes to Ah Hong, "if you're feeling better now, it's time to get up, do chores, and learn about God's way."

The flat blankness had now returned to Ah Hong's face. She had not looked like that at all on the ship. Maybe it was something she'd adopted since her purchase at the basement auction and perfected when hundreds of gweilo dirtied her. Now she could put it on whenever she needed it.

Miss Moore shook her head, saying no more. Yizheng, however, was able to interpret her wordless reproach into Cantonese: "If you don't embrace God and pray to him, you will never be clean. You will keep looking as dumb as you are looking now." Then she turned her eyes to Sixiang and Ah Jia. "You two disobedient girls, come with us."

Punishment was no dinner. They were led directly to the prayer room to kneel before the portrait of Jesus. During morning study, Miss Moore had taught them that Jesus was scourged, crucified, and bled to death "on our behalf, because God loves and forgives us." Sixiang couldn't understand why the almighty God would allow bad men to torture and kill his own son. Nor could she think of any god or goddess in China who would allow that kind of thing to happen to their children. And if Jesus's suffering at the hands of traitors and evil-doers should be honored, why not Ah Hong's suffering at the hands of the gweilo mobs? Why was her suffering unclean while Jesus's was not only clean but revered? If God loved and forgave them, why were they punished for visiting a sick, lonely friend who had suffered no less than Jesus?

They could smell dinner across the hallway. "Why am I always so unlucky?" Ah Jia sniffled. "I thought you were okay, but the first thing you did was get me in trouble again. I'm so hungry. I'll starve because of you. Why did you have to go see her? She looked half dead anyway. And we'll soon end up just like her."

"I'll give you half of my breakfast tomorrow," Sixiang said.

Ah Jia considered this but did not look consoled. Maybe breakfast was simply too far away. How could they survive this hunger through the long night and then the chores and prayers in the morning before finally reaching the stingy scoop of congee? Or half a scoop for Sixiang.

Was it worth it? Now that Sixiang knew it was indeed Ah Hong, as she had feared, what was there to do?

THE NEXT MORNING, as Sixiang and Ah Jia waited in line for their scoop, they heard a wave of mumbles behind them. Ah Hong was standing at the end of the line. Her face was not blank like yesterday in the sick room, but aware and apologetic, as if shy of inserting herself. Or perhaps she knew everyone was staring at her as if she were still without a shred of clothes, crawling in covered with blood and bruises. She knew they wouldn't see her now without seeing her then.

Miss Moore let Ah Hong sit next to her, on the opposite side from Yizheng. "Everyone, this is Ah Hong. Let's thank God for her recovery."

For the rest of the breakfast, Miss Moore sat straight, unsmiling. She seemed to be steeling herself for something. Her left arm next to Ah Hong's right arm looked rigid, tugged in.

Later in the study room, when the daily question was asked, "What dirt will God clean from your heart today?" Ah Hong looked down and said, "Filth," in Cantonese, lightly, but everyone could feel the weight of the word.

Day after day, she would say the same: "Filth. I hope God helps me clean it."

She became the most fervent prayer among them. She would kneel before Jesus in the prayer room even during the one-hour recess, the only time they didn't have to work or study. Even during the fifteen-minute break after dinner, she would go there to kneel, her head lowered to her folded hands, as if it were broken from her neck. She also took her time washing herself. There were only three bathtubs for the girls to share once a week and there was never enough hot water, but Ah Hong would take the longest to scrub and scrub.

She continued to wear the sorry look on her face, which Sixiang wanted to wipe away so that Ah Hong could be the girl she had been on the ship—when she hadn't cared about a thing, not even food. That was pride. Sixiang would do anything for food. Everyone else she knew would do anything for it too. Her mother and grandmother had literally sold her for food. That was how important food was, but Ah Hong had forgone food for several days. And later, after little Ah Fang had been dropped into the churning water, Ah Hong had come and lain down on the death-stained berth with Sixiang, unconcerned about the germs that had killed Ah Fang. She had not cared. But now she cared too much.

Sometimes, watching Ah Hong pray, Sixiang imagined putting an arm around her shoulders that were slumped like a haggard woman's, but she was also angry at Ah Hong for being that way—so much older than Sixiang herself but so helpless, as if she were no stronger than a child such as Meimei. And Sixiang was glad when Ah Hong pulled her away.

IF SIXIANG'S WORLD had been small at the Chens', now, enclosed entirely within the walls and fenced yard, it felt even smaller.

Besides threat notes from the tongs slipped in under the front door demanding the release of certain girls, the Mission Home was also vandalized routinely with crude drawings and wildly scribbled English words on its windows and walls. Sixiang soon learned what those words meant.

It was not until the oak leaves turned bronze and rusty that Sixiang was allowed her first outing. But Miss Moore and Yizheng didn't take them toward the heart of Chinatown, where Sixiang hoped to see Daoshi sitting by his desk outside the pawnshop. Instead, they walked away from Chinatown to a white people's park, which Miss Moore said would be safer for them.

There were seven of them besides Miss Moore and Yizheng: four younger girls including Sixiang and Ah Jia, and three older ones including Ah Hong. The rest were scheduled to go out another time. They walked close together, holding hands in twos or threes, looking around with both fright and delight.

As they climbed up the hilly block and turned east toward the blue harbor, they heard noises from behind them. A group of white boys, ranging from early to late teens like themselves, were coming hard on their heels. They were joking and laughing riotously, one holding a Chinese brush and a bottle of ink in his hands, like they'd just robbed a letter-writer from Chinatown.

Soon after the girls stepped onto the corner park's green lawn, an older girl jumped and shrieked, moving a hand to her bottom. They looked back and saw the boys picking up stones from the park's gravel edge and aiming at them dramatically, eye squinting, arm swinging, foot hoisted in the air. They were aiming at specific spots on their bodies. The older girls got pelted the most. Yizheng wasn't spared either. "Stop that," Miss Moore shouted at the boys, "you good-for-nothing ruffians!"

"*You* stop that, you Chinaman-lover," one boy yelled back. "Why do you have these Chinese whores with you?"

"I'll show you who is the dirtiest whore in the world," the boy holding the ink and brush said. Then, dipping the brush in the bottle, he lunged toward Ah Hong and swept the inky brush across her face twice.

Ah Hong froze. The rest of the girls screamed and scattered. The rest of the boys cheered and clapped. Miss Moore, who had covered her mouth with her hands, now pointed her finger at the boy: "You'll go straight to hell!"

People in the park were turning to look at them. The boy splashed the remaining ink in a wide arc toward the rest of the girls and threw the empty bottle at Miss Moore's feet. Then he ran away, followed by the rest of the cackling gang.

Ah Hong dropped to her knees on the grass, her face pale against the black ink streaks across it. She wasn't making a sound, her eyes not directed anywhere but hanging blank and dull. Sixiang wanted to shake her, to wake her up. She wanted Ah Hong to cry or curse like the rest of them.

"I said she shouldn't have come out with us," Yizheng said in Cantonese to seemingly no one. She and Miss Moore had been speaking loudly in English, in a kind of furious and agreeing way.

Ah Jia took Sixiang's hand, holding her to where they were standing, which was a few feet away from Ah Hong, as if the ink still running down her face would run onto theirs if they got any closer.

Sixiang did not pull her hand from Ah Jia's grip and cross the few steps to help Ah Hong wipe away the stains. Now Ah Hong wore a silly smile on her face, which was not just weak and sorry but seemed to contain something new, like a kind of recognition, as if she'd finally confirmed something she had been asking herself. She looked insane with that silly smile and those blank eyes and black streaks. What had befallen Ah Hong seemed so thick and dark it was overflowing. Even the grass she knelt upon seemed to be wilting away.

Miss Moore was quiet on their way back, her neck held long and stiff. The two older girls walked side by side with Ah Hong. They'd helped pull her up and wipe her face with a kerchief. But they would need water and soap to clean away all the stains.

That night in her dreams, Sixiang was kneeing in front of Ah Hong, trying to wipe the two brush strokes off her face, but the moment she wiped away the stroke from the top right corner to the bottom left, the one from top left to bottom right would reappear. Sixiang woke up in the middle of the night knowing what she had not done. Since the day Ah Hong came down the stairs, Sixiang had not gone over to her once. It was as if after she'd found out that the sullied girl was indeed Ah Hong, Sixiang no longer knew what to do with her. Because she had wanted a friend, a big sister who could care for her like she'd done on the ship, not someone who needed help herself.

A FEW DAYS after the outing, right at the beginning of their afternoon recess, Ah Hong walked over to Sixiang and asked her to come to the backyard with her. When Ah Jia grabbed Sixiang's hand, Ah Hong said to Ah Jia, "You can come too. I know you two are best friends." Ah Jia seemed pleased by that, but maybe deciding against being seen with Ah Hong, she stepped away.

Ah Hong led Sixiang to the oak tree. Its rusty leaves had begun to fall. "You don't need my help here," Ah Hong said, her eyes following a leaf twirling alone in the wind. "You're young. They like the younger ones. You'll do just fine," she said with a touch of envy, but when she looked at Sixiang, her eyes were soft and open. Sixiang had not seen her eyes this way since they landed on this shore.

"I—" Sixiang started, thinking about all the things she had not done.

"This is a good tree," Ah Hong continued. "Remember what I said about little Ah Fang being reborn into a whale? I'd like to be reborn into a tree. All it does is grow and grow. It sheds its old leaves so it doesn't need to remember anything." She touched the rough, cracked bark.

Sixiang touched it too. It felt dry and bumpy and hard. "You won't die. It's not too bad here. We have food to eat, and no one beats us." She realized that she was repeating what Ah Jia had said to her.

"I know. But look at how better off the tree is. Whatever happens to it, it feels nothing. And it's always clean. It doesn't need to pray for their God to clean it," she said with a chuckle in her voice, as if she was laughing at herself, at all those hours of kneeling and praying.

THE NEXT MORNING before the bell ring, Sixiang awoke to the mourning doves' cooing and a thump in her chest. She lifted the curtain and saw a bare body swaying under the oak tree, in the blue air, not falling or rising. On her forehead where the sun landed, a golden glow gathered as if it was bursting out from inside her. Leaves had covered the ground and continued to fall. One landed on her shoulder, balancing there for a moment, as if to say goodbye. Fourteen months after her attempted leap into the sea, Ah Hong had finally done it—here in this empty backyard where the oak tree held her, so that her body could be seen by all, bruiseless now, clean and bold in the cold air.

Miss Moore and Miss Webb moved a ladder to the yard. Again, they put a blanket over Ah Hong before moving her, this time down onto the ground. The girls talked with quick, shivering voices. Yizheng hushed them. Then they whispered, their eyes quivery.

After two policemen came and took Ah Hong away, Miss Moore and Miss Webb gathered everyone in the prayer room. "What Ah Hong did was a transgression," Miss Moore said with hands clasped tight at her chest, her voice shaken and shrill, her eyes red. "Only God can take away a person's life because God gave the person her life."

Yizheng translated her words with a dazed look. Then Miss Webb played the organ, and Miss Moore led the psalm.

They sang, "Cast your cares on the Lord and he will sustain you; he will never let the righteous be shaken."

They sang: "If I ascend up into heaven, thou art there; if I make my bed in hell, behold, thou art there."

When they were let go, Ah Jia talked about hell, its firepit, ice blocks, serpent nests—how Ah Hong had to go there now, there was no helping it. Sixiang stopped her: "Aren't you afraid her ghost will haunt you if you say bad things about her?"

Ah Hong wanted to be reborn into a tree. An oak tree that would always be clean, no matter what others did to it. It would always feel nothing. Even if it was chopped into firewood and burned into flames, it would simply rise to merge into the air. Even if it was cut down and carpentered into a piece of furniture, it would simply sit, fine and still.

Ah Hong must have been looking at the oak tree these last few days. This hadn't been a rash attempt like the one on the ship. This time, she had first tried to live, by taking pains to crawl to this place and offer herself to the wavy-haired God—only to learn that he wouldn't help her either. So, she took her own path: she took off her clothes to be as bare as the tree and she kept her eyes open so that she would watch her way to the tree world. She had to, as she was all alone on this journey.

Morning after morning, Sixiang would awaken to the doves' cooing, deep and limpid, and she would shake her head so that she didn't have to see Ah Hong's dangling body under the oak branch. Instead, she tried to see a sapling somewhere safe in the forest.

SOON, ACORNS BEGAN to fall in abundance, hitting the girls during their recess. It was not hard for Sixiang to imagine someone up there, invisible to their eyes, aiming acorns at them in mischief. One dropped right on the center of Sixiang's head. Was that Ah Hong saying hi to her, saying things were fine, that she had been reborn into a tree, was no longer hurting and would never be? Or was she a little mad at Sixiang for having let her go without ever trying to help her? And for being still down here, feet on the ground, food in the belly? Sixiang hoped it was the first message.

Every day after breakfast, they continued to answer the question about what dirt God would clean from their heart. Now Sixiang was answering it in English like most of the girls. "Disorder" or "heathen beliefs," and then, "I pray to God and he can wash my heart clean." More and more, she felt they were just empty words.

Ah Jia made a point to talk to Sixiang in English only. "We should practice as much as we can," she said, "because it makes Loumou happy."

Then came the Christmas show, the biggest annual event at the Mission Home, which they'd been rehearsing for months. About two dozen donors and trustees from the church were present. The girls sang hymns, recited the scripture, and above all, reenacted their rescue scenes.

Sixiang played herself. One of the babies played Meimei for her to carry on her back. One of the women in her twenties played Mrs. Chen. At the end of the show, Sixiang thanked God and the Mission Home for her new life. She was supposed to cry in gratitude, but she had trouble squeezing out tears. She felt uneasy in front of so many white people. Even though the men wore suits and ties, the women wore lacy dresses and ribbons, and they smelled of cigars and flowers, they did not all look friendly. Some had frowning faces. Some looked quizzical, as if they were examining a colony of strange insects. The girls all spoke English in their reenactments, which also made it difficult for Sixiang to feel anything other than nervousness. But she was also slightly proud that some of the white people seemed to understand her, as they were nodding or shaking their heads.

Ah Jia outperformed them all. So deep in her role, she looked like she was living it all over again. She cringed tremblingly when an older girl pretended to burn her with a candle and then sobbed openly. When she showed her big scar to the audience, several women in the audience gasped, dotting their foreheads with kerchiefs.

Then Ah Jia said proudly, "I thank God that he led me to this place. I am very happy, for I do not have those troubles which I had before. God has given me the Bible to read, which teaches me, 'Strait is the gate and narrow is the way that leadeth unto life.'"

They had just learned the quote. Miss Moore said it meant vice was a far easier path than virtue. The path to salvation was narrow because the pious were besieged by sinners, which was why they must ask God to clean their hearts every day and must always be on guard against temptation of sins.

All were given dolls as Christmas presents. They compared their yellow-haired, pale-skinned, round-eyed dolls to vote on which was the cutest, which were the runners-up. Though they all looked the same to Sixiang, making the girls holding them look darker-skinned and smaller-eyed.

Then came the news: Ah Jia got a sponsorship from a white gentleman who had been at the show and was so moved by her suffering and transformation he decided to send her to a boarding school in Philadelphia all the way across the country, so that she would receive a real education. Ah Jia was the only girl at the Mission Home to have ever been bequeathed such a generous gift. Even Yizheng, the leader of them all and the longest resident among them, must not have dreamed of anything like this. But it was Ah Jia, the least popular girl at the Mission Home and Sixiang's only friend, who had been chosen.

Ah Jia changed after that. When the older girls were mean to her, she would say, "You better look out. My American papa will give it to you!" And it worked. They left her alone. Even the food-duty girls gave her a bigger scoop, and gave Sixiang a slightly bigger scoop too, for being Ah Jia's friend.

FOR SPRING FESTIVAL, they swept the last fallen leaves, twigs, and acorn shells left by the squirrels into a large pile and lit a bonfire. They sat around the fire listening to the firecrackers and drums and dragon dance procession meander through Chinatown. They watched fireworks light up the sky.

The oak tree stood still, its bare limbs bearing the cold night, but it had no complaints, nor had it prayers to utter or resolutions to make. When the fireworks died down, the girls looked back at the flames in front of them. Some started to talk about their lives before the Mission

Home, or before Gold Mountain altogether. Some talked about what would happen to them in the coming lunar year: What kind of white families would they be sent away to serve? What kind of men would they be married to?

Ah Jia talked about the school she would soon be attending, where she would eat biscuits and drink tea with milk and sugar. There would be pies and cakes too, and uniforms and leather-bound books. She had met with her sponsor once, who picked her up in a carriage in front of the Mission Home. He wore a pink carnation in the buttonhole of his checkered suit, his chestnut hair oiled and combed back. He took her to Golden Gate Park, where they tossed flat rocks to see them bounce in the water. He'd given her an English name too, Grace, which she asked everyone to call her now. She kept asking Sixiang to ask her questions about that outing, even though she'd already told Sixiang every detail. "Ask me again."

"But I already know."

"Just do it for me, please."

Spring came with new leaves sprouting out of the old branches. The tree looked happy with its tender, yellow-green baby leaves, even though it had not been sad before. Each day began again with the doves' cooing and the bell's ringing, and then the scoop of congee and heart-cleansing lessons. The lessons meant less and less to Sixiang. They were just things to memorize, to repeat. What actually echoed in Sixiang's mind was this: What would happen to her? What was there to look forward to? After Ah Jia left for her great, thrilling adventure in the big world, what would be left for Sixiang?

She longed for the faraway too, but not the other unknown coast of America. She wanted to make the voyage back to the moist air and winding river and green fields of her village. In her vision, the village spread out in the endlessness of time, where episodes of floods and famines did not end lives but were only intervals—where villagers had returned and rice had ripened again, and her mother and grandmother were waiting for her to come home. Sixiang would touch the pouch of silver coins and the furred edges of her father's photo nestled by her heart and pray that Daoshi had not forgotten his words. She prayed not to God, but to Daoshi himself, for him to hear her, to remember his promise that he would help her find her father across the mountains so that she could bring him home.

Morning after morning, the doves' cooing reached Sixiang through the window with such lucidity she felt she could trace its sorrow to her own beating heart.

Daoshi

1877

DAOSHI STOPPED TELLING FORTUNES. THE FORTUNES AWAITING his countrymen who came to open their palms to him weren't all that different to tell. Those cross-stitching lines, caked in dirt and callused by toil, wouldn't pronounce much transcendence or deviation from their shared fate—die in fear, die without dignity, or keep living in fear, living without dignity. Like himself that night, pointing a dull ornamental sword at the floor, too weak to even consider lifting it. While little Sixiang leaned against him in the dark, all he could do was put his arm around her and listen to the wreckage through the door and his own weak heartbeat.

Then, as his countrymen picked up still-usable things from the debris, salvaged small remnant lives from the ashes, cultivated their shames, resurrected their angers, and divined their revenges, he knew he couldn't keep the child here with him. He knew too that her owners would dump their rage on her. He had to act quick. He'd heard about the Mission Home and the missionaries' rescues. The fact that their building was intact save a couple of broken windows while all the Chinese businesses were either torched, looted, or ransacked also made it seem like a safer place for the girl, at least for the time being. He'd promised to find a way to help her, and that was the only way he could think of, at least for now.

The afternoon when she walked past him, hands gripped by the white missionary lady and a Chinese girl with a haughty look, Sixiang looked into his eyes to search for an answer. She tried to free her hands from them, to come over to him and ask all her questions. She turned her head twice before they pulled her around the corner.

Daoshi looked back at the palm spread open before his eyes: messy lines, more haphazard days ahead, more disappointments, likely premature death. He did not want to name a harmless caution. Avoid water. Chew raw garlic. Eat sautéed chicken livers. All would sound foolish and futile. "Your lines look just fine," he said. "I have to call it a day. You won't be charged."

ALL THROUGH THE past year, the Six Companies had been urging everyone in Chinatown to write letters home. They called it a "Letter Writing Campaign to Discourage Immigration." They created a template for everyone to copy:

"Please do not make the long sea voyage to the United States and bring trouble on the community. The reason we have been subjected to all kinds of harassment by the white people is that many of our Chinese newcomers are taking jobs away from them. And yet, if we take a look at the wages of the Chinese workers in the various trades, we can see that they are shrinking day by day. This is also due to the large number of our fellow clansmen coming here. If up to 10,000 people come here, even if they do not take away 10,000 white men's jobs, they will still drive down the wages of 10,000 workers in various trades. It's inevitable. If this trend is not stopped, not only will the white men's harassment continue, causing a great deal of trouble for our community, but even skilled Chinese workers will have difficulty finding jobs and will lose their livelihood. If it is hard for the Chinese who are already here, imagine how much worse it will be for the newcomers."

They thought that was a smart move, one stone to kill three birds: no more trouble from the whites; no more shrinking of wages; no more competition with newcomers. Everyone would benefit.

Except that no birds were killed. Denis Kearney, who himself came to this country no earlier than many Chinese here, only shouted louder at the ever-expanding sandlot rally, "There is no means left to clear the Chinamen but to swing them into eternity by their own queues, for there is no rope long enough in all America wherewith to strangle four hundred million of Chinamen."

The Six Companies had learned by now that all their gestures of appeasement, respectfulness, assimilation, and population control, all their mitigations of the tong rivalries that the whites were overzealous to highlight in their newspapers, had come to no avail. The mobs had attacked them and would continue to do so. And when they did, the rich and the poor in Chinatown were all subject to looting and ruining—the rich even more so because they had more to loot. The pawnshop owner was one of the Six Companies' leaders, a self-made man who'd prospered through importing labor and who now owned a hardware store and an antique store in addition to the pawnshop, all ransacked during the riot. Daoshi went with him to the Six Companies' headquarters on 917 Clay Street.

Among the leaders seated around the square table was Chang'er. His path for the last decade had been a fabled one: from a bereaved railroad man to a vice-trade tong soldier to the founder of his own tong. It was a unique tong too, allegedly founded on one agenda: kill a gweilo for each of the Chinese men murdered in the Los Angeles mass lynching in 1871. A life for a life. Not the tong-war kind in which Chinese fought Chinese, but Chinese against gweilo. Though no one knew if Chang'er's secret tong had succeeded in killing eighteen gweilo for the eighteen Chinese lynched, dismembered, or shot by the five hundred mobsters, many were said to have joined Chang'er—fathers, sons, brothers, uncles, friends, all bereaved and enraged like himself. Word had it that all his tong members got day jobs and did their secret killings on the side. It was a tong nobody could put their fingers on, particularly not the white police squad patrolling Chinatown.

Daoshi had also heard that Chang'er had gone to Truckee to stage revenge last year—after six white men attacked a Chinese logging camp, killing a logger and wounding four others, and were,

unsurprisingly, freed by the court. Daoshi had heard about the car-
nivalesque trial: how a cannon was fired for each of the criminals announced not guilty and how the white townsfolks cheered. Guifeng's
face had surfaced then as if he was involved in the whole thing. But
Daoshi did not make the effort to ask Chang'er about it even when
he ran into him at a bar or saloon. They hadn't really talked since the
railroad days.

Chang'er took the floor. He hadn't changed much, but more than
ever seemed right in his righteousness. "We're in a war. Have been in
it since we came here. If we continue to hide our head in the sand, we'll
keep losing. We need guns. Lots of guns. Not kowtowing, not hiding
behind doors, not asking our countrymen not to come, but fighting for
a place for ourselves. Why do people from Europe keep coming? They
stay and join the mob to chase us away. We have to fight for our place.
They kill us; we kill them back."

Chang'er paused in his speech, looking at Daoshi. "What do you
think, Daoshi? What's Laozi saying here? Another wuwei strike? The
gweilo would love it if we quit all our jobs for them to take."

Indeed, what would Laozi say? Daoshi had been asking himself
the same question. What would be wuwei now, the effortless action
performed according to Dao, when Dao seemed to be the Dao of violence, of killing so as not to be killed? Laozi seemed as out of place
now as he had been two thousand years ago. No wonder throughout
history hardly any rulers adopted his worldview, because as long as
there were humans, there would be wrongful actions breeding more
wrongful actions.

Chang'er's teeth-for-teeth method did not win the majority vote,
nor did more letter-sending concessions. One too radical, the other
turtle-like. The middle way won, which was to use legal channels to
sue the city and the vigilantes that instigated the riot. Meanwhile, they
would form Chinatown's own vigilante group to protect the community. They would also stock up on weapons and ship them to other

communities for self-defense. Riots were spreading across the West Coast. Chinatowns in Truckee, Los Angeles, Sacramento, Carson City, and anywhere where there were Chinese all needed to gun up.

"I'll ship weapons to Truckee. I know that town somewhat," Daoshi volunteered.

He had lived in this land for twenty-two years now, had performed death rituals to soothe the soul and comfort the living a little, had told people harmless fortunes to ease their lives a little. He drank some, whored some. He told himself he was practicing wuwei—not accumulating more than the bare minimum, nor craving more than a few diversions. It was not a colorful life, but he was not looking for colors. He, at thirty-nine, felt neither young nor old, neither a failure nor a success, neither too lonely nor particularly comforted. Then the child crossed the street to him. "Can you tell this person's fortune?" And then he was pushed into his small room with the child to protect, whom he promised to help. How? He would go to Truckee and find out. He would ship weapons too, which he didn't think would be of much use, but was better than doing nothing. There was simply no place for non-action or effortless action in this world.

"When you go to Truckee, you might want to visit our old friend." Chang'er caught up with him as he stepped out of the headquarters.

"Who?" Daoshi asked, though he already knew.

"Your disciple, Guifeng. Have you forgotten him? He took all your Laozi teaching to heart and has been practicing wuwei in the opium den." Chang'er shook his head, his eyes mocking. Then he looked up at the sky, which was open and clear, with white clouds foregrounding its boundless blue. Chang'er's gaze was now long and laden, as though it carried many unappeasable souls and their skyward longing.

6

Wood and Fire

※

1869–1876

Guifeng

THE ROOM SMELLED OF PAINT AND PINE. A FULL BED, A TABLE, two chairs, a trunk. A room for couples. "This room," the photographer said, "was built for my own family, but things happened, so it's now for rent. It's more luxurious than a boardinghouse bunk, less expensive than a hotel room, perfect for lovebirds." He looked at them and laughed, "Just kidding."

He had been eyeing them. He told Guifeng he looked familiar and then focused his gaze on Feiyan. He was the same photographer who'd taken Guifeng's photo three years ago, at the same studio on the now expanded Jibboom Street. Guifeng and Feiyan had just gotten off the train and walked a block down west to Truckee's Chinatown, past the old bathhouse, barber, and brothel, and then a couple of new diners and merchant stores.

The room was a vertical expansion of the one-level photographer's studio where the carved high-back chair and small end table still sat, although in the place of the stirring narcissus was now a braided lucky bamboo. It might be careless to stay on the main street right above a conspicuous shop run by someone who had a keen eye for faces, rather than find a crack to hide away in. But did it matter? Guifeng had slept a few hours on the train and was once again feeling the rightness of it all. All his toil and sweat sucked up by the railroad felt worth it for this crossing alone—for the two of them to reach where they were now.

The bed with the blue linen sheet was not the sleek plum one they'd glanced at but left alone. This bed held a wedge of twilight slanting in through a corner of the curtained window. It was waiting for them.

THEY DID NOT leave the room until after nightfall. Guifeng had offered to go out and get food while Feiyan stayed in.

"No, I'm going with you," Feiyan had said. "I'm not going to be trapped in a room again."

He understood and wished he'd thought of it before Feiyan had to say it. He was only thinking his own thoughts: be a provider and keep her safe and unbothered by men, any men.

She put on his clothes again.

"I'll buy you new clothes."

"I like these. I like dressing as a man."

Guifeng felt the gap in their thinking again, as if thinking was a kind of running, in which she was always ahead and he, always catching up.

Lanterns and oil lamps lit the streets. Though smaller and sparser than the one in Big City, Truckee's Chinatown was just as bachelor-oriented and rowdy at night. Men fell into the same types: merchants and clan leaders in satin *changshan*, tong soldiers in black jackets, and laborers in coarse cotton, who made up most of the population, whether here or there, and with whom Guifeng and Feiyan blended right in.

They stepped into a rice noodle shop. A group of tong soldiers eating and drinking at a table did not even cast a glance at them when they walked in. Guifeng felt as if the two of them were invisible—not only to others, but to their own past and future. They seemed to have obtained a magical power that was shielding them within the safety of the present moment, which kept expanding yet was in no danger of burst.

Feiyan held her face straight when the server set down a bowl of noodles in front of her. Then she beamed at Guifeng. It occurred to him that she must have never eaten at a restaurant before. She picked up the chopsticks the server left on the top of the steaming bowl, lifted a strand of noodles, and blew on it before taking it to her mouth with an air of solemnity. There would be many more firsts for her, Guifeng thought to himself, and he would be overjoyed to experience all of them with her. But as he, too, brought the hot noodles to his mouth, his delight was suddenly muddled by something else—something cloudy and achy. *Not now*, he said to that ache. He didn't deserve to feel it right now.

After dinner, they walked back to the attic room. With Feiyan in his arms, it was easier to push any unwanted feelings aside, easier to draw a circle around the two of them and name everything either in or out. Earlier when their bodies finally joined for the first time in the wedge of twilight, their eyes looking into each other to confirm it was real, he'd felt something he had not quite believed to be possible. More than his past and future, he had felt freed from himself. He touched her with an astonishing assertiveness as her want swelled up to complete his own. He kissed the whip scars on her back and buttocks, almost with the belief he could erase them. Now he held her tight again to reclaim that certainty.

THE THIRD MORNING, Guifeng was startled awake from a dream. His daughter whom he'd never met looked at him out of two sunken eye-sockets. "I'm hungry," she said, her small face all bones. "I want some of your rice noodles. Can Mama and I have some of your noodles? And Grandma, she's hungry too."

Guifeng did not reach for Feiyan so that he could once again enter their protected, prolonged moment. His mother was in the dream too, her lips forming silent sounds, which seemed to be her story: nobody ever listened to her, but she kept talking. His wife was also there, sitting on the red lacquered chair she liked to sit in, washing her feet in a basin, going through the tedious steps of unwrapping, soaking, and trimming. Her pointed feet looked like two darts, pale and dank, but full of aggrieved vigor, aiming, flitting toward him.

ON HIS WAY to the labor contractor's office, Guifeng saw men gathering in front of the bulletin board. The poster was newly pasted on, the glue still wet and bumpy under the paper. On the poster were two portraits, crudely drawn but recognizable, and below them, Guifeng's real name and Feiyan's alias, Ah Hua—he, a "kidnapper"; she, "property of Red Peony." A reward of fifty dollars was offered for information.

If his pre-dawn dream had cracked the spell that managed to hold them inside the ever-expanding present, now the spell was completely broken. Guifeng must reenter this moment-by-moment succession that wouldn't stop just because he was in love.

He came to the contractor's office. "It's your lucky day." The middle-aged man behind the counter wore a Western suit over his satin changshan. "I need a tender, up the mountain above Lake Tahoe, to herd the flume. Great pay: a dollar a day."

Guifeng had heard that flume-tending was dangerous work in the lumber industry, almost like dynamiting in the railroad. "What about wood-chopping? I've done that a whole winter before."

"No wood-chopping. Those are good jobs. White men want them too. You need to work yourself up the ladder. Either flume-tending or nothing. Decide soon. Any job goes away fast."

It wouldn't be safe to leave Feiyan here in Chinatown, as tong soldiers would soon be chasing them down. It wouldn't be possible to bring her to a men's camp either, for obvious reasons. *But why not?* Guifeng could hear Feiyan say. *I'll keep wearing men's clothes.*

What about your hair? You can't wear the hat all the time; you'll have to take it off eventually.

I'll cut my hair and say the whites cut off my queue. Many got their queues cut, right? Nothing is impossible here. This is Gold Mountain, not Yunteng Village.

What about bathing? How are you going to do that?

It can be done, okay? I'm going to work and get paid, like you.

You have no muscles.

I'll get them.

Why not? And besides, what were the alternatives?

"Okay, I'll take the job," Guifeng said to the contractor. "A cousin of mine is looking for work too. Can we both do it?"

"Only one position. The white boss is not paying two heads for this, but if you want to split the work and wage, it's up to you. Board is free. There's a cabin right by the flume. The current herder needs to move on and is waiting for his replacement. I can take you up there now."

Why not? Why not the two of them living in a cabin in the woods? The tong soldiers wouldn't think of going there to hunt them. She would dress in his clothes and work with him in the daytime, and at night she would be a woman for him alone. *Why not?* This Gold Mountain was a place where you came up with wild ideas and saw no reason not to follow them.

Guifeng ran back to the attic room, glad the photographer was occupied with a customer, and he could sneak upstairs without having to talk to him. Had the photographer seen the wanted poster yet? If he could remember Guifeng's face from three years ago, he would no doubt see the resemblance in the portraits.

The room was empty. The bed was made; Guifeng's trunk and bedroll leaned against the wall in the corner, same as for the past two days; but besides a few wispy scents of hers, there was no trace of Feiyan. Had she run away again? It wasn't the first time Guifeng had the feeling that none of this was real: things had simply been too extravagant to be real. How could all these outlandish experiences, these *why-nots*, happen to an ordinary man like himself? Standing in the middle of the empty room, where the morning air from the half-opened window was erasing even the last scents of their togetherness, something else was also rising in him, something close to relief. The comfort of going to sleep without being haunted by his daughter's sunken eyes or his mother's emptily moving mouth or his wife's darting, agonizing feet. The ease of not having to sustain a moment to its bursting point as he'd done these last two days. Yet already, he wanted her. His body was hollowing in its want for her. He sat down on the bed, touching the linen sheet that had touched their skin, doubting himself.

After what could have been an hour or just ten minutes, the wooden stairs creaked. The door swung open, and she came in, holding something wrapped in paper. She ignored his question of where she'd been, unwrapped the package, and showed him a porcelain bowl featuring a pair of painted wood ducks. "You and me." She pointed at the vivid ducks known to never part.

THE CONTRACTOR SIZED up Feiyan. "Such a slender build, like a girl. Can you work? But never mind, it's one person's pay as I said."

He lent them a horse to ride together and led them out of the town and up a ferny trail into the woods. When the sun-filled fog began to fade, they saw through the branches a flume of rushing water winding down the mountainside like an exposed vein. They rode in silence. Pines and spruces rose above them, breaking the sky into small patches of grayish blue like shadows on water. Birdcalls and crickets swelled among the leaves. The horses trotted in soft, steady steps. Feiyan pressed her face against Guifeng's back.

After half an hour riding like this, they came to a cabin in a stump-studded clearing. On one side of the cabin was the flume and the sonorous rushing water. On the other, a pile of cordwood five or six feet long each.

A middle-aged man limped out of the cabin leaning on a stick, one of his feet wrapped in what looked like an old pair of underwear tied up with a rope. "Finally," he said to the contractor. "I was expecting my replacement two days ago." He looked at Guifeng and Feiyan. "It's two men's work for sure. How come you didn't pay me double?"

"Because two of them are getting the pay of one," the contractor said, handing out his pay. "This extra dollar is for training them, and for your pain."

The herder had fallen off the flume's narrow plank trying to unjam three logs and got swept down the miles of snaky chute all the way to Lake Tahoe. The flume was shaped like a V, with two wooden boards joined perpendicularly at the bottom, designed to make the logs move faster and less prone to jam than the old retired U-shaped flumes. "But don't be fooled," the herder said. "You still need to step up there and unjam the logs with this." He picked up a short-handled pickaroon. "If you fall, you'll be lucky to only break one leg."

The cabin was located half a mile from the main camp, where men felled and chopped trees into logs and drove oxen to haul them over to the flume. As the contractor sat on a tree stump smoking a cigar, the herder showed Guifeng and Feiyan how to use the pickaroon to herd the logs from the stacked pile across the clearing and down the flume, and how to position the curved, beak-like hook to wrangle the jammed logs. He signaled Guifeng to step onto the narrow plank of wood, which was about four feet above ground, the lowest if he looked up and down the flume, where some planks seemed as high as a mature pine. The herder held his walking stick as if it were a pickaroon and balanced himself on one leg for a second. "Keep your balance," he said, "or you're in for a wild ride." Guifeng looked down into the loud, splashing water where the sunlight danced and pranced. His legs shook.

After the man hauled his bundles and bedroll onto the horse and rode off with the contractor, it was only Guifeng and Feiyan within half a mile's radius. Dozens of logs still needed to go down the flume. They made clumsy attempts, experimenting with new ways to maneuver the pickaroon, comparing techniques. They wiped sweat away and laughed.

In the midafternoon, two men and four steady-footed oxen came with new cartfuls of logs. Guifeng introduced himself to them as "Ah Fook." Earlier today, when the contractor asked him to put down his name on the registry, he'd written down his surname Liang before remembering the bounty bill, and then, without knowing why, he put down Ah Fook's given name. It was strange to hear himself say the name out loud.

He told the two cartmen that he and Feiyan, who now went by Ah Fei, were cousins and had come to Gold Mountain not long ago. Feiyan waved and said hi, her voice coarse, and she looked like she was enjoying the faking.

Before dusk, a traveling merchant came. With Guifeng's remaining money, they bought a week's supply of rice, vegetables, and dry goods.

When the westward sun candled the trees alight, they were cooking their first meal together in a firepit outside the cabin. Water kept running down the flume. Crickets kept chirping. Once in a while, a branch fell, or a deer whisked through the low-hanging twigs. The sounds made the quiet quieter. After they finished dinner, they could see a quarter moon rise above the shelves of leaves. They stepped into the cabin and lit the oil lamp.

THE THIRD DAY, a drizzle came with the gray dawn. A dull ache throbbed in Guifeng's head as they worked, and dampness weighed down their clothes. Shortly after the morning carting crew unloaded more logs and drove the oxen away, a man on a horse miraged out of the misty woods. The flume's loud splashes had covered up the horse's trotting until the man was a dozen feet away from them in the clearing.

Guifeng set down his pickaroon against the side of the flume and, holding his hands in front of his chest, bowed the way he did to respectable elders. "Uncle Chang'er," he said.

Feiyan stood by him, still holding her pickaroon.

Chang'er dismounted from his horse. It had been two years since Guifeng last saw him. He'd aged more, the loss of his son engraved more deeply in his face. A face Guifeng could not see without seeing Ah Fook's wide eyes staring up at him from the granite bottom of the tunnel.

Chang'er did not return the bow. Instead, he gave Feiyan a quick, knowing look. Through the opening of his unbuttoned black jacket, a revolver flashed on his belt. Guifeng had heard: Chang'er was a tong soldier now, one who wouldn't hesitate to kill.

Feiyan still clutched her pickaroon. From her tightened jaw, it was clear she knew he was a soldier, if not the typical type—older than typical, but nonetheless a determined man who would do what he'd made up his mind to do. Had he made up his mind about what he would do to them?

Guifeng had never known what to say to Chang'er after Ah Fook's death, which was now clouding his vision, tightening his throat. Feiyan looked at him, waiting to see what he would do about this moment presenting itself, replacing their prolonged, protected moment that they both had known would not last.

"I heard you were in Big City. What business brought you here?" He managed to pretend.

"My business is your business. If you two were not here, I wouldn't need to be. You know what I know, right?" Chang'er stepped closer to them, glancing at the cabin. "I heard you go by Ah Fook now. Why is that? Do you think my son would have done what you did?"

"I—" He felt foolish to have used Ah Fook's name. Chang'er must have recognized it right away on the contractor's registry. Was this borrowing an insult to his memory and his son's shortened life? Was taking Ah Fook's name not unlike taking the life that Ah Fook could have lived had Guifeng not urged him to step back into that accursed tunnel, that dark hole of no return?

Guifeng felt small and brittle again—the feeling of a straw dog, spent and disposable. He felt he was back on the summit: Chang'er's hammering on the coffin outside their tent as Ah Fook lay covered head to toe on his cot; the clutter of graves on the ocean-facing slope; the sky an altar waiting for its sacrifice. Death that came before and after Ah Fook's and was likely to happen now—all so numerous in the blink of an eye. And Guifeng had the audacity to love a woman and dream of being free, of expanding a moment, as if his life was more precious than others'.

Even Feiyan looked pale now, weary, like she'd already been locked back inside that flimsy room with the gaudy bed.

Chang'er unfolded a piece of paper from his pocket: the wanted poster with their portraits. "I kept thinking this is a big country, but small for us Chinese. I would sooner or later run into someone I know. And what would I do then?"

It was clear that Chang'er still hated him. Perhaps more so than ever—as if hate was a high-interest debt that would only accumulate with time. Perhaps now was the time he wanted Guifeng to pay it, once and for all.

"She is not mine to give, or yours to take." Guifeng looked at Feiyan. He would grab Chang'er and pin him down to give her a head start, and she would run as fast as she could ever run. She seemed to be considering it. She was wearing the cotton shoes he'd gotten her, which wouldn't last long on the bumpy forest floor. They had been talking about buying her a pair of boots once they received their first pay, which wasn't due until three days from now. They had been making plans: how much to spend, how much to save, not looking too far into the future, but into a future nevertheless. He might not see her again if she set out running. But he would do what needed to be done.

Chang'er eyed him. "No fighting." He looked amused, reading Guifeng's mind. "Only a few months ago, right down the mountain in Truckee, two tongs fought for a whore, putting up such a show for the gweilo to enjoy. 'Kill them. Kill them.' They were betting on which side would win, which would lose, which side would lose more or kill more. It was all a joke for them, and we Chinese their jesters. Proud to entertain you. Delighted to be at your service. We kill each other because we prove to be too stupid to kill them." Chang'er spat on the ground. "I'm not here to kill you. Or her."

Guifeng felt a relief, although the relief felt unreliable. The straw-dog brittleness was still stuck in his throat, and in his chest a pre-felt sorrow was settling, as if Feiyan was already running away even though she hadn't yet moved. Her posture stayed tense, leaning slightly away from him, toward the deep woods, as if readying for flight.

"You don't have to thank me," Chang'er went on. "Because I'm not letting you go for free. I have a condition: you owe me this one. When I need your service, you'll say yes no matter what it is."

This time, Guifeng nodded. Again, he held his hands in front of his chest and bowed, the way Daoshi had done to see him and Feiyan off, not quite a week ago. But Guifeng felt no wuwei or Dao in his own gesture. He felt fated to fail somehow, fated to act in some foreseeable future with the great effort of defeat.

Chang'er nodded back. "You need a rifle." He looked around them. "There're bears and mountain lions. But humans are the wildest. Of course, you know that."

He got on his horse, clucked his tongue, and left. The woods, dark, dense, and forbidding, closed behind him.

Feiyan

THE SUN WAS NOT ABUNDANT BUT PLENTY IF YOU SEIZED IT. IN THE early morning, it glided over the eastern slopes through the cabin window, and she would reach to him in its leaf-speckled light. Sometimes outside the cabin, in the broken streaks of the noon sun, with the logs flushing down the flume casting sideway glances at them, he would pull down her men's pants or she would draw him to her. They would have each other right there in the clearing, their bodies stirred by the growing things around them. After lovemaking, she would keep her body bare in the sun awhile, for each inch of her skin to get a taste of the light. She was taking back her share of the sun denied to her for the past five years.

She bought boots and thick canvas pants from the traveling merchant with her half of the wage. They picked blackberries, mushrooms, and miner's lettuce for salad, sautéed dandelions and clovers, and foraged pine nuts from cones. They flattened kerosene cans to patch the leaky roof, punctured holes in bean cans for strainers, and fashioned a shelf and bench with the old flume boards lying idle by the cabin wall. When they had saved enough, they bought a rifle as Chang'er had advised, and shot rabbits, squirrels, and deer. They perfected the way to cook them in the open firepit. She had craved greasy meat at the brothel, where meals were bland and punishment was hunger. Now there was plenty of meat to eat. They ate what they could and salted and canned the extra for the winter months.

They still talked about back home, as if to talk into being the home they could no longer go back to. He'd asked her how she ended up in Gold Mountain, and she told him about the beating, her escape, but kept the ash bucket and ashen face out of the telling. That part was something no one needed to know. "I heard he died," he told her. "They said bandits had killed him and taken you away."

"Ha" was all she said, and left it there.

She didn't ask him, but he volunteered the information. He had a family of three to feed back home: a mother sick with worry, a wife he barely knew, a daughter he hadn't met. That was not the back-home the two of them talked about. Their version of back-home was the home before she was married off and he had three empty mouths to feed. Their back-home was a home they were re-making now. With their bare hands and accumulated tools, with the pennies they were saving and seeds they were collecting. It was a home in the becoming.

She wore men's clothes, did men's work, her muscles building. All around her, trees grew patiently toward the sun, their roots clutching deep into the earth. These trees seemed to be telling her to stay put. She wanted to plant, to put her hands in the soil, which used to be part of her existence, as natural and necessary as sleep and food. Already the soil was turning cold. She saved seeds of the vegetables they'd bought from the traveling merchant: tomatoes, cucumbers, green beans, squashes. She wanted to see them rooted and grow.

In spring, after the last frost, she planted the seeds in pockets of dirt hugged by tree roots. When, a couple weeks later, the dirt spotted dashes of green, her joy overflowed. When the leaves grew fuller, the stems sturdier, and some began to cast tendrils and vines, she felt a stirring in her belly. A bubbling up, soft knocks at the bottom of her chest. Along with an unease, a frail dizziness, a muddling in the head. She wasn't sure until her period was ten days late. Her upper stomach revolted.

Before she could even decide whether she was ready for a child, or whether she should be happy, Guifeng tripped while unjamming the logs. He fell down the flank but managed to hold on to a log that was flushing down the chute. She ran. When the log paused at the bend, she reached down with her pickaroon and pulled him up. But she bled later that afternoon. The baby was gone. He held her while she wept.

When they walked the two miles to Truckee Chinatown, Fei-yan lingered in the merchandise store, by the table displaying the few choices of fabrics—black, dark blue, light blue. She bought two yards of light blue cotton. The bulletin board on Jibboom Street now hung other men or women's sketches. Chang'er had kept his word: they were proclaimed "Dead," their portraits and names crossed through. They saw it the first time they came down from the mountains to the town, and when they walked past the photographer's shop, he seemed surprised to see them. Was he the informer, and had Chang'er then gone to the contractor to find out who got the latest work? Standing by his door, the photographer pretended not to know who they were. They pretended the same. All was well. To the world, they no longer existed, but they had hardly existed in other people's eyes anyway, although they had never felt more alive to themselves and to each other.

By summer, about a year into the job, they had saved seventy dollars between them: she fifty, he twenty. He'd been mailing money to his family—all he'd made minus food and supplies in the past, then eighty percent after she'd lost her first pregnancy to the race with the downhill current. "What about us?" she couldn't help but ask.

Their plan was keep saving until they could buy a plot of land in town. Or until she became pregnant again. They would quit herding the flume and find another way to make a living, one that wouldn't risk her losing a child again. She had not been paying enough attention. She was playing a man, but her body had betrayed her.

Before either prospect could happen, the contractor came up unexpectedly one day at sundown. Feiyan had just bathed and changed into the dress she'd made with the light blue fabric. She had started to wonder if her wearing men's clothes was stopping her from getting pregnant again.

"I had my suspicions," the contractor said, still in his hybrid changshan and Western suit. "A Hua Mulan, I thought to myself, but who cares as long as you get the work done? This is Gold Mountain: we're all shapeshifters. But people are talking. Real men are looking for jobs to feed their entire families, and here you are." He asked them to start packing and get ready to leave when he brought their replacement the next day.

They had accumulated things over the year, made a nest with each object they owned, unlike in the past when not even their own lives were quite theirs to keep. The pair-duck bowl was only the first. Then there was the new quilt she'd sewn up with fabrics and ginned cotton bought in town, the new pillows made of husks, the new wok in which they'd cooked their meals together. There were also the shelves and benches that they'd made but were too heavy to take. They couldn't take with them the little vegetable garden they'd fenced up either. Nor the sunny spots in the clearing that had tanned their skins and solidified their bones and muscles, as if they'd been like the trees, not having to question their will to grow or doubt their abilities to root and reach.

IN TRUCKEE, THEY rented a shed on Spring Street from a grocery store owner and his family, one of the dozen or so households with a woman and children in the majority-bachelor Chinatown. Guifeng got a wood-cutting job in the logging camp through Li Shu, his old friend from his railroad days. Feiyan cooked for a restaurant on Jibboom Street.

Six months later, they had saved enough to rent the two-story house next to the grocery store. It belonged to Fong Lee, the richest man in Chinatown, who had, years before, purchased several lots on the block from the railroad tycoon Charles Crocker. Feiyan had been eyeing houses since they moved into town. The one next door to their rental used to be a hardware store owned by two partners who closed shop and went their separate ways due to some disagreement. With the help of Guifeng's co-workers, they converted the ground level into a diner. Buffet style, so that Feiyan could manage all by herself. Every morning she would make six dishes and one soup and keep them warm on small stoves till they were sold out; in the afternoon, she would make more dishes for dinner. Customers liked her homestyle food and her company too. There was only room for eight tables in the diner, and they got filled up quick. Still, men waited in lines. Some ate sitting on stools outside.

After the last frost, she turned the dirt in the backyard, fertilized it with kitchen waste, and started a vegetable garden. As daytime lengthened with stronger sun, the garden began to yield fresh edibles. But it was not until the second winter when Feiyan became pregnant again. This time, she cherished even the nagging nausea. She made sure not to move too suddenly, cut down the number of dishes she cooked every day, and saved the heavy lifting for Guifeng when he came back from the logging camp. She hoped it was a boy. Though she was Guifeng's second wife, she was confident she could give him a son.

When, nine months later, the midwife apologetically told her it was a girl and handed her the blood-stained bundle, Feiyan looked at the baby's red wailing face and thought of her mother. How her mother had looked away when her father and brother tied her hands and feet and threw her onto the donkey. How hunched her back was, the knots of her spine pushing out through her threadbare blouse. Out the window, the autumn wind blew, scattering leaves like they were abandoned children. The baby cried in Feiyan's arms, thumb-sized shoulders shuddering, as if they had to carry all the impossible pains passed down from one mother to another.

But Feiyan was not her mother. She knew her strength and knew what belonged to her and what she would never give away. She named her daughter Duofu, "many blessings," to counter all the hardships and misfortunes likely in store for her. She closed the diner for a month to take care of herself and Duofu. When she opened it again, she changed the diner's name from Hometown Diner to Duofu Diner—red characters on a golden plaque, proudly hung on the lintel. She cooked and served with Duofu strapped on her back. Her goal remained the same: own this lot, make it their permanent home.

When the baby was a year old and began to attempt stumbling steps on her own—her little feet testing the ground as if to know it inch by inch—they had finally saved enough for the down payment and bought the house from Fong Lee.

THEY NO LONGER needed to talk about back-home now that they had their home right here and now. They continued to save. Now she had a new goal: pay off the loan so that the house became theirs entirely. Duofu who was born here would be growing up in this house that belonged to them alone.

The new autumn arrived early. A cooler rain swept through the trees and dyed them gold and amber. Then, a row of dry, brittle days came with cold mornings and quick sunsets and dense death chirps of mating crickets among the leaves. One night, closing the diner, Feiyan saw a half moon above the dark branches, quiet and glowing. A directionless sorrow rose within her: she felt as if she were only half here and half elsewhere. Even Duofu's bubbling words and shrieking laughter as Feiyan gave her the routine bedtime tickle felt only half real.

Later that evening, with Duofu sleeping in the crook of her arm and Guifeng on her other side, she dreamt she was back in the kitchen of Red Peony, where Ah Gu was stirring the pot of steaming congee. Round and round her spatula went, and her face, which had never failed to shock Feiyan, was in red tendrils, as if old flames were reignited and burning her flesh once again. Feiyan could smell the dark smoke and feel the melting heat reaching toward her. She opened her eyes to red flames crawling up the walls and window frames. She thought of egg whites. Were there still eggs in the kitchen? Eggs she had planned to stir fry with cucumbers in the morning for one of the six dishes? She pushed Guifeng awake and grabbed Duofu in her arms and ran down the stairs. She was hacking when she ran out of their burning house.

Theirs was not burning alone: the whole block was aflame. Smoke was pushing and billowing out of the entire row of roofs and windows. People were screaming and scampering out of smoke-choked doors. In the frenzy, Feiyan ran her fingers over Duofu's face, which was wet from bawling. She looked at Guifeng's face, clenched but unsinged. She then touched her own. At least they didn't need egg whites, not for now.

But nothing could save their house. She looked at the four windows of fire. She could see all that belonged to them burning into char—the bed, the quilt, the pillowcases she'd embroidered, the clothes she'd sewn, the tables and chairs, the chopsticks smoothed by fingers, the wok she'd oiled every night. All including the walls and roof that were crumbling now in the punching flames. This home that had once been theirs was gone.

Guifeng
1876

AH LING RAN OUT INTO THE NIGHT FIRST, A BUCKET IN HAND TO fetch water from Trout Creek. Guifeng was only three steps out of the burning cabin when he heard the shot and the heavy thud as Ah Ling fell, the bucket dinning on the ground of the clearing. In the next second, amid the flames' crackling and his other cabinmates' scampering, a voice drifted from behind the shrubs on the entrance side of the campground: "Here comes another rat." By the wind-blown sparks, Guifeng caught a blur of hats, a shift of shoulders, a squinted eye or maybe glint of metal, before he heard the second bang and felt his own leg falter. He reached down and touched the warm liquid as he fell.

He curled into a fetal position, as more shots and shouting and scuttling wheeled around him. "Get up!" Li Shu caught his arm, pulling him. He limped on one foot with Li Shu into the woods. They threw themselves behind a tree trunk on the gnarled forest floor. The cabin where they'd been asleep just minutes ago now blazed as if it were offering itself to some raging god. *Fire! Fire!* How many times did Guifeng have to hear the word and awaken to red flames licking the walls? Just minutes ago, when he woke up in the smoke-choked cabin, he'd first thought he was back in the old house with Feiyan and Duofu in the previous year's fire.

The shooters lingering behind the shrubs were talking among themselves. In the firelight, Guifeng seemed to see their teeth, eyes, gun muzzles, all hard, glinting. They must not think of themselves as straw dogs. They must think of themselves as something solid, durable, destined to set others on fire and kill.

In a momentary lull, the wind carried a singular sound through the burning. A man was peeing and humming at the same time—a simple tune that sounded strangely delicate, like a lullaby. When the humming stopped, Guifeng heard boots crushing leaves. Then the shooters were gone.

As the fire spread toward where they were hiding, Guifeng and his campmates held or leaned against each other and crossed Trout Creek. They examined the injured. Four were shot: Ah Ling in the belly, Guifeng in the lower left leg, another in the right arm, the fourth in the shoulder. They tore off strips of cloth from their shirts to wrap around the wounds. Their hands were shaking.

Across the creek, the cabin roof had buckled, walls collapsing. Guifeng felt stupid for not having taken his rifle with him out of the cabin—and for having thought the fire was an accident, like the Chinatown fire last year. It was surely easier to think that than to believe some people hated them so much they'd set them on fire in their sleep. But as Chang'er had once warned him, "Humans are the wildest." The rifle he and Feiyan had bought following Chang'er's advice must be melting now.

LAST YEAR'S FIRE had swallowed everything they had, not even sparing the little rag duck Feiyan had made for Duofu. For days, Duofu cried, "My duckie, my duckie." Feiyan had much more to cry for. All that she'd gathered piece by piece was burned to ash. Even the cucumbers, beans, and lettuce she'd planted in the backyard curled into smoke.

No one knew for sure how that fire had started. The town's white folks blamed them because it had spread to four or five white businesses bordering Chinatown. Those in Chinatown, on the other hand, didn't know who to blame. They tracked the inferno down to a few houses that had been the first to burn. A laundromat owned by a father and son, who swore they'd gone to bed leaving no candle or kerosene lamp on. A saloon insisted that they'd doused all embers in the kitchen stove.

They had no one to blame. And Guifeng and Feiyan had no

insurance to cover their loss. They had not purchased any as none had been available for them to purchase.

But they rebuilt with a high-interest loan taken from the loan shark Luo Laoda. As long as they still had the plot of land, they must trust it could hold up another house. Guifeng worked extra hours at the lumber camp so that they could pay off the loan faster. He lived in the cabin most of the time, going home only a couple nights during the weekdays and on Sunday mornings. More and more, he avoided going back on Saturday nights, the meeting time of the Caucasian League—a club formed by the town's white folks soon after the fire. Their agenda was loud and clear: Drive out all Chinese from Truckee. Already, they had been making rounds at lumber camps, hollering, "The Chinese must go!" It had become a routine for the league members to go about town after their weekly meet harassing Chinese. On a previous Saturday night, a Chinese woodcutter was found dangling under a lamppost in the white part of the town.

Guifeng had not minded spending the nights in the cabin with Li Shu, Ah Ling, and the other three campmates. It reminded him of his railroad days, the simpler times when all he had needed to do was work and mail money home and call it fulfilment of purpose. His cabinmates still did just that, sent most of their wages to their families, and smoked or gambled or whored the rest away. They had developed the philosophy of living one day at a time, as things tended to be out of control the next. They kept their belongings to the minimum, their valuables on their bodies, so when they had to run away, they wouldn't have much to lose.

Sometimes Guifeng wished he could still be like them, living the simpler life with simpler goals. But Feiyan wanted more: a plot of land, a two-story house, a diner, a vegetable garden—a real home of their own. Was that too much to want for a Chinese in this land? But he knew it wasn't just Feiyan: he wanted all that too. Perhaps somewhere inside him, he believed if he devoted himself to the building of this home, with this woman he truly loved and their child he saw born and grow, he would be spared from thinking of his family back in China. As if his devotion to this new home would redeem him for forgetting the old one. He hadn't sent money to them for three years now, ever since Duofu was born. Let them think he was dead, like what had happened to his own father, like what was possibly happening to him right now, as blood continued to ooze out of the bullet hole in his leg.

LYING NEAR HIM, Ah Ling had stopped cursing, the way he often did when he lost a fan-tan game, swearing fervidly before holding his tongue to silently accept his bad luck. Ah Ling was a regular of gambling dens and liked to say that surviving Gold Mountain was itself a gamble, the wager being one's own life. Whenever he had an extra dime, he threw it for a grasp of luck. He said karma was an outdated idea and chance was what ruled here: each time he tried his luck, it was like reacquainting himself with living or dying. Li Shu piled up more dry leaves for him to lie his head on. Ah Ling closed his eyes, accepting.

Guifeng was in and out of consciousness. At one point, eyes closed, he saw trees at noontime shooting up emerald light. Feiyan undressed in the middle of the clearing, her skin aglow in the sun. At one point, he was cutting trees. A centuries-old redwood toppled down. From earth to heaven back to earth. Was it a sigh, a groan, a final shout as its life came to an end? Guifeng and Ah Ling had spent several hours cutting it, which was not all that different from drilling a hole into the granite with Ah Fook. Hours of toil, of repeated, rhythmic motion made by their small straw-dog human bodies, back and forth, back and forth, muscles rotating, tensing, grinding the bones and air. Motions reminiscent of lovemaking, of his and Feiyan's bodies' tremendous rubbing, not to tear anything down, or kill a centuries-old thing, but nevertheless to reach a final moment of breaking as something new was released, something perhaps not unlike the soul of the ancient tree, a kind of fire. Green flames fell all around them.

At one point, he was on top of the mountains shoveling snow for the rail track. He felt cold to the bone, and his thoughts were full of cold longings. He did not yet know he was going to tumble down the mountainside, to be wrapped in snow and wind. None of that had happened yet. He opened his eyes, shivering. The remains of the cabin continued to burn; so did the trees and bushes around it. Fire was what reigned now, not ice. Nonetheless, all were made of straw, all were straw dogs sizzling, barking their last barks in their death throes. Because the universe did not care, and in the eyes of heaven and earth, the ten thousand things were the same. The fires he and Feiyan built and those set upon them, in heaven and earth's eyes, were no different. All were straw dogs' doing.

He leaned back on the pillow of leaves Li Shu had made for him and looked up through the dark canopy at the sky's small punctures, where a few stars emerged, as if out of mercy.

7

Housekeeping

✳

1881

MRS. TURNER SWEPT HER EYES ACROSS THE LIVING ROOM ONE more time before gesturing for Sixiang to open the door. Two ladies from her church were paying a visit. Both wore frilly dresses buttoned up to their chins like Mrs. Turner. The abundance of laces and ribbons made them look like three heads afloat above seafoam. Sixiang had learned that beneath the soft fabrics of their dresses were metal molds tight around their torsos, but none of them showed any discomfort. They must have gotten used to such an arrangement for their bodies—the way Chinese women like Mrs. Chen and Sixiang's mother and grandmother grew accustomed to the tight bandages around their feet.

Sixiang served tea and biscuits before going back to wiping the stairs. Mrs. Turner had instructed her to wipe each step with a rag. The mop was no good, she'd said, as it left smudges on the varnished wood. "It's essential to keep everything spotless clean," she liked to say, "because God doesn't visit a dirty house." As a result, Sixiang was often on her knees.

Earlier at breakfast, Mr. Turner had read an article in the morning paper out loud: "Chinese servants and laundrymen are carrying germs into the households of white families, creating a perfect network of contagion and infection." As Sixiang poured coffee into his cup, she could sense Mrs. Turner's eyes on her, as if she was diagnosing the germs Sixiang could be carrying. Although Mrs. Turner wore a habitually amiable face—unlike Mrs. Chen whose face had looked either lethargic or enraged—it wasn't difficult for Sixiang to imagine something hard within, like what underlay her lacy dress.

Now the three ladies were talking about the newspaper article. "It's just unbelievable. They found a Chinaman with smallpox working in a slipper factory. He must have contaminated thousands of slippers," the tall, plump visitor said. "I had been wearing a pair of those slippers. They were real pretty, embroidered all over with glass beads. But after I read the article, I tossed them in the trash can. And I wiped my feet with alcohol."

"Good for you," the thin visitor said. "The way they make cigars is downright disgusting. They take a cigar in their mouth and put spit on it, their Chinese polish. That's just nasty. After Mr. Louis read that, he swore he would only smoke white cigars from now on."

"Not just that," Mrs. Turner said, "the Chinese laundrymen will spit on the laundry as they iron. I'm only having Cindy do the laundry now." Cindy was the English name Mrs. Turner gave Sixiang. She'd said there was no way she could pronounce Sixiang and Cindy was quite close.

Sixiang could sense all three ladies' eyes on her, when the thin lady asked, in a muted voice: "How old is she?"

"Fifteen," Mrs. Turner said. "Is that right, Cindy?" she called out to Sixiang.

"Yes, Madam," Sixiang answered from the stairs.

"She was not one of those—?" the thin lady continued her audible whisper. "Mrs. Burn's boy got the worst case of syphilis from a Chinese brothel. Those stupid young boys spend their pocket money on—"

"Oh, no, of course not," Mrs. Turner said with a hint of indignation in her voice. "Cindy was a slave girl, rescued by the Mission Home when she was only eleven. She's clean."

"That's good," the tall lady said. "I'd say it's better to have a maid than a houseboy. I never feel quite safe leaving my children with them, especially my girl. They get uppishly too. The first one I interviewed was just brazen. You can't imagine what he said to me when I told him I would call him Charlie—just like everyone else does. He said, 'I'll call you Mary then, since both are common names.' Who did he think he was? I asked him to leave right away."

Sixiang finally finished the stairs, relieved to be able to stand up and leave the ladies' sight. Since she was sent here to work for the Turners, she had not been asked the daily morning question, "What dirt will God clean from your heart today?" The questions now were more specific and literal: "Are your hands clean?" "Have you washed them with soap after you used the privy?" "You won't spit when you do laundry, right? Is that a cultural tradition?"

In the hallway mirror, Sixiang caught a glimpse of her face—a face shockingly different from the white ladies' with their distinct, self-possessed, commanding features. Sixiang stood in front of the mirror and stared at her reflection: this was the face that the ladies saw and thought of germs and prostitutes. Sixiang had not really thought much about her face in the past, as the majority of faces she'd seen were those that looked like hers, even though there were many varieties of them. There was her mother's face with the two long front teeth that made her look smiley even when she was sad. There was the young, even-featured face of her father in the photo. There were the fleshy, sulky face of Mrs. Chen and the unclely face of Mr. Chen when he was in a good mood. And there was Daoshi's face, how to describe it? A quiet, sparse, thinking face, a face Sixiang thought of almost as often as her mother's face since the riot night. And at the Mission Home, besides Miss Moore and Miss Webb's faces, the rest continued to be the same kind as Sixiang's. They all agreed that the best-looking among them was Ah Juan, who was so pretty that even Miss Moore and Miss Webb talked to her softly. Like Sixiang, she too had been placed in a white household to learn about their housekeeping, to build "character, habits of industry, independence and self-reliance," as Miss Moore told them. Would even Ah Juan feel startled to see her own face in a mirror, with her masters' imposing white faces constantly hovering by and their eyes detecting germs and filth in her? Could even a beautiful face like Ah Juan's withstand the weight of their scrutiny?

As she dusted the upstairs bedrooms, Sixiang thought of Ah Hong's bare body dangling under the oak branch. "It doesn't need to pray for their God to clean it," Ah Hong had spoken of the tree. Her pale body had had a blue hue; it looked clean, but where was the life in it?

THE WALLPAPER IN the living room repeated its countless roses and leaflets, while a day was countable by the tall grandfather clock that announced the arrival of each hour, sparing not even the night. Not until her second week at the Turners' could Sixiang sleep through the night without been startled awake by the clock's hourly booming chimes.

Now, morning did not greet her with the doves' cooing from outside the window where the oak branch swung sometimes empty, sometimes weighed down in Sixiang's mind. And there was no more fighting for wash water or waiting in line for a scoop of congee or conjuring up new dirt for God to clean from her heart.

Now, she woke up to an alarm clock's dinging by her bed. She would lie with her eyes open for a few minutes, taking in her surroundings in the narrow room—a small desk, a chair, sandy wallpaper, wooden floorboards. Of all the rooms she'd slept in during her fifteen years of life, this room felt the emptiest.

At five o'clock, she started the fire, then cooked the mush, brewed the coffee, set the table. Then she woke up Mrs. Turner, who would cook the sausages as Sixiang boiled the eggs. Then she brought the newspaper in and left it on the end of the table where Mr. Turner sat. Then she woke up the children, Luke, ten, and Sally, seven, whom Sixiang helped dress. Sally was a serious-looking girl who liked to correct Sixiang's English: "Not a 'not,' but a 'lot,' look at my tongue." She would hold Sixiang's chin in her little hands and study Sixiang's tongue. Mrs. Turner would burst into laughter at her daughter's precocious ways.

Luke tended to regard Sixiang with inquisitive eyes. "Do you eat rats?" he'd asked her the day after Sixiang's arrival, when she was serving dinner under Mrs. Turner's instruction.

"No, I don't," Sixiang said, although she wouldn't have minded doing so after the flood, had the rats not all fled from her starving village.

"That's a rude question," Mr. Turner said to Luke.

"But they say at school that their Chinese servants eat everything with legs except the table."

Both Mrs. and Mr. Turner laughed. "Are they going to eat me?" Sally asked, alarmed. "I have legs. Are you going to eat me, Cindy?"

"Don't be silly," Mrs. Turner said, but they all looked at Sixiang as if expecting her to assure them she wouldn't do such a thing.

"Please excuse me" was all Sixiang could say. She remembered the day when she was led away from the Chens', she had asked Yizheng the same question: "Are you going to eat me?" "That's the stupidest thing I've ever heard" was Yizheng's answer. Sixiang thought that would be a good answer to Sally's question too. But obviously she was in no position to say it.

"Change is good," her grandmother had said after making the deal with Madam to sell her. "Change makes a tree die and a person live." Life had not stopped changing for Sixiang, and she had continued to stay alive. And perhaps out of habit, she continued to measure each change by the quantity and quality of her meals. During the first weeks of her post, Mrs. Turner had taught her how to make cherry pies, strawberry shortcakes, beef stew, roasted chicken, and fish fry. They all tasted rich, flavorful, substantive, but now, a few months into such a diet, Sixiang found herself missing a simple bowl of congee for breakfast and rice and sautéed vegetables for lunch and dinner. Even the meager food at the Mission Home she'd detested so much didn't seem that bad in retrospect.

But food was not the only thing on her mind. Sixiang had not forgotten what she was really in Gold Mountain for. It was not just to put food in her belly and stay alive—but to find her father and bring him home, so that her family would be whole again. How to find him? She hadn't seen Daoshi since the afternoon of her rescue four years ago. Once, after Ah Jia had left for the boarding school in the East Coast, Sixiang had asked Miss Moore to let her accompany her to a grocery store in Chinatown. They'd walked past the pawnshop, but Daoshi was no longer there.

At the Mission Home, Sixiang poured herself into study. She wanted to learn as much as Ah Jia was learning at the real school in Philadelphia, as related in the few letters she'd written to Sixiang. But some of the subjects Ah Jia was studying, such as Latin and science, even Miss Moore and Miss Webb didn't know much about. Sixiang understood there were only two paths ahead of her—to be married to a Christian man or to be sent back to China for missionary work. She would choose the latter, but first try to find her father somehow. If that was impossible, she would go back alone and support her mother and grandmother with the stipend she would receive as a missionary. After all, with or without her father, her family had managed for ten years. Now that she was an adult, they could certainly manage more easily.

Besides learning English through Bible studies, Sixiang learned Chinese with a college student who came from a rich family in the provincial capital Guangzhou and volunteered two hours of her time twice a week to teach Sixiang and a few other select girls how to read and write in Chinese. Miss Moore said that to become a successful missionary in China, one must be literate in both languages. Only girls with good brains and clean bodies were eligible candidates. "God has a higher purpose for some of you," Miss Moore said to Sixiang after she was baptized.

Sixiang received her baptism in her first spring at the Mission Home. Baptism had always felt like a privilege there: those who'd received it carried themselves with a kind of pride, an invincibility. Even though they continued to be asked the question "What dirt will God clean from your heart today?" they spoke of their dirt with a marked aloofness, as if they knew they would end up in heaven anyway.

At her baptism, as Sixiang tilted her head back until she felt the shock of water, and then further down until her face was half submerged, she somehow thought of the drowned woman knocking on the side of their tub during the flood—her hair pooling out like spent wings, just like Sixiang's own hair now soaking and spreading. She begged for God's forgiveness for such an unclean thought: this image from the past was clearly hellish, while Sixiang was now being saved from hell. She tried to envision heaven where everyone would be dressed in glowing white and moving about without a fear. She would be looking for her family there, but could she find them? How could they be there if they were not baptized? Did that mean she would be separated from them eternally? She in the Christian heaven inhabited by white people and a dozen Chinese girls searching in vain for their families. She wouldn't be able to find Ah Hong there either, as she had been condemned to hell due to her transgression.

Still, baptism was a crucial step for Sixiang to be sent back to China. Sixiang studied Chinese with zeal. She wanted to write a letter to her mother. She'd seen the old envelopes her father had sent them and remembered the way their village name was written, as well as her grandmother's name that the letters had always been addressed to. With the tutor's help, Sixiang wrote a letter, and with Miss Moore's permission, she mailed it out. But she had not received a response back. It could be that the letter got lost. It was after all such a small thing among so many other letters and parcels, cargos and people, first crossing the monthlong ocean and then the delta and river. It could also be that her village no longer existed. It had already been disappearing when the boat took Sixiang away and all she could see was the green mountain that stayed big and fat as people shriveled and died. But she would not allow that second thought to linger. She must believe the village was still there and so were her mother and grandmother. She would find out for herself when she went back to China.

This servant work was part of the training. All the clean older girls were sent to a white family to learn Christian ways of housekeeping. They would not only serve and help, but more importantly, as Miss Moore told them, learn. Miss Moore said this was an education and their masters were their teachers. After successfully serving their as-signed household for two years, they would return with a recommen-dation from their master-teacher. The recommendation would help the Mission Home decide if a girl was fit to wed or proselytize.

Sixiang's post was in Grass Valley, a town in the western foothills of the Sierra. With Ms. Webb as their escort and two other girls as-signed to families in a nearby town, Sixiang rode a train along the rail-road her father had built. The mountains appeared in the window and then loomed larger and larger as the train rumbled forward, blocking where her father must be on the other side. When the train stopped at the bottom of the Sierra, a wagon sent by the Turners picked her up at the station. She didn't know how or when she would get back on the train and keep riding until she crossed the mountains. But she had come this much closer.

ONE DAY, SHORTLY after the church ladies' visit, Sixiang stepped into the front yard to water the plants and saw a young man trimming the evergreen bushes across the fence, as he always seemed to be doing. He had an unmistakably Chinese face but neither a braid nor shaved forehead. Mr. Chen had called Chinese men without a queue "cow-ards," and Mrs. Chen had echoed him by calling them "men who'd lost their way."

Sixiang had thought about this young man. She'd seen him on the day of her arrival in Grass Valley, even before she met the Turners. After the wagon picked her up at the train station and took her to a spread of houses not jumbled together with shared walls like those in Chinatown but set apart with gardens and lawns, it stopped right past where the young man was trimming the evergreen. He looked up from the bushes. He was about seventeen or eighteen, her father's age in the photo that she continued to carry with her. There was something similar about their faces too—the evenness of the eyes and mouth perhaps, along with a sort of fortified composure. The more Sixiang examined her father's photo, the more she felt he was not actually as calm as his face had initially suggested, but rather was forcing a poise onto his face, which made him look both lonely and a little sad.

When Sixiang got off the wagon, the young man nodded at her slightly, his face opening only a little from his thoughts, as if the sight of her was not so remarkable. But she had never felt more concrete about her grown body, which she'd been carrying like a strange armor. At the Mission Home, she had observed the older girls: some carried themselves upright with a showiness well matched by their curves; some slouched like their budding flesh was nothing but extra weight to bear. Sixiang vacillated between the two approaches but decided to settle upon the middle: to be fine with her body without showing it off; to carry it with both confidence and modesty. But the quick glance and aloof nod of this young man, the first Chinese boy she'd seen in what seemed like years, made her feel both conspicuous and commonplace.

Since then, whenever they both happened to be in their separate front yards, he would nod at her but never say a word. His name was Michael, the Coles' adopted son, Sixiang learned from Mrs. Turner.

Now as Sixiang watered the roses, she pretended not to see him. Her hair was curled into bouncy tangles, the result of sleeping with rag strips and poking pins the last few nights. Mrs. Turner had shown her how to do it and commented every morning: "How lovely! Don't you think?" At first it had just been the Western dress, a present from Mrs.

Turner the day after her church friends' visit. "I only wore this once or twice before it got too small on me. Now it's yours." Mrs. Turner had helped Sixiang with the strings, buttons, puffs, and laces. "That's a start," she'd said, stepping a few steps back to appraise Sixiang. "We'll fix your hair next. It will be so much fun. You're going to look just like an American girl."

Sixiang had felt proud. In the mirror, all that was left to be Americanized was her face. Maybe they would ignore the face if she wore the Western dress and curly hair? Maybe they would no longer think of her as someone who carried germs and diseases? Maybe they would think of her as almost American and certainly Christian?

She'd been diligently imitating the way they spoke English too, parroting their inflections, trying out their little filler words that made their speech sound so natural. She had heard Michael speak English with Mrs. Cole in their front yard before. It sounded quite authentic: had she not known, she wouldn't have guessed he wasn't white. Did people think of him as a disease-carrier too?

He was looking at her when she lifted her head from the rose bushes. "Don't let them turn you into a monkey," he said across the fence, a dozen feet away from her, hand clutching his clippers. He looked almost angry, as if he was personally insulted by her, as if she, whom he neither knew nor had exchanged a word with, was bringing shame upon him.

"What?" she said, but she knew exactly what he was saying. He was looking at her curled hair as he said it. His eyes ran down her tight dress as well, which, she became aware again, was constricting her breath. Back home in the market by her village, she'd seen a monkey dressed in baby clothes made to perform funny tricks for the audience. When the monkey did well, its owner would grant it a bite of banana or a pat on the head. Sixiang couldn't believe a young man not much older than she was had just said such an ugly thing to her. "What about you?" Sixiang said. "A Chinaman without a queue."

He looked like he was going to respond with something vindictive. His mouth opened halfway but closed again. His face settled into a mocking smile that could have been directed at Sixiang, or himself, or both. He lowered his eyes and returned to the trimming of the bushes, which were not the typical oval or globe or square she'd seen in the neighborhood, but had ebbs and flows, like waves.

WHEN SIXIANG STEPPED back into the house, Mrs. Turner was waiting to teach her how to make a chicken potpie. After that, she would teach Sixiang how to make a quilt. Mrs. Turner seemed to have a to-do list for every hour of the day, a list she wouldn't allow to end. She kept adding new items, new things for herself to do, which also meant for Sixiang to do. The way Mrs. Turner looked at Sixiang was something Sixiang recognized in Miss Moore too. The planning, agenda-driven look. It seemed that Sixiang was not just Mrs. Turner's servant and student, but her new project as well, which would remain a work in progress, even after her regular list of things was completed. Since her church friends' visit that day, Mrs. Turner seemed to have seen potential for an expansion of that project and embraced it with fervor. Calling Sixiang Cindy and teaching her how to cook and do chores and speak better English was only the beginning. She had more work to do. She would change not only Sixiang's accent, diet, manners, but also her clothes and hair and everything that was changeable. She would transform Sixiang into an American girl—an agenda Sixiang had welcomed too. Until the boy called her a "monkey."

"That adopted son of Mrs. Cole's," Sixiang asked Mrs. Turner as they kneaded dough for the potpie, "does he not have a job? Why is he working in the yard all the time?"

"That boy can't keep a job." Mrs. Turner seemed to perk up at the question. "Mr. Cole let him work in his bank earlier this year, but after just a couple months, Michael stopped going. Mrs. Cole said it was because the other employees complained about having a Chinaman in their midst. But, you know, there could be other reasons. Frankly, that boy is not known for having the best temperament. He's in fact quite prone to angry outbursts, which was why he got expelled from school in the first place. He'd gone to the same high school as Jason, our oldest, who is now attending Harvard, the best college in the world. But Michael, that strange boy, has been staying at home doing nothing but some household chores for Mrs. Cole. Poor Mrs. Cole, one night a few years ago, the boy threw a big fit. We could hear every word he said: 'I wish you had left me there to die with my real parents.' That must have broken our poor neighbors' hearts. Mr. Cole wanted to kick him out, understandably, but Mrs. Cole wouldn't let him. After all, she'd brought him up, treated him like her own. Now that her real children are all married and living away, she keeps him around like a big baby, and so of course he'll never grow up.

"But you, my darling, you're a different story. Only three months, and you've learned to keep a house sparkly clean like us and cook our food just right. Look at you—" Mrs. Turner leaned back to look at Sixiang's coiled hair and confining dress. "At the end of these two years, I have no doubt you'll become one of us."

NIGHT WAS SIXIANG's alone. In her narrow room, after taking off her tight, heavy dress, she dampened her fake curls with a wet towel and saw them straighten and fall onto her shoulders. She saw herself in the boy's eyes, monkey-like, a Chinese girl trying to be white. But what was wrong with trying to be white? Hadn't all her days since her rescue been spent to that end? Wasn't that the price to pay for not being a mui tsai, or "slave girl," as the white people called them? "Slavery was abolished in America in 1865," Miss Moore told them. "The country fought a war for it. We're not going to let heathens bring the inhumane practice back here." Sixiang had been saved, and she needed to be as white as she could to show her gratitude for being free and her worthiness of that freedom. She had spent four years of her life learning the scriptures to be close to their God. Now a year and eight and a half months remained to learn to live and keep a house like them. That was what she needed to do, and she had done it with such sincerity it had never crossed her mind that she was turning into a monkey in someone's eyes.

She decided to ignore the boy who couldn't even speak Chinese, who spoke and dressed like a white man but did the typical Chinese houseboy work and dared to insult her when he himself had been turned into a monkey. She wrapped locks of her hair around the rag strips Mrs. Turner had given her. She was not going to stop curling her hair just because he thought she was turning into a monkey. She did it for herself, she decided, not for anyone else.

But throughout the night, while her hair was being shaped into those correct curls, the word "monkey" rang loudly in her head.

THE FURNITURE AND things Sixiang wiped daily reminded her of those her family had once owned when she was little. The walnut dining table brought back memories of their *hongmu* table with legs shaped like lion's paws. The glass-topped coffee table recalled their tea table carved entirely out of a tree root. The sets of china displayed in the glass-paned cabinet featured a similar gold-inlaid floral pattern as their antique bowl set. Sixiang had almost forgotten all about these things. She had learned not to become attached to material objects, as they had the tendency to disappear from her life. But Mrs. Turner did not seem to have that kind of anxiety about her possessions. It did not seem she had ever had to worry about them being taken away from her piece by piece to be traded for food. It must have been good to live without having to worry about losing things.

During the four years at the Mission Home, Sixiang had seen a dozen girls married off. Dressed in white, the color of death and funeral for Chinese but of weddings for Christians, the bride would stand by a man she hardly knew in the Mission Home's parlor. The rest of the girls would each hold a lamp and sing: "Are your lamps all trimmed and burning? Should the Bridegroom now appear?" Then each of them would get a piece of white cake as sweet as Ah Jia had described, and the bride and groom would descend the steps to the street, into a carriage that took them away, never to return.

If she were to marry a Christian man, would she also have these sparkling things around her? Would she stay here in Gold Mountain, wear a corset and bustle, curl her hair, go to church, and have children who spoke perfect English and knew all the idioms, like Luke and Sally? But even if that were true, her children would still look just like her, seen as either disease-carriers or monkeys. Anything but real Americans.

She must keep her path in mind. She would serve the Turners well and receive a good recommendation so that Miss Moore would send her back to China as a missionary. Maybe she could even ask the Turners to help her find her father, as Mr. Turner went out to work every day and must know many people. Maybe out of Christian charity, they would be willing to help.

Sixiang and Mrs. Turner were making a rhubarb pie the next afternoon, using Mrs. Turner's grandmother's recipe. Mrs. Turner was talking about her own father. She often told Sixiang the same stories of her life, over and over again. But this one about her father was new. He hadn't been home much when she was young, but now that she was her father's age, she could understand his absence better, because just like Mr. Turner, her father had to hold up the entire family. She told Sixiang that she alone, of all her siblings, could bring a smile to her father's face after he came home from a tired day.

"I've been hoping to find my father," Sixiang said quietly, not sure if this was a good time to bring up her request.

"What did you say?" Mrs. Turner looked at her. "I thought you were an orphan. They told me you were all orphans."

"I'm not, Mrs. Turner. My mother lives in China, and my father lives here. I came here to find him and bring him home."

"Oh." Mrs. Turner looked lost for a moment. She arranged the rhubarb pieces Sixiang had chopped in the pie crust, her fingers agitated. "I can tell you were not paying attention to what I was saying. Of course, my life doesn't interest you, but this is also part of your education. It's good for you to learn what a Christian family is like, how we do things, how we think and talk about things. Don't you agree?"

Don't you agree was what ended many of Mrs. Turner's remarks. A question in the negative form that allowed no negative answer. Sixiang could never say, "No, I don't," but instead, "Certainly, Mrs. Turner, I completely agree."

Her father didn't fit in Mrs. Turner's project, just as he hadn't fitted in Mrs. Moore's. In their project, Sixiang needed to be an orphan, alone and helpless in this world, so that she could be entirely dependent on their charity, shaped whichever ways that suited their fancy. A father would only give her a reverse anchor they had to pull her away from. It would spoil their reform mission.

Sixiang had humored Mrs. Turner the way she had with Miss Moore, because both held the power to decide her future. She had told herself that whatever she was going through was nothing compared to Mrs. Chen's yelling and pinching. This was much better, or at least not as bad. And she had been fine with it all, until the boy's words fell on her like a blade: "Don't let them turn you into a monkey."

She did not curl her hair that night. It wasn't because of what the boy had said, she told herself, but because she didn't like how uncomfortable the pins and twirls felt when she was sleeping. The next morning, putting on the corset, she realized just how shallow her breath became, how constantly she felt the hard spiral steel against her body.

"What happened to your hair? Forgot to do the curls? And did your dress already need washing?" Mrs. Turner asked the moment she saw Sixiang.

Sixiang had anticipated the questions, but she couldn't think of anything to say except the truth: "I'm not really used to them, Mrs. Turner."

"Darling, it takes time to get used to new things. Don't give up so quickly."

"I just don't really feel comfortable in the dress and curls. Thank you though."

"Okay, if you say so." Mrs. Turner's face hardened for a second and then turned almost pleading. "But the dress and curly hair looked really nice on you. Don't you agree? They make you look more American. Don't you want to look more American?"

There was no saying "no" to her questions, so Sixiang lowered her eyes and said, "I'm sorry, Mrs. Turner."

For the rest of the day, she regretted apologizing.

A FEW DAYS later, when Sixiang was raking the first autumn leaves after an overnight storm, Michael stepped out of the house next door with his clippers. He walked straight toward her, and, before she could turn away, said, "I shouldn't have said that the other day."

Sixiang looked up, and he continued, "I lost my queue when I was little, soon after I lost my parents. The Coles took me in. You know what the kids used to call me? 'Michael the monkey without a tail.'"

He told her his Chinese name was Qinglong. He remembered his parents calling him that, and he knew it meant *green dragon*. He said the two Chinese words exactly the way a Cantonese would say them.

And with that, Sixiang forgave him. She told him her Chinese name too.

"Sixiang," he said, then said it again as if to remember it.

Now when Sixiang looked at the bushes he was going to trim, she saw what the wavy shape resembled: "It looks like the back of a dragon in the dragon dance."

"It's a dragon without a head. Everyone else think it's only waves."

Just then, Mrs. Cole opened the door. She was a slender woman with a frail build. "Michael," she called, her voice frail too, "can you help me with something inside?"

She didn't look at Sixiang, not even a glance.

A dragon without a head. A man without a queue. A dragon without a head is a dead dragon. Without a queue, a Chinese man in China would get beheaded, and without a queue, a Chinese man in Gold Mountain was neither a Chinese nor an American.

Sixiang decided when she saw him again, she would call him Qinglong, the way his parents had called him. The name must be lonely without anyone calling him by it. Just as he must be lonely not being called by his real name. If he and his name could finally meet again, would he feel more like himself?

THE NEXT DAY, on her way to the grocery story, Sixiang heard her own name called—"Sixiang." She turned and saw him walking toward her. She called to him too, "Qinglong." Surprise came to his face, and then he nodded, as if to welcome his name back.

He asked her about China, what she knew, how her life had been, how she'd gotten here. She talked about her village and the river where she'd tried to catch a fish or shrimp but ended up eating an earthworm that tasted like dirt mixed with one drop of fat. They laughed at the things the Turners' children asked her, such as Luke's question, "Do you eat rats?" And Sally's, "Are you going to eat me?"

"Ah, they still ask the same questions. I was asked those things when I was a kid. Just say, 'Yes, you look yummy. And rats? We pick them up with our chopsticks and chomp them down raw.'"

At the store five blocks away, where most of the shoppers were either Irish maids or Chinese houseboys, Sixiang had received unwanted attentions from both the shoppers and the shopkeeper who was in the habit of following her with his eyes. If she asked him a question about some produce, he would appear not to understand her. "Speak up," he would say. "I don't get your mumblings." Now he looked tickled by the sight of Sixiang walking in with Qinglong, a smirk on his face, as if he was savoring a private joke. Sixiang quickly filled her sack with a few potatoes and onions, a bag of flour, and some sugar. Qinglong put some potatoes and onions in his sack too. Neither could wait to get out of the store and be alone on the sidewalk again.

Qinglong told Sixiang he didn't know for sure what had happened to his parents. All he could remember was the fire, the choking smoke, and the smell of scorched flesh. For a while, he thought the memory had come from a nightmare. But one of the Coles' children, the older girl who had been watching him with a frosty face, said to him, "Remember we're the real children in this house; you're just a homeless yellow child my parents took pity on, a stray we let in. Your real parents used to do our laundry. They died in a fire." He was about four, not long after he'd been taken in, new to the language, but somehow he could understand every word she'd said.

He was sent to school with the Coles' two children. The questions were always like these: "Where is your pigtail? Do you wear it on your butt like a rat?"

Qinglong had watched a dragon dance once at San Francisco Chinatown when the Coles took a vacation in the city. "I saw some Chinese boys in the audience," he told Sixiang. "They all wore queues and spoke Cantonese with their families. I remember envying them, but at the same time thinking to myself, well, they do look like rats." He had that mocking smile on his face again, the one Sixiang wasn't sure whom it was directed at. Now she felt it was perhaps directed at all of them, all Chinese living in Gold Mountain, himself most of all.

"I used to wish I could be a dragon dancer," he added after a few minutes of silence, his face even and lonely again.

For the next few days, they continued to walk together to and from the grocery store. Qinglong would wait in the Coles' front yard until she stepped out of the Turners' door. Then they stepped out of their separate gates onto the sidewalk, which was bordered by other people's gardens and lawns and occasional wagons on the road. They continued to learn about each other, about their narrow place in this world, as they walked side by side on this skinny sidewalk covered with fallen leaves.

The autumn sky, however, was broad and open. The pale green, rolling mountains stood in the distance with their snow-capped peaks shimmering in the sun.

He asked her to teach him Chinese. He told her that sometimes shadows of sounds visited him in his sleep. In a dream or memory, he was in a wooden shack with a woman who was his birth mother, who swung a straw bird above his eyes while singing a song.

Sixiang taught him to say "*niu*," *bird;* "*fei*," *to fly.* She wanted to bring the tones and shapes back to those faded words tucked away somewhere in his mind. When other pedestrians walked past them, they would simultaneously lower their voices, as if they were speaking in code and they wanted to keep their secret safe between them.

She would quiz him across the fence when they were both doing yard work, which they timed carefully. But as the weather turned colder and the yard needed less tending, it became harder for Sixiang to find excuses to be out in the garden. On a Sunday, after church with the Turners and lunch preparation and cleanup, she asked Mrs. Turner for permission to go out and take a walk.

"With Michael?" Mrs. Turner asked, bluntly. She had of course seen them together and had complained about how long it took Sixiang to do the grocery shopping and how many chores needed to be done that she couldn't do all by herself. But she had not objected openly.

"Yes," Sixiang said without meeting her eyes.

"Promise me you'll be prim and proper. You know what I mean, right?"

Sixiang nodded.

Mrs. Cole had asked Qinglong questions too, and Qinglong

told her he was learning Chinese with Sixiang, to which Mrs. Cole responded with something like a shock: "Why do you want to learn Chinese?"

Why would I not want to learn Chinese? Am I not Chinese? Qinglong had wanted to say to her but restrained himself. Mrs. Cole had been kind to him, and he owed it to her to speak kindly. "There're certain things she just doesn't get," he told Sixiang. "I have to accept that."

He had been keeping his hair long, tied in a ponytail, or sometimes, like today, letting it fall on his shoulders. Strands caught in the late autumn wind, flowing like black silk. Sixiang wanted to reach out and touch it.

They walked to the nearby park where there was a small wood, and beyond it, in the distance, the Sierra peaks rose to the limpid sky. Sixiang told Qinglong her plan: she would one day find her father on the other side of the mountains and take him home to her mother and grandmother. The words didn't sound convincing even to herself, as they rolled too easily off her tongue, and as the rugged mountains, cold and unsurpassable, blocked the horizon. But she tried to keep her voice free from doubt.

"That's a good plan," Qinglong said quietly.

Sixiang seemed to detect a touch of envy in his voice. Perhaps he too wished to have a plan like hers and a father who was alive and could be found across the snowy mountains. Perhaps living with a plan was something that had been denied to him. What did he have to look forward to? Day after day, the tending of the bushes, trimming down new growth that would always come back, even in late fall, always disfiguring the perfect contours of the dragon without a head.

He said he remembered a few things about China, even though he had never been there. There were pictures in his head, not just the things he'd seen in Chinatown, but things he couldn't have actually seen anywhere here, such as rice paddies with water buffalos, misty rivers by dreamy tile-roofed houses. They must be things he remembered from his mother's words. But they felt real, even if separated from him by mountains of waves.

At night during her hours alone, Sixiang found herself reimagining her dream with Qinglong in it. In several more months, he would be able to braid his hair into a long enough queue and shave his forehead if he wanted to. He would be able to speak enough Chinese and no one would doubt that he was one of them. Then they could go back to China together, where they would blend right in wherever they went. No one would single them out and throw stones or ugly words or angry stares at them. They would finally be home.

SEVERAL DAYS BEFORE Christmas, Jason, the Turners' older son, came home for his winter break from Boston. He wore a full goatee that made the rest of his face appear strangely young and fair. He was the same age as Qinglong, and they'd been in the same class at the same school before Qinglong was expelled, Mrs. Turner had told Sixiang, and now Jason was a freshman in the country's best college, studying law.

Sixiang had not met a young white man who wasn't the hooligan type, the kind who took pleasure in harassing Chinese, such as those who'd thrown stones at them and smeared Ah Hong's face. "They're God-forsaken people," Miss Moore had said about them, "but they belong to only a tiny slice of the American population. The majority are good God-loving, God-fearing citizens."

Jason wore a three-piece suit and bowtie even at home. He never failed to say *thank you* and *excuse me*. But there was something that seemed at odds with his elegant clothes and flawless manners. Some agitation just below the surface, some unease or dissatisfaction that seemed to stop him from standing still or sitting still. He was constantly moving his body, shifting his legs, his hands fluttering tirelessly in the air.

At dinner, he argued with his father about "socialism," "the labor movement," about Washington and the "Chinese question." Mr.

Turner's throaty old voice and Jason's tense young voice clashed over the dishes, while Jason creaked the wooden chair he was sitting on and waved his hands that held the fork and knife. Sixiang couldn't quite follow their argument: some words used by Jason sounded especially unfamiliar. But it seemed to Sixiang he was not against Chinese people. While his father talked about "laws and legislations," Jason talked about "hypocrisy," "equal rights," "mockery to the constitution." From time to time, as she took away plates, served desserts, or poured coffee, Jason cast glances at her, as if to make sure she was paying attention to what he had to say.

One day when Sixiang and Qinglong were talking across the fence, Jason stepped out into the front yard. "Hey, Michael, long time no see." He paced toward them, reaching out his hand to Qinglong like they were old friends. "How's life treating you?"

"Fine." Qinglong hesitated before taking Jason's hand and giving it a loose shake. He was not smiling.

"We should catch up sometime." Jason kept his overzealous tone. Then he nodded at Sixiang and walked back in.

Inside the house, Jason seemed to be everywhere. When Sixiang prepared breakfast in the early morning, he would appear at the kitchen door in his robe to get coffee. When she wiped the stairs on her knees, he would move about in the living room, flipping the newspaper, putting it down, pulling out a chair, sitting for a second and standing back up again. All the while, he seemed to be glancing at her from the corner of his eyes, while there were many more steps for her to wipe on all fours.

One afternoon, after Mrs. Turner took the children out shopping, he stepped into the kitchen where Sixiang was chopping carrots for a beef stew. He didn't leave after filling his coffee. "Is there really a maze of underground tunnels in San Francisco Chinatown?" he asked, and seeing Sixiang perplexed, added, "I mean the opium dens. They're all underground, aren't they?"

"I don't know," Sixiang said. "I've never been to one."

"Oh, don't get me wrong. I think it's grand, actually. I'd like to take a trip there and find out."

Sixiang didn't know what to say, so she just nodded. Jason still leaned against the kitchen counter, sipping coffee. He didn't hold his mug like other people did. He put it down after each sip so that his hands didn't need to stay still. "I actually have another question," he said, rubbing his hands. "Why do you folks leave food at graves for the dead? Do you think the dead actually eat it?"

"Yes." Sixiang remembered how on Qingming Festivals, her grandmother and mother would bring fruits and pastries to the ancestral graves. After they burned paper money and paper houses and said prayers, they would take the food back home with them. "Our ancestors ingest the flavor out of the food."

Jason laughed, as if she'd been joking.

Sixiang didn't laugh back. "It's no different from you bringing flowers to your ancestors' graves so that they can smell them."

"That's a good one. You got me there." Jason clapped his hands and threw them in the air. Then they reached toward Sixiang as if he was going to hug or grab her. Sixiang stepped back. "You're smart," he said, retrieving his hands, and left the kitchen.

The days around Christmas kept Sixiang busy inside the house. She cooked, served, and cleaned, as the family opened presents and feasted on one meal after another, as the children ran around and yelped, as Mr. Turner and Jason argued, made peace, and argued more, and as Mrs. Turner came up with new chores for Sixiang to do.

Meanwhile, Sixiang had been revising her dream so often and with such rich detail it now felt like the only possible version. The destined one. She would go back to China with Qinglong even if she couldn't find her father. They would live with her mother and grandmother. They would farm and support the family. She didn't even need to wait for Miss Moore to grant her the wish of being sent back to China. The only problem was money. She still had nothing besides the six silver coins of her own sale money, which was far from enough to buy a boat ticket. She had been working since she landed in this country five years ago but had not made a single penny. She supposed it was the same story for Qinglong. He worked for the Coles like a houseboy but was unpaid. They were servants without a salary. Did that not make them another kind of slave? She'd like to talk about all this with Qinglong.

IT WAS NOT until the third day after Christmas that Sixiang was given a break by Mrs. Turner. She walked with Qinglong to the park. There had been a freezing rain the previous night and the trees' bare branches were coated in ice. Qinglong seemed distracted. He looked behind them from time to time, as if someone might be following them. There was something different about his right boot too. A sheath was riveted on the outer side where a knife's wooden handle stuck out.

"Why are you carrying a knife?" Sixiang asked.

"All Chinamen need to carry a weapon of some sort. I would be carrying a gun if I had one." He had not called himself a "Chinaman" before, and he said the word without mockery, as if he'd decided to claim the term as his own.

He talked about the weather—how it was the coldest, gloomiest winter he could remember, which made Sixiang feel colder. Her coat was an old one Mrs. Turner had given her for Christmas. It was made of wool but not the thick kind, and she was shivering.

She couldn't say what she had hoped to say. The Sierra, covered entirely in snow, rose high above them—an immense, relentless mass that made her dream seem fragile and tenuous. She feared it would turn to mist if she spoke of it out loud. She spoke a little about how her village must look this time of the year: it would be sunny, green, and warm, nothing like this frozen land. She taught Qinglong Cantonese phrases people would say during Spring Festival, though it was still a month away and when it came, there wouldn't be any celebrations in this white neighborhood. But the Cantonese words added a bit of color and comfort to their walk in the icy, desolate park.

It was after they paced into the woods that they heard footsteps not their own. They turned and saw three men approaching on the trail, crunching dead leaves underneath their boots. Jason and two other young men, all in long woolen coats, felt hats, and black leather gloves.

"Look who's here—Michael, the monkey without a tail," one of them, the stout one in a plaid coat, hollered.

"Be civil," Jason said, gesturing with his gloved hand. "We're all grownups now, aren't we?"

Sixiang could feel Qinglong tense beside her. She could hear both their hearts rattle.

"Who is this girl? Your Chinese bride?" the third man with a long red chin asked with a laugh.

Jason said nothing, as if he didn't know her. Instead, he reached a hand to his hat and tipped it at Sixiang.

"Hi, Michael, have you grown back your tail now? Remember the good old days when you pulled down your pants for us to check?" the stout man asked, then looking at Sixiang, said, "Miss China doll, have you taken a look at his tailbone yet, where his queue grows?"

"Be nice." Jason waved his hand again. "As I said before, we're not kids anymore, are we?" But his fake serious tone seemed to be only doing the opposite—goading his friends on, as if he wanted to see how low they could go and how Qinglong and Sixiang would react. His eyes were appraising, amused, moving back and forth between Qinglong and Sixiang.

"Michael, you've always liked to share things with us, why not now?" the one with the long chin said.

"Right, share! Is her thing really horizontal like they say?" the stout man said, giggling.

Jason put a hand before his face as if embarrassed by his friends, but at the same time, he was giggling and laughing with them. These three, so well dressed, but the way they talked and laughed was no different from those shabby-clothed ruffians harassing Chinatown and those boys pelting stones and smearing Ah Hong's face.

"Leave her alone," Qinglong said. He bent down and drew the knife from his boot, the weapon he believed all Chinamen needed to carry. Now, it occurred to Sixiang that Qinglong had not thought of carrying a knife before Jason had walked across the yard toward them, his restless hand stretching out to Qinglong for a shake, as if they were equals.

"Oh my, my, our Michael is getting mad. Is he also threatening our lives with a knife?"

Still pointing his knife at the men, Qinglong turned to look at Sixiang. "*Nei ʒau liu,*" he said in Cantonese, one of the expressions she'd taught him and one that she had said to him when they had to say good-bye, except that was "*Ngo ʒau liu,*" *I leave now*, not "*nei,*" *you.* He was now saying it so clearly as if he had always known how to say it. Or as if he had known he would have to say it someday.

You leave now.

"*Nei ʒau liu,*" he said again, louder this time, and there was something irrefutable in his eyes, something also beseeching. He wanted her to leave, needed her to.

She shook her head even as she started running, circling past the three men, running as fast as her trembling legs could carry her. She was saying *no* even when she slid on a patch of ice, fell, got up, and ran again. She didn't stop running when she heard the fight break out behind her, and shouts, cries, kicks, and grunts. She ran out of the woods and called out to a white couple who were sauntering across the frozen lawn, "Help!" But they tossed a glare at her and walked on. She saw a white maid on the sidewalk who spat at her even before she could form a word. So Sixiang kept running, as if by running fast enough, she could outrun the future unraveling before her.

She banged on the Coles' door, calling, "Mrs. Cole," knowing that besides herself, this woman was the only one in the living world who loved Qinglong. "They are beating him." She grabbed Mrs. Cole's hands. "Quick, they're going to kill him." Sixiang had not let the thought come close to her, but out her mouth the words came. "Don't say things you don't want to happen," her grandmother had warned her since she was a child, "because if you do, they will happen for sure." But Sixiang had said it. She had just made another mistake.

Followed by Mrs. Cole, and with the burden of the words she shouldn't have said, Sixiang ran back to the woods. He was lying where she had left him. The knife he'd been holding while saying *Nei ʒau liu* was stuck in his chest. Blood had soaked through his coat, trickling onto the dead leaves beneath him. His eyes were open but could no longer see her. In them, two tiny pools of icy branches and empty sky. His hair that she'd wanted to touch shimmered lightly in the pale sun. Mrs. Cole was screaming and howling, shaking his shoulders as if to awaken him. Sixiang reached out a trembling hand and touched the strand of hair on his face. It felt silky smooth but cold.

THE TRIAL TOOK place a week later. On the witness stand, Sixiang was questioned by a man with eyes the color of flint. Why were you alone with a man in the woods? What were the two of you doing? How long and how often were you seeing each other? Like the shopkeeper, the man kept asking her to repeat herself, to speak louder or clearer, and kept interrupting her in mid-sentence.

Jason was the next to speak. Waving his hands in the air as if conducting an orchestra, he told the court that Michael and Cindy had been engaging in indecent acts in the woods when he and his friends happened upon them. He kindly asked them to stop, but Michael pulled a knife from his boot and started a fight. The three of them tried to defend themselves, and in the chaos, Michael stabbed himself with his knife, which caused his death. Cindy was not there when it happened: she had run away the moment Michael pulled his knife. "It was an unfortunate accident," he concluded.

Besides repeating Jason's statement, the two other men said that Michael had always been aggressive, even during the years when they were in school together. One of them pointed at a cut on his cheek. The other pulled up his sleeve to show a slash on his arm.

The principal from their high school testified too, confirming that Michael had been "an impulsive young man, prone to violent conduct, which was why he was expelled from the school two years ago. Conversely, these three young gentlemen," he said, pointing at Jason and the two other men, "are from respectable families, of good lineage and upbringing. They excelled at high school and have just completed their freshman year of college."

Mrs. Turner was next. She had asked Sixiang to stay inside her narrow room during the week before the trial, excusing her from all the household chores since she was "in an unstable condition." Or was it perhaps because Mrs. Turner feared Sixiang would get close to Jason and do something dangerous to him? Now Mrs. Turner talked about Sixiang's "slave-girl past," her "heathen background." "I have tried my best to reform her, to teach her Christian ways of living. So many times, we took her to our church with us and let her sit next to our family as if she was our own, but unfortunately, she rejected the scriptures. She wanted to go out and take a walk with Michael—that poor boy, God bless his soul—and I asked her again and again to be prim and proper. I trusted her . . . but look at what happened." Mrs. Turner paused to wipe her eyes with a kerchief, then continued shudderingly, "Our dear neighbors Mr. and Mrs. Cole tried so hard to raise Michael right, to give him a good life, but then this Chinese girl came. I should have known better than to bring her into my household, into our neighborhood and community. Miss Moore of the Mission Home warned me that it is a most difficult work to tame barbarians. I certainly see that now."

When the judge pronounced the three men innocent, the court cheered. Mrs. Turner embraced Jason, who cast a glance at Sixiang and looked away. With a smile frozen on his face, he patted his mother on the back and then each of his friends on the shoulder.

Mrs. Cole did not testify. She was ill at home. Too sick to appear in court, said her husband, who didn't testify either.

Sixiang was sent back to the Mission Home the next day. "I believe we're all God's creatures. Even if we are not the same kind, I pray for the strength to love those who are less fortunate than us," Mrs. Turner said before the horses were whipped away from their gate.

Sixiang turned to look at the bushes that Qinglong had trimmed, the rolling dragon back. Cold days had thwarted the growth of new shoots, so the shape remained the same, but the green had turned weighty and weary. As if these bushes, too, were grieving for their companion, who had been there, trying to implant through them a wish in this world that had been so eager to kill him.

8

Chinaman's Chance

※

1876

Guifeng

GUIFENG WATCHED DUOFU KNEADING A FACE INTO A LUMP OF dough. She was sitting cross-legged on the floor, in the far corner of the bedroom, away from the bed where he was lying. She glanced up at him from time to time, cautiously, as if she was afraid what he'd got— the loss of a leg, the bedridden frailty—was contagious. It was both sad and heartening to see his three-year-old daughter already possessing such a strong sense of self-preservation.

He had survived, again and again, even now minus a leg. "Life or leg, you choose," the doctor had asked him. "Life" was Guifeng's answer. Maybe he could have chosen both. Maybe had the doctor not been white, or a member of the Caucasian League for that matter, he would have chosen both for Guifeng too. But this doctor, who'd once served in the Union army, had not hesitated to cut off his leg. He wouldn't even look Guifeng in the face, as if he could barely stand being there, among four bleeding Chinese in the servants' quarters of their boss Joseph Gray's mansion. "Where is their herbalist?" he'd asked Gray when he

walked in, laughing without humor. "Why didn't you send their heathen herbalist to treat them?"

Gray gave Guifeng a week's pay as compensation for not taking
him back—more than Guifeng had expected from a white man, which
was nothing.

Feiyan took him in her arms at night when he kicked his phantom
leg and woke up covered in cold sweat. Her pity weighed on him. Already, he couldn't quite find himself worthy of her love. So many young,
capable men circled around her in the diner downstairs, each hoping to
score a look or smile from her. Each more capable of giving her the love
she wanted and deserved. At night, when her body heat shrouded the
bed, Guifeng felt ugly and grotesque, a helpless weakling who had allowed himself to be smoked out and shot, his leg cut off like that of a hog.

Maybe that was why so many men stayed solo in this land. They
kept their wives an ocean apart to sustain a feeble, but dignified, tie
through their monthly letter and check. Their women would not need
to see them humiliated or mutilated. In their letters, they would continue to stress that they were doing fine, and as long as they could keep
their families fed and sheltered, their dignity would remain intact.
They would die knowing they'd done all they could.

But Guifeng was not one of them. He had abandoned his family years
ago. Lying in bed upstairs, he overheard Feiyan talking with her customers about their village, Yunteng—the days-long flood and months-long
famine. It wasn't the kind of news she would pass on to him, but he'd
heard it clearly and knew even more clearly that there was nothing he
could do. It would have been easier if he had died, like Ah Ling, whose
family would learn about his death in less than a month and would revere
him on their ancestral altar and burn incense for him every day. Guifeng,
on the other hand, would only be remembered as an unforgivable son,
a despicable husband, a useless father—that is, if his family had been
lucky enough to survive the flood and famine. While here, in this new
life for which he'd given everything, he was now being regarded by his

new child with distance and caution, and tolerated by his new wife with pity and benevolence, which would sooner or later run out.

Feiyan brought opium home to ease his pain, and carefully controlled the dose so that he wouldn't develop a habit. She also ordered an artificial limb from Big City so that he could walk. Where did she get all that money? They were still paying off the high-interest loan for the new house, and the diner's earnings were certainly not enough. He didn't want to think too much about it, but it was all he could think of. And all he could do was either lie in the upstairs bedroom or sit on a stool in the kitchen chopping vegetables, adding firewood to the stove, or keeping soup from boiling over. He wanted more opium, but his leg was healing; the pain was not real.

THEN CAME A miracle. All seven white men got caught. Joseph Gray and a few other lumber bosses had raised one thousand dollars for a bounty. The Truckee Chinatown had raised two hundred on top of it. The lead investigator, Constable Jack Cross, tracked down the murderers and jailed them all. Two confessed. A trial would be held in late September.

One of Gray's houseboys, Ah Lu, came to the diner with the news that Guifeng could testify at the trial, which was yet another miracle. For twenty years, Chinese had been banned from giving testimony against the whites. Guifeng would now be one of the first Chinese to take the stand in a white men's court. The seven white men who had smoked them out with every intention to kill might actually be hanged. The thought itself was incredible.

During the next month, he practiced his testimony with Ah Lu, who was born here, spoke good English, and liked to come over during his free time to enjoy Feiyan's cooking. When Guifeng worked on his English with Ah Lu, he was almost able to accept the loss of his leg. Maybe the doctor had indeed to cut it off to save his life. Maybe Guifeng had been too distrustful of white men. Not all of them were

bad; actually, most of them were all right. They just didn't want anything to do with the Chinese whom they saw as strangers, which was
not that hard to understand. Hadn't Punti treated Hakka the same in
Guangdong, laughing at their barbarous traditions, forcing them to eke
out a living in the hills, and waging war on them when their numbers
grew? Wasn't it human nature to resent newcomers? But the trial was
promising. It was going to be held in the big courthouse in Nevada
City, the county seat of Nevada County, and reported in the newspapers so that the whole country would know that the whites could not
get away with burning and killing the Chinese.

Guifeng would tell the court what had happened that night. The
fire; the shooting of Ah Ling, himself, and his two other campmates.
He would not describe the dark trees soaring up into the sky and pouring more darkness onto them, or the sharp smell of blood mingled with
the sharper smell of smoke as they watched the flames leap like tigers
in the burning cabin where they had been soundly asleep just moments
earlier—how he could almost see himself still lying in there, melting
and charring on the blazing cot.

He would leave those details out and stick to the facts, which
should be enough to bring the killers to justice. He would testify with
dignity, even with one less leg. The white folks would see for themselves that the Chinese were not all that different from them—they just
wanted to make a living, have a family; they worked hard and wanted
to rest after work with all their limbs intact. Maybe this would be the
last blatant killing of Chinese, and from now on, they would be left in
peace, and their children who were born here, like Duofu, would be
Americans just like white children, left alone and unharmed. And then,
Guifeng would be able to live again.

SEPTEMBER 25, 1876. The grand two-story granite and brick courthouse in Nevada City. To arrive here, they had to first take a train and
then a wagon, but many came. Besides Li Shu and Guifeng's other

three surviving former cabinmates, Fong Lee, the richest man in Chinatown, was here; the contractor who had fired Guifeng and Feiyan was here; the loan shark Luo Laoda was here; even the photographer who had housed Guifeng and Feiyan during their first fugitive days was here. But among all the Chinese faces in the courtroom, one stood out like a jutted tooth: Chang'er, whom Guifeng hadn't seen since that misty morning by the splashing flume seven years ago. What was he doing here?

Guifeng had heard outlandish tales about Chang'er at the logging camp—that he had founded a tong different from all others. Chang'er's tong would only kill white men, specifically white killers of Chinese men whom the white men's laws would do nothing about. He'd assembled a dozen assassins adept in kung fu and fast with guns. Guifeng's campmates had loved talking about Chang'er's tong, although they differed in their opinions. Li Shu, for example, said that each time a Chinese man killed a white man, eighteen times more Chinese men would get killed in return—as demonstrated by the Los Angeles Massacre of 1871, which allegedly had been triggered by the accidental killing of a white saloon owner at the hands of a Chinese tong soldier, and which ended with eighteen Chinese men lynched and maimed. The whites were the majority, they the minority; the whites the wolves, they the sheep. Fighting back would merely get them killed quicker. Opposite to Li Shu, Ah Ling the gambler had called Chang'er an outlaw hero and had said he would join his tong one of these days. Perhaps he could do so in spirit now.

Why was Chang'er here? Had he already predicted the outcome of the trial? Was he already plotting to take matters into his own hands?

"Which one of these men do you accuse of shooting Ah Ling?" the defense attorney, Charles McGlashan, asked Guifeng on the witness stand. Truckee's number one celebrity, McGlashan was not only the town's most prominent attorney but also the publisher of the *Truckee Republican* and leader of the Caucasian League. He combed his thick handlebar mustache with his fingers as he spoke.

The seven men fixed their eyes on Guifeng. They wore smirks or shook their heads as if amused, as if they were daring him to point his finger at any one of them. Guifeng remembered parts of a face lit fleetingly by fire sparks. A squint eye, a hard jaw. He'd seen glimpses of that partial face in his head and in dreams, but in front of these daylight faces that were either bearded or newly shaven, he could not identify the man. Like white people's claim that all Chinese looked alike, these gweilo also looked alike to Guifeng. Whether their faces displayed defiance or indifference, malice or curious naivete, they looked like they could be either decent everyday folks who wouldn't do harm unless provoked or coldblooded, remorseless murderers.

"It's him." Guifeng pointed at Jack Reed, whose cold eyes lingered on his empty pant leg. Guifeng did not wear the artificial limb Feiyan had bought him, so that he wouldn't have to take it off to show what they'd done to him. It had to be this man, because the coroner had testified that Ah Ling's wound matched the wire shot loaded in Jack Reed's rifle.

"Are you sure?" McGlashan asked.

"I think so."

The white people who filled most of the courtroom booed.

"You think so? As you said earlier, the fire and shooting took place after midnight. It was deep in the woods. There were no light sources except for the fire. How could you see any of the perpetrators unless they stood right by the fire? But you said they hid behind shrubs away from the cabin. Were the shrubs on fire too?"

"I saw his face in the firelight. The wind carried sparks to where they stood—"

"How could a spark or two light up an entire face in the dark? The truth is you did not see any faces that night. You certainly did not see the faces of these seven men standing here. You must not incriminate an innocent man just because some other men have committed abhorrent crimes."

Then one by one, fifty white men were called to the stand. Each swore on the Bible that one of the seven men was with them playing cards or visiting a brothel or drinking at a saloon during those specific deep-night hours on that Saturday night. Fifty of them conjured up fifty alibis for the seven men: some looked at the ones they were defending with fraternal affection in their eyes; some laughed out loud as they spoke their alibi. The courthouse turned increasingly festive. The white audience clapped their hands and cheered as each alibi was produced. The all-white jury did not hide their glee either. One shouted out loud: "I can hang a Chinaman for killing a white man but can't hang a white man for killing a Chinaman!"

As each defendant was pronounced not guilty, a cannon was fired outside, shaking the courtroom's paneled walls and polished floor.

AMID BOOS AND slurs, Guifeng limped out of the court on his crutches. He was now quite sure it was Jack Reed—the man he'd pointed at— who had shot Ah Ling and then leveled his rifle at him. The man's cold eyes and stony jaw matched those that had flashed in Guifeng's dreams. Was it his fault to have hesitated and spoken without conviction?

As he was climbing back onto the wagon, a voice came from behind him: "What a show!"

He turned and saw Chang'er astride on a horse, looking down at him. "I hope you're not surprised by how they do justice here. But wait till it's our turn. I'll catch up with you soon," he said and rode away.

Guifeng and his former campmates did not talk much as the wagon took them down the dusty road to the train station. The one who'd gotten shot in the arm said he was going back to China: "I've had enough of this shit." There were agreements, sighs, and swears. But for the most part, they were quiet.

Now that Guifeng knew the seven men's faces, he would not fail to recognize them again in the future. But what was the use of remembering these men who had just been freed? He wished he could talk to Chang'er, who had ridden far ahead of their wagon and was now a black dot in the distance, like a bullet aiming at an invisible target. Guifeng wanted badly to hear Chang'er talk about their "turn" of justice. He would cling to every word Chang'er had to say about rage and revenge.

When the train took them back to Truckee, a bloody sun was setting fast behind the mountain peaks. Guifeng's former campmates were heading toward the opium den. "My treat." Li Shu patted Guifeng's shoulder. "What's better to do now than get lost in the clouds?"

It would be good to not care or know that you had lost yet again. To not judge yourself or distinguish dignity from shame. In the stupor of opium, it was all the same. All were made of straw—white or yellow, one-legged or two, those who got away with inflicting pain or those who continued to suffer. He could almost see the world through heaven and earth's eyes and see that wuwei was not all that different from what he was doing now—lying down on the cot, inhaling the vapor into his lungs, and then, doing nothing at all—and Dao was not all that different from this calm already spreading in his remaining limbs. What would Daoshi say about this? Probably that this calm would not last, that once the stupor was gone, Guifeng would be in a sorrier shape. But who and what could make Dao last? Even that strike, thoroughly planned, widely participated in, at the cost of so much gusto, so much hope and pride, ended up a failure. Now, his month-long preparation for the trial, his impassioned study of English, his foolish optimism, was nothing but a failure again.

But as he floated down into the easeful numbness, Daoshi's words became more comforting. "In the end, it will all even out," he was saying. All that would remain in the end was this free emptiness Guifeng was entering now.

WHEN FEIYAN CAME to the den and shook him awake, she didn't scold or advise. She just told him it was time to go home. He followed her down the night street. He wanted to talk to her about wuwei, about how he finally understood why so many of their countrymen indulged in this habit, not hesitating to spend all their labor's worth on it. But Feiyan was not Daoshi who could elevate everything into a philosophical inquiry. Feiyan was the breadwinner of their household for the last three months. She was his woman who held him in her arms when he whimpered like a child in his nightmares, who touched his body to show her love. But he had not been able to touch or love her back. He could already feel the disdain that she hadn't yet shown. He felt it when he overheard her chitchat with her customers in the diner and pictured the way her eyes rippled like sunlit water. Guifeng felt it as her life continued to flourish while his own life shrank away.

The next day, he took a dollar from their money jar tucked in their bedroom's chest of drawers. As he limped down the stairs into the diner, he saw her talking to a young, able-bodied man. "I'll be back" was all Guifeng said, and he knew she knew where he was going.

Feiyan

WORD HAD COME. SHE LEFT DUOFU WITH HER NEIGHBOR AND RAN to Joseph Gray's big brick house. Cool morning, so much sky. She wanted to scoop up some of the blue and gulp it down until she felt nothing but the empty air. She should be thankful that he was still alive, that he was not Ah Ling lying on the cot next to him, inches away from death. Guifeng tried to form a little smile, to let her know that it wasn't too bad, that losing a leg wasn't the worst thing that could happen to a man. The white doctor said it had to be done, Guifeng told her, or the infection would spread. But who could trust the words of a white doctor who was also a Caucasian League member, who, for all she knew, could be finishing off the shooters' work—by taking not Guifeng's life but his leg and livelihood, to kill him slowly?

For what could Guifeng do with one leg? He wouldn't be able to chop wood or herd the flume. When jobs were rare and newcomers were plenty, no one would hire a one-legged man. The houseboy translated the boss's words: "We'll find the criminals and put them on trial. We'll make sure they get hanged." A good gweilo, Guifeng had said about Gray, who was known for paying his Chinese workers the same as his white workers. But he wouldn't take Guifeng back. His goodness had its limits.

Now it was all on her. She had to get up well before sunrise to start working and not stop until well after sundown. She was tired, and his tossing and groaning at night made it hard for her to get her needed rest. Meanwhile, she also knew that their lives could end anytime—whether it was after the next Caucasian League meeting or the white men's next impulse to burn and kill. She had to learn to live in the present. They still had this new house that they'd built after the last fire. They still had each other. She was still able to work and feed the family. They were all alive and all was livable, except that Guifeng was in pain. She bought opium for him so that he didn't have to bear it on his own. Darkly, she thought there might not even be enough time for him to get addicted before the next fire and next gunshot.

She found him in the opium den after the trial. It had been hours since she'd heard the verdict from her customers. She closed the diner early, left Duofu with her neighbor, and found him where she feared he would be.

She could have said, "Don't do this. You'll ruin the whole family," but did not. She knew his pain. Pain after pain was what he had to bear. If he needed to forget the pain and this was the only way, how could she not let him?

So she let him. She didn't blame him. It was his way of living in the present. But what was hers?

In one of the few brick buildings in Chinatown, the loan shark Luo Laoda put down his account book on his metal counter. "I would give you an extension if I could, but what about my loss? It's a hard time for everyone, not just you." He walked from behind the counter to stand an inch away from Feiyan and lifted her chin. "Unless—"

She got an extension from him, and the next day, to mute the feeling of disgust, she took a young man who frequented her diner. She flipped the sign to Closed and locked the door from the inside. She led him to the small storage room by the kitchen. She didn't say a word, concentrating on her body's pleasure. She felt cleansed afterward, her body recovering its worth and assurance.

The next day, she did it again with the young man, and when he didn't show up the day after, she did it with another man. And then another. They brought gifts. "Just money," she told them. "That's what I need." She would be her own madam. This was a place where there was little time to live, many chances to die, and she had to adapt to survive. One moment she was trapped in a brothel, and the next she walked free in men's clothes. One moment she saved enough to buy a house, the next, it was burned down to ashes. One moment she had a man who couldn't get enough of her body, the next, he lost a leg and the courage to touch her.

Many men wanted her, and she wanted the sensation of running, of being fully there in her body, open and faultless. She wanted to be easeful, to be indifferent to all but her own sense of ease, and to do that, she must be so focused on the present she could merge into its coming and going. The act of lovemaking, done quickly and breathlessly, gave her a semblance of that.

She wouldn't call any of the men lovers. They were her customers. She served them food and received payment to make more food. She served them sex and received both payment and pleasure. She hid away the money jar but would leave a dollar in the chest of drawers for Guifeng to obtain his own dose of pleasure, so that they could both live in the present. But she knew that he would soon need more money to maintain his sense of ease, while she had no interest in having more sex than she was having. Already, the sensation was neither new nor free.

Duofu looked at her strangely. Her fast-growing daughter seemed to know everything, her eyes not skipping any surface but digging deep beneath and making you meet her there. She sniffed like a dog in the storage room every night after Feiyan picked her up from her babysitter. "Mama, this room smells bad. I don't like it." Should Feiyan start using lemon again, to cover it up?

Then her babysitter, the wife living next door with two children of her own, pulled Feiyan to a corner of her cramped room when she came to pick up Duofu. "I can't watch your girl anymore if you keep doing this," she said with pursed lips.

"Doing what?"

"You know what." She looked away, as if embarrassed for Feiyan.

"What do you expect me to do to feed everyone, to pay off our loan, to pay for my man to go to the den?"

The wife shook her head and sighed.

Then one day, a customer wanted more for his dollar. He called Feiyan a whore, and she said, "So what? I'm a whore, and you're a limp dick."

She started to yell at Duofu. She had been strict with her before, but now there was real meanness in her voice. She started to yell at Guifeng too when he came back at random hours to get money for his next dose of opium. She stopped leaving a dollar in the drawer.

"Please," he would say, "just this one last time. I'll feel better. I'll get a job."

She would end up giving him the dollar so that she could get back to work, or so she and Duofu could go back to sleep so she could get up the next morning to do the cooking, selling, serving, cleaning, all over again, all on her own and without joy. She was losing her present too. Not only had she no future to wish for, no past worth remembering, she was losing the only moment she had left to depend on.

THREE WEEKS AFTER the trial, Chang'er showed up at her diner. She had never liked the man. It certainly wasn't out of charity that he'd let them go seven years ago—but because he wanted to indebt Guifeng, to let him owe his life, and hers too, to him. Guifeng had told her about Ah Fook, and she knew Guifeng wanted to feel that indebtment. He needed it to lessen his survivor's guilt. Where did all those unnecessary feelings come from? If she allowed herself to be inundated with all those fine shades of feelings, she wouldn't be able to go on living. Now Chang'er stepped into her diner and sat down, his hard eyes as unforgiving as ever.

She served him two plates with each of the six dishes she'd spent the whole morning making. "On the house," she said.

"Where is Guifeng?" he asked when she came back to add tea. "Or does he still go by Ah Fook?"

"At the opium den," she said without emotion. "Are you looking for him?"

"Yes."

"What for?"

"Just a chat," he said.

She knew it must have something to do with the debt. She'd heard about his secret tong, his mission to kill white men. She would be all for it if she believed this kind of killing would free them. It was different from her kind of killing. She freed herself from being tied to the shabby bed in the rickety shed. She ran away. Where would she run now if she had to? Not back home, because no home was back there for her anymore. Nor to another part of the country, because it would be all the same. The whole country, large as it was, was trying to get rid of them. What was the use of killing white men? It would only bring the white men's hatred to another boil and get more Chinese killed.

"He's lost a leg. He is an opium-eater. He can't do what you want him to do." She allowed pleading into her eyes. "And we have a child."

"We all have or had a child." Chang'er got up and left.

Guifeng

HE DIDN'T STIR WHEN HE HALF OPENED HIS EYES AND SAW
Chang'er's face above him. This composure was something he didn't
use to have. This non-distinction: it made no difference to him whether
the face belonged to Chang'er, or his creditor, or another regular, or
a total stranger, or even Feiyan who had not come to take him home
for a while now. She had stopped yelling at him too, replacing anger
with silence to show she'd given up on him, which, in turn, only made
him care less. He had no need to say anything or act in any way, even
in front of Chang'er and all the things this man stood for. Such as the
untimely death of Ah Fook, the extraordinary escape Guifeng had
somehow managed to achieve with Feiyan, the extravagant passion
he'd once felt entitled to, and last but not least, the debt he owed him.
Chang'er sat down by his missing leg on the cot. "What do you think
Daoshi would say, seeing you here?"

"Daoshi will say," Guifeng said, smiling, suddenly overcome by
nostalgia, "good, I see you're practicing wuwei here."

Chang'er burst into a hard laugh while slapping his knee, a gesture
Guifeng remembered from their early Sierra days. Days when he could
still call Chang'er uncle and death had not yet stalked them so closely.

"That must be it." Chang'er stopped laughing just as abruptly.
"And we all know what practicing wuwei leads us to. So, I say, you
need to get up and do something."

"There's nothing to do."

"Yes, there is. You owe me a debt. Now it's time to pay."

"You can see I have nothing. Unless you want my other leg." Guifeng elbowed up to take another pull from the pipe.

"Who wants your damn leg." Chang'er snatched the pipe out of his
hand: there was only so much humor he was willing to spare. His eyes

swept across the den, which was not yet busy at this early afternoon hour. "Listen up." He lowered his voice. "I need you to kill one of the gweilo who killed your buddy and wounded you and the other two. Kill one of them, then your debt is clear. Understood? Kill not for me, but for yourself. Take your pride back. Don't be a dope-fiend lying here smoking away your woman's hard-earned money."

Guifeng knew it was coming. Sometimes in his half stupor, he'd even dreamed of doing it—pointing the rifle that hadn't yet melted in the fire at the white men who'd sat in the courtroom looking at him with disdain. Sometimes when he woke up, he thought the act had already been done—bullets already discharged and lodged into those murderers' bodies—only to see his empty pant leg on the cot. "How do you expect me to do it? I can hardly walk."

"All you need is a gun. I asked you to get a rifle. Did you listen? Had you had one with you, you could've killed one or two of them in the woods."

"I did have one . . . but who'd have thought they'd kill a white boss's workers?"

"You stupid ass, you thought working for a white boss was protection? All those deaths on the Sierra clearly didn't teach you a thing, so you had to learn it the hard way, by losing a leg. Look at yourself!" Chang'er looked at Guifeng hard, with disdain as well. "But I'm not here to teach you how to be a man. You pay your debt, kill one of them. That's all."

Was Guifeng capable of killing? Not just in dreams or thoughts, but in reality? He wasn't sure. Compared to killing, smoking opium was more doable. It was easier to let it all go, to not distinguish criminals from victims, cowardice from manhood. But now, it was not up to him to choose. He had a debt to pay. "How do I find them?"

"You were in the court. You saw their faces." Chang'er took out a piece of paper from his jacket pocket and unfolded it: on it were the names of the seven men and their whereabouts. Jack Reed had become the new constable, which Guifeng had heard. The bullet removed from Ah Ling's body matched his rifle, but apparently the town decided that a Chinaman-killer was more fit to be the law-enforcer than the previous constable, Jack Cross, who'd caught the seven men. "He's known as the fastest shooter around here. You probably don't want to mess with him." Chang'er pointed at the next name, William O'Neill. "This guy frequents the Buffalo Saloon, a drunk and easy target." He looked at Guifeng, cutting into his eyes. "It will do you good. You'll never get back on your feet if you keep smoking your life away like this."

Chang'er had never forgiven him, Guifeng could tell, and never would—not until Guifeng killed a white man as he was instructed to. Not until then would his guilt of not dying in Ah Fook's place in the nitro misfire be exonerated. Not only was Ah Fook's death on him, but Ah Ling's too. In fact, all the deaths caused by white men were on him if he failed to kill a white man. Why did Chang'er do this to him? Dumping so many deaths onto him without the slightest pity? But did Guifeng still expect pity from others? Wasn't it pitiful to still indulge such an expectation?

"Can I have my pipe back?"

"You must take a chance." Chang'er held the pipe out of his reach. "The Chinaman's chance. Gweilo think the Chinaman's chance means no chance. But we must think the Chinaman's chance is our chance to take."

"My pipe, please." Guifeng reached forward.

"Say you will take the Chinaman's chance first."

"I will take the Chinaman's chance," Guifeng repeated after him. Maybe he did still expect pity from others. Maybe he didn't care whether he was pitiful or not as long as he could get his pipe back and go where action or nonaction made no difference, nor revenge or letting-be. Earlier today, he'd begged Feiyan for a dollar so that he could reach that place. Now he needed Chang'er to give his pipe back, so that he could once again reach where their contempt did not matter. Where nothing mattered. Where a straw dog did not even know that he was a straw dog, and he would not strive, nor contrive a plan to kill a white man and settle an old debt—no, not with one leg and a body hungry for one thing only.

Chang'er shook his head as he stood up. His eyes once again swept across the den, which was filling up more. A few men were propped up on elbows inhaling; a few lay close-eyed against a wall. They were Guifeng's mirrors, but Guifeng would not look at them and see himself there. His pitiable, despicable, and maimed body was not the real him; the real him was curling up somewhere inside, peaceful like a baby.

"This is why they call China the Sick Man of Asia. They got us drugged there and now they're getting us drugged here." Chang'er dropped the pipe on the greasy pillow, where Guifeng would soon rest his head and forget.

Feiyan

SOMETIMES WHEN HE CAME BACK FOR MONEY, SHE WANTED TO SLAP him. Sometimes she wanted to take him in her arms, holding him till he put down all his pains, faced up, and stayed here with her. Then, together, maybe they could make the present tolerable again.

"Did Chang'er find you?" She tried to keep her voice low. Duofu was sleeping in the big bed with her, had been since Guifeng started spending the nights in the den.

"Yes, he found me." He headed directly to the chest of drawers.

"And?"

"Nothing, just catching up." He lied like a child. His back hunched as if he wanted to shrink back into being a child as well—as if that would make him blameless and make her leave him be.

"Whom did he ask you to kill?" She knew he couldn't do it. If it had to be done, she wouldn't mind doing it for him. She'd done it already, after all. It would just be one more life on her, one more possible ghost to be haunted by. But Guifeng, no, he couldn't do it. It wasn't in him to kill. He was too soft. She'd known that since they were children. Once when the kids in the village set a rat on fire, he'd quietly stepped away, while the rest of the kids, including herself, watched the little thing carry the flame on its back and listened to its horrible shrieks. She'd caught his eyes when he turned away and the pain in his eyes made her feel the rat's pain as it burned. But she did not turn away.

She wouldn't mind killing the white man who'd put a bullet in his leg and broke apart their family. She would do it if she was only living for herself and no one else. But here was Duofu sleeping by her side, her three-year-old sleeping face as sweet as when she was a newborn baby. "Answer me." Feiyan got off the bed.

He stood bent, rummaging in the drawers. She had not left any money there for a couple weeks now, but he continued to go there first to avoid asking her directly.

"What do you mean?" He continued to avoid looking at her.

"I know all kinds of things. People talk, you know. They don't just eat. They talk."

"No, they certainly don't just eat." He turned his eyes to her now, eyes full of barbs. Then, as if deciding it wasn't worth it, he lowered his eyes and went back to the rummaging. "He just asked how I was doing."

"Revenge, that's what it's all about. Why can't he do it himself? He has two legs and no family."

"Don't think too much of it. It's men's business."

"Men's business? Isn't it men's business to support their families instead of ruining them? Who are *you*, talking to me about men's business?"

Duofu woke up. "Mama," she said from the bed, her eyes begging and accusing all at once. Her daughter, her conscience, born out of her body, was telling her to stop yelling. To believe that there had to be a future somehow where the child didn't have to look at her father with wariness and her mother with disappointment.

Guifeng was now tossing the whole contents of the drawers onto the floor, one by one, and when he was done with the last, he leaned against the dresser top and covered his face with his hands.

Feiyan stepped back to the bed, reached under the mattress beneath her pillow and retrieved a dollar from a small bundle. She handed it to Guifeng. "Money doesn't drop from the sky."

"I know that." He took it without looking at her and headed to the door.

"Look at me." She followed him.

He didn't turn his head.

"I asked you to look at me." She walked up to him and took hold of his face with both her hands, forcefully, to turn it toward her. She had failed to believe in tomorrow, the way he had failed, but there had to be one in the family who still believed in it. Or the family would just crumble like a burned house, and there would be nothing left but ash.

"Stop it, woman!" He threw her hands off his face and limped out of the room, dragging the fake leg she'd bought for him.

Guifeng

HE DIDN'T WANT TO GO HOME—IF HE COULD STILL CALL IT A home—because he didn't want to catch a man in her bed, which was once their bed, a man providing the cash for his next dose of opium. Guifeng could think of it all as wuwei on his end: he didn't need to do anything; let them do the doings. Let Feiyan enjoy the sex and get the money for him so that he would be out of her way, and she could be guiltless. What a solution. Was it perhaps even an act in accordance with Dao? Everyone got what they wanted. Except that everyone wanted more and more as they headed faster and faster toward hell.

How to kill? He no longer had the rifle. The other gun they had, which they'd bought after they rebuilt the house, was a revolver that Feiyan kept close to her at the diner. He had no money to buy a gun. He had no desire to kill anyone either, the white murderers included. He didn't even want to feel the hate he felt. He'd rather not feel anything.

But Chang'er came the next day, and the day after, which felt almost like love. Because despite his anger and disdain, Chang'er was the one who took the effort to shame him—not Feiyan, who gave him money and let him be. The fourth time Chang'er came to find him in the den, he poured a glass of cold water onto Guifeng's face. "Wake up," Chang'er shouted at him. "You idiot. If you can't be a man, why don't you at least kill yourself?"

Guifeng wiped his face with his sleeve, realizing he was wrong: no, Chang'er did not love him, not a bit. In his eyes, Guifeng was nothing but a coward, whose life had no worth unless he managed to kill a white man. The only way for him to redeem himself was that action, and that alone. "I need a gun," he said. "Get me a gun, I'll kill and disappear. Haven't you always wished it was me who had died instead of Ah Fook, or at least that I'd died with him? I'll do it for you, so you don't have to wish it anymore."

Chang'er looked at him long and hard. "You stupid donkey," he spat finally and shook his head, but there was no denial in his eyes. "Okay, if you say so. I'll get you a gun."

THE FOLLOWING NIGHT, Guifeng walked out of Chinatown to Front Street where the Buffalo Saloon was located, the hangout spot for William O'Neill, the second man on Chang'er's to-kill list. That afternoon Chang'er had given Guifeng a gun and an earful of righteousness: "You think your father died of natural causes. No, he was killed by gweilo for sure. Those kinds of undocumented deaths were all caused by them. You were spared for a larger purpose, which was not this wuwei nonsense to smoke your family's livelihood away, but to avenge yourself, your father, your countrymen. To make your life mean something."

Chang'er made it sound as if he was doing Guifeng a favor. He had let him live seven years before just so that Guifeng could learn his lesson. And now he entrusted Guifeng with this killing so that he could fulfill "a larger purpose." It could indeed be a goal in Guifeng's goalless life. He would kill a white man for Ah Ling's life, Ah Fook's life, for his own leg and livelihood. Let one white man pay for it all. It could be as simple as that. He himself would be dead for sure after the killing, but he was already half dead anyway. In so many people's eyes, he was already nothing—useful to nobody, not to his family here and certainly not to his family back in China. Maybe they would finally forgive him when he was really dead, relieved of all his unfulfilled responsibilities. Maybe to kill and die was his only chance.

Guifeng's artificial leg drag-clicked with each step he made in the dark, foggy street half lit by oil lamps. At the door of the saloon with a buffalo skull nailed to the lintel, he glanced inside: all white men, all looking alike.

"Hey, aren't you the one-legged chink who tried to get us hanged?"

A sudden hand landed on his shoulder. Guifeng turned and saw a big white man in a scruffy suit too small for his frame. He had been one of the seven men at the court's defense table. He'd stood out to Guifeng as he was the biggest among them but also appeared to be the least menacing. There was something innocuous, almost dully friendly, about his face. Now he regarded Guifeng with a childlike curiosity, his hand on Guifeng's shoulder big like a loaf of bread but heavy as a rock. "What are you doing here?"

"I'm . . . just taking a walk." Guifeng moved away from his hand.

"In our place? Careful you don't lose the other leg too." The man giggled.

Maybe Guifeng could pull the gun out of his pocket and aim it at the man's chest. Then, he would pull the trigger and get it done with. But he felt faint. His phantom leg ached, and his good leg trembled with dread. He dragged himself back to Chinatown. In the lantern-lit velvet dark, he limped to the house that he could no longer call home, and looked up at the one lamp burning in the upstairs window.

THE IDEA CAME to him after he inhaled his first lungful of opium fumes later that night. He thought of explosives that had blasted rocks a hundred times harder than bones—and that were responsible for the deaths of hundreds of Chinese railroad men. Including Ah Fook, whose name Guifeng had used even at the trial and whose destiny he had inherited. Guifeng could imagine what Chang'er would say: "How many of our folks were killed by those misfires? How can they ever rest in peace with their enemies left unpunished? The gweilo are all the same: the rich who fatten their wallets and build their mansions on our lives, the poor who have nothing to their names but blame us for taking away their livelihood, those idiots and their politicians who despise them but tell them they're voicing their voices—all of them want us dead and all deserve to die."

Guifeng could see the seven men in the courthouse, cold-blooded killers who enjoyed the sight of Chinese men burning and bleeding to death, and their pretend witnesses, their lawyer and jury, their audience who cheered for their crimes. They were all the same. All wanted to see the Chinese burn and die.

It wouldn't be easy to get hold of nitro. But Chang'er could surely secure some black powder before Saturday night when the Caucasian League met again. Guifeng would carry that load on him to avenge all, to kill all of them at once.

Before slipping into dimness, he saw Ah Fook's wide eyes like two deep wells. Had he gazed into them long enough before closing them with his hand, Guifeng would have perhaps seen his own destiny. If only he could believe he was doing this for his loved ones: a final action, and then it would be nonaction for good.

IN HIS HOTEL room, Chang'er asked Guifeng to take off his jacket. As carefully as he'd handled the nitro in the Sierra tunnel, he fastened around Guifeng's waist a fat, heavy cotton belt sewn with pouches of black powder, all of them connected to a fuse. "Remember we Chinese invented black powder," Chang'er was saying. "But we got too busy making fireworks instead of guns and cannons. That was why we lost the Opium Wars and got kicked around by gweilo."

When two days earlier, Guifeng had found him in the gambling house to tell him his plan, Chang'er response was just as he'd expected. "A genius idea!" He'd slapped his knee. "You finally got it right this time. It's not just about the seven men. They are only the gunmen for the Caucasian League. All of them want to kill us. So, do it. Kill as many as you can."

In an hour, Guifeng would light the fuse and run into the rallying crowd in front of the town hall where the Caucasian League gathered every Saturday night. He would do so as fast as his good and fake legs could carry him. His bits of bones would become bits of shrapnel. His bits of flesh would be stuck to the Chinese-haters' bits of flesh. Skin colors would matter no more; all would become indistinguishable pieces of nothing that heaven and earth didn't give a damn about.

Nobody would need to mourn him. There would be no funeral, nor anything to bury. He would die in hate, turn himself into the loudest, most explosive firecracker. What a celebration! What a manly thing to do and a manly way to die. Would Feiyan finally be proud of him? Would he forgive her? Yes, he would. There wouldn't be a thing for him to feel.

A last blast, making tunnels in human flesh. He wouldn't be a straw dog cast away, trampled upon, or burned for its final disposal. He would throw himself into the pit and light the fire himself.

HE AND CHANG'ER snuck into the night. With each stumbling step, Guifeng felt the homemade bomb jabbing his ribcage. The stars in the sky were as cold as those above the Sierra. Guifeng wanted to go up the mountains one more time, just to lie down on the hard granite and look at the stars with nothing between his eyes and the pinpoint brilliance.

He wished Daoshi were here—to tell him, them, that this was headstrong striving. It was against Dao. Surely, this killing couldn't be natural. How could this blasting of human bodies be the natural course of things? The natural course is to live and let live, not to die and end lives.

"Are you sure you want to do this?" Chang'er asked all of a sudden. His eyes revealed a hint of pity.

But pity was not what Guifeng wanted anymore. "Yes," he said.

They kept walking, now in the white part of the town. White men were stepping into bars and saloons. They were really not all that different: Chinese drunks or white drunks, Chinese gamblers or white gamblers. All drank to hide away from their lives or gambled to simulate life's capriciousness.

Guifeng could hear the rally gathered in front of the town hall and the usual tirade carried in the wind: ". . . parasites . . . rat-eaters . . . dirty heathens . . . must go . . ."

Anger had more dignity, more yang. Chang'er was right. Wuwei was a ludicrous idea when you were the target of hate.

Chang're led him to a clump of evergreen bushes on the edge of the square. He unsheathed a dagger from his belt. "Take this just in case." A parting gift? He'd taken back the gun Guifeng had failed to use in his last attempt to kill.

Guifeng took the dagger. "You will protect my family?"

"Yes, you have my word." Chang'er looked into Guifeng's eyes as if waiting for him to say more.

But Guifeng did not. Soon, he would be dead. All would die sooner or later, and there was nothing he could do about it.

HE HID BEHIND the bushes, waiting for the crowd to gather. Waist rounded by dynamite, he was the bomb itself. All he had to do was light the fuse and plant himself in the crowd. Powerful. Even if he had failed throughout his life, he would be powerful in this final moment. Even if he had not fulfilled his duties to his families, he would at least serve a larger purpose for his countrymen. He had chosen defeat for too long; now he chose anger. He was tired of being a maimed man. He would feel one last burst of pain and then it would be over.

A man paced over and stopped two feet from the bush behind which Guifeng was crouching. The man unbuttoned his fly and started to pee. He was humming a tune, one that Guifeng had heard before. In the woods as blood had poured out of the bullet hole in his leg, as he bit down on his lip to stop himself from groaning, one of the killers had been peeing and humming a tune that sounded like a lullaby. Since that moment, Guifeng had been losing himself, first one leg, then half of his brain, then his heart, his family, and soon, any moment now, whatever little was left. The tune, the pee, the ammonia smell permeating the dark air. Holding the dagger Chang'er had gifted him, Guifeng lunged forth from behind the bush at the peeing man. Stabbing and covering the man's mouth to muffle the scream, Guifeng acted so fast and fluidly it felt as if he had been trained, or fated, to do so. As the man collapsed, Guifeng pulled his body behind the bush. He knelt down, dazed by the man's face: even in the dark, he could tell it wasn't one of the seven men in the courtroom.

The rally was swelling. The new speaker was yelling about the "tumor of California," the "disease of the country." The crowd echoed with the familiar shouts of "The Chinese must go!"—their weekly dose of hate, as if by injecting it they would love themselves more. They went on and on, and Guifeng continued to look at the face of the man he had just rendered lifeless. No life would be lived by this man anymore. He wouldn't pace back into the crowd, join in the hate, or act upon it. He wouldn't burn or kill. He would only keep humming that lullaby until he was reborn as a peeing baby in his mother's arms.

Guifeng had killed the wrong person, a man who was once a baby. The humming continued to echo in Guifeng's head, as he looked at the dead man with his fly open, his penis flopping to one side. A giant child whose life Guifeng had just ended. If only this man had deserved to die. If only this were justice.

The black powder heavy in the explosive belt around his waist, the fuse idle, his phantom leg throbbing, his good leg numb, Guifeng knew he couldn't act any further. He could no longer turn his body into a bomb to explode and kill. His body that had been given by his mother whose blood ran through it and that had given life to two daughters. This body wanted to live and let live, not die and end lives.

9

Reunion

1876–1882

Feiyan

HE CAME HOME SMELLING OF BLOOD AND BLACK POWDER. CAME
home not just his lost self but with a dead soul clinging to his chest. He
talked about the debt, the killing, and got on his knees, begging her to
help him: "Tie me to the bed, lock the room. I want to quit."

She did what he asked. She put him in the small room upstairs,
locked the door from the outside, brought water and food, cleaned his
mess, endured his cursing. For a whole week she did this, all while still
running the diner downstairs, cutting down the dishes by half, which
was all she could manage, and leaving Duofu with the babysitter till
bedtime. She sat by his bed as he tossed and sweated cold sweat, and
told him he would feel better soon.

Once Guifeng recovered, once he returned to her, Feiyan tried to
imagine their future, but there was a white man's ghost lodged between
them. She burned incense at the Guanyu altar downstairs: "We're
starting new. We don't need a ghost here. Please make it leave." But
Guifeng was absent and slow when he tried to help her in the kitchen,
his hands moving as if against a hefty weight. She had to yell, "I need

that cabbage chopped now." "That soup is boiling. Can't you hear?"
She knew that he wanted the opium back, wanted it more than he
wanted her, more than he wanted their daughter. This craving was
the dead soul's grievance and revenge: it was muttering into Guifeng's
head, "Want, want. Go get it. Go get it. There's no future. Don't dream
of a future that's not yours. All that you build will burn down. All that
you gather will fall apart."

But Feiyan wouldn't allow those mutterings into her own head too.
She had a child who was growing and must continue to grow. She had
to think of the future even if only the next minute, the next hour. Even
if the present was constantly crumbling, she must believe in the future.
Even when she was tied to a donkey by her father and brother and then
to a bed by the drunken man, she had believed that. Had she not, she
wouldn't have killed the old man. She did not regret it, even though she
often wished it hadn't been necessary. But she did what she had to do
to go on living.

Now Guifeng had killed too, and he too wanted to go on living.
But the ghost wouldn't let him. At night, the house held its breath. It
seemed to be waiting for the next fire to consume it, each beam bracing
for the next burning, the next collapsing into ashes.

She took him in her arms to snatch him away from the ghost's hold.
She didn't know how long it would last. This reunion.

Daoshi

1877

Chang'er had told him where to find Guifeng—at Duofu Diner, named after their new daughter and run by his new wife. "Either there or the den." Chang'er had told him about the shooting, the amputation, the trial, the opium. Daoshi came to the diner first, which was easy to find, a popular hangout with tables spilling out. He had just finished his official business, delivering two dozen Henry rifles hidden in crates of rice to Fong Lee, leader and the richest man of Truckee Chinatown, who was recruiting vigilantes to do rounds in the community. White gun sellers all across California had been boycotting the Chinese for years now, but the Six Companies managed to bypass the boycott by hiring white men to do the buying.

Inside the diner, Feiyan couldn't be missed—the one woman in a lychee-colored blouse among the horde of plain-clothed men. She stood behind the counter where dishes were kept warm on stoves. Daoshi had only seen her once before, dressed in men's clothes, hat brim pulled low to cover her forehead. She was still straight and lean, but now wore her womanhood out loud. She seemed to be presiding over the men temporarily released from their day of labor, the one woman sure and confident among all the lonely bachelors. She was looking at him. He walked over to the counter, greeted her, and asked for Guifeng.

"He hasn't been here for months." She looked unsurprised by his inquiry. "Was clean for two weeks and went right back to it."

She made a plate for him and seated him at a table with a quarter unoccupied space. When the other three diners at the table were done and left, she came over with a cup and a jar of rice wine. She poured it and put the cup in front of him. "Guifeng told me you're a daoshi, a

real one. Exorcise him. He's possessed. I'm sure you'll see that when
you find him."

THE BASEMENT DEN was owned by Fong Lee, who controlled most
of the vice trades in Truckee Chinatown. It was windowless, airless,
and skyless. If one didn't see the sky for a while, it would probably
just disappear from one's head. Daoshi had to search around the den
for Guifeng, as all the men looked similar, all resembled Daoshi's own
father—the way they reclined in their cots, smoking with eyes closed;
the way they slumbered like children in the bodies of old men.

He found Guifeng only because a prosthetic leg caught his eye.
It lay on a cot by an empty pant leg. He walked over and checked the
man's face. Briefly he saw a flash of the young man who used to be so
bright-eyed and nimble-limbed, whom Daoshi had liked the way he
liked his own younger self with the due tenderness obtained over time.

This older Guifeng did seem possessed. There was a moldy green
energy about his sunken, blistered face, and his shrunken body in his
twisted clothes that were desperately in need of a wash. Even in stupor,
he looked haunted and ill.

When Daoshi was still Fuyao, besides funeral rituals, he had
watched his father perform exorcisms on sick people who were supposedly possessed by malignant spirits. He'd pressed his father to tell him
if he'd seen those spirits, actually seen them. And his father's default
answer was this: it didn't matter; what mattered was the ritual itself,
and the belief in it. It was not about whether this pair of eyes saw it
or not; it was this eye, he pointed at the center of his forehead. And it
didn't matter what the evil spirits looked like. What mattered was that
Fuyao memorize the verses and incantations and practice the steps and
dances to lead the spirit away, either by force or trickery, to the clear
sky realm where they could finally rest and leave the living in peace.

But despite the verses and dances, many of those his father had
exorcised continued to ail, and some even died. Including Fuyao's

mother. Then his father lost himself in opium, possessed by his own de-mon, which no one could exorcise from him. As far as Fuyao knew, nei-ther his uncle nor his elder brother even tried. Instead, they sustained his father's addiction by busying themselves making others believe that their rituals still worked.

Daoshi considered leaving, walking away before Guifeng woke up only to sleep again—the way he had left his father behind twenty-two years ago. Now was then again. But there was one thing he had to do. He leaned over and gave Guifeng's shoulder a pat.

Guifeng opened his eyes and looked at him without surprise, as if he'd been expecting to see him. "I was just talking to you," he said, rubbing his eyes. "You were telling me about straw dogs, and I was thinking, so be it, I'm made of straw, and this smoke helps me burn. I was telling you that this slow fire was at least set by myself." He el-bowed himself up, smiling deliriously.

Earlier that morning, on his train ride across the Sierra, Daoshi had thought about his railroad days, how sometimes he'd felt so close to the sky he seemed to be able to see the orbiting of Dao as clear as the coursing of the sun and moon, and how sometimes when he sat still, he could almost feel Dao flow through his own body. He had not felt like a straw dog in those moments.

He sat down on the cot. "Your daughter Sixiang is here, in Big City. She's been looking for you."

"What?" Guifeng let his smile hang like a dead leaf on his face.

"There was a famine in your village. She was sold here as a mui tsai. We met a few months ago and I told her I would help her find you."

Guifeng leaned back down on the cot. He turned to the wall, put-ting a forearm across his eyes.

Daoshi waited, and as he began to wonder if it was better to get up and leave, Guifeng said to the wall, "I have no daughter, no family. I have not even myself. You're talking to a straw dog that has no life of its own. The sacrifice is done." He kept his eyes shielded with his arm so that the rest of the world, including his daughter, could stay out of his sight.

Daoshi couldn't do what Feiyan had asked him to do. How could he isolate a person's miseries and turn them into clouds? No one could really do that. And no one would really be cured. Life had a tendency to stay tight and narrow, especially in this world where your life was not even seen as human life. The centuries-old incantations he had hardly committed to memory could dissolve no afflictions here. They were merely words, as hollow as straw.

Guifeng

HIS DAUGHTER WHO HAD INVADED HIS DREAMS WITH HER SUNKEN-eyed pleading: "Can Mama and I have some of your noodles?" The daughter he had stopped feeding years ago but whose hunger he continued to sense all too well. How could he be a father to her now?

What did Daoshi expect him to do? He, a cripple and opium-eater, useful to no one? Had he killed himself with the pouches of black powder, he would have already been in hell, tormented by many white ghosts instead of just one. What would Daoshi say about that? Daoshi had left him in the den without saying much, disappointed in him like everyone else.

What would Laozi say? If heaven and earth were indifferent to any of them, be they white or yellow, and if in the eyes of the universe, rocks and dust were all the same, wouldn't hell be no different from what was here and now, with flesh and bones still gathered together, no matter how temporarily?

He knew he was nearing the end of it all. The one thing that kept him alive was the desire for that feeling. The way the vapor filled his lungs and infused the rest of his body, first the torso, then the limbs, then the neck and head, so that he could become a hollow man. All emptiness, all calm and still, where nothing could damage him or shame him, where he had not been hunted down, nor made to kill, where the dead man's humming did not ring in his ears.

When he'd asked Feiyan to help him after he limped home that night, he had decided to come back to life from hell, to bring his body that had almost turned into a bomb back to her. As he tried to help her with the diner, young, capable men eyed her, flirting when they thought he wasn't within earshot, but he had decided to forgive her when he decided to live. He forgave her for what she had done as he asked for her forgiveness.

Then news came to the diner: a white man's body was found floating up the Truckee River, someone last seen over a week ago, stabbed in the back through the heart, some stranger passing through the town.

It must have been Chang'er who had taken the pains to return to the bushes, remove the body, and dump it into the river. That night, he had come on a horse to where Guifeng was hiding, after the Caucasian League ended their rally, their words of "Kick them out," "Set those shanties on fire" still reverberating in the air. Chang'er had looked at the body, and without saying anything about Guifeng's botched mission, pulled him up and helped him get on the horse. He kicked the dirt around to get rid of their footprints before getting on the horse himself. He took them to his hotel room. "I need the bomb belt back. It'll be useful in the future." Then as Guifeng turned to leave, Chang'er said, "You don't owe me anything now. Go live your life. Don't go back to the den."

A guiltless man who had happened to pass through the town on his way somewhere northwest, who had happened to stop by the rally and needed to pee, who might have had a family somewhere and been mailing money to them every month. Guifeng had killed him.

The night after the man's body was found, a young Chinese man, a teenage houseboy working for a white family, was lynched by a white mob in the white part of the town. The league members had decided that the white man must have been killed by a Chinese because he was last seen at the anti-Chinese rally, and that the first Chinese man they came across on the street must be responsible.

So it was not just one but two deaths on Guifeng. Their enraged souls clawed and gnawed at him, urging him to quit trying to pretend to be good. They nagged every inch of his body to go back to the den, to go back to being bad and real, despicable and hopeless—a punishment he couldn't help but embrace.

After he was left with the news about his daughter, Guifeng went back to talking to Daoshi in his head, asking what Daoshi expected him to do. *Famine, sold, mui tsai.* What else had happened to his daughter Sixiang, whose name Guifeng had chosen? But he didn't want to know more. He kept asking Daoshi to repeat the Laozi quote that heaven and earth saw no difference in anything. All were the same, and all would die in the end. Striving or not striving. Suffering or not suffering. And he kept asking Daoshi if what he was doing was doing nothing, nonaction, wuwei. In his head, Daoshi was more patient than he had been during his short visit, which, for all Guifeng knew, could have happened in his dream, and his daughter could still be in China, with her mother and grandmother, in Yunteng Village, surviving somehow. Was it a dream or not a dream? He couldn't quite tell.

HE WAS IN the den when the fire started. A new fire in the new year, but it was not all that different from the ones that came before. When he stumbled out of the den, he could see the same fire catching all things burnable in its insatiable mouth, the same hissing and melting, the same orange heat, black smoke, and unrelenting radiance. He could stand there on the street and watch it all burn, until the whole world was nothing but ash and ember. But something stung his heart. He stumbled toward the direction of home, if he could still call it that.

Feiyan and Duofu stood side by side, watching the charred beams crumble. Beside them were a few salvaged chairs, a couple of quilts and pillows. When Duofu saw him, she called out, "Baba," uncertainly, as if he was something rescued from the ruins. Feiyan did not look at him, refusing to—refusing to even say, *Where were you when our house was burning to the ground?* He wasn't even worth her anger.

This time, there was no rebuilding on the lot they still owned. The Caucasian League led a mob of five hundred men and women to Chinatown and tore down what the fire had not destroyed. Then they signed a petition to Nevada County, demanding the whole Chinatown be relocated to outside of Truckee's town limits across the river, so that the site "would soon be covered," as McGlashan put in the *Truckee Republican*, "by delightful residence, and possibly business houses, which would add greatly to the appearance of the town." Had Guifeng killed them all that night, would Chinatown have been spared? He had indeed taken the Chinaman's chance, which was no chance at all. Taking it or not, no chance. Killing or not, no difference.

When a town was burned, the den was always the first to resurrect. It took no time to transform from a shack patched together with salvaged boards back to its old furnished self. Even as Guifeng wished that all the opium within his reach were burned to vapor and dissolved into the air so that there was nothing for him to creep back to, it was already there. One thing you could count on. No matter how the whites bullied and sullied you, burned down and tore down your life, opium had the magic power to reemerge from the ruins and lead your nose to its luring knot.

He stayed away from his family as much as he could. Once or twice, he paused in front of the new house that Feiyan had once again rebuilt, with the help of her customers or lovers this time. Guifeng had played no part in its building, but he still felt the pull of just one dollar from there, for just one more dose. It was a good thing that he had no key to the house.

He tried to scrape by. For a few months, he had a job tending kilns, which did not require two working legs. But he couldn't show up on time, his need for opium striking at random hours. Sometimes he got an odd job for a couple of dimes, cleaning bathtubs or barber shops or privies. He scavenged food and slept in shacks or tents in shifts. Once, when he was scavenging in a trashcan outside a grocery store, Feiyan and Duofu stepped out. He turned away to hide his face.

When he was desperate, he sometimes asked Li Shu for a dollar or two. Li Shu no longer cooked for the logging camp. After the farcical trial, their old boss Joseph Gray decided to sell his company to another lumber boss and left town. The new boss was also a Caucasian League man and, out of principle, replaced all the Chinese workers with white men. Li Shu found a job cooking for a white boardinghouse. On his days off, he would sometimes invite Guifeng to go fishing with him in the river. They would chat about the old days on the Sierra: the summit, the tunnel, the storms, the cold. In retrospect, the cold had become tolerable, the pains bittersweet, because they had survived it all. Those were simpler days when Guifeng was still able to fulfill his duties and lived honestly.

"You need a purpose," Li Shu would say.

Guifeng would stay quiet until Li Shu said something else.

Sometimes, in the moments before he drifted off in the den, Guifeng would talk to Daoshi again. "I killed a man. I can still hear the tune he was humming when I stabbed him in the heart. A simple tune, a childlike tune. He was just peeing."

Daoshi would look at him in his understanding way.

"What would Laozi say about this?" So Guifeng would continue. "That we're all straw dogs? Killing and being killed make no difference in heaven and earth's eyes?"

"Indeed, what would Laozi say? He would probably say, 'Let it be. What's done is done.'"

"That's what I'm doing. I'm letting it be." With that, Guifeng would ease himself into the dimness where thoughts could no longer reach him.

Sixiang

1882

THE OAK TREE IN THE BACKYARD HAD SHED ALL ITS LEAVES ONCE again. Its squirrel nests, now bared and disheveled, looked like tangles of knots. If Ah Hong's spirit lived up there amid the old, crooked branches, her home was a meager, dreary one. Sixiang swept away the last leaves on the ground, each shriveled and brittle.

Miss Moore and Miss Webb had offered no words of consolation when the wagon took Sixiang back to the Mission Home. An aloof "welcome back" was all they'd given her. Sixiang could imagine what Mrs. Turner had told them, perhaps reiterating what they'd told her in the first place: "It's a most difficult work to tame barbarians."

Sixiang was no longer allowed the privilege of taking Chinese lessons or attending the extra Bible study reserved for missionary candidates only. Between the regular morning studies and the afternoon sewing, she was assigned cleaning chores around the Mission Home, and was made to do so alone, not paired with another girl as was often the case. The girls looked at her the way they had looked at Ah Hong once: quiet all of a sudden, or half covering their mouths to whisper among themselves. Sixiang had been one of them. She had not reached out to Ah Hong when she was all alone. Back then, Sixiang had wanted to be safe with the rest of the girls who could still be cleansed—and to be liked by Miss Moore and Miss Webb, who decided which among them could be saved, and which could not. When the daily question was asked, "What dirt will God clean from your heart today?" Sixiang was now the one being stared at, and the word "filth" with all its weight was what was now expected from her tongue.

"Cowardice," she said instead, day after day. "I hope God helps me clean it."

But if God meant to teach his believers a lesson with the torturous death of his son, what did he mean by Qinglong's death? That the killers could get away with it, and even blame Qinglong for his own death, because they were God's chosen people? That as long as they said so, a murder was a tragic story of a Christian family's sacrifice and a heathen ex-slave girl's corrupt presence?

Sixiang was guilty, not of what she was accused of, but of cowardice. She had run away from Qinglong when he most needed her. She had left him to suffer and die alone.

SOON IT WAS spring again. The oak tree shed its stringy tassels like old tears. One afternoon, as Sixiang was sweeping the last tassels in the backyard, Yizheng stepped out to her. "You're getting married," she said in English, in Miss Moore's and Miss Webb's commanding tone. "We're finding you a husband."

She pronounced "we" with pride. She was wearing a Western dress and her bangs were curled into frizzy locks, but nobody ever called her a "monkey." How furious Sixiang had been when Qinglong used that word on her. Had he not done so, perhaps he would still be trimming the evergreen bushes in the Coles' front yard, sculpting a dragon's back he could not ride on. Perhaps she would have stayed at the Turners' to finish her two-year "housekeeping education," to be a good pet for them so that she could return to the Mission Home with a good evaluation and get sent back to China. Had Qinglong not called her a "monkey" in the first place, they could have perhaps both survived, ignorant or feigning ignorance.

THAT NIGHT, AFTER the Mission Home had been dark and quiet awhile, the girls now snoring or mumbling lonesome words or clenching nervous jaws, Sixiang got up to pack. The trunk she'd used to travel to the Turners' had been passed on to another girl for the "housekeeping education." Sixiang still carried the now dog-eared photo of her father and the six now tarnished silver coins in her inside pocket, which she'd sewn into all her undergarments. She put her few belongings in a cloth bundle, leaving the blond dolls given by the donors at Christmas and the Bible and cross given by Miss Moore upon her baptism in the basket under the cot.

She tiptoed down the stairs and through the parlor. Then she unlatched the front door and walked out. It was that easy. There was no lock on the inside to stop them from leaving, and no one had dared to leave before. Where could they go? But Sixiang had to believe there was somewhere for her out there, where she would find her father and bring him home.

The night sky hung clear and high. A slender moon looked like a slim boat, drifting alone in the dark blue. Carrying the cotton bundle on her shoulder, Sixiang headed toward the pawnshop in the center of Chinatown. The streets were thinning, shops nearing their closing hour. She looked away from men's stares and quickened her steps at someone's whistle. She didn't know if Daoshi still lived in the backroom of the pawnshop. It had been five years since she last saw him.

The man tending the shop was not Daoshi, but Sixiang snuck in anyway when the man turned away from the door to chatter with a customer. She had no other choice but to find out, no other place to go but the small room where she'd stayed with Daoshi during the riot nights, sheltered from the mobs set loose as if from hell. She had felt safe then, the way she had during the flood when she was in her mother's arms under the oilcloth, separated by a wooden tub from the hungry ghosts in the raging water. And the way she had felt when she was younger still, held tight by her mother against the bandits hunting for gold in their house. Devils took many forms and could be unleashed anytime. If only she could return to those arms.

She half expected to see the paneled screen depicting the Four Great Beauties, behind which she'd hidden when she was a younger, smaller runaway who held fast to a sounder and sturdier dream. Now, she felt tired above all and wished for nothing more than to lie down in a safe, quiet place and sleep for a long time. She took cover behind a shelf until the shopkeeper turned to walk the customer out. Then she found herself in front of the same door that had shielded her years ago from the mayhem of the world. She turned the knob, and as if by magic, it opened for her again.

She closed the door behind her and stood there in the dark. Slowly, by the dim lantern light filtering in through the small window, she could make out the bed where she had once fallen asleep, the wooden trunk also functioning as a table, the single chair by the door in which Daoshi had sat, and his black robe hanging on the wall. The same room with its same sparse contents. But as she stood there, she also sensed something different. It was the smell, a stale, loose mixture of liquor, sweat, and dust. She had not remembered this smell to be part of the room.

She sat down on the bed and groped for the match box on the trunk. She waited till the shop was closed outside before lighting the oil lamp. Empty bottles idled on the trunk. Clothes were draped on the chair arms. The bed was unmade, the quilt rumpled and unclean. Dust gathered on every surface. For the past five years, Sixiang had been inspected every day for cleanness. She had learned to make her bed so neat it looked as if it had never been slept on, and to clean her face, mouth, and fingernails as thoroughly as if one single smudge would reveal a moral failing. Already, she imagined what Miss Moore and Miss Webb would say about this room—about heathen habits and barbarians.

The books on the trunk were also covered in dust. She picked up the one with the drawing of Laozi on the cover. At the Mission Home, when she was still allowed to take Chinese lessons, she'd hoped to see the book again and find out if she was able to read it now. She blew off the dust and opened it to the first page. "道可道, 非常道; 名可名, 非常名。" She read it out loud. What is this Way that cannot be told or named?

She put down the book and, leaning back, lowered her head to the pillow, which needed washing. But as she was lying there, her body recognized an older, homebound feeling, a comfort and care remembered by her childhood self. From two deaths ago, before her eyes were trained to linger on the surface of things and her heart had to carry much more than a wish.

She pulled the quilt over her and closed her eyes. Sleep descended like a drop of dark sap that wrapped her up so tight she no longer needed to fight it.

Without quite wakening, she heard the door open and close, and then a few steps. She didn't need to open her eyes to know it was Daoshi. He was looking down at her in his quiet thinking way. She'd rather keep her eyes closed and stay inside the dense sap of sleep. She hoped he could see with his fortune-telling eyes everything that had happened to her during the past five years—so that she wouldn't have to bear it alone, and so that in the morning when she woke up, she would not have to say anything. Daoshi would know and he would tell her about the Way that couldn't be told or named.

Daoshi

HE WAS DRUNK WHEN HE CAME BACK TO THE SHOP. SOMETHING felt different, but it took him a moment to see it: a slice of light slipping out from under his door. Inside, he saw a girl sleeping in his bed. Something stirred in his mind. He recognized her, the way recognition worked in dreams when you knew who a person was even though they had a different face. How long had it been now? Her eyelids trembled but did not open.

Her face looked soft and clean, unlike the bedding that was overdue for a wash. Daoshi had not bothered to do laundry. The most he had managed to do lately was wash his face in the morning and open the pawnshop and tend to it. The Laozi book had been removed from its original spot on the trunk, its coat of dust lifted. He had seen dust gather on it and had done nothing about that either. The act of wuwei. No action. Just being and letting be. He had planned to lie down on his bed without undressing or lighting the lamp, and sleep the rest of the night away, with the comfortable numbness he had nursed since sundown. But here in his bed lay this child who was no longer a child, who had tremors in her eyelids, sorrow between her brows.

He sat down on the chair. About five years ago, he had sat here while Sixiang slept, a little person determined to find her father and take him home. Now Daoshi knew for sure that this dream of hers would not come true.

Feiyan had asked him to exorcise Guifeng, but Daoshi left without saying goodbye to her. There was nothing he could do about Sixiang's father, who, like Daoshi's own father, was a lost cause. When he came back from Truckee, he did not go visit Sixiang in the Mission Home either, because he didn't want to lie, and he knew the girl could see through him. So he let her be. He'd heard it wasn't bad there. They had their own system, which at least was not prostitution or slavery—much better for sure; after all, it was called a "rescue."

But the girl found her way back here. Why? What could have happened to her at the Mission Home? Was she still determined to find her father and return home? Most likely her folks were either dead or still struggling not to die, not unlike here. The Chinese Exclusion Act would be passed soon, and white mobs were readier than ever to be inflamed into killing sprees. Meanwhile, the tongs were at war with one another again, knifing, hatcheting their own strong-limbed countrymen away. The rest smoked or drank or succumbed to disease. Whether it was self-destruction or self-preservation, self-love or self-hate, each seized their own remedy to reconcile with the ending of it all.

DAOSHI HAD SHIPPED weapons to five different towns before quitting the job. Guns would not protect them. They might arm some vigilantes and deter the mobs awhile. But gunned up, they would still be outnumbered, still seen as lower and lesser, and still wouldn't be left alone. In Truckee, soon after the whites learned about the rifles he'd shipped, they formed a new club, the 601: six feet under, zero trial, one bullet. They flooded Chinatown with red ribbons to show they were out for blood. Then, along with the town's famous Caucasian League, they burned it to the ground.

After the weapon-shipping trips, Daoshi got his job back tending the pawnshop, except now working the day shift. At night, he visited brothels, played games of cards and fan-tan, and drank. At first he only drank at night, but soon he found himself keeping a bottle underneath the shop counter, stealing a swig from time to time when he thought no one was watching. But the pawnshop owner had started to notice. "Don't pass out on the job," he said, "and be kind to your liver."

Be kind—Daoshi would like to. But in the end, a liver was just a piece of furniture. So was a heart, a head. All grew old, wore out. He'd once had certain ideas about Dao and could sometimes visualize a path between the ground under his feet and the sky over his head. A path that went beyond the tightness, ignorance, and laziness of this paltry existence. But visions did not take him far. He took the shortcut of forgetting.

If Sixiang opened her eyes now and asked, "Why didn't you help me as you'd promised?" what would he say? He was not in the mood to explain or justify himself. In fact, he felt almost irritated at the girl for keeping him from dropping his head on the pillow and closing his eyes, like last night and the night before. Even a routine such as this, lousy and lame as it seemed, could be a comfort, and something to live for.

But there was something else he felt. It was shame. About the condition the room was in, its disarray matched by his own being, and foregrounded by Sixiang's clean, sleeping face. He had prided himself in being tidy, in keeping things simple but clean. The least he could do was honor the sky that always returns to clear blue.

He blew out the oil lamp and leaned his head against the wall. He had become a version of his father who burned his robe while dancing for the dead, as if he himself was entangled in the hell flames. Guifeng insisted that he was a straw dog, burning slowly in a fire he had lit himself, as heaven and earth looked on without a care. So be it. One step in hell. Burning there or here. Life here or death there. The threshold a breath thin.

Sixiang

SHE OPENED HER EYES TO THE FIRST BLUE STREAMING THROUGH the threadbare curtains. Daoshi was sleeping in the chair by the door, head slumped to one shoulder, mouth slightly open, deep furrows between his brows. She wondered if she could still trust this man who slept in such a troubled way. She doubted that he had been able to see what had happened to her last night, and she was not going to tell now.

He woke up under her gaze, straightening his body in the chair.

"Can you help me find my father now?" She did not allow herself to hesitate. All that had happened during the past five years had changed nothing; all would be redeemed if she just picked up her old dream, found her father, and brought him home. Qinglong would be restored. Ah Hong would be resurrected. They would both be miraculously waiting for her on the other side of the sea.

"What if he does not want to go back with you, or cannot go back? Things change, you know. Home changes too."

She knew, but she didn't have any other home than the one she had known across the ocean. Was it still there? She must believe it was. Otherwise, what did she have? Qinglong had no home. He died in the frozen woods. She must have a home so that she could give him one too. While home changed for other people and there was nothing one could hold on to, she must believe that her home had stayed still, firming itself up for her return.

"Take me to him." She looked at Daoshi until he nodded.

10

The Dance

✳

1882

Feiyan

THE GIRL STEPPING IN WITH DAOSHI LOOKED VAGUELY FAMILIAR:
the sharp cheekbones, the thin nose, the willow-leaf eyes. A resemblance that made Feiyan ache a little, reminding her of the back-home
that she and Guifeng had talked about once upon a time—before all the
fires, all the burned houses, and the ones rebuilt, each smaller, barer,
keener in its knowledge of perils, as the echo of that back-home faded
away further.

She seated them at a table. "What brought you here?" She looked
at Daoshi.

Daoshi looked at the girl, who was looking at Feiyan, her eyes
searing. "This is Sixiang," he said, pausing. "Guifeng's daughter. She'd
like to meet him."

"I see the resemblance." Feiyan poured tea into Sixiang's cup,
meeting her eyes, which had the clarity of Guifeng's eyes from his
younger self too—but not the love he'd once shown her unsparingly.
In its place was something akin to hatred. "You can't find him here."
Feiyan turned her eyes back to Daoshi. "He doesn't live here anymore."

Daoshi took it in knowingly. He had the look that made you want to say things to him, to just sit down and let it all out, and he would be there looking at you. Not judging you, nor offering any advice, because there was nothing else you could do that you hadn't done already. And then he would just be gone. It would be like talking to a well, but you would feel lighter anyway.

He'd made her feel that way last time he was here, five years ago, and she'd asked him to exorcise Guifeng, to free him from that white ghost. But Daoshi hadn't done it. Maybe he had known what Feiyan had suspected, that Guifeng couldn't be helped.

Now here was this daughter, whom Guifeng had long stopped feeding and who had nevertheless survived, crossed the ocean, and ended up here. No longer a child who needed feeding, but old enough to marry and bear children of her own. What was she doing here? To dump blame on her father? Was Feiyan to be blamed too? Well, she had once made Guifeng commit more to this family here, their future together, their back-home, their daughter Duofu who had lived through two infernos and few blessings.

Duofu was sitting on her heels on a chair by a corner table, shelling peanuts, her chore. She was gazing at Sixiang, as if she had sensed a kinship between them. Her daughter, her heart, her justification to pressure Guifeng to reallocate his obligations. But the past never just went away; it came back to assert itself.

"Where can we find him?" Daoshi asked.

"Same spot, I figure."

Same den. Its manager a customer of hers. He would let Guifeng smoke on credit sometimes and then get it back from her. "Your man owes too much. I'll lose my job if I keep letting him."

"Not my man anymore, nor my business."

Still, she let the guy leave without paying her. It was filthy, but it saved her from feeling bad for not doing more for Guifeng. Last time she saw him, he was picking a rotten apple out of a garbage can outside of the grocery store. For a while she couldn't eat without thinking he was starving. But new and old angers bonded together to drive him out of her mind. She had let him go, and as a result, she was nobody to this girl.

She brought them two bowls of soup, rice, and two plates with each of the buffet dishes. "My treat," she said and turned away.

Sixiang

THIS WOMAN WAS POSSIBLY HER MOTHER'S AGE BUT LOOKED SO unlike her mother. Big feet, quick and sturdy legs, straight neck, she wove through the male customers, pouring tea, bantering a bit, agile and sure. She was in control of her smile, the degree of it. She carried herself in a way Sixiang hadn't quite seen women do before, so comfortable among so many men, who seemed to respect and adore her at the same time. Sixiang could only imagine what her mother would think of this woman, and how jealous and self-doubting she would feel. While her mother had been abandoned across the sea, starved to bones her bound feet could barely carry, this woman who was feeding dozens of men must know no hunger. And the woman's daughter, the little well-fed, well-dressed girl watching Sixiang from the corner of the diner, must know no hunger either, while at her age, Sixiang had to fish in a corpse-strewn river and dig up earthworms for their one drop of fat.

She should resent this woman on behalf of her mother, who had to sell her in order to put food in their bellies. This woman, on the other hand, looked like she could survive anything and would make sure her daughter survived too. She would not allow her daughter to be taken away from her. But she took away Sixiang's father, her mother's husband, and then kicked him out.

"Your father has been through difficult things," Daoshi had forewarned her on the train. He'd told her about the fire, the gunshot, the loss of a leg, about another woman and another daughter. When the train began to climb up the mountains, Daoshi changed the subject to the railroad. How her father and other Chinese men had laid the tracks through hard rock, hammer by hammer, shovel by shovel. The dark, cold tunnels the train entered threw their ghosted reflections back at them.

"I hate Gold Mountain," Sixiang said after the train crawled out of the longest tunnel. Through the window, snow peaks glowed gold and copper in the western sun, but their beauty was not for her.

Only five months ago, Sixiang had pointed at these mountains from the western foothill, telling Qinglong she would cross them one day to find her father on the other side and bring him back to China. Where had she gotten that kind of confidence? Perhaps she was only saying it to make herself believe it, and to make Qinglong want to be part of it. It was a dream she had to keep feeding so that it wouldn't wither away. Now, she was alone with it again.

She liked the food this woman made. She hadn't had a real hearty meal since she'd been taken to the Mission Home. She felt guilty enjoying the food cooked by a woman her mother would surely resent. She ate quickly, as if that would somehow excuse her betrayal. When she and Daoshi finished their meal and rose to leave, this woman, whom Daoshi called Feiyan, followed them out.

"You go find him and bring him here," she said to Daoshi. "It's not a place for her to go." She turned to Sixiang. "You can stay here with me." And before Sixiang could say anything, Feiyan took her hand.

"I'm going with him." Sixiang slipped her hand away.

"You stay." Daoshi looked at her. "Your father may not want you to see him where he is."

Was the "same spot" Feiyan had referred to what Sixiang suspected? An opium den? She knew there were plenty of them in San Francisco Chinatown and wouldn't be surprised that they were here too. There had even been one in her village, Yunteng. She'd followed other kids by stepping on a rock to look through its window and seen the village's top opium-fiend slumped in a cushioned couch, elbowing up for a mouthful of vapor. Within a few years, the man would smoke away everything his family had owned: first the furniture, then the porcelains, the quilts, the clothes. During the famine, Sixiang saw his skeletal body by the river, with nothing but undergarments on, and a palm leaf meant to cover his face half lifted by wind.

Had Sixiang's father also been smoking away his family's possessions, so that this woman had to throw him out? But that couldn't be the case. Clearly this woman had plenty, if she could feed all these healthy-looking men around her, eyeing and admiring her.

Feiyan didn't take Sixiang's hand again. But if she was offended by Sixiang's rudeness, she didn't show it. She led her back to the diner, and directly to where the little girl sat. "Duofu, this is your sister," she said and left the two of them there.

The way she said the word "sister" sounded almost casual, as if it might have nothing to do with blood and family. But still, the word softened something dense and heavy in the air. Sixiang sat down across the table from the girl, her half sister, connected with her by a father absent from both of them.

Quietly, they shelled the peanuts together. The girl peered up at her when Sixiang was not looking and looked away when she did. When the peanuts were done, Feiyan brought a basket of green beans for them to destring, leaving it right on the table between them, and they got right to it. Sixiang had done all this when she was the little girl's age, helping her own mother prepare food for cooking.

"Sister," the girl finally said, "who is your mama?"

"She's in China," Sixiang said.

"And your baba? Where is he?"

"I hope to see him soon," Sixiang said after a few seconds. *Where's yours?* she thought to ask but didn't.

But the girl seemed to have heard her thought. "The den. Where he feels better about his leg. How many legs does your baba have?"

Sixiang didn't know how to answer the question; she touched Duofu's hand lightly.

"Your baba? Does he have both his legs?" Duofu persisted.

"I don't know. I haven't met him."

"Never?"

"Never."

"Are you going to meet him one day?"

"Yes, I hope so."

Sixiang glanced at the door of the diner, her heart jumping at each man stepping in. She checked their faces and their legs. Feiyan brought a bowl of fried salted peanuts she'd just made for them to snack on. After they finished the peanuts, Duofu went upstairs to fetch a book to show Sixiang. It had pictures and Chinese characters. "My mama found this in the shop. My baba can read, but he isn't here. Can you read?"

It was *San Zi Jing*. Back in her village, Sixiang had seen the book held in the hands of the boy next door while he dozed off on a stool in their front yard. He was supposed to recite verses from the book for school. Sixiang snuck it out of his hands but couldn't read any of the words. The boy woke up, snatched the book back, and sneered at Sixiang, "Don't pretend you can read. Long hair short wit." At the Mission Home, before Sixiang's "housekeeping education," the college girl from Guangzhou had used the Chinese version of the Bible to teach Sixiang and other select girls Chinese, starting from simpler characters to the more difficult ones. Sixiang had studied hard, still believing that those characters held the promise of a future where everything would be resolved. She missed those afternoon hours when things still felt possible.

"I can read some," she said to Duofu, and read the first few lines, pointing at each character as she read along:

"人之初，性本善。性相近，习相远。"

"What do they mean?"

"At the beginning of life, our nature is kind. We're all similar, but habits form and set us apart."

"What habits?"

"It's like people eating different food, wearing different clothes, praying to different gods."

"Do you and I have the same habits?"

Sixiang thought about this. "Yes, I think we have similar habits."

"We're not apart."

"No."

Duofu chuckled. Sixiang too. She saw Feiyan looking at them from behind the counter, a smile on her face. A smile that could have almost come from Sixiang's own mother.

Guifeng

WHEN DAOSHI'S FACE APPEARED ABOVE HIM, IT FELT AS IF IT WAS only days ago when Daoshi had last found him in the den and told him about his daughter.

Guifeng had just gotten his dose of opium. He'd rummaged through a dead man's pockets to find the last dollar. For a few years now, he'd been hanging with the homeless at the edge of the new Chinatown, between the mountain foot and the riverbank, in tents made of salvaged canvases and used wood boards, living on occasional squirrels, rabbits, and fish if there was a catch, along with discarded food picked from trash cans. Earlier today, he woke up to find his tentmate, who'd been coughing up blood, dead. Guifeng was relieved when he pried the last dollar from his dead buddy's pocket, and then cried all the way to the den, wiping his face and nose with shirt sleeves hardened by filth. The sun was swinging down, his eyes filled with its blood of light.

"Your daughter is here. She's with Feiyan at the house right now," Daoshi said.

What was in his eyes? Pity? Disdain? This man was good at keeping his emotions to himself. Wuwei, straw dogs. How many times had Guifeng comforted himself with those words he'd learned from Daoshi, using them to justify one more day of his existence, one more dose of opium? Especially since he hadn't bothered Feiyan and Duofu for over three years now, not robbing from them or sucking their lives dry, as Feiyan had accused him of doing.

"I'm almost done. This straw dog here," he said, patting his gaunt chest, "is finished soon."

"Not yet. You still have unfinished business." Daoshi held out a hand to him. "Your daughter needs to see you. You need to wake up."

When Guifeng ignored that hand, Daoshi took his arm and pulled him up. He looked impatient, almost angry. The rare emotional display surprised Guifeng into obedience. He let Daoshi drag him off the cot, out of the den. It was night already. Trees that had been candling in the sunset when he came in had returned to darkness.

Daoshi held his arm tight. "First you take a bath." He was leading them toward the bathhouse.

The bathhouse owner glared at Guifeng: "I told you I don't need you here anymore." Guifeng had scrubbed those bathtubs for a few dimes and sometimes cleaned himself in the muddied water. Since he lost that job months ago, he hadn't taken a bath, unless he counted the rushed cold washing in the river, which should be warmer now that spring had come. He remembered seeing pink-purple clusters of crocuses poking out of the frozen ground. How many doses ago was that?

"He's here to take a bath." Daoshi handed a coin to the owner.

Guifeng took off his grimy clothes, his fake limb, and climbed into a dim corner of a less occupied tub. The hot water pushed open his pores as if to fill him with it. He closed his eyes and felt both the contour and the weight of his body, which he had thought of ending on his way to the den so that it would stop feeling the craving that was never-ending. As he rubbed off months of dirt, he kept his eyes closed, to not think, just let the body feel what it was feeling, the simultaneous drowning and buoying up, scathing and lightening.

Daoshi came back with a set of new clothes. "Barbershop next."

Once upon a time, Daoshi and Guifeng had done this routine together, visiting the old Chinatown from their mountain camp for the weekly respite. They'd first soak in the hot bath and then have the barber's practiced hand shave their foreheads and clean and braid their hair. It had felt delicious to be touched and cared for that way after their weeklong labor.

Now, he sat in the chair as Daoshi waited, chatting with the barber. No longer the old barber, but his then apprentice, who was talking about the last fire. How his *shifu* had run out with the shaving kits in his arms and flames on his back rising taller than his body. All charred, save the kits that the new barber was using.

Guifeng wanted to shut off the voice and blank out the image of burning, although fires had never really ceased burning in his head. Already, he longed for the vapor, to blur all the charred remains of houses and soften the ashen ruins into a fog. Fog, that was what he wanted to have in his head, not the image of a tall fire carried on a man's back.

"Stay still," the new barber said. "If not for Daoshi here, I'd charge you double for such filthy hair."

Guifeng glanced at his reflection in the mirror the barber held in front of him and looked away. One glimpse was enough: sunken, sallow, chapped lips, cracked nose, coarse and aged skin. His old beard and filth had camouflaged his face well to keep it away from both others and himself. Now, this was the face his daughter would see, for the first time in her life. He wanted to run away. Run as fast as his fake leg could carry him, away from Daoshi who was determined this time to make him face his daughter and see all his failures in her eyes.

But meanwhile, in this body that was now light and clean, he felt a longing that he hadn't allowed himself to feel for a long time. It was strange to find it still there, like a nocturnal plant, waiting to bloom secretly in the dark.

They walked into the night. The dark river flowed patiently beside them, renewing itself after one more day of witnessing all that took place on its banks. Or was it as indifferent as heaven and earth? They walked down the block, and stopped in front of the house he had not dared to call home.

Sixiang

IT HAD BEEN ALMOST TWO HOURS SINCE DAOSHI LEFT. THE DINER'S crowd had thinned to only one occupied table where two men nursed their last cups of wine. Feiyan was cleaning the kitchen. She had not stopped working, her eyes turning to the door from time to time, which comforted Sixiang a little, knowing she was not the only one waiting for them to return. When Daoshi said, "Wait here. I'll bring him back," Sixiang had trusted him, but somewhere in her head also lingered the fear that he would leave and not come back, dumping her here as a temporary solution rather than offering the real help he had promised. There was that in him, she felt, a tendency to wash his hands of something, as her father had done.

The restaurant was empty when they came in. Feiyan was leaning over the counter, sipping a cup of rice wine, and Sixiang was reading another line of *San Zi Jing* to Duofu. Daoshi walked in with him—a stranger whom Sixiang would never have recognized based on the photo she was still carrying with her. He limped in, bone-thin, his face bruised and chapped. He looked like someone emerging from a famine, even though he was wearing brand-new clothes with fold lines clearly visible. But the new jacket and pants recalled the stiff clothes put on a dead person's body for the mourners to view. The thought was so stark Sixiang stopped it in its tracks and forced herself to stand up and show respect.

This man, her father, cast a glance at Feiyan first, and as though scathed, glanced away. He turned to Sixiang. Lamplight scattered in his eyes, so they looked fractured. And Sixiang recognized him then, the eyes, those even eyes in the photo that she'd suspected were hiding something. They were hiding this fractured gaze that was directed at her now.

He stepped to her with his hands reaching out, but instead of taking hold of hers, they paused in midair before dropping onto the table, as if to steady himself. "Sixiang," he called her by the name he'd given her.

But Sixiang couldn't open her mouth to call him "Father." The father she'd had in mind held certain meanings that she couldn't assign to this man, who had caused her to leave her mother and grandmother. If they were seeing him through her eyes now, would they still think of him as a son and a husband?

"Baba?" Duofu asked tentatively, as if she, too, had to reconnect this man with the one she'd once known, or thought she knew.

"Duofu." He reached an uncertain hand to the girl, touching her head, relieved to turn his eyes away from Sixiang.

Daoshi

DAOSHI HAD HEARD THE AWFUL SOUNDS OF WITHDRAWAL BEFORE. From his father, four or five times at least, each lasting a week or two. Where was his father now? Was he still smoking? Still suffering? "If you leave now, don't ever think of coming back" were his father's last words to him. And Daoshi had mumbled to himself, "I won't." He hadn't sent a letter home since. He did not want to be dutiful. He had drifted away, in the name of self-searching, and when he was made to confront his homelessness here, he told himself there was no turning back. The ocean was no longer crossable. Because not only had he denounced his duty as a son, he had also denounced his guilt. If the reasoning behind all that seemed flimsy, it was also convincing.

He was going to leave the next day, back to his feckless, guiltless life in Big City, to be among the pawned furniture, utensils, clothes: the detached objects people sought attachment from. He only needed to buy and sell, attach a price tag to give them an arbitrary value. He did not need to hear the tormenting sounds Guifeng was making.

Two nights ago, a bath, new clothes, and a shave had not done much. A pained meeting. No recognition in Sixiang's eyes, nor in Guifeng's. A pair of strangers who were nevertheless father and daughter. Sixiang had refused to call him "Father," a word that could have bridged some distance or at least signaled certain acceptance. Despite what Daoshi had told her on the train, despite his effort to prepare her, her dream seemed to be burning itself up right in front of her. And Guifeng, as Daoshi had feared, looked wearier, as if he'd rather make the last sprint to the ether than stay here.

So Daoshi couldn't leave. Not yet. He knew Guifeng would go right back to the den, now with more burden and despair to push him that way. And Sixiang, what would she do? Daoshi had done what he'd said he would do, bringing her to her father. He kept his word, but was that enough?

On the third morning, after he woke up from the cot in the storage room Feiyan had tidied up for him, he went out for a walk by the rustling river. Rising in the southwest were the cold, rugged peaks. The twelve hundred dead Chinese men who built this railroad could still be up there haunting the tunnels and cliffsides that would shake each time a train rumbled by. Daoshi had performed death rites on makeshift altars to appease them, imagining that they floated up the pined slopes, the snow caps, and merged into the open sky like clouds. He had performed to comfort the living too, who grieved for their lost ones and feared for their own lives. He had picked up the family trade he'd left behind, turning himself into a real daoshi on the mountains.

But he had never performed an exorcism. He'd seen people his father and uncle had supposedly cured continue to sicken and die, and seen his father continue to be possessed by his own demon. Daoshi had dismissed it as trickery. But he was too young then, ignorant of the depth of pain and the persistence of suffering. Since he'd left home to meet his life in this land, he had felt the thick, heavy grievances of many hungry ghosts drifting among the living—footless and sightless, attaching themselves to lives already suffering, as if suffering could be redeemed by suffering more.

So generations of daoshi had been putting on their robes and hats and chanting and dancing to let the living and the dead know they were all suffering but all would be cured. They led the restless spirits to an open space where their anger and anguish would be neutralized by air, and they let the living believe their afflictions were gone, that they had been tended to and eased. It was an offering of care, for both the living and the dead. The care itself must be what mattered, no matter what it could or could not do.

Daoshi would need a peach-wood sword with or without a dragon carved on one side and a tiger on the other, like the one his father had wielded in his hand. He would also need a bronze bagua mirror, which his father had held in his other hand. Daoshi would need to try.

Sixiang

ON THE THIRD NIGHT, FEIYAN ASKED HER TO COME UPSTAIRS TO her father's room. Sixiang had been sharing the big room with Feiyan and Duofu next door, while Daoshi stayed in the downstairs storage room that Feiyan had turned into a bedroom not unlike the one at the back of the pawnshop. During the last two days, Daoshi and Feiyan had been in and out of her father's room, and when they left, they locked the room from the outside. Sixiang had heard her father's tossing, cursing, and moaning through the wall most of the previous night. She steeled her heart to it. She couldn't make herself pity him. She would lose something if she did, something that was tightly hugged inside her, although she didn't even know what it was. She just knew it would be gone if she let herself pity her father. She clenched her jaws and hummed inside her head to shut out the terrible groans and swears coming out of her father. In the daytime, she stayed downstairs and cooked and cleaned and did all the things Feiyan could use help with. When Feiyan asked her to take a break, she took Duofu outside to the river. They turned rocks to catch crabs and tossed stones into the water. They didn't talk about their father.

In the evening as the diner was emptying out, Daoshi came back with a longish bundle in his hand. He said something to Feiyan and went upstairs. Feiyan saw the last customers off and flipped the sign to Closed. After disappearing upstairs for several minutes, she yelled for Sixiang and Duofu to come up. "Duofu, you stay in that room and close the door. Sixiang, you come here with me."

Her father was writhing on the bed. He was tearing at his hair, sobbing and shaking. His fake leg had fallen off. The empty pantleg flopped like a newly gutted fish.

The room was smoky with agarwood incense. Daoshi was wearing his black robe and black silk hat. In his hands, he held a wooden staff and a fengshui mirror.

Feiyan gripped her father's hand and asked Sixiang to grip the other. Sixiang did what she was told. But her father was yanking his hands away. He was trying to get off the bed and limp to the door. "Why do you all want to do this to me?" he was yelling.

Daoshi and Feiyan grabbed his arms, pulling him back to bed. "Stay," Daoshi said. "You'll feel better soon."

Feiyan once again clutched his hand and asked Sixiang to do the same from the other side of the bed. Sixiang caught hold of her father's slipping hand, and this time, she held it so tight her jaws clenched as if with hate.

The incense thickened. Gray clouds gathered in the small room. Daoshi opened the window, and then, waving the staff in one hand and the mirror in the other, he started to dance. The dance didn't look real. It looked make-believe, like some kind of show Daoshi was putting on, his face unsure, noncommittal, the way he'd looked years ago when Sixiang turned her head to search for an answer in his eyes while being taken to the Mission Home. Care and not care. That was what the dance looked like: a spectacle meant to care but without conviction. Sixiang lowered her eyes from Daoshi's faltering steps, as if embarrassed. She didn't want to look at her father either, though her hands continued to clasp his hand tight, finger bones fighting finger bones.

But when she looked up again, things had changed. It was like something had burst out of Daoshi's dancing steps and chanting voice, his shifting mirror and brandishing staff. Sixiang felt a force, a kind of pulling and tugging within her father too. She felt cold sweat oozing out of the hand she was holding and his hard, brittle bones tingling beneath his skin.

Daoshi chanted and danced, his steps frantic but also disciplined, his eyes bright and fierce. He was inviting divine power from the deities to help him lift the aggrieved spirits from her father's body, to guide them to the ether outside the open window so that the yin-yang balance would be restored and her father would stay put on this earth, with them.

Duofu had snuck in, hiding behind her mother's back, peeking at Daoshi and her father. All four of them were here to help dispel his demons. Sixiang recognized the awe in this moment, the preciousness of the life she was holding—her father whose blood ran in her and pulled her to this moment of holding him to the life he must continue to live. His pain was so immense it seemed to contain all her pain, and all her mother's and grandmother's pain. And all Qinglong's pain too, his pain and pride, his pleading command: *Nei ʒau liu*. And she ran away, out of cowardice, or love, or both. It didn't matter. The fact was that she ran away while he was dying.

She held her father's hand, which was quiet now. She held Qinglong's hand, which did not hold hers back. She held her mother's hand until it slipped away as she was dragged onto the boat. Daoshi held the staff and mirror and continued to dance, as if the dance could redeem all that was lost, all that was slipping, all who knew the bitterness and despair of love but still held on to it because there was nothing else. *Let live, let love*, Daoshi's now steady dancing steps seemed to proclaim. He continued to chant too, addressing the spirits directly: "Go home. Go where you belong, where you will be at ease . . ."

Daoshi chanted and danced as sweat beaded his forehead. Her father lay exhausted on the bed, his damp hand lying still in hers. As she felt her own energy begin to drain, Sixiang saw the aggrieved spirits floating above them, tight and lonely, wrestling still or drifting footless in the incensed air. Ah Hong and Qinglong were among them. They were the quiet ones, the ones she could see most clearly. Orphaned ghosts who could still be living had she been there for them. Had she been stronger, kinder, wiser than she was.

They were floating close by around her, as there was no one else for them, only her. She couldn't abandon them again as she had done before. She didn't want them to leave her, to be exorcised out of her. They were hers to carry. Their pain her pain. Their weight hers to bear.

She would not move on, like her father had done. Because those who were gone from your sight deserved to be carried still in your heart, or they would indeed be lost. If you continued to hold them, in whatever way possible, they would have no choice but to stay alive.

Sixiang let go of her father's hand and, balancing Qinglong and Ah Hong on each of her shoulders, stepped out of the room.

Feiyan

As Daoshi danced, chanted, waving the staff and mirror, she saw hungry ghosts with their mouths of ashes, mouths of screams and knots, flitting around her. She had tried to run away from them or to keep them at bay, with her sheer will to live, to not be crushed. She had done what she must do: cook, serve, clean, make love without loving, eat while knowing a loved one was starving, sleep to wake up for another day's toil, and above all, rebuild after another burning. Ashes had followed her—from those she'd dumped onto the old man's face to those choking her own. The mountain ghost hollered in laughter: "Let me see how far you can outrun your fate now." The chamber ghost continued to quibble, lonely and bitter: "Once a whore, always a whore."

She saw the ghosts Guifeng carried too, those who had been pulling him on a leash to the den: the white man's ghost turning hungrier and angrier each day, and the lynched Chinese man Guifeng had invited to himself, needing more guilt.

Daoshi was chanting an enticement: "Go where you belong, where you will be at ease." *Ease.* Such a good word. How good it would be if the heart was at ease. No more churning thoughts, no more stirring and mixing them into a concoction of poison and learning to feed on it without dying. Daoshi was saying there was a place, a better place, for the spirits to go. It was no good for them to stay in this world with the living who couldn't help them. They would be better off moving on and ascending into the empty sky where all pains would dissolve.

It was almost tempting to go with them. But no, it wasn't her time yet. She had to keep living, and she knew she would never choose death over life. That had never been her. Not even in her most tortured hours had she wished she were dead. She wanted to run. To get up at the first light of dawn and go out running along the river before everyone else awoke. It would feel as if she was back in her childhood village by the other river, having carried two buckets of water home on the shoulder pole, running along the river to the foot of the mountain. Why hadn't she done so while there was a river right here by the house? She could let all her crowded thoughts, all that made her twisted and murky inside, settle into the rhythm of running and a steadying heartbeat.

That was what she wanted to do as Guifeng broke into a sweat and stopped fighting, his face easing, eyes closed. The ghosts on his chest lifted, gliding toward the open window, to where the wind and air were beckoning.

But her own ghosts lingered. "Please go," she said to the ashen one. "You were not a drunk until you became one. You had not turned wicked before you were poisoned by despair. Please go rest."

Then she looked at the mountain ghost. "I heard your howling, I know your anger, I appreciate your taunting me to run. Easy now. Let go of your pain. You don't have to suffer anymore."

"You, girl." She turned to the chamber ghost, "I've finally got you a daoshi. He's guiding you to where there are no knives and no killing, just ease and comfort. Go, girl. It's your time."

Feiyan saw them waft up from her, lighter already, floating to the window, to outside, the home where they belonged.

Then she felt the spirits around Sixiang, the ghosts she carried, not embittered, spiteful ones, but sad. Sixiang was not letting them go. She held on to them. She was pleading, it seemed, for them to stay. She must not believe that there was a better place for them to go.

For a moment, Feiyan feared they were the ghosts of Sixiang's mother and grandmother, but they were much younger, about Sixiang's age, a boy and a girl. What could have happened to this firstborn of Guifeng's who carried two deaths with her? Based on what Feiyan had learned from Daoshi, Sixiang had not suffered too much in this land. A year as a mui tsai, abused certainly but not for long, and then five years at the Mission Home, which Daoshi had said was safe. All in all, it was nothing like what Feiyan had gone through. When she was Sixiang's age, she had been beaten and raped and had to kill a man, and then she continued to be beaten and raped, and she had to carry all of that on her own, with no one to turn to. Yes, she'd kept herself busy. She had worked and fucked and never stopped moving to keep herself from feeling down, from being crushed by all the things that had been crushing her.

"Let them go," Feiyan said.

But Sixiang was not listening. Daoshi continued to chant and dance. He must have sensed their presence too. But Sixiang was keeping them. She stood up and stepped out of the room, carrying her ghosts.

Daoshi

HE HAD GONE TO SEVERAL STORES AND ALL HE COULD FIND WAS A staff made of oak and a feng shui mirror made of wood and glass. But as the familiar smell of agarwood incense rose in the room, waving the staff that was not a sword and the mirror that was not bronze, Daoshi began to dance. First, he stumbled along, half remembering, testing, trying out steps the way his childhood self followed his brother, as if it was all a game. He looked into the mirror and saw Guifeng's wrestling body reflected in the polished glass. He tried to look inward, to see through the inner eye on his forehead, but saw no restless spirits crawling under or along Guifeng's skin. What he saw was what he had sensed all along, the moldy green energy's tight grip. It was the same energy that had gripped his own father who had danced to exorcise other people's demons, the same that Daoshi saw himself inherit as he drank night after night into oblivion.

Remembering, improvising, he let half-forgotten incantations stagger off his tongue. He invoked divine assistance to reason, to negotiate and bargain with the unruly spirits. He promised them a rightful place in the open air where their grasps would be loosened once and for all. And the afflicted would be left alone, detached from what they'd mistaken to be theirs all along.

Daoshi had never imagined he would do this since he left home, but he was doing it now, unfolding the past with the unpracticed steps and faltering verses excavated from memories that he'd thought were long gone.

As he danced, he thought of the home he had decided not to return to but seemed to be returning to now. He was doing what he had been brought up to do, what he had abandoned. He had to trust that his body could do the right thing, that he would become the dance, the wish, the air, the vast and open. He danced and felt the rightness of his dancing. He was doing what he was supposed to do. He danced till he felt loosened from all grasps, as emptiness filled his body.

Guifeng

HE HATED THEM FOR WANTING TO SAVE HIM BECAUSE THEY WERE saving him for their own sakes. To turn him into the good husband, the good father he was not. Why did they insist on keeping him here where he did not belong? And why was Daoshi meddling in other people's business while he himself chose a life of no responsibility? Why not just let Guifeng be? He wanted to escape but was held down by two pairs of female hands, held down because they wanted him to be more than what he had been, this weakling who'd allowed demons to take him over. He felt an ache in every inch of his body, a pounding sickness from the top of his head to the phantom toes of his lost leg.

Daoshi danced, filling up the space from the ceiling to the floor, between the bed and the table-turned-altar where packs of agarwood incense burned. As the room was clouded with smoke, Guifeng seemed to see his pains on Daoshi's robe, in his frenzied steps, his chanting voice. Daoshi was contouring Guifeng's pains with his waving staff and flickering mirror. He was wrestling with them. Guifeng saw no demons except the white man lying by his foot, the childish humming pushing out of his half-open mouth into a harsh wail. And Guifeng saw the teenage houseboy hang above his head, neck broken, youthful eyes pained and blaming.

Guifeng shut his eyes so he didn't have to see. He heard Daoshi calling the two lost souls, cajoling them, beckoning them to the open window, to the dark night where the cold wind blew.

Guifeng let out a breath and felt his body—a weak hollow not made of straw, but flesh and bones. He lay frail on the bed, shivering. His body continued to ache, but the aching was now keeping him still.

He was not sure if he had been released from the demons, or if he was the demons themselves forced into rebirth.

FOR THE NEXT few days, he stayed in the curtained room. Feiyan came in and out to check on him, changing the chamber pot, adding water to the jar, leaving a bowl of congee, the only food he could keep down. He feigned sleep when she was near. He couldn't yet face her eyes, her judgment, or, worst of all, her forgiveness.

On the seventh day, he woke up and saw the sun wedging in through a corner of the curtain. The light was straight, level, not swirly and looped like the days before. It made him think of the wedge of light in the attic room above the photographer's shop, where Feiyan and he were finally able to let their bodies meet.

He got out of bed, walked down the flight of stairs, and saw all of them there. His family. Feiyan and Sixiang were preparing breakfast, Duofu setting the table, Daoshi making tea. Daoshi looked up at him and said, "Morning."

Guifeng said it back and as he walked toward them, it felt like that morning years ago, after the night of fire and blood, when he stumbled out of the woods and its dark shadows onto the meadow.

11

Two Fish

✳

1882–1885

Sixiang

A fountain dried up. Two fish are stranded on land. They blow bubbles to wet each other. They feed each other with their saliva. It's better they forget each other in rivers and lakes.

SIXIANG HAD READ THIS STORY FROM *ZHUANGZI*, ONE OF DAOSHI'S two books. Holding the little orphan Minnie in her arms, Sixiang wondered if the baby's mother was in a lake now, forgetting her, so that she wouldn't be weighed down by what could not be helped. But whatever it was that couldn't be helped, the baby would not forget, nor could she swim away from where she was stranded. She opened her little empty mouth, not much bigger than a fish's, and wailed, her dark blue eyes bloodshot, her red face shuddering, while the rest of her body wrapped in the swaddling cloth couldn't move an inch.

Ada, the boardinghouse owner, was a stout woman with cornsilk hair and thick shoulders. She said she'd tried to feed the baby cow milk first and then breadcrumbs soaked in milk, but Minnie had coughed up both. "What an idea," Ada said, "leaving a baby in front of a boarding-house, with all the itinerant folks coming and going!" It was Li Shu, her cook and the earliest riser at the establishment, who'd heard the bawl-ing outside the gate and woken Ada up. "I said to him, 'Don't hand it to me.' I have no time to take care of a baby. This is a boardinghouse, not an orphanage. But who else would they hand an orphan child to but a woman? And guess what? I haven't gotten one good night's sleep ever since. I need my sleep, and I don't need any of my lodgers to think I'm not the boss, carrying a crying baby like that all the time. Now you fig-ure out how to feed her." Ada threw her hands in the air, which Sixiang took to mean that she was hired.

The night before, Li Shu had come to Feiyan's diner with news about the job—a nanny and cleaner position, at the boardinghouse where he'd been cooking for the last five years; fifty cents a day, food and board included. Sixiang had tried but failed to find a job in Chi-natown, and although Feiyan told her she could just help out at the diner, Sixiang figured that Duofu was already the help, and she wasn't needed. Besides, she wanted to earn wages. She had devised a new plan to replace the old, unattainable one, and to implement it, she needed money. She would not forget in rivers and lakes. Why did it have to be either dying together or forgetting separately? Why couldn't one fish swim back to where the other was?

Now in the boardinghouse kitchen, with Minnie strapped to her chest, Sixiang slow-cooked congee to liquid, which was what the women at the Mission Home fed the littlest ones. Minnie had finally dozed off sucking on a rag soaked in sugar water. Carrying her re-minded Sixiang of carrying Meimei and her little brother at the Chens' when she herself was still a child. Now the baby's weight on her grownup body felt small, soft, and trusting. She felt almost glad to carry such a warm bundle of life so close to her skin. When the congee was done, she dipped a corner of the rag in the bowl, blew it cool, and offered it to Minnie. Minnie touched it tentatively with her lips, looking forlorn for a moment, but took it anyway.

The boardinghouse was a three-story brick building laid out not all that differently from the Mission Home—except it was a lot rowdier and smellier, and occupied mostly by adult white men. With Minnie asleep on Sixiang's chest, Ada gave her a tour. "All babies do is sleep. You don't need to fuss over her. Your main job is to keep this place clean." She pointed at the crimson-wallpapered parlor, the dining room with two wooden tables each as long as the one at the Mission Home, the large bedroom with many cots, the smaller bedrooms, the stairs, the corridor covered by loud, worn carpets, and more rooms lining up on each side.

As they walked down the corridor, two white men in bowler hats and off-white linen shirts stepped out of a room. They tipped their hats at Ada, stepping aside to let them pass, but just as Sixiang was passing, one jumped in front of her. "Hey, Chinese bitch." He sneered.

That night, on the bed in a closet-sized room next to Ada's, with Minnie lying in the crook of her arm suckling on a sugary rag, Sixiang thought she needed to buy a pair of boots and carry a knife with her, the way Qinglong had done. She imagined drawing the knife and pointing it at the man's face earlier. "Watch your mouth," she would have said before Ada said it. And she imagined pointing the knife at the ruffian with the stolen brush and ink bottle in his hands, before he swept the brush across Ah Hong's face. She imagined drawing the knife as Qinglong had done in front of Jason and his friends. Had she carried one that day, she wouldn't have run away. She would have fought side by side with Qinglong. Wouldn't she have?

Two weeks earlier, Daoshi had danced to dispel the ghosts. Sixiang carried hers out of the room because she didn't intend to let them go. Without them, who else did she have? She revised her failed dream by replacing her father with her two ghosts. Why not take the two dead home in the place of one living?

She did not call him "Father." She couldn't do it without thinking of her mother's dull eyes, like the dead fish's on their flooded floor. Her mother had been left behind but was not forgotten. Sixiang would continue to carry her to sustain her life, and she would carry her the way she was carrying her ghosts, by keeping their images airy. Because the solid would bleed when stabbed by a knife, or hang dead with a noose made of a bedsheet, or collapse with no food in the belly. They were safer, and more durable, if they were three floating clouds in the shapes of themselves.

When Sixiang held her father's hand that night while Daoshi danced, it felt like seeing her father lying at the bottom of a dark hole. Those weak moments of her father's were also the moments she'd felt closest toward him, despite the keen knowledge that she could no longer bring him home.

But after he recovered, he avoided Sixiang, making no attempt to atone or apologize. Instead, he poured all his regained life onto Feiyan, clinging to her like she was his new opium. But he also glowed. He looked almost good again, more like the photo that Sixiang no longer carried with her. His love for Feiyan was so showy it made Sixiang feel shadowed and small.

Sixiang had taken a walk with Daoshi by the river when her father's weakest moments seemed to have passed. *What now?* she wanted to ask Daoshi but did not. She had to figure it out herself. The river, although rockier, reminded her of the river flowing through her village. Had it finally run clear and free of corpses now?

"What's happening in Guangdong? Is the famine over?" she asked Daoshi. At the Mission Home she'd asked the same question of her tutor, who told her there were always famines somewhere in the rural areas.

"I suppose so. Famine doesn't last forever," Daoshi said.

"Why haven't you ever gone back?"

"What's there to go back to?"

"Your family. Don't you have a family?"

"It's been a long time. I don't know if I still have a family or not."

"So that's it? You tell yourself they're gone so you don't have to think of them again?"

Daoshi did not answer. He looked at the river.

River here or river there. They flowed and rippled on while the families living by their banks lay down, turning to mud.

That night, she read the "two fish" passage in *Zhuangzi*. She had been reading Daoshi's two Daoist books and learning more Chinese with him. She asked Daoshi why—why it was better to forget in rivers and lakes. "Why not?" he said. "When remembrance only brings sorrow, why not set the other free?"

She was not surprised by his answer, because for him, forgetting must be easy. He could just leave people behind, forget, and be free.

EARLIER IN THE morning, Daoshi had walked her across the bridge to the boardinghouse. "You're not going back to Big City, are you?" she asked him.

Both Feiyan and her father had asked him to stay. Feiyan had transformed the storeroom into a real bedroom, taking stuff out, replacing the pallet with a wooden bed, adding an end table and cushions for the chair. But Daoshi had not said if he'd stay put.

"What if I do go back?"

"You'll find me in the pawnshop's backroom again." Sixiang meant it to be a joke, but her voice sounded serious even to her own ears.

Now, lying in the dark in this white people's place, holding a white orphan newly abandoned by her mother, Sixiang already missed Feiyan's diner across the bridge. That was how she thought of it: not her father's house, but a place run by the sure-footed Feiyan, and kept together by Daoshi. If he left, they would fall apart again—she would be the extra, the outsider; her father would run out of his love for Feiyan and go back to the den; and Duofu would grow up into the lonely, gloomy-eyed girl who she had already halfway become.

Sixiang missed them all together as a whole, even though sitting with them and sharing food at a table had made her think of those who were absent. Those hungry ones who were possibly still saving the last grains of rice, picking bamboo seeds, or boiling grass to extend their last breath. And she thought of the two who could no longer eat, who sat on her shoulders like a pair of mourning doves cooing. It was difficult to think of them only as clouds.

It would be easier to forget, to eat and drink and start anew in rivers and lakes, forgetting those stranded on the land. But she would not.

Daoshi

SIXIANG TOLD HIM HE WAS A QUITTER BY THE RIVER. HE SAID nothing in response, because he knew he was perhaps the only person in the world she could openly blame. Not her mother and grandmother who had sold her, no matter the circumstances; nor her father who had abandoned her and continued to disappoint her; nor Feiyan who had taken her father away. Sixiang couldn't blame any of them because they were either too far away, too far gone, or not hers to blame.

He recognized that, so he said nothing. What could he do, after all? He couldn't replace her father and go to China with her to fulfill her old dream, which even she knew could be blown away by a single breath of doubt.

What he could do was find a job for both the father and daughter. A job was real: it could feed you, keep you occupied, tire you, and push despair out of your mind. Daoshi went to Fong Lee, with whom he'd left the gun shipment years ago. Although the guns hadn't helped them keep the old Chinatown, Fong Lee was still the richest man in the new Chinatown.

"I could use an extra soldier. Is he able-bodied? Can he kick?"

"He lost a leg to gunshot at Trout Creek in '76. Ah Fook, you must have heard about him." Chang'er had told Daoshi about the peculiar pseudonym Guifeng had decided to use when he settled in Truckee.

"I heard he'd become a fiend."

"He had certainly been a faithful customer of yours," Daoshi said, and then laughed to be amiable. "But he has just quit and is making a fresh start."

Fong Lee gave Daoshi a charitable look. "He can work at my cigar factory. I've got four workers there already, more than enough, but I'll do this for you."

"His daughter, sixteen, is also looking for work. Can you hire her too?"

"Girls are trouble. I don't want my employees to have wet dreams at work."

The night when Li Shu came to the diner with the job prospect, it didn't escape Daoshi that Sixiang looked at him, not her father, for advice. And the way she looked at him made him see her at once as the young adult she was now and the child she once was, glancing back at him while being taken to the Mission Home. Both trusting him and challenging him to deserve her trust. Back then, he'd believed that even if the Mission Home was not the best solution, it was the best available at the time. But Sixiang had found her way back, older, sadder, bearing something heavy and agonizing with her. A burdened girl, who had once been weighed down by a child on her back, and who now carried herself straight as if balancing some invisible weight on her shoulders.

"What do you think?" Daoshi responded by asking her.

"I'll do it."

"Are you sure you want to work for a white boss?"

"I'll give it a try," she said with steel eyes.

THAT NIGHT, LYING on the bed in the room that Feiyan had started to call his room—after he'd been out for a few drinks with Li Shu—Daoshi thought it was about time for him to leave. He had done all he could for Sixiang and Guifeng. It was time to go back to his old life. Was there anything about that life to look forward to? Maybe not. Or maybe that was the wrong question to ask. Maybe looking forward itself was a delusion. It would just be another day, the sun moving across the sky at its predictable pace, and him moving across the shifting shadows cast by the sun. Life like that was wuwei easily observed. Or at least that was what he'd told himself when the drinking became too heavy, and he woke up with a hangover, irritated to find himself in the midst of another day.

The next morning, when he walked Sixiang to the boardinghouse to start her job, she asked him if he was going to leave. "You'll find me in the pawnshop's backroom again," she said. And he felt the trickling of water in his head again, stirring something that had thickened there, something that wished to clarify.

When he returned to the diner, a young man was talking to Feiyan at the door. He looked at Daoshi's topknot and bowed: "Can you please exorcise my uncle? He's ill and has been talking nonsense day and night." Without hesitation, Daoshi went to his room, put on his robe and hat, took the staff, the mirror, the remaining incense, and left with the young man. He felt the clarity in his head spread. He improvised more on top of the dance steps and incantations recovered at Guifeng's exorcism. He had to make it real and believe it to be real. And he did it, again. And again, it felt right.

During the following days, more people came to him, for a sick child, a diseased father, an injured uncle, an addicted brother. They came to the diner and asked for him and when they saw him, doubt did not crawl onto their faces.

So he wrestled with demons that would surely come back, as conditions were not about to change, and relief was inevitably temporary. Temporarily, the afflicted stopped battling. They lay still. They felt better—not because Daoshi was able to expel the real demons from them, but because they felt that he had. They felt they had been cared for, that their lives, deemed so insignificant in this land, were worth saving. So Daoshi performed, dancing and chanting, coaxing or snatching the dark energy from the suffering ones, telling them they were fine now, what troubled them would trouble them no more.

For payment, he accepted whatever they could offer. If it was food or household items—a bunch of green onion, a slice of pumpkin, a few tomatoes, an oil lamp, a bar of soap—he gave them to Feiyan, the first person who had believed he could do this.

He believed or half believed himself, performing the rituals that his father and uncle and elder brother had performed. So had his grandfather and great-grandfather and great-great-grandfather. All of them must have doubted themselves like him, but nonetheless learned to put conviction in their dancing steps. As he danced, Daoshi could almost feel all his forebears' ringing chants joining his own.

Guifeng

THE CIGAR FACTORY SAT RIGHT ON TOP OF THE DEN, WHIFFS OF vapor slipping through the floorboards. The factory was just a small room with a beat-up table where Guifeng and four other men rolled cigars. Each of the men had suffered a debilitating injury like Guifeng: one had fallen off a platform while sawing a fir; one got crushed by a branch thicker than three men; one was burned in a fire; one was beaten half dead. They were the dredges of Chinatown's workforce, no longer capable of doing the manly, better-paying lumber work, but still able to use their heads and hands. They were Fong Lee's charity project, although they were paid so little it didn't feel like charity to them. They complained about their paltry wage, but never loudly. They were supposed to feel grateful even though they felt used, but what was the alternative?

Besides Guifeng, they were all bachelors. Two still managed to send money home; two had forgone their duties. One was a drunk; one was a gambler; two visited the den in the basement, bringing up more opium smell that clung to their skin and clothes. They were all lost in some way, but not as lost as Guifeng once had been, nor did they need to be saved as he had been.

That morning after stepping out of the room lit by a wedge of sunlight, after having breakfast with his expanded family, he followed Feiyan upstairs to clean the room. They peeled off the soiled sheet and spread a clean one on the mattress, stretching, smoothing it together. Then, Feiyan drew the curtain and opened the window wide. The sun flooded in. He came to where she stood and felt the sun in his eyes, on his forehead, over his palms. He raised his hands and touched her arms.

"Look at me," he said, looking at her till she met his eyes.

One step at a time was all he could take. All the tenuous love he could summon, which was not meager, he gave to Feiyan. Every day, he endured the test of opium vapor emanating through the floorboards and his co-workers' pores. He brought his earnings to Feiyan, handing over the two quarters as if he were paying dues for his redemption.

He had taken the job eagerly, wanting to be of use to the family, and wanting to feel deserving of Feiyan's love when they were alone at night. He lived for their time together, letting that longing guide him through the day of rolling cigars, like rolling one minute onto another. Her wanting him back was confirmation of another day worth living.

He gladly took the job also because he wouldn't have to face Sixiang all day long. Not that he didn't want to see her: he looked at her when she was not looking, such as when she was cooking with Feiyan or chatting with Daoshi or teaching Duofu words from *San Zi Jing*. He thought about how to make amends, but finding no answer, he looked away. He couldn't do the same as what he'd done with Feiyan, looking into her eyes and asking her to look into his. There were too many years and too much distance between him and his daughter for that to work.

Daoshi had given him a rough sketch of her life. To fill in the details would involve information he might not want to know. So he avoided asking questions. He resorted to small gestures and safe remarks. Such as the time when he noticed Sixiang liked the beef and turnip stew Feiyan had made but was too polite to get herself a second serving, and he got up and added a scoop to her bowl. "It's my favorite too," he said, but stopped himself from saying that his mother, Sixiang's grandmother, had made it the same way. He wanted to connect with his daughter, but whatever delicate ties he could possibly form with her seemed to point right back to his unforgivable past.

ONE DAY WHEN he came home from work, Sixiang had a brush, an ink bottle, and a sheet of rice paper spread on the table in front of her. She pointed at two characters on the paper, 云腾, and asked him, "Is this how you write our village name?"

He said, "Yes."

She wrote down a few more words. "Is this how to write my grandmother's name?"

He said, "Yes," again.

"What about my mother's name?" Sixiang looked into his eyes. "Can you write her name for me?"

Guifeng took over the brush, dipped it in the ink, and slowly moved it to the paper. In his past letters home, he had put down his mother's name on the envelope, and in the letter itself had addressed his mother and wife just as "mother and wife," not by their names. He realized that he had never once written his wife's full name before, nor had he ever thought of it, and now, he had forgotten what her name was, except her diminutive, Ah Yu. He couldn't possibly tell his daughter that he'd forgotten the full name of her mother, his first and foremost wife in title. So he wrote down her diminutive, 阿玉.

Sixiang must have noticed his hesitation and known what it meant. She took the paper back, looking at the two characters. "Will this reach her?" she asked without looking at him.

He didn't answer or ask what she would write in the letter. Daoshi had told him that she'd written a letter home before but never received a word back. That was enough information for Guifeng. This daughter would not forget the place she'd come from, like the name he had given her—the wish he had imparted on her without quite knowing what it truly meant. Was it some kind of prescient hope that his daughter would do what he could not?

Then when Li Shu came to tell them about the job across the bridge in the white people's world, Sixiang gazed at Daoshi for advice. She had not even thought of looking to Guifeng. Maybe because she thought that advice was something he was more fit to receive than give? But it was probably for the best. This daughter he'd abandoned had found herself a new father, and a much more capable one for that matter.

"How do you like your boss?" he asked her when she came back from work on Sunday.

"Ada is fine," Sixiang said. "She curses a lot. I've never seen a white woman curse so much. *Goddamn it*," she said in English, in an older, louder voice, and they both laughed.

Then she talked about the baby Minnie under her care. "She's sweet," she said. Her face looked sensible, calm. His daughter whom he had not cared for a single day was now an adult, no longer his responsibility, and that was a relief.

Feiyan

SHE HAD STARTED RUNNING AGAIN. EARLY IN THE MORNING, before the busyness of the new day rushed in, before anyone else in the family woke up, she would go out and run by the river. This was her home. She would not leave. She had a whole family here. She would not let it fall apart again. These thoughts merged with the rhythm of her running steps, her steadying heart, her breathing in of the clear crisp air.

Guifeng had come back to her. Their lovemaking made her think of their youthful days in the mountains, between the root-crawling earth and cloud-drifting sky, surrounded by the trees' green light. But this lovemaking had something new to it too. It had the tenderness of cherishing—of being fully aware of its preciousness while not knowing when it would end. It made her forgive everything, even the fires, even his lost leg, and all the burned and lost things she'd once claimed to be hers. When she held him, she was holding more than his body. She took all his losses and hurt in her arms, in acceptance.

She was saving again. With the money she made from the diner and the wage Guifeng brought home, she was hoping to buy land again, and, this time, build a real farm. The soil was fertile in the Truckee River basin. Already, in her backyard, a new batch of lettuce she'd seeded less than a week ago was sprouting. Potatoes she'd sliced and buried with their eyes up were poking sturdy leaves out of the soil. Green beans were flowering on the lattices. Tubes of green onions were fattening, peppers' red and orange hues ripening. They grew and took in the sun and rain without a doubt.

She shouldn't doubt either. Even though the country had just passed a law to exclude them, Duofu was born here, in this very land. And every year they'd lived here was one more year they had become accustomed to the land's climate and seasons, its dirt, water, and wind, which made no distinction about the colors of skin.

She wanted to be a better mother to Duofu, which, with Guifeng here now, wasn't as difficult to do. She also wanted to be a good stepmother to Sixiang, to make it up to her by including her in the family. "Help me with the diner. I could use some extra hands here. You don't need to go out and work," she'd said to Sixiang when she was looking for a job, and said it again when Li Shu came with the news about the one across the river. "It's not safe there. You don't want to work for the white people."

But the girl didn't listen. She looked at Daoshi and said she would take the job. She didn't look at Feiyan or Guifeng. They were no parents to her.

Once a week on Sundays, Sixiang came back for her break. A quiet girl with her ghosts. Not only did she have her father's features, she was also like him inside. Both took in too much and let it all stay. But there was something more about this girl. She was stubborn. Maybe because she hadn't had a mother since she was Duofu's age. If she wouldn't accept Feiyan as her stand-in mother, Feiyan hoped Sixiang could at least think of this place as her home. A back-home that was right here.

Sixiang

MINNIE COULD NOW EAT CONGEE WITH A BIT OF DICED PORK AND spinach cooked down to semiliquid. When the cleaning wasn't heavy, Sixiang strapped the baby on her back, her little warm, solid body grounding her. Carrying Minnie also seemed to make most of the lodgers leave Sixiang alone. While some still gave her vile looks, they refrained from slurs and harassment, as if the white baby's presence was a reminder to act decently. When the work was heavy and required much bending, such as washing and room cleaning, Sixiang would either put the baby down in the center of their bed so that she wouldn't roll off, or hand her over to Ada.

Ada didn't like to be seen holding a baby while managing the boardinghouse. "It makes me look like a maid or a housewife," she said. "I'm neither." But it was also clear that she liked the child. She'd already submitted the paperwork for legal guardianship, and she gave Minnie mouthy kisses every night after the baby was fed and bathed for bed. "Got myself a baby at forty-eight," she'd say, while leaving most of the caretaking to Sixiang.

Alone, Sixiang would speak to Minnie in Cantonese, the way she had with Meimei, talking the same baby talk she knew innately, maybe because it was how her mother had talked to her when she was a baby. In the beginning, Minnie's fair skin and strawberry hair had made Sixiang speak to her in English, but that didn't last long. Just as quickly as the baby attached herself to Sixiang, Sixiang's stilted, formal English slipped back to the smooth undulation of Cantonese. And Minnie understood her. She looked into Sixiang's eyes and responded in her infant tongue.

Once when Sixiang was cleaning the empty parlor and saying something in Cantonese to soothe Minnie back to sleep, Ada stepped in. "Don't talk to her in that gibberish. She doesn't need to know your language. She won't know who she is. I don't need to protect another Chinese in this place."

"I don't need your protection," Sixiang blurted out, even though she hadn't intended to confront her boss in any way.

"Then I won't," Ada shot back.

One day, several weeks later, while Sixiang was cleaning a checked-out room, a man appeared at the door. "Can you help me with something?" He pointed at the next door. "I had a spill."

The man wore a three-piece suit, a necktie, and a goatee that made his complexion look very fair in contrast.

"I'll be there in a moment," Sixiang said. When the man stepped away from the doorway, she bent down and pulled her knife from her boot sheath. She'd bought a pair of boots and a knife after she'd received her first week's pay, and had since worn the boots and carried the knife every day when she was on this side of the bridge. As she stepped into the man's room, she held the handle of the knife, hiding its blade in her sleeve.

There was indeed a spill of milk on the floor. When she bent down with the rag in one hand, she made sure she was facing the man. But he didn't close the door or jump on her. She did not have to use the knife.

ON SUNDAY EVENINGS, at Feiyan's diner, after everything was cleaned up and the rest of the family went upstairs to bed, Sixiang would sit alone with Daoshi downstairs, the books, ink, and rice paper spread on the table between them. She had many questions to ask Daoshi: How much would it cost to buy a boat ticket? How much to keep a family of three alive? How much to buy a piece of land? How much to hire a farmhand? Could she become a tutor or letter-writer now that she could read and write? Or would they still prefer a man in that line of work? What could a woman do to make a living and support a family in China? Besides the cost of a boat ticket, Daoshi's answers tended to be vague. He hadn't lived there for almost thirty years, he reminded her. Things had changed. Here or there, things never stayed still.

No, things did not stay still. The father in the photo that Sixiang no longer carried had once remembered her mother's full name and cared for her enough to send that photo home. But her father had stumbled and fallen into a hole in Gold Mountain and in his place climbed out this man with his new love—this woman who walked on big feet that her mother did not have, and who kept a revolver under the food counter and took it upstairs with her every night. Sixiang could accept this changed man as Feiyan's husband and Duofu's father, but not as her own father or her mother's husband. His forgetting her mother's full name only erased more of her mother, whose face was already fading in Sixiang's memory, and there was no photo of her mother for Sixiang to carry.

She had asked Daoshi, not her father, to look at her letter and correct any miswritten words. She continued to learn Chinese from him, reading *Laozi* and *Zhuangzi*. "道可道, 非常道; 名可名, 非常名。" What was the way for her to follow? The way that led her to where she would finally belong? The answer given by the books was as vague as Daoshi's. It had to do with following the natural course of things. But the most natural course Sixiang could think of was the one her mother had laid out for her at her departure: *Find your father and bring him home.* Now that she'd found her father and knew that she could not bring him home, there was only one part of the course she could still follow: return home herself.

One Sunday night, Daoshi told her that he'd gathered some information about her village, Yunteng. Many had indeed died during the famine and many who had left never returned. A man from the village had inquired about Sixiang's family on Daoshi's behalf in his letter home. The answer had just come back, albeit an indefinite one: Sixiang's grandmother and mother no longer lived there; no one seemed to know where they were.

"They're not dead?" Sixiang asked.

"No, the man's family didn't know that, or didn't think so. They could have moved on to a different village, maybe your mother's home village."

Sixiang vaguely remembered visiting her other grandmother with her mother in a different village when she was little, but after that grandmother passed, they'd stopped going. "Where is my mother's home village?" she asked Daoshi, as if he would know, as if he was still the fortune-teller she had once believed knew everything.

Sixiang didn't want to ask her father again. Daoshi said he would ask, but the answer was just as she'd expected. Her father wasn't sure.

Had Sixiang heard her mother talk about her home village? It had not occurred to Sixiang that her mother was from somewhere else too. She too had been sold, from a village she had called home to a strange place called Yunteng. Sixiang had thought her home was where her mother was, but it turned out that her mother herself had no home. Her mother was a wanderer like her, except without her big feet, her leather boots, and a knife she wouldn't hesitate to draw.

SIXIANG DID NOT have to draw the knife again until the next spring, after Minnie had begun to take stumbling steps. It was a Saturday night, a few hours after supper. Sixiang had fed, cleaned, and handed Minnie to Ada, and was mopping the parlor floor, her last chore for the day. The parlor was empty. The lodgers had either retreated to their rooms or were still out enjoying the weekend night. When Sixiang was finishing up, a man staggered in, a big drunken man with a neck as thick as his head. "Hey, celestial girl, why are you here all alone?" The man came toward her, and, as Sixiang stepped away, he grabbed her arms and pushed her to the crimson-papered wall. His head came down next, his foul face shoving into hers. Mouth muffled, arms pinned, Sixiang couldn't yell, couldn't move, let alone reach down for her knife.

She had never felt so relieved when she heard Ada's curse and

Minnie's cry from the parlor entrance. As the man turned to look, his body momentarily loosening its weight and grip on her, Sixiang lifted her knee into the man's groin with all her might. The man wobbled back. She reached down to her boot sheath, pulled the knife, and without a moment's pause stabbed it into the man's leg.

Squealing, swearing all at once, the man threw himself at Sixiang. He clutched her arm while reaching for her blood-dripping knife. As Sixiang's arm was going to break, Ada picked up a shovel from the fireplace and brought it down on the man's head. "You motherfucker," she shouted. "You mess with my maid, you mess with me." The man's eyes rolled back, legs buckling. He collapsed onto the floor.

Sixiang looked at her hand that still held the knife: the red, sticky blood had dribbled onto her fingers. She felt faint, her insides churning, but over her loud pounding chest, the thought rang out clearly: she had done it; she had not backed off this time.

That night, with Minnie asleep in her arms, she talked to Qinglong. *I did it, I fought back*, she tried to tell him, as if one knife stab into a villainous white man's leg could bring Qinglong back to life. But of course nothing could bring him back. She trembled again, remembering the sticky blood on her fingers and the sensation of the knife slicing into the man's flesh only to be blocked by bone. Even though the man had been taken to the jail for assaulting her, thanks to Ada's testimony, Sixiang feared he would somehow get out and break into her room with an ax and cut her leg off the way they'd done to her father. Or he would rape and cut her open, as Jason and his friends would have done had she not run away. It was out of mercy that Qinglong had asked her to leave, because her staying would not have saved them. But she would never know that for sure. She could never forget.

Guifeng

LI SHU WAS DESCRIBING WHAT HAD HAPPENED AT THE BOARDING-house. How Sixiang had held a bloody knife at the big, groaning white man. Li Shu was gloating, full of pride for "our girl."

Sixiang smiled a pained little smile. *Don't go back there anymore*, Guifeng wanted to tell her. *It's not safe.* But he stopped himself, knowing that he still couldn't take care of this daughter of his. What right did he have to tell her what to do?

A few months earlier, Daoshi had asked him about Sixiang's mother's village, having taken it upon himself to inquire about the family Guifeng had left behind. Guifeng's memory of the village name was not reliable. Was it Longhu? Or Longwan? A village upstream, a poorer one, was all he could remember. "Is Sixiang still looking?"

"Yes," Daoshi said.

"Tell me what to do."

"If only I knew."

Later that Sunday after Li Shu told them about the stabbing, Guifeng made himself linger downstairs at night. When Daoshi stepped away to the kitchen to boil more water for tea, Guifeng went to the table where Sixiang was practicing writing. "Sixiang, quit the job," he said. "It's not safe."

Sixiang looked up at him. "I'm okay. I can protect myself."

"If it's money, there's plenty," he said. "We're all working. You can help Feiyan. She wants you to help her with the diner."

"I want to make my own money. I'm saving to go back," she said, looking away from him.

HIS OTHER DAUGHTER, Duofu, continued to watch him warily, as if any moment he might slip away from them again. She watched him when he felt his weakness ooze out of his spine and his craving crawl under his skin. He feigned wellness, but somewhere deep down, he wanted to stop trying. He wanted to succumb, to be a useless straw dog again and left alone, without any eyes looking for signs of his wavering, or trusting him to be strong.

The opium smoke slipped through the floorboards as he busied his fingers with the cigar-rolling, as his co-workers chatted and joked to make the hours go by. One day, they were joking about the women in Chinatown, one by one, moving from the prostitutes they'd patronized to the few wives. "Your lady is hotter than the whores," one said, and the rest laughed. In the past, such a remark would have triggered a punch in the face, but this was not the past. Guifeng shook his head. He kept rolling the cigars.

Perhaps he didn't even need his co-workers' sneers for doubt and jealousy to seep back into his heart. The more love Guifeng gave to Feiyan, the more he felt she did not love him back enough. Those strong-limbed men he suspected she'd slept with already were still frequenting her diner. He had never asked her directly about it. He had only made suggestions to let her know that he knew, so as to manipulate her into giving him money to smoke away—to hurt her as she had hurt him—and hurt her more by being the mess he had been. But now he had to trust that with their new beginning, bygones were bygones, and all that he had done and all that she had done had canceled each other out. They just needed to hold on to the present by looking into each other's eyes. The seeing, the baring, the lovemaking at night, was all that mattered.

The jealousy and doubt, he recognized, were the residues of the demons. So were his desire to smoke and his feelings of failure, as a father, a husband, and a son. The demons that Daoshi had danced to expel didn't want to release him. With each new day, what lingered behind in him continued to beckon them back.

This struggle was his life now. Guifeng must continue to dance Daoshi's dance by himself. It was a battle dance between the two forces inside him that held each other in a tortuous embrace. Between their unceasing pushing and pulling and their exhaustion and temporary truce, he must learn to take a breath and fortify himself for the next let-it-be.

Feiyan

GUIFENG LOOKED PAINED AS LI SHU RELISHED IN THE DETAILS OF the stabbing, bragging as if he himself had done it. Daoshi, too, had shadows in his eyes. Both seemed to be seeing their failure to protect their girl, leaving her in harm's way.

But did they not see that Sixiang was growing tougher? She was learning who she could truly be, and how to trust that being and welcome the freedom in that trust. She was becoming her real self, so that in situations like these, she didn't need to think, but just act.

Feiyan had to find out how to become her real self too. And to find out, she had to run, because the running was her knowing. It was what gave her knowledge of herself. During the five years at Red Peony, she had almost lost her imagination of running, which meant she was losing herself. So she had to run away even if that meant death.

But no matter how real you were to yourself, you would never be safe in this land. Not safe before or after being driven to this side of the river, or before or after the passing of the Chinese Exclusion Act. Feiyan had been paying attention. She'd heard about the purges up and down the West, sparing no place where there were Chinese. Darker things would not spare Truckee just because they'd already had their share of darkness. As long as the white folks were angry, they needed to vent their anger on someone. As long as they were hurting, they needed to hurt someone so that they didn't have to feel their own hurt. That was their addiction. But when it became commonplace—when killing Chinese men and raping Chinese women became as normal as hunting deer or slaughtering cows—there would indeed be no future for the Chinese in this land.

So you had to fight back each time you were cornered. You had to stab and draw blood, so that they would open their eyes and see you were not their feeble prey. Feiyan almost wished it was she who had done the stabbing. What came to mind with Li Shu's description was the white man sitting his big ass on her chest at Red Peony, choking her while spitting nasty words into her face. Feiyan wished she'd had a knife then. Then her body would have stayed clean and proud and asserted its rightful place in this living world.

Feiyan brought a pot of rice wine and cups to the table, an additional one for Sixiang, who hadn't had liquor before. Feiyan wanted to turn this into a celebration, to let Sixiang know that she had grown. She had rightfully protected herself, acting the way she should. Feiyan poured the wine in Sixiang's cup. "You did the right thing," she said.

Sixiang looked at her as if to make sure she meant it.

"Cheers." Feiyan held up her own cup.

The thing was that Feiyan didn't really know. It would have been the right thing if she herself had done it, but for Sixiang, her husband's daughter who insisted on carrying her ghosts with her, it might not be. Sixiang's eyes still held traces of panic and bewilderment, as if she were still replaying the act her body had done that caught her by surprise— even though she must have been preparing for it, carrying that knife in her boot for months now. But right or not, this wouldn't be the end of it. There would only be more danger and harm when the girl stepped back into the white men's world the next morning.

This girl needed someone, a real living young man who could hold her and let her learn to love what was right here. Then she would let go of her ghosts along with her dream of going back to a home that was no longer there. She would stay here with them on this side of the river and be a real part of the family.

One of the diner's recent regulars, a young man born in California like Duofu, had made it a habit of coming for both brunch and dinner every Sunday when Sixiang was around. His eyes would follow Sixiang as she helped serving the tables, and Feiyan thought she'd seen Sixiang glance back at him. Who wouldn't? He was a handsome young man Feiyan would have fallen for had she been Sixiang's age. Not old, not a drunk or a gambler, the exact opposite of what Feiyan once had to live with.

"I can tell you like my stepdaughter," Feiyan asked him one night when he showed up on a weekday.

"I do." The young man blushed.

"What can you offer her?"

"I'm saving up to open a shop."

"What kind of shop?"

"A tea shop. My uncle is in the tea import business."

"When will you save enough?"

"In a couple of years."

Feiyan told Sixiang about the conversation the following Sunday when they were in the kitchen together.

But Sixiang shook her head. "I don't want to marry," she said without looking at her.

Why? Seventeen years old. Not wanting to live a life with a real young man, but stubbornly choosing the dead. Feiyan had never done that. She had never wanted to be in the company of ghosts if she could help it, while Sixiang chose to carry them, to let her youthful years be burdened by the lost and dead. But maybe it was safer that way: the lost and dead would not be lost or die again, unlike the living. While the living were what Feiyan had to carry, to keep safe—with a loaded revolver always within reach and a will to make a home here, a will that she must renew every morning, with every running step she let fall on the river-washed dirt.

Feiyan asked Daoshi to talk some sense into Sixiang. "Among all of us, she only listens to you."

Daoshi did the talking and came back telling Feiyan what she'd already known: Sixiang was still saving to go home.

IT WAS ALSO safer to carry your home in your head. But unlike Sixiang, the only home Feiyan's daughter Duofu knew was this home that bore her name on the lintel and had been burned down twice already. Duofu still screamed in nightmares, "Fire, fire," jolting up from bed, staring into the dark for the familiar red tongues to lick everything into ashes. But Sixiang did not think of this home as her home. She carried her ghost-home with her ghosts, safer that way because it couldn't burn.

This house here that sheltered them, that gathered warmth in the sun and could be touched by feet and palms, was all the home they had. This house wanted to give. But in Duofu's dreams, the house kept burning. And in Guifeng's sometimes distant eyes, the house was not enough. Already, he was craving something not here, distrusting this present with her lying by his side, and that the house was still standing and one more day had been lived without tragedy. Sometimes when they were making love, she felt they were holding the distrust between them, while from the next room, Duofu's periodic screams punctured the dark: "Fire! Fire!"

What did Daoshi think of this house? He seemed to be the one holding this expanded family together, keeping Guifeng's ghosts at a controllable distance, balancing Sixiang's absent presence with his present detachment. He continued to perform exorcisms, continued to have his pleasures and disciplines. He seemed to have figured it all out, but there was a lostness about him too.

Only she, Feiyan, felt grounded by this house, which was here to hold her, all of her, and all the family she had now. A house waiting for her to come home every morning after she ran. She ran away at dawn so that she could run into its arms as the sun wiped away the darkness.

Daoshi
1885

EARLY DECEMBER. LATE NIGHT. THEY HEARD THE NOISES AND listened: the shouting, the stomping, the same four words, "The Chinese must go!" yelled in unison like the scraping of metal.

Eight years earlier, Sixiang had asked Daoshi what it was they were shouting, while he pointed a dull sword at the floorboards in the room of the other city. Now she would know.

He looked around the diner. He could go to the kitchen and grab the meat chopper or fish knife. He wished he had a gun, that he had kept one for himself during his five gun-shipping trips years ago. Or had purchased one after news came in September about the murder of twenty-eight Chinese in Rock Springs, Wyoming, or in November about the driving-out of seven hundred Chinese residents at gunpoint from their homes in Tacoma, Washington. Things had been brewing here in Truckee too. The town's newspaperman, attorney, and Caucasian League leader, Charles McGlashan, was propagating a new strategy: no more fires, he claimed, no more bloody shootings for the national headlines to capture and lawsuits to follow. Even though in the end no white men would be convicted, they did not need more negative public attention if they could help it. This time, the "better class of citizens," as he put in the *Truckee Republican*, would lead the Chinese expulsion campaign. They would legally drive out the Chinese by boycotting all Chinese businesses and products, as well as all white employers who hired Chinese workers. Freeze them out. Fire had been disastrous. Now it was time for ice.

But the shouting and stomping sounded like the same old faceless mob with their same combustible rage. Daoshi had been foolish to not be more prepared for this. He had not quite believed in guns, as there would always be more white men with more guns to outnumber the Chinese. But here he was, again with Sixiang, again finding himself weaponless and helpless as he had been eight years ago.

It was their weekend night together, their routine. For the last three and a half years, they had been doing this, sitting together at a table in the diner after the rest of the family had gone upstairs to sleep. Sixiang had been learning Chinese with him from *Laozi* and *Zhuangzi*. The words in the two books kept altering, transmuting their meanings, and as Sixiang learned them, Daoshi was unlearning and relearning them. So instead of him teaching her, he felt it was more like they were teaching each other and learning together. During the week, he visited the afflicted and performed exorcisms, performed death rituals as well when needed. When he was free, he helped Feiyan at the diner or taught Duofu Chinese and the limited amount of English he knew. At night, he spent time with the family or visited wineshops or teashops, and occasionally brothels. If he drank, he watched the amount he was drinking. He was content, but sometimes found himself counting the days to the weekend when Sixiang came home.

Unlike her childhood self who had hidden her face in his arms, Sixiang bent down and pulled the knife from her boot. She had used this knife two and a half years before to draw blood from a white man's leg. Daoshi had asked her not to go back to the boardinghouse then. But she said she had to work and save so that she could go back home. Even after learning that her mother and grandmother had left her village, she held on to her dream, refusing to let it go or embrace instead a young man's love. "I'm not going to marry someone here and forget where I'm from."

So she kept saving. "How much is enough?" she kept asking him. "Not what you've got," he told her, as if to keep her here longer—even though there was hardly a future here to count on. As he'd learned again and again.

The rally easily contained hundreds. *Why are we still here?* Sixiang seemed to ask him with her eyes. *Why allow them to shame us again and again?*

Feiyan came down the stairs holding her revolver. She didn't need to ask the question why they were still here. This was her place. She had claimed it and would not let them take it away from her. She would rebuild again if they burned it down again. There was no shame on her face—fear, yes, but not shame. Fear and rage. "Those devil mother-fuckers," she said. "We need more guns."-

Duofu came down hiding behind her, followed by Guifeng, who was limping, but with no shame on his face either. They had given birth to a child here, had made up their mind to make it a home. "Let me have the revolver," Guifeng said to Feiyan. "You take Sixiang and Duofu upstairs." Sixiang and Feiyan looked at each other. "Please, for Duofu's sake." Guifeng looked at them both.

Feiyan handed him the revolver, took a knife from the kitchen, and went back upstairs with Duofu. Sixiang followed them. Guifeng barricaded the door with a long table and blew out the oil lamps. They waited in the dark.

And Daoshi? Had he also claimed a place in this land that he wouldn't quit fighting for till the end? He had been a temporary dweller, until this family gave him a home. A home that had put his heart at ease. If that was not worth fighting for, he could not imagine what was.

Guifeng

SITTING WITH DAOSHI IN THE DARKENED DINER, WAITING FOR THE mob to make their next move—be it setting the house on fire or kicking the door open—Guifeng resolved to shoot the revolver's six bullets into six men. Then, if he was still alive, he would wield the knife he'd picked up in the kitchen and keep fighting. There were no other alternatives, and there was satisfaction in doing what he had to do, the purpose simple and true, no conundrum, no battle to fight within himself.

He had been rooting himself here for the last three and a half years, with each meal he ate with his family, each time he made love with Feiyan, each word he taught Duofu, each talk he had with Daoshi, each Sunday spent with Sixiang here. Each gesture of care he'd given and received had deepened his connection to the space they were occupying, this green valley by the river, this clear-flowing water by their house. The rooting was precious because he knew they could be uprooted too easily.

Guifeng had done what he could do. Throughout November, he'd walked with Daoshi and Fong Lee to the other side of the bridge, where he would rather never set foot. He had the best English among the three of them and translated their words to a dozen white business owners: "Our two worlds can exist side by side with each other. You hire us to do your work. We get your work done and get a wage and buy merchandise from your shopkeepers. You buy products from our factories, which are well made and more affordable, such as our cigars. You sell them for more and make a profit. We benefit from each other, don't we? It wouldn't help either side to boycott us."

A few did listen: three white shopkeepers pulled their ads from the *Truckee Republican*. But most did not, including one who took the time to explain, "I understand, but that's not how things work here. It's about principle and community. We need to protect our kind."

Fong Lee put up a notice on Chinatown's bulletin, listing all the white businesses that had joined the Caucasian League's boycott committee, whom no Chinese should patronize again. It was their counterboycott. But there were always more white stores and white people whose committee visited every white employer of Chinese and every white merchant who bought Chinese products, invoking community spirit, threatening boycotts and public shaming. As McGlashan put in his newspaper:

Let our mothers, wives and sisters draw their skirts as they pass them on the street. Let them teach the little ones to abhor a Chinaman or his upholder. Let the little fingers be pointed at them, and the first words that fall from their baby lips be "Shame, you China lover."

More and more Chinese workers were getting fired. They came to the diner for their last meal before moving on. Some were heading home, with hurriedly bought presents, without much in the pocket, but at least still a fit body that could work. Many had to stay, because home was no longer there across the ocean. Like Guifeng, they'd lost their homes one way or another, so the only home was somewhere here in this country that had been trying every means to drive them out. They had no choice but to find the next crack to set down their bedrolls and eke out a living.

But where in this country would they be spared from torchlight rallies like this—and the crouching in a dark house, waiting for it to be over, or fighting it out till the end? If this was the end, so be it.

The rude shouting and stomping reached their front door but did not stop there. It did not turn into kicks, bangs, gunshots, or flames. The rallying men and women continued on, sending their loud commands down the streets and alleys, into darkened rooms, letting their torchlight snake across the windowpanes, their rancor spread in the cold river air, and left.

Guifeng couldn't go back to sleep now. He stayed downstairs with Daoshi. He wanted to talk, to get some perspective. Something about Dao and wuwei, something that could point to a path forward for them, or at least shine some light on the spot they were at. They relit the oil lamp, brought a bottle of wine from behind the counter, drank, and talked.

Guifeng wanted to see a larger picture. Here, or China, or the whole world, the universe, as seen in heaven and earth's eyes. What do they see? One dynasty overthrowing another. One race expelling another. One tribe warring with another. One tong fighting another. One human opposing another. Tooth for tooth, fist for fist. That's the truth of the human history. If you don't kill, you get killed. Thus, the killing spree begins. You gang up to kill more. They gang up to kill back. One gang wins and the killing begins within the gang. Humans cannot stop themselves. They want, they worry, they fear, they kill, they regret, they want more to dull that regret, and round and round again.

"So what is Dao in such a world?" Guifeng asked.

"Maybe that's why people keep returning to *Laozi*, to look for an answer to that question. Because Dao is unattainable; it remains elusive."

"Or does it all boil down to survival? Doing whatever it takes to stay alive?"

"It sure looks like it. Though things change. We'll have to wait it out."

"Waiting it out is not wuwei, is it? It's surrender to bullies. Surrender is not wuwei, it is not nonaction; it's an exercise of fear, an action of submission."

"Is it? Fighting back at the cost of our lives doesn't do much either."

"We're the Hakkas who were defeated in Guangdong by the Puntis. Karma, you could call it that."

"Except that the Hakkas here are targets too. To the whites, we're all the same, just like the native tribes in their eyes, all destined to lose."

"Should we then accept our loss even before we completely lose, or should we put up a fight before we lose? Which is the right thing to do? What is Dao here? What would a sage do? What kind of non-doing would get the doing done? What is the doing for us in this land?"

They talked until they were drunk, until they could no longer make out their questions.

Daoshi

THE NEXT MORNING, ON CHINATOWN'S BULLETIN BOARD WAS
nailed a bold-lettered poster in all-capital letters:

RESOLVED: THAT NOT ONLY THE LABORING
MAN, BUT THE ENTIRE COMMUNITY, DEMAND
THAT ALL INDIVIDUALS, COMPANIES AND COR-
PORATIONS SHOULD DISCHARGE ANY AND ALL
CHINAMEN IN THEIR EMPLOY BY JANUARY 1, 1886,
AND REFUSE THEREAFTER TO GIVE THEM WORK
OF ANY KIND.

A race war. It was again not white laborers against Chinese laborers, but the country against the Chinese in the country. Fifty million
against ten thousand. And it was again Chinese fending for Chinese.

Daoshi had come to Gold Mountain because it was the other side of
the world, the farthest place his younger self could have possibly con-
ceived, where the sun set as it was rising in China the next day. Twelve
hours behind. Stepping back to see the world larger, its movement
slower and in panorama. He came to this far-off land to meet himself
but ended up finding himself in an ongoing war against him and those
like him—miners' tax, riots, ordinances, lynching, massacres, laws,
and now this new Truckee Method to starve them out.

Last night after the rally died down, he and Guifeng had sat drinking and talking about Dao, or the Dao of staying alive. Daoshi had
sometimes thought that life didn't have to boil down to nothing but the
grubbiness of mere survival. He could look up at the sky, hold a piece
of it in his chest, and let it expand. He could try to envision what it

would be like to look down from up there. He had tried. But the truth
was that he saw himself and this family he had formed and cared about
hiding in a darkened house, holding their breath.

He went to Fong Lee and bought a revolver from him. Weapons,
according to Laozi, are malignant instruments that should be detested
by followers of Dao; but if one has to use a weapon, one must use it
calmly.

Last night, before the white men stomped down the streets with
shouts and torchlights, Daoshi and Sixiang had been talking about
Zhuangzi's butterfly story again, one of Sixiang's favorites. Zhuangzi
dreams he is a butterfly, and when he wakes up, he doesn't know if
he dreamt he was a butterfly or if he was a butterfly dreaming it was
Zhuangzi. Daoshi had read this story as a parable of non-distinction,
no boundary between *I* and *you*, the dreamer and the dreamed. There
were moments in his life he'd felt this kind of collapsing and merging.
Such as years ago when Sixiang opened her palm to bare her father's
photo in front of him, different lives—his younger self, Guifeng,
Sixiang, his then older self—all seeming to converge and unify for a
moment.

"What about the living and the dead?" Sixiang asked. "Is there no
difference between them either? Could the dead be the butterfly, the
living Zhuangzi?"

Daoshi could tell this girl was carrying something. Years ago,
when he danced to exorcise her father, she had stepped out of the room
before the ritual was over. He'd first thought Sixiang carried too much
anger at her father, but it was something more shattering and mournful.

During the past few years, Daoshi had danced and chanted again
and again, in the incense smoke, to provide solace without promising
outcomes. When asked, "Can you really cure him?" he would say,
"Let's give it a try." To try was all he was able, and willing, to guarantee. Before the ritual, he would ask questions, letting the sick tell
him how they felt, or what might have sickened them. As they talked,

pouring out their hurts and grievances, they already felt less burdened, more supported, cared for. When Daoshi began to dance, they believed that he was isolating their afflictions into a tangible demon and coaxing it away from them, for good.

"Tell me about it. Who is the dead to you?" he asked Sixiang.

She met his eyes for a moment, as if considering where to begin, but then shook her head and looked away. She still wasn't ready to tell him, if telling meant letting go.

Her boardinghouse boss was now among Truckee's last dozen white employers who had refused to fire their Chinese workers. And Sixiang refused to quit. Now, with the January 1 deadline drawing close, things were becoming more dangerous.

During the last week, Daoshi and Fong Lee had wired the Six Companies in Big City, asking them to pressure California's governor to put a stop to this Truckee Method, which would surely spread if left unchecked. But unsurprisingly, Governor Stoneman responded by blaming Chinese for "crowding the Caucasian race out of many avenues of employment," and explicitly told them, "I cannot prevent meetings of citizens."

Now Daoshi had a gun. Sixiang, who still worked among the "Caucasian race," would need it more than he did. But was it a good idea to give it to her?

When she came back for the weekend, they walked into the woods at the foothill. He showed her how to use the gun. "If you have to use it, use it calmly."

"If only I had this back then," Sixiang said.

"Back when?"

"When I was weak." She wouldn't say more.

Daoshi could not decide whether it was a good idea to give her the gun. He kept having dreams about it. In one dream, the gun got into the hand of an attacker; in another, the bullets were missing; or it wouldn't shoot when Sixiang needed it to; or it backfired, hurting her instead. There was no leisure to dream of butterflies or contemplate who was dreaming or who was being dreamed of. In this world, it was all too real. In this world, you either found yourself hunted down or pointing a gun at the hunter.

Sixiang

THE LAST DAY OF THE SOLAR YEAR. WHITE PEOPLE WERE CELE-brating. A train from the East Coast with eight special cars of white cigar makers was passing through Truckee en route to San Francisco, to replace Chinese cigar makers there. As the train refueled at Truckee train station, the church bell rang. A parade of white folks and their children, led by the fife and drum corps, marched up and down the platform where banners and posters hung loudly from the station front:

SUCCESS TO ANTI-COOLIE

NO CHINESE NEED APPLY TRUCKEE STEAM LAUNDRY

WHEN THE COCK CROWS THE CHINAMAN GOES

Some banners had pictures too: a crudely drawn rooster; a buck-toothed man with his queue held in a white man's hand like a whip; a cigar box on top of a burning torch.

Sixiang could see all these from a second-floor window of the boardinghouse, which was quite empty, with most lodgers out joining the festivities.

Ever since the wind had turned crisp and the poplar and aspen leaves began to drop, Ada had been visited by the Boycott Committee. "Think on behalf of the whole Truckee community, not just your own profit," they told her.

"You don't tell me whom to hire and whom not to hire," she said.

"Think of your white brothers and sisters, your fellow citizens. The Chinese are sucking our blood dry."

Sixiang's father had lost his job: the cigar factory closed because no white stores were buying Chinese-made cigars. Feiyan's diner had grown quieter and quieter the last few Sundays when Sixiang went back, as more and more woodcutters, teamsters, cleaners, cooks, and launderers had been fired by their white bosses and left town.

The white folks were planning an even bigger celebration for January 1. In their vision, the new year would be a year rid of the Chinese, so that their paradise could be restored, and they would live happily ever after.

Yet Sixiang was still here, still had not left this country that was dying to throw her out. *Why?* she asked herself. Because the home that she had hoped to leave here for was no longer quite there. And each time Sixiang thought it was finally time to go, she faltered. When she had saved enough for the boat ticket, she told herself she needed to save more for a house if the old one was no longer there, or theirs. She would also need to save the money for a couple mu of fields and all the necessary expenses for farming, since she was unlikely to get a job as a woman. So she continued to stay and tell herself she needed to save more. Once she went back to China, one thing she knew for sure was that she wouldn't be able to come back. The Exclusion Act passed in 1882 banned all Chinese laborers from coming to the country; and even before that, as she'd learned from Daoshi, the Page Act passed a decade ago had banned entry of all Chinese women. The only way for her to come back here would be the same way she had come here in the first place—with fake papers and a fake name.

Once she was gone, she would be gone for good. She would never see them again—this family she'd been a part of every weekend in this house that had felt like the closest thing to home, with no Ada yelling at her or lodgers harassing her, with the sure-footed Feiyan who had been kind to her, and with her father whose eyes were gentle when they were not evading hers. With the fast-growing Duofu who called her sister. And with Daoshi.

But even if she continued to stay, how much longer could she and this new family of hers do so, with the whites so desperate to chase them away?

SIXIANG WAS GIVEN the rest of the New Year's Eve and the entire New Year's Day off, which could mean that she was off for good. Minnie, who never liked goodbyes, was more insistent this time. "*Nei mau ʒau, nei mau ʒau*," she whispered to Sixiang in Cantonese, the language they spoke in private, especially at night with Minnie cuddled in her arms. At those moments, Sixiang felt less a nanny to Minnie than a mother. She would miss this child and she knew the child would miss her too. *Nei mau ʒau*, Minnie said every time Sixiang left for her weekly break. *You don't go.* The opposite of what Qinglong had said to her that day, when he asked her to leave.

Holding Minnie's hand, Sixiang found Ada in the parlor. On the crimson wall near the door was glued a crude drawing of a woman stripped, tarred, and feathered. The words "China-lover" were scribbled in red above the drawing. A group of lodgers, who must have just returned from the parade, stood in front of it, pointing and laughing.

Ada pushed through her lodgers to the wall. She stood on tiptoes to reach for the drawing, tore it off and into pieces. Sweeping her eyes across the snickering men and women, she put her hands on her hips, shouting, "No one will tell me what to do!"

Then she saw Sixiang standing behind the crowd, waiting to hand over Minnie to her. "Don't stare at me, you idiot," she yelled at Sixiang. "I'm not firing you yet. I'll put a bullet in whoever made this first."

Li Shu, coming to the parlor to walk Sixiang home, shook his head at her to urge restraint, and then pointed his chin to the door. Sixiang handed the sniffling Minnie to Ada without saying a word and headed to the door.

"It won't be long," Li Shu said after they stepped out of the boardinghouse. "They want us gone for good this time."

The streets were crowded with loitering white folks, many with a kind of aimless gaiety on their faces. As Sixiang and Li Shu headed toward the bridge, they passed a saloon with a noose hanging down its awning. A queue was tied to the bottom of the noose by something red. It was a red ribbon that looked like blood. Sixiang could almost see a head there, hanging loose in the air. She saw Ah Hong's head bent under the oak tree as if thinking. And the open-eyed, open-mouthed man noosed with his own queue that Daoshi had tried to shield her from seeing after the riot nights.

Li Shu cursed under his breath. They hurried toward the bridge.

"Hey, Chinaman and Chinese bitch, want a haircut for free?"

Sixiang glanced back and saw three men, one of them holding a knife in his hand, all dressed in shabby work jackets, unlike the three men years ago in tailor-made woolen coats and leather gloves—but in their eyes, the same. "Let's run," Li Shu said, quickening his steps.

But running away was not the answer. It never had been. Sixiang could hear them following closely, laughing and joking among themselves, the way Jason and his friends had done that winter day in the woods.

Sixiang reached under her coat and drew the revolver from her waistband holster. She had been carrying it since Daoshi taught her how to use it two weeks before. She turned, pointing the gun at the men, her finger on the trigger. She was trembling. *If you have to use it, use it calmly*, Daoshi had told her.

The men paused in their steps, guffawing faces freezing, mouths hung open.

Sixiang drew a breath to will her arms steady. She aimed the gun at the ground a few inches from the feet of the knife-wielding man and pulled the trigger. The men jumped and scattered.

Sixiang drew another breath. The revolver was hot and smoky in her hands. Her head throbbed, but she was still.

THAT NIGHT, SIXIANG lay awake with Duofu in their room. She had not stayed up with Daoshi downstairs. She'd said she was tired and came up to lie down so that she could think it through by herself. Li Shu, like last time after the stabbing, had told the family what she'd done first thing as they stepped into the diner, and Daoshi had looked at her strangely, his eyes both relieved and grave.

What had happened today felt different from the stabbing. This time Sixiang was shaking too, but she was also still. She had taken out the gun and used it calmly to protect herself and Li Shu. She shot at the brick pavement in front of the knife-wielding man's feet. She didn't hurt any of them, just killed their ego for a moment.

She had carried Qinglong and Ah Hong through all of this— Qinglong like a lover and Ah Hong like a big sister, talking to them, keeping them company so that they knew she had not forgotten them. Was she able to show them today that she was finally brave? Did they still want her to carry them, which meant that they had to continue witnessing the cruelty of the world? Or did they want to close their eyes and rest?

Sixiang got out of bed, wrapped herself with a blanket, and tip-toed out of the room and down the stairs. Standing in front of Daoshi's room, she turned the knob. He was sleeping. She stepped to his bed and looked at him—the way he must have looked at her that night in the backroom of the pawnshop, which was not all that different from this one. A room floating in the dark, cold air where all would eventually go and rest. In the slice of moonlight gliding through the window, his face wore a frown, as if he was negotiating away some pain.

She knelt down, touching his brows to smooth them. He opened his eyes, and blinking away sleep, he called her name in his quiet way. He took her hand and covered it with his.

"Can you guide Qinglong and Ah Hong to where they belong?" She had not been able to tell Daoshi about them in the past, because each time she wanted to do so, to feel lighter through the telling, she also feared that she would lose them. But now it was time for them to go. There needn't be any dance, or wrestling, or persuasion, she said to

Daoshi, because they were not her enemies. They were her friends. She told him about Ah Hong's bare body dangling in the morning air and Qinglong lying on the ice-coated leaves. They were tired of staying in this world. They needed to be gently guided away to the sky realm. Rest, and be free.

Daoshi nodded as she talked. Then he got out of bed and stepped to the window. He opened the frame as the night air rushed in. Cold and clean. The sky was dark, edgeless.

As Daoshi recited a verse, Sixiang said, *"Nei ʐau liu,"* first to Ah Hong, then to Qinglong, the last words he had said to her. She was freeing them in rivers and lakes.

12

To the Land of the Lost

*

1886

Daoshi

IT MUST HAVE BEEN AROUND MIDNIGHT WHEN SHE CAME INTO HIS room—between the last hour of the last solar year and the first of the new. Daoshi was dreaming something, a dream where Sixiang was running down the few streets of Chinatown, which were dark and empty. She was holding the gun he'd given her. The gun had run out of bullets, but she still held it. Three white men were chasing her, their boots hitting the brick road. Where was Daoshi? He was not there helping her run away or stopping the men from their chase. He had given her the gun, which she'd used earlier that day and which, for the moment, seemed to have saved her. But the chase was not over. The hunting went on.

He opened his eyes. She was there by his bed, wrapped in a blanket, her fingers touching his brows. He took her hand in his own and listened. It was about those she had been carrying with her, the invisible weight she'd finally decided to let go.

She had witnessed two deaths because of his decision to have her "rescued" by white people, and because of his inability to care more than he had. But she continued to trust him. Despite what he had put her through, she continued to believe he was someone worthy of her trust.

He got off the bed, and putting a blanket over his shoulders, came to the window and opened it. The cold air rushed in as if it had been waiting.

The moment felt like a dream within a dream. In this better dream, Sixiang was not in danger, not being hunted down holding the useless gun he'd given her, and he was not uselessly dreaming, watching but unable to protect her. In this dream, she was here with him, letting go of her ghosts whom she'd been carrying for four years, even longer than the advised three-year filial mourning period.

Daoshi did not need to dance, or wrestle the ghosts away from their host, as he'd performed time and time again in this river basin. He had sometimes felt weakened by all the wrestling and cajoling, felt tempted to succumb to those moldy green presences and give up the effort. But tonight, he only needed to open the window and let the air, the deepest blue, beckon them.

No butterfly in this dream, only invisible beings taking flight. A window separating and connecting the seen lives and the unseen, the dreamers and the dreamed, those who were still staying and those being released.

Daoshi let the cold air fill his lungs and chanted a verse about emptiness and ease. Sixiang came to stand by him in front of the window. "*Nei ʒau liu*," she said to the air, and looked out into the night.

A waning crescent was rising in the east, casting a lace of gold on the river. Above the river, the snow-covered Sierra and its dark forests were glowing lightly. The earth was large and beautiful with so many places to go, but which place called out to them? Where could they be safe and free?

"Do you still want to go back to China?" he asked.

"Yes." She turned to look at him.

"I'll go with you."

All the straight and crooked paths he had followed, stumbled through, and groped along had led him here, to this beginning of a new path he had not known until now. And how right it was. He would go with her, whose dream was strong and big enough to hold his. They would return together, to a home that might be long gone, but they would find it somehow.

Feiyan

FEBRUARY 4, 1886, THE FIRST MORNING OF THE LUNAR NEW YEAR, her twenty-second year in Gold Mountain. Feiyan stepped out of her house and looked at the sky. Gray clouds scattered like pieces of coal yet to burn in the rising sun.

She had tried to make it and had made it till now. Last night, all the folks in Chinatown who were not yet gone came to her diner for the New Year's Eve feast. They'd brought what they could spare ahead of time—a bag of rice, a last chicken or duck or goose, a rabbit they'd caught or deer they'd shot, the last potatoes or cabbages or carrots they'd saved. She and her family had spent the whole day cooking, and after sunset, the six dozen people, less than one-tenth of Chinatown's old population, came for their final meal together. She'd moved the tables into long rows and borrowed benches so that everyone got a seat, with a plate and wine-cup in front of them.

Duofu Diner was the only restaurant left in Chinatown. During the last five weeks, the other owners had closed shop one by one and moved out of Truckee. But that didn't mean Feiyan had more business without the competition. There were very few people around and even fewer who could afford to eat out, and she had fewer groceries than ever before to cook with. The only grocery store still running for the last two weeks belonged to their neighbor who had depended on a white man they'd secretly hired to buy meats for them from the white stores across the river. But the man was gone, caught by the Caucasian League or the 601 or the Boycott Committee, stripped, tarred, feathered, and run out of the town. Besides the scarcity of meats, Feiyan's vegetable cellar was almost empty, as were her rice jars.

She had come up with the idea of pooling everything together for a last communal meal. Despite everything, she would not let the Spring

Festival go without any festivity. They would eat, drink, cheer, and talk even if it was for the last time.

And they did just that. Some talked about China, where they were heading back for good. They'd gone to the mountainside cemetery buried in snow, exhumed the bones of their dead, and secured them in urns for travel. They raised their wine-cups for a toast to Daoshi, who had helped them at the cemetery, performing rituals for the excavation. Over the last month, Daoshi had received hardly any requests to exorcise the living, maybe because when perils were right in front of you, even your demons held off their mischiefs to ensure you stayed alive. Instead, Daoshi had been busy serving the dead, asking their permission to have their bones exhumed and praying for their safe journey across the ocean.

Daoshi and Sixiang were going back to China too. Sixiang had quit her job at the boardinghouse the day after the incident with the revolver. They planned to leave once Daoshi's service was no longer needed here. Like Daoshi, Feiyan would cook and serve until there was no one to serve or cook for. They were the last holdouts, but the last days had come.

If Feiyan could, she would move the whole family back to China together. But her home was not back there, but in the farther unknown places.

People had been talking about this place called New York. To get there you would need to take the train all the way across the country to the shore of another sea, where there was another Chinatown, a smaller but fast-growing one. At last night's feast, folks were talking about the legendary Ah Ken, the founder of New York Chinatown, who'd made a fortune selling three-cent cigars, and then opened a boardinghouse for the Chinese, and employed them at his cigar factory. This was how New York's Chinatown had grown from a dozen people to thousands. They talked about a giant statue of a white goddess towering at the harbor to welcome immigrants to the shore. "Well, not welcoming us," they said, "only the white folks. But we'll make ourselves welcome anyway. That's what we'll do." They laughed and cheered.

"Will I like New York?" Duofu asked her when Feiyan tucked her in after the party was over.

"Yes, you will," Feiyan said. "It'll be a better place than here." This was the New Year and Feiyan had not stopped believing in good wishes. She'd named her daughter Duofu, and in spite of everything, there had been blessings in their lives. Especially these last few years when they had all been together, caring for one another and being cared for in return.

Now, she ran along the riverbank she had gotten to know well— the big rock shaped like a turtle, the two quaking aspens with leaves flipping like shiny coins in spring, gooseberry's red lantern flowers in summer, and sagebrush's silver stems all year around. Her shoes had touched every inch of the dirt as she ran, and she had seen many sunrises as she ran back to the house that had been her home.

She had been packing but there was only so much they could take with them. If she tried to picture what would be needed in the Chinatown across the land, the whole house would be needed, including each pillar and each beam she had seen hauled into place, and each window and door she had opened and closed.

She felt tired thinking about all the places she'd had to run away from. "Let me see how far you can outrun your fate," the mountain ghost had once goaded her. And Feiyan had heeded her command. She had been running toward the unknown to outrun her fate, but could she ever outrun it? Or was this running itself her fate?

The coal-like clouds were now burning red in the east. The sky looked like an immense stove. What was cooking on it? Feiyan couldn't see but must believe it was food. She must believe that as long as there was a burning stove, food would be on it cooking. And, as long as she kept running, there would be a house welcoming her home.

Guifeng

The family stood at the train station, bidding farewell. Soon, he, Feiyan, and Duofu would board the eastbound train, while Sixiang and Daoshi would, a little later, board the westbound one.

Sixiang hugged Duofu, hugged Feiyan, and hesitated in front of him. He knew words were insufficient, but there wouldn't be any other chance to say them. "I'm sorry for what I did to you and your mother," he said without any expectation of forgiveness.

In China, the second day of a New Year is the day when a wife takes her husband and children to her home village to visit her family. With Daoshi by her side and her dream stubborner than any he'd known, Guifeng suddenly had no doubt that his daughter would find her mother against all odds, even though he didn't know where his own journey would end.

Daoshi hugged Duofu, and then, holding his hands in front of his chest, bowed to Feiyan and Guifeng as he had years ago when he saw them off in San Francisco Chinatown, Feiyan in men's clothes and Guifeng still a young man unacquainted with too much pain. Back then, Guifeng had not known what was awaiting them either, but they had managed to survive every peril. He must trust they could do it once again.

It had only surprised him momentarily when Daoshi told them he was going back to China with Sixiang. This old friend of his who had hardly talked about his family in China nor expressed any interest to return nevertheless decided to return with Sixiang. But then, it also seemed to be the natural course of things. By helping Sixiang follow her path, Daoshi was following his own. It was his wuwei.

How could they be straw dogs? They were flesh and blood and felt so alive during the last few weeks that they knew were their last ones together. They talked quietly, looking each other in the eyes, committing what they heard and saw to memory. Then, they all celebrated the dawning of the New Year with abandon. They ate as if there were no tomorrow and drank and cheered. At midnight, they all went outside the diner and set off firecrackers to scare away demons and lit fireworks to attract good luck. How the eyes loved the brilliant red and golden sparks lighting up the sky and the river, no matter how briefly. If they were straw dogs, they cherished their moments to rejoice, because they knew the moments were passing.

As the train started and Guifeng leaned out of the window to wave at them one more time, Sixiang was running along the train, reaching a hand to him, calling, "Father, Father."

Father. The first, last, and only time she called him this. But it was more than enough.

Father. There were days when he had felt the hungry ghosts that lingered inside him would never be satisfied unless he snuck back into the den and lost himself again in the numbness. He would walk home feeling everything was crumbling, even though all appeared to be the same on the outside. Until he stepped into his house and saw his family: Feiyan running the diner, holding the home together, Daoshi and Duofu helping. And on Sundays, there was Sixiang, coming home one week older than before, her features more defined, her steps surer— one week less his once abandoned daughter, and more her own brave, independent self. All of that had kept him going, giving him the courage to continue the dance Daoshi had danced for him. And none of that could have happened had Sixiang not come into his life. He had felt lucky to be her father.

Feiyan put her hand on his. He took it. The sun was setting, blazing in their eyes.

Duofu, seated on Feiyan's other side, had cried quietly on the platform when Sixiang and Daoshi bid their farewell. Now she was trying to hold back her tears, wiping her face when she thought no one was watching. She'd grown half a head taller this year, no longer thinking of herself as a child, and was acting accordingly. Seated across from them were their neighbors: the grocery store owner, his wife, and their two children. The wife gave Duofu and her children each a piece of ginger candy. Duofu said thank you. She put the candy in her mouth and closed her eyes to focus on its sweetness.

The train moved along the frozen river for a while before entering the snow-covered desert. The flaming sunset had now been erased by inky clouds that were moving fast in the sky, as if they too were on a migration. Feiyan took out a bundle from their food basket and shared the rice cakes she'd made among the two families. They were talking about New York, about the Chinatown there. How hard would it be to open a diner or a grocery store? What kind of competition would they be facing among the Chinese? What would the white people be like? Would there be expulsions too? Fires? Boycotts? But they glanced at the children and told each other not to worry too much. No sense in worrying until they had to.

When the dark fell, Duofu rested her head on Feiyan's shoulder, and closed her eyes. Feiyan wrapped her arms around Duofu, letting out a deep sigh, and closed her eyes too. The one oil lamp hanging from the ceiling cast the passengers' reflections in the windowpane. Guifeng found Feiyan and Duofu's sleeping faces there, smoother now, swinging with the train. He saw his own face too and looked at it as if to learn who he was. Then he moved his eyes closer to the pane to look into the dark night outside.

Sixiang

THEY STOOD BY THE SHIP RAILING, WIND AND SALT ON THEIR faces. The ship had sailed away from the seagull-flitting shore. Gold Mountain was shrinking once more to a whale's back, and soon there was only sky and sea. She knew that the land she was returning to was also full of holes—the porous land where things grew fast in the bountiful sun and rain, but famines ate them up.

She looked at Daoshi. A strand of hair was loosened from his topknot, caught in the wind, shimmering.

The night when he'd said, "I'll go with you," Sixiang had nodded because no words could speak to how she felt. She put her face on his chest and put her arms around him. She held him tight, as if she were holding a home she had finally found and would not let go.

She forgave her father. Because now she understood his love for Feiyan. She forgave him even on her mother's behalf, because she knew her mother would understand too, had she ever felt that love herself. As the train took him away, Sixiang ran, calling, "Father." She had found her father after all.

Day and night, the ship surged forward, backtracking the old sea miles she had traveled a decade before—where Ah Hong climbed down from her top bunk to lie beside her; where Ah Fang's little body was dropped off deck into the deep water. When one day on the deck, Sixiang pointed at a family of whales frolicking out on the horizon and said, "Look," to Daoshi, she thought one of them could be Ah Fang, reborn into a whale and having found a home for herself after all.

Far away now, in the land Sixiang and Daoshi had left behind, her other family must have already arrived in New York. She hoped that they would soon be able to build a new house and hang the red-gold plaque of "Duofu Diner" on the lintel. Duofu, who looked more and more like Feiyan, would be working side by side with her sure-footed mother. Their father would be working at Ah Ken's cigar factory, and when he came home at night, his sad eyes would light up seeing his family. Sixiang hoped there would also be a river nearby, which Feiyan could run along at sunrise, a river to remind them of all the other rivers they had lived by.

And in the old west, in what was left of Truckee, Minnie would have a new nanny by now, and the Cantonese she had learned from Sixiang would soon fade away. But if one day it happened that she found herself in a place where Chinese continued to live, and heard the tongue spoken, she might reach into her memory and find some of those distant words that had once been spoken to her, with love.

Farther west, on the other side of the Sierra where spring had already come, Qinglong and Ah Hong's bodies lay underground, held tight by dark earth that was warming again. In no time, their light would push out of the dirt and burn through the green grass into the air, making a fact of itself.

Acknowledgments

My thanks to Caroline Eisenmann and Megha Majumdar, for believing in the book even before it was done; to Kendall Storey, for making it better; to Wah-Ming Chang, Megan Fishmann, and Rachel Fershleiser, for helping to bring it into the world.

I'm thankful for the many books about the nineteenth-century Chinese American experience that I have drawn upon, especially Gordon H. Chang's *Ghosts of Gold Mountain*, Jean Pfaelzer's *Driving Out*, Benson Tong's *Unsubmissive Women*, Wendy Rouse Jorae's *The Children of Chinatown*, Julia Flynn Siler's *The White Devil's Daughters*, and Sue Fawn Chung's *Chinese in the Woods*. Chapter 5 borrows details from the life stories of Sing Kum and Tien Fuh Wu.

Thanks to Shawn Flanagan, Rachel M. Hanson, Michael Nelson, Laurie Stein, Brian Castleberry, Ian Case, Mary Alice Mills, Jess Camara, Kevin Stemp, Tsung-Hui Yang, He Jiawei, Paul B. Roth, Lisa Russ Spaar, Emily Pittinos, Amy Foley, Yune Tran, Peggy Reid, Fumiko Yasuhara, and Akio Yasuhara, for their care and support.

Thanks to my mother, father, sister, and my great-great-grandfather, who had been here; and to Mike and Mira, with all my heart.

YE CHUN is a bilingual Chinese American writer and literary translator. Her debut story collection, *Hao*, was long-listed for the 2022 Andrew Carnegie Medal for Excellence in Fiction. She is also the author of two books of poetry, *Travel over Water* and *Lantern Puzzle*; a novel in Chinese, 《海上的桃树》 (Peach Tree in the Sea); and four volumes of translations. A recipient of a National Endowment for the Arts Literature Fellowship, a Sustainable Arts Foundation Award, and three Pushcart Prizes, she teaches at Providence College and lives in Providence, Rhode Island.